Just An Act
A NOVEL

by
TAMARA TILLEY

Just an Act
By Tamara Tilley

Copyright © 2017 Tamara Tilley

All rights reserved. No part of this publication may be reproduced, stored in a retrieval system, or transmitted in any form or by any means without the written permission of the author, Tamara Tilley.

Library of Congress Cataloging-in-Publication Data is on file at the Library of Congress, Washington, DC.

ISBN 10: 0692832262
ISBN 13: 978-0692832264

This book is a work of fiction. Names, characters, places, incidents, and dialogues are either products of the author's imagination or used fictitiously. Any resemblance to actual events or locales or persons, living or dead, is entirely coincidental.

Cover design by Scott Saunders
Cover images by Shutterstock

ARCHER PRESS

OTHER BOOKS BY TAMARA TILLEY
FULL DISCLOSURE
ABANDONED IDENTITY
CRIMINAL OBSESSION
BADGE OF RESPECT
ONE SATURDAY

TO WALTER
I am so thankful for your
love and encouragement.
♥

Acknowledgements

Thank you to my family, friends, and readers. You are a continual source of encouragement, and it's your support that keeps me going.

A special thank you to Michele, Nancy, and Charlene for helping me with the editing process.

Thank you, Scott, for another great cover.

Thank you to my Lord and Savior, for the stories you allow me to tell.

Chapter One

"I've made up my mind, Jerry. You knew this was coming. I told you I needed some R & R. Some time to clear my head." Mitch Burk—aka superstar Simon Grey—stood in the middle of his high-priced agent's office, his arms crossed over his chest.

"Okay. I get it. You need a break," Jerry said as he stretched back in his massive leather chair and stroked his chin. "I'll make arrangements for you to stay at this exclusive retreat I've been hearing so much about. It's very discreet. You'll be able to relax in complete privacy while you sort out whatever it is that's bothering you. The place even has counselors. You know, if you need a little extra help."

Mitch shook his head. "I don't need help. I need time. Time away from here to think. Time to myself." He grabbed the envelope from Jerry's desk. "Thanks for getting this for me," Mitch said as he thumbed through the large stack of bills.

"You didn't give me much choice," Jerry grumbled. "Besides, it's your money. It's not as if you couldn't have withdrawn it yourself. It's obvious you don't need me anymore."

Mitch felt a twinge of guilt. He and Jerry had been through a lot together. They'd weathered the good and the bad before Mitch had become Simon Grey—overnight heartthrob.

But Jerry didn't get it.

He didn't understand that success and fame weren't all they had cracked up to be. At least not for Mitch.

Being a success, being recognized wherever he went—having his personal life scrutinized and put on public display—was more than

Mitch had bargained for. He was feeling claustrophobic. He thought he'd prepared himself for stardom, but Mitch had only masked his introverted demeanor to fit the persona Jerry had created for him. Now he needed some time to figure out what he wanted to do with the rest of his life, reevaluate where he was headed, and make a decision about his future.

Mitch extended his hand across Jerry's desk but instead of shaking it, Jerry stood, pushing his hands into his pockets. "This is a mistake, Mitch. You walk away now, and you can kiss your career goodbye. Studios aren't going to stand by waiting for you to *find yourself.* They'll get themselves another 'Sexiest Man Alive' to throw their money behind. You'll have the solitude you want. That's for sure. In six months, no one will remember who Simon Grey is or even care for that matter."

Jerry's words were cold and callous, but it wasn't anything Mitch didn't already know. Together they had created Simon Grey: movie star, sex symbol, globetrotting playboy. Mitch thought it was the life he wanted—and had enjoyed it for a while—but now he needed to figure out who Mitch Burk was before he drank himself to death. Something definitely needed to change.

Before it was too late.

The next morning, Mitch studied his reflection in the mirror while he towel-dried his hair. His signature blond locks were now dyed a dusty brown—his natural color—and a shade similar to the scruffy beard he'd been growing for the last few days. Going back to his original color, as well as his real name, would help him blend in, that, and his low-budget wardrobe. No more Saint Laurent jeans or Bruno Magli shoes. Wranglers and Roper boots were now his labels of choice.

Mitch grabbed his duffle bag and phone—then thought better of it. Studying the piece of plastic that had been a natural extension of his hand for so long, he realized he no longer needed or wanted it. Tossing his phone on the entry table, he jogged down the front steps and out to his latest purchase. The old 1986 Suburban he'd picked up at a used-car lot looked like a pile of junk. Its fenders were rusty and the paint was peeling, but it ran like a top. That was all that mattered.

Mitch stood back and looked at the three-story ultra-modern home he'd acquired four years ago. He could still remember how he'd felt the day he bought it. It was the same day Simon Grey had been named the highest paid box-office actor. Worldwide.

He had made it to the top.

He was number one.

However, when Mitch studied the house that stood as a symbol of his success, it looked like a facade from a movie set. It was as fake and phony as the name Simon Grey.

Mitch didn't care if he ever saw it again.

Pulling from the driveway, Mitch once again felt guilt nudging his conscience. Even though he'd told Jerry not to worry—assuring him he would be back in three or four weeks—he had no intention of returning. He'd straight-up lied. It was the only way he could get out from under Jerry's thumb. If his agent knew his top-grossing client, along with the hefty paycheck he represented, was walking out the door, Jerry would fight him every step of the way. Mitch didn't want to fight. He just wanted to live his own life. Make his own decisions. Mitch would be forever grateful for the persona Simon Grey. It was because of his alter ego that Mitch had the finances to do what he wanted with his life. To find a small, quiet town somewhere in Middle America where he could just blend in.

Live a quiet life.

Be Mitch Burk again.

Chapter Two

"I dare you!" Curtis goaded Shane as he took a swig of beer and swiped the back of his hand across his lips.

Shane Justin looked at Curtis and glared. He grabbed the pistol Lucas was holding and turned it over in his hand.

"What's wrong, Shane? Haven't you ever held a gun before?" Curtis taunted.

"Of course, I have!" Shane snapped.

"Yeah, well, we're talking about the kind that shoots real bullets, not airsoft BBs or buckshot," Lucas added as he gave Shane a shove.

"Knock it off, Lucas. I said I would do it, and I meant it."

Shane tried to talk a good talk for a sixteen-year-old, but wasn't sure he could follow through with the dare. His heart beat furiously in his chest, making it hard to breathe. Shane looked at the pistol in his hand and told himself he had nothing to lose, but when the sound of an approaching vehicle grew louder, he felt like he was going to throw-up.

"It's now or never," Lucas said as he pushed Shane from behind.

"Knock it off!" Shane shoved him back, wanting to punch him in the face. He could take Lucas. He was bigger than his friend and definitely more muscular, but that wasn't the point. Shane wanted to fit in and prove to them he was as just as tough as they were.

Shane turned around and peered over the long, dried grass growing on the side of the road. He watched as an old Suburban headed their way, pulling an Airstream trailer, going slower than slow.

"He's driving too slow. What if it's someone old? I can't shoot at someone old. They could have a heart attack or a stroke or something."

"I knew you couldn't do it! You're nothing but a coward and a momma's boy!" Curtis yelled.

"Oh yeah? I'll show you who's a momma's boy."

At the last moment—before the Suburban had passed—Shane bolted out of the ditch, crouched along the side of the road, aimed the gun at the windshield, and pulled the trigger.

Lucas and Curtis took off the minute the report of the gun echoed, but Shane couldn't move. With his eyes glued to the Suburban, he watched as it swerved back and forth across the road, completely out of control. When Shane realized it was headed straight for him, he squeezed his eyes shut, knowing he was about to be hit.

Tires screeched and the acrid smell of burning rubber stung his nose. He opened his eyes just in time to see the Suburban and trailer jet across the two-lane road and land in the ditch across from where he was standing.

When the truck's door swung open and the driver staggered out, Shane realized he needed to get out of there. Fast. He dropped the gun and took off across the open field behind him. He could hear the guy running behind him—panting and cursing—as his pounding footsteps closed the distance between them. The man tackled him to the ground with a thud, and lay spread eagle on top of him. Shane struggled to get away but couldn't. The guy was pure muscle.

Yelling obscenities and grabbing Shane by the collar, the man spun him around and shoved him into the brittle grass. His brown-green eyes sparked with anger and blood dripped from a gash on his head.

"You stupid little punk! What were you thinking? I could've been killed!" The man clung to Shane's collar, shaking him violently with every questioning accusation.

Shane couldn't disguise the fear he felt or hide the tears clouding his eyes. The guy was going to kill him. He just knew it.

Finally, the man stopped his assault on Shane and rolled over on to the rocky soil. He lay on the ground, his chest heaving as he grabbed for his head.

Shane scrambled to his feet, ready to run, but he couldn't. The stranger lay on the ground, blood oozing from his forehead, eyes closed, his chest rising quickly with every breath.

"Dude, are you going to be okay?" Shane asked, but got no response. He bent down alongside the guy and shook his shoulder. "Don't die on me."

"I'm not dying!" the man yelled, shoving Shane's hand away. "Now stop shaking me before I puke all over you."

Shane sat back on his heels, not sure what to do next. He could run, knowing the guy wouldn't have the strength to catch him. But if he left and the stranger died, it would be his fault.

I guess I am a coward.

Swearing under his breath, Shane pulled his flannel shirt off and yanked his grungy t-shirt over his head. With the pocketknife he got for Christmas, Shane cut his worn undershirt in to strips, then wadded up the tattered material and pushed it against the man's forehead.

The man flexed in pain, obscenities flying, his hand latching on to Shane's wrist.

"I'm just trying to help!" Shane shouted. "I need to stop the bleeding."

The guy held Shane in his stare for a moment before he released the hold on his wrist. Shane pressed the bloody material against the man's forehead and wrapped the second piece around his head.

"So, do you think you can walk back to your truck?" Shane asked, still not knowing what he was going to do with the guy. The stranger looked at him, hatred in his eyes.

"Yeah, I think so." He sat up, swaying slightly.

Shane extended his hand to the guy. Hesitantly, the stranger looked up at him before allowing Shane to pull him to his feet. The man was tall, nearly collapsing on top of Shane when he took his first step. Taking a minute to steady the stranger, Shane looped the man's arm around his shoulders. Slowly, they made their way across the field. When they got back to the road, the man picked up the gun where it lay on the edge of the pavement. Shane swallowed hard,

JUST AN ACT

wondering what the man was going to do with it.

"Consider this my insurance policy," the man warned as he gripped the gun. "No more trouble, okay?"

"Okay," Shane answered, knowing his trouble had just begun.

It was slow moving, getting the guy back to his vehicle. He stumbled over the uneven ground and nearly took a header when he ran into the fender. Looking at the damage of his Suburban, he cursed and hollered up a storm. When he slammed his hand down on the hood, he moaned and grabbed his head.

Shane waited until the guy was done throwing his fit, then helped him navigate the ditch as they circled the passenger side of the old jalopy. Swinging the door open, Shane brushed the shattered glass from the front seat, then lowered the man to the torn interior. Slowly, the stranger swiveled his long legs around until they settled on the floorboard. Shane slammed the door shut and took a step back, staring at the man through the broken window.

"So, is that it?" the man asked. "You're just going to leave me here as I bleed to death?" The guy moaned, then rested his head back against the worn seat cushion and closed his eyes.

"No!" Shane snapped, even though that was exactly what he wanted to do.

He took a few steps back and looked at the Airstream that now rested precariously in the ditch. "Great!" There was no way he was going to be able to pull it out. The Suburban didn't have enough power.

After jumping up and down on the hitch, and wrestling with the winch, Shane was finally able to unhook the trailer from the truck. He walked to the driver's side and yanked the door open. Wiping the rest of the glass from the seat to the floor, he climbed in and slammed the door.

"Do you think you could slam it any harder?" the man hollered.

"Sorry," Shane mumbled as he turned the key in the ignition. The engine whined and squealed, but didn't turn over. He tried a second and third time with no luck.

"You're going to flood it," the man said, with his eyes closed, his head leaning against the doorframe. "Pump the accelerator three or four times, then turn the key halfway. When you feel the engine grab, floor the peddle."

Shane turned to fire off on the guy. He didn't need him explaining how to start a stupid truck. He opened his mouth to tell the man what he could do with his advice but decided against it. He was the reason the man was hurt, and his vehicle was in a heap. Getting the engine to turn over was the least of his worries.

He pumped the accelerator four times, turned the key halfway, and listened as the vehicle roared to life. When he dropped it into gear, the man opened his eyes. "Do you know what you're doing?"

"Yeah. I think I can drive your piece of junk." He turned forward—looking through the shattered windshield—and gunned the engine.

It took him three attempts, but finally, the Suburban lurched and groaned, and with a burst of power, Shane was able to get the beat-up vehicle out of the ditch and back onto the road. Shoving the gearshift into park, Shane got out of the Suburban.

"Where are you going?" the man asked.

Shane ignored him as he walked around to look at all four tires. He then pressed his belly to the asphalt to inspect the undercarriage. He didn't see anything wrong, so he got back in, shifted into drive, and started down the road.

"Where are you taking me?" the man asked, looking dazed and ready to puke.

"Home."

"No way!" The man protested, trying to sit up straighter. "I'm not going home with you. Take me to a hospital or something."

"The hospital is fifty miles away, and I'm not sure this piece of junk of yours will make it that far."

"Then take me to the sheriff's office or the town vet. Anywhere would be better than your house. Your family is likely to make me disappear so I can't press charges."

"You're not the one who needs to be worried." Shane glanced at the stranger and then back to the road. "By the time my mother gets done with me, I'll be the one needing police protection."

"Then she should've thought about that before she decided to raise a juvenile delinquent."

"Hey, my mom's not like that!" Shane hollered.

"Yeah, right. Excuse me if I don't believe you." The guy turned toward the passenger window, but silence lasted only a moment. "Where did you get the gun, and why were you out on the highway shooting at people?"

"Passing time."

"Passing time?" he repeated with a sarcastic chuckle. "Geez, I hate to see what you do for real entertainment." Again, there was only a moment of silence before the stranger asked, "Who were those other boys with you?"

"What other boys?" Shane answered coolly, keeping his eyes on the road.

"I saw them take off on four-wheelers. Who were they?"

"You must've been hallucinating. I was the only one out there."

Shane slowly turned down the long gravel driveway, his stomach churning, his heart racing. He shifted the vehicle into park just short of his front porch. He watched as the stranger leaned forward to get a better view of the house.

"For what it's worth, I'm sorry," Shane said.

"Why'd you do it then?"

He looked at the man and shrugged. "What does it matter?"

Shane got out of the vehicle and slammed the door. Walking around to the passenger side of the truck, he saw his mother approaching from the barn. Leaning on the frame of the window, he crouched down and stared directly at the stranger. "I know you think I'm some punk kid, and that's fine. Just don't take it out on my mom. This is my fault, not hers."

Mitch studied the kid's face. Try as he might, the teen wasn't the delinquent he pretended to be. Mitch recognized something in the kid from his own childhood; he was struggling.

After one more look at the quaint clapboard house, Mitch turned to say something to the kid, but the woman walking toward him completely upended his thoughts.

She couldn't have been more than five-foot-three, maybe five-five if you counted the heel on her dusty cowboy boots and the beat-up straw cowboy hat perched on her head. Mitch watched as her hips swayed in worn jeans that hugged her slight frame like a glove. *No way is that the kid's mother.* She was too young to have a teenage son; not to mention she was drop-dead gorgeous. Mitch had expected to find a toothless, overweight woman with a cockeyed snarl and a shotgun perched on her hip. Not a bombshell in boots.

Glancing at his lap where the gun lay, Mitch figured wielding a weapon would not be in his best interest—at least not until he knew her frame of mind. The woman didn't know him from Adam, and if she saw the gun, she might jump to the wrong conclusion. Mitch quickly shoved it deep within the upholstery of the bench seat. He could always pull it out later if things went south.

The woman approached, her blonde ponytail bobbing from shoulder to shoulder. Mitch watched her pleasant smile turn into a frown when she took in her son's appearance.

"Shane, why is your shirt unbuttoned and where's your t-shirt?"

Before the kid could answer, she crossed her arms over her chest and turned her attention to Mitch. "What's going on here?"

Chapter Three

"Mom, I can—"

Before Shane could explain the unfamiliar truck, and why he was with a complete stranger, he watched as his mom zeroed in on the guy's bloody t-shirt and the blood-soaked bandage over his eye.

"Oh my gosh! What happened? Who is this?" She hunched down to look at the man through the busted window. "Are you all right?" Without waiting for an answer, she turned back to Shane. "What happened?"

He tried to answer, but his mom jumped from one question to the next without giving him a chance to say anything.

"Mom, stop!" Shane yelled in frustration. "Give me a minute to explain!"

She quieted immediately, looking shocked at his outburst, then snapped, "Don't you dare take that tone with me, Shane Justin! Now, tell me what the heck is going on."

He softened his pitch. "I was on the road . . . hanging out . . . looking for something to do . . . when—"

"Wait a minute. What do you mean, 'looking for something to do'?"

"Looking for something to do, Mom! Something! Anything! This place is the most boring—"

"Okay!" She put up her hands to stop him. "I get it. You were bored. Just tell me what happened."

Shane slumped his shoulders and stared at the dirt drive. "I—"

17

Mitch felt sorry for Shane—why, he didn't know. But when it was obvious the kid was going to give himself up, Mitch interrupted. "I had an accident just up the road."

Mitch paused and looked at the defiant teenager. He could tell from the set of his jaw, Shane was bracing himself for his mother's reaction. Mitch should've just unloaded on the woman. She needed to know what a jackass prank her son had pulled. After all, he could've been killed. But when Mitch looked at the kid again, he could see through his belligerent façade. The boy was terrified—of his mother, or of him, he wasn't sure—so Mitch decided to change tactics and see how things played out. He turned back to the woman and said, "Your son saw me go off the road and stopped to give me a hand."

Shock was evident on Shane's face while a look of pride washed over his mom's. She smiled at her son before turning back to Mitch. "Are you all right?"

"A little dizzy, but I'm all right."

Mitch slowly climbed out of the Suburban as Shane and his mother took a few steps back. He held on to the doorframe for support while his stomach rolled and pitched. He focused on the woman's worn cowboy boots and tried to stand up straight. When her boots began to spin, Mitch had to use every ounce of strength he had not to spew his lunch all over them.

The woman reached for him just as he closed his eyes. "Are you okay?" He heard her say, but before Mitch could answer, his knees buckled.

"Shane, grab his arm."

Mitch never blacked out, but he was definitely seeing stars. Shane and his mom guided him toward the house and helped him navigate the porch stairs. Mitch got as far as the living room when he felt his stomach clench. He could actually feel the color draining from his face, replaced with perspiration. His eyes darted from left to right. He needed a bathroom. And quick! As if reading his mind, the woman answered his question before he could even ask it.

"First door on the right."

Mitch pushed away from Shane and his mom, then stumbled through the bathroom door.

Beth listened to the violent heaving and knew the man was in pretty bad shape.

"Shane, did you see what happened?" she whispered.

When he hesitated, her chest tightened. In her gut, Beth knew there was more to the story. "Shane, please tell me Lucas and Curtis didn't have something to do with this."

He just looked away.

It was all the answer she needed. "I knew it!" Beth threw up her hands and began to pace. Shane had been getting into more and more trouble lately, so naturally she feared the worst. And the worst always seemed to include Lucas and Curtis. Not wanting the stranger to overhear, Beth took a deep breath and lowered her tone. She would have to whisper her lecture instead.

"I've told you over and over again, those two are no good. Listen to that man." She pointed to the bathroom door. "He could be seriously hurt, and those idiot friends of yours are somehow to blame. When are you going to see for yourself those two are nothing but trouble?"

The toilet flushed, and the man stepped out into the hallway. Beth turned to him and saw that his skin was still a sickly shade of gray, and he had to lean against the wall for balance. But it was the blood that bothered her the most. There was so much of it. She knew head wounds were notorious for heavy bleeding, but somehow that didn't make her feel any better.

"Why don't you take a seat on the sofa," Beth said, motioning to the den. "I'll call Dr. Bradley and see if he can stop by." When the stranger didn't argue, she worried even more. She'd never met a man who would willingly go to the doctor or be seen by one. It could only mean one thing. He was in even more pain than she first thought.

She watched as the man shuffled into the living room and slowly lowered himself to the worn leather couch. Beth pulled her phone from her pocket and dialed while studying Shane. He paced the room like a caged animal. Not quite the actions of a hero, she thought to herself. More like the behavior of an offender. Her stomach clenched. Her son was turning into a delinquent before her eyes, and she seemed powerless to do anything about it.

"Hey, Doc, it's Beth Justin. I need you out here at the Diamond-J. No, no, Shane and Charlie are fine. No, it's not for me either. There seems to have been some sort of accident on the highway. I have a man here with a head injury. I'm not sure how serious it is, but he's light-headed and nauseous. I could bring him in but—Okay. I'll see you in about thirty minutes."

Beth laid her phone on the coffee table before walking to the kitchen to get her first aid kit. Returning to the living room, she heard Shane whispering to the stranger. However, when Shane made eye contact with her, he clammed up and moved to the other side of the room. He was hiding something, but Beth decided to wait and find out what it was later. Right now she needed to see what she could do to help this man.

"Dr. Bradley will be here in about thirty minutes," Beth said as she took a seat on the couch. "I'm sorry, I didn't catch your name."

"Mitch. Mitch Burk."

"Well, Mitch, let me see if I can clean this up in the meantime."

She brushed away a few random curls that rested against the wad of cotton tied around his forehead. She pulled the makeshift bandage from his head, causing him to flinch.

"Sorry," Beth said as she got her first look at the gash—a very nasty gash. "This is pretty deep. I can clean it up, but you are definitely going to need stitches." She tried to swab away the blood with a piece of gauze, but Mitch recoiled every time she made contact. Finally, he grabbed her wrist and pulled her hand away.

"Why don't we wait for the doctor?" he snapped.

Beth withdrew her wrist from his hand. "I'm sorry. I was only trying to help."

"I know," His words were cool and measured. "and I appreciate it, but my head feels like it's about to explode and your poking and prodding isn't helping any."

Beth watched as Mitch closed his eyes and sunk back against the couch cushions. He lay there, his chest rising slightly with every breath. She waited for Mitch to open his eyes, for him to say something, but he just lay there for several minutes. He was still. Too still.

She shook his arm, startling him.

His eyes flew open. "What are you doing?" he barked.

She jumped back. "I'm sorry, it's just that you shouldn't sleep if you have a concussion. I would feel better if you stayed awake until the doctor got here."

He sighed and closed his eyes again. "Don't worry. I'm not going to die on you."

"Where are you from?" she asked.

"What?"

"I asked where you were from."

"You know what, I really don't feel like chit-chatting, lady. So if you don't mind, I'm just going to rest here until the doctor shows up."

How dare he!

"Yeah, well, I can't say that having a stranger puke all over my bathroom and lay half-unconscious on my couch is how I would've chosen to fill my day, but here we are."

"Wow, I see where your son gets his charming disposition."

Beth was speechless. Stunned. She didn't even know what to say. When he opened his eyes, she couldn't tell if what she saw was a smidgen of remorse or if he was going to puke again.

He sighed. "Hey, I'm sorry. That was uncalled for. Let me start over. To answer your question, I'm on vacation."

"Okay, so when you're not on vacation, where are you from?" Beth persisted.

"I'm originally from New York, but I've been living in California."

"Well, I'm Beth Justin, and this is my son, Shane. So, do you even know where you are?"

"Somewhere in Kansas."

"Triune, Kansas, to be exact," Beth clarified.

"So, what do people do in Triune, Kansas?"

"Raise cattle mostly."

"Is that what you and your husband do?"

Beth bristled at his assumption. "The Diamond-J has been in *my* family for years. I have four hands that work the ranch, besides Shane and myself." She hoped she'd made her point.

"So, how old are you, Shane?" Mitch asked as he shifted his attention.

"Sixteen."

"What does a sixteen-year-old do for fun in Triune, Kansas?"

"Nothing. There's no such thing as fun in Triune." Shane shot to his feet and stomped upstairs.

Beth watched her son's outburst and cringed. She didn't know why she felt the need to apologize for his behavior, but she did. "I'm sorry. Shane's going through a—"

"Save it." Mitch held up his hand. "It's none of my business."

When the pounding on the stairs reprised, Beth turned to see Shane coming back down the stairs. He stormed toward the front door as he pulled a clean t-shirt over his head, then turned back to where she and Mitch sat on the couch. "I've got chores to do," Shane said. "Sorry about your crash. I'm sure Doc Bradley will have you fixed up in no time and you can be on your way." He then pushed the old screen door open and let it slam behind him.

Beth sighed.

She glanced out the large picture window and watched as her son stalked toward the barn. *I'm losing him.* Beth knew she was, and felt powerless to do anything about it.

"So, what happened?" Beth turned her attention back to Mitch. "To your Suburban, I mean?"

Mitch answered with his eyes closed. "Something hit the windshield. I kind of lost control and landed in a ditch. My trailer's still there. Does Triune have a mechanic? I'm going to have to get my truck and trailer checked out, and get my windshield replaced."

"Triune doesn't have a mechanic, but I can have my foreman take

JUST AN ACT

a look at your rig. He's pretty good with old cars." Beth picked up her cell phone from the coffee table and pressed speed dial.

"Hey, Uncle Charlie, I need your help. There's this guy here who had a... well... he had a fender bender on the highway. He's going to need his windshield replaced, and it looks like he might need his front fender pulled out. Other than that, I'm not sure." Beth paused, then glanced at Mitch before turning away and whispering into the phone. "He's sitting right here. No, I'm fine, Uncle Charlie. Doc Bradley is on his way over, and the guy can barely stand up. Believe me, he doesn't have the strength to try anything. Okay, I'll see you in a little bit."

When Beth hung up the phone, she turned to see Mitch staring at her. *Shoot. He probably heard me.* Nervously, she attempted to make small talk. "My Uncle's also my foreman. He'll be over later. He's a ways out."

Mitch's eyes stayed fixed on her, making her feel self-conscious. She cleared her throat. "You said you were vacationing. Is someone expecting you?"

"Expecting me?"

"I mean, is there someone I should call? To let them know you've been delayed."

"Nope."

Beth wished Shane hadn't stormed off like he had. It was awkward having a stranger in the house, and there was something about the man's demeanor that bothered her. His answers were vague, and she had the distinct feeling she wasn't being told the whole story. Then again, Shane wasn't telling her the whole story either.

"Look, I have some things to do in the barn. Dr. Bradley will be here soon. Do you think you can stay awake until he gets here?"

"I'll be fine. Thanks for your help."

"No problem."

Beth walked outside and released the breath she'd been holding. Pressing her hands to her cheeks, she could feel the heat rising in them. *I don't know who this Mitch guy is, but I'll be glad when he's gone.*

When Beth walked into the barn, she saw Shane was in the loft pitching down hay. Climbing the ladder, Beth watched him as he worked, staring at him, purposely trying to make him feel uncomfortable.

"Are you going to tell me what *really* happened?" Beth finally asked as she shoved her hands in her pockets, her eyes riveted on her son.

"Why? You never believe me."

"I want to believe you, Shane, it's just that ever since you started hanging around Curtis and Lucas, these little *incidences* keep happening." She walked in front of Shane so he couldn't avoid looking at her.

"He told you what happened. I saw him go into the ditch so I helped him out."

Beth knew Shane was lying, but instead of getting angry she felt defeated. Little by little her son's anger and bitterness was eating away at their relationship. He didn't have a father and he blamed her. Shane didn't understand, and Beth wasn't sure she wanted him to. She'd rather he blame her than find out the truth about his father.

Beth moved from stall to stall, filling the troughs with clean water and putting down fresh straw. She really needed to go back to the house. Leaving a complete stranger alone wasn't the brightest thing to do. *Right this very minute, he could be snooping through my things or eyeballing the place so he can come back later and rob me blind. That is, if he hasn't already fallen into a state of unconsciousness.* But she just couldn't sit around making small talk with him. Because, try as she might, Beth couldn't stop staring at him. And it had nothing to do with the gash on his forehead.

The man was gorgeous. Hands down, step-out-of-a-magazine handsome. And Beth was sure—if she sat with him much longer—she would do or say something stupid. So, she was better off keeping her distance until Doc showed up.

Just then she saw Uncle Charlie ride across the yard on his Palomino, Hammer. *Thank goodness.* As she walked out to meet him, Charlie got down, lapped Hammer's reins over a post, and gave her a squeeze.

"So, where's this stray of yours?"

"In the house. That's his vehicle over there."

Charlie looked over to where the Suburban was parked.

"He also has a trailer stuck alongside the highway."

"I'll get to that soon enough," Uncle Charlie said as he made a bee-line toward the house. "First, I want to get a look at this guy who magically showed up out of nowhere." He barged through the door—the old screen creaking in protest—Beth right behind him.

Mitch turned toward the slamming door and saw a burly man fill the doorway. He decided right then and there if that was the doctor, he'd take his chances with the gash on his head and a couple of band-aids.

"Mitch, this is Charlie Justin. Uncle Charlie, this is Mitch Burk."

Slowly, Mitch leaned forward and extended his hand. The guy had a fierce grip and shook his hand a little harder than necessary. Mitch knew the old man was making a point.

"So, that heap outside is yours?"

"Yeah. How long will it take to find a windshield for it?"

"I could probably have it replaced in two or three days," Charlie answered.

"Three days! That long?" Mitch did little to hide his annoyance.

"In case you haven't noticed, hotshot, my name's not Manny, Moe, or Jack. I'm a car guy, but it still takes time to find things."

"I'm sorry, I didn't mean to sound rude." Mitch quickly changed his tone, not wanting to get on the hefty man's bad side.

Charlie glance at Beth, then back at him. "I'm gonna go take a look at your vehicle. Beth said something about a trailer. Where's that?"

"It's in a ditch alongside the highway, but you're going to need something big to pull it out."

"Gee, thanks for the advice, cowboy, I might have taken Shane's bicycle or something."

Beth rolled her eyes at Charlie's sarcasm, then gave Mitch an apologetic smile before following her uncle out the door. She quickened her steps to catch up with his long strides and then gave him a half-hearted slug in the arm.

"What was that all about?" she asked.

"I don't like him," Charlie grumbled.

She laughed at his directness. "How could you not like him? He barely said ten words to you."

"I just don't like him, okay?"

Beth tried to hide the smile on her face while Charlie headed around the back of the barn where the old tractor was parked. "Where's Shane?" he yelled, before the motor roared to life.

"He's in the barn. I'll get him."

Charlie was already halfway down the driveway when Shane hopped aboard the tractor. Beth walked back to the house surprised to see Mitch standing at the refrigerator. She let the screen door slam shut behind her, drawing his attention.

"I was looking for something to drink. I hope you don't mind."

"No, not at all."

Beth watched as he ducked his head behind the refrigerator door. She could hear the clinking of glass as he moved things around. It was clear he wasn't finding what he wanted.

"If you're looking for alcohol, there isn't any."

Mitch mumbled something under his breath as he reached in and pulled out a soda.

Beth was annoyed. Mitch had all the signs of a concussion—could barely even walk—but having a drink seemed to be what he cared about most. She looked at the clock on the wall, wondering what was keeping Doc Bradley.

Chapter Four

Beth watched the doctor put away his instruments then listened as he gave Mitch instructions. "Son, you need to stay put for a few days."

"Stay put? Where?" Mitch asked.

Doc Bradley turned to Beth with an empathetic look. She nervously shook her head, knowing exactly what his caring eyes were suggesting.

"I would take him home with me, Beth," Doc said, "but Betsy and I are celebrating our anniversary this weekend."

Beth motioned for the doctor to follow her into the hallway.

"He can't stay here," she tried to whisper, but her frustration got the better of her. "I don't even know who he is. He could be a dangerous maniac or a serial killer for all I know. I can't have someone like that in my house, around my son."

"I'm not a serial killer or a maniac," Mitch hollered from around the corner.

Beth cringed as she and the doctor walked back into the living room.

"Look, doctor," Mitch directed his attention to Doc Bradley. "Just give me a ride into town. I'll stay in a hotel while my vehicle is being fixed."

"What hotel, son? The nearest town is fifty miles from here, and you're in no condition to be by yourself. What about Charlie and Sarah?" Doc Bradley asked Beth. "Maybe he could stay with them? Or what about Travis? Maybe he could stay at his house for a few days?"

"Look, this is ridiculous," Mitch interrupted. "If Ms. Justin will allow me to park my trailer somewhere on her property, I'll take care of myself. I'll set my alarm and wake myself up every hour if I have to. And then, as soon as I can get my vehicles fixed, I'll be out of here. How does that sound?"

Beth was about to say something when she heard the tractor out front. Looking out the picture window, she saw it was pulling an Airstream. Charlie pulled the trailer next to the Suburban, then walked over to the truck and popped the hood.

Beth turned her attention back to Mitch. "Look, I'm sorry I said what I did about you being a maniac or a serial killer. You seem like a nice guy who's just having a run of bad luck. You can stay here. I'm sure with Dr. Bradley, Charlie, and the rest of the hands knowing you're here, you'll be on your best behavior."

"Gee, thanks for that vote of confidence," he said sarcastically. "I'll make sure to tell all my serial killer buddies how hospitable the people are in Triune, Kansas."

Beth glared at him for a second, then followed Doc out into the yard. They both stopped along the Suburban where Charlie was bent over the engine. "So, how bad is it?" Beth asked.

"Not bad at all, really. The fender needs to be pulled out, and a couple of the hoses replaced, but the engine's fine. The alignment took a pretty hard jolt, but he'll be able to limp along and get it looked at on the way to wherever it is he's going."

"So, what's *your* prognosis?" Charlie asked Doc.

"He should be fine in a day or two. By the time you get his rig fixed, he should be ready to be on his way."

"And until then?" Charlie asked, his expression telling Beth he wasn't going to like the answer.

"Uncle Charlie, he's going to stay here; in his trailer. It will only be for—"

"Oh no, he's not! I'm not letting some stranger stay so close to your house. We don't know a lick about this guy."

"Uncle Charlie, it's not your decision to make." Beth held up her hand to stop his lecture before he got started. "Look, I appreciate your concern, but I'm a big girl. I can take care of myself. Besides, he's in no shape to try anything stupid."

Beth waved to Doc as he disappeared down the long driveway. When she turned around, she looked at where Mitch's trailer sat in the yard still hitched to the tractor. *What would it hurt to take a look around?* Beth nervously bit at a hangnail on her right thumb. *If I find anything among his things that I think is questionable, I'll call the police and let them deal with him.*

She slowly walked to the Airstream trailer and pulled on the door handle with a tug. Beth craned her neck to look inside, expecting to see old dilapidated upholstery and worn-out appliances but was greeted by what appeared to be brand new everything.

Wow. This is pretty nice.

Climbing inside, Beth picked up a few things that had obviously tumbled from the cupboards in the accident. Laying them on the bench seat, she glanced around and slowly moved toward the back of the trailer. Beth slid the accordion door open to reveal a small but tidy bathroom. The shower and vanity weren't what she considered full-size, but it was certainly larger than the bathroom units she'd seen in other trailers.

Thinking she heard something, Beth stopped and listened. After waiting a second or two, she shrugged. *Must have been the wind.* When she pushed back the collapsible door in front of her, Beth saw the sleeping quarters. The neatly made queen size bed took up most of the room, along with built-in lamps and nightstands on either side. The closet door to the left was open slightly. A few pairs of shoes had tumbled out, again, probably because of the accident. Beth reached down to push them back inside, but not before noticing an expensive pair of cowboy boots. Very expensive. She reached for one of the boots and turned it over in her hand. *Lucchese. These have to be fifteen hundred dollar boots.* But they were broken in pretty well. The leather creased, the sheen dull.

Weird.

Beth didn't know why the boots bothered her so much, other than they didn't fit the profile she'd subconsciously conjured up regarding

Mitch. That, and the fact that no sensible cowboy would wear such an expensive pair of boots for everyday work. From the looks of them, they'd taken quite a beating.

She felt the Airstream rock slightly, jostling Beth from her thoughts.

The wind must be picking up. She glanced at her watch. *I'd better get back inside anyway, so I can figure out what I'm going to make for dinner.*

Beth shoved the boots back inside the closet and pulled the door shut. She took a step back into the hallway so she could close the bedroom door, then turned around and ran smack dab into Mitch's chest.

"Find anything interesting?" His words were calm, but she could tell by the way his arms were crossed against his chest Mitch was irritated she was there.

Beth took a step back, trying to put some space between them. "No. Not that I was looking for anything. I was just . . . making sure nothing got damaged . . . in the accident." The pitch of her voice did nothing to camouflage her guilt.

"So, you were worried my clothes or maybe my shoes got broken?" he questioned, without even a hint of humor in his voice.

Beth shoved her hands in the back pocket of her jeans to keep them from shaking. "I'm sorry. I know it looks like I was snooping, but that wasn't my intention. I was expecting this to be an old worn-out trailer, and when I saw everything was so nice and new, I started looking around. Your closet door must've slid open, and some of your shoes had fallen out. I was just putting them back inside."

Brushing past Beth, Mitch opened the bedroom door and took a cursory look around. He knew she hadn't had any real time to snoop, and he'd been careful to keep his personal items locked up somewhere safe. With one final glance, he slid the bedroom door shut and looked at Beth.

She was pressed up against the wall, barely enough room to stand opposite him. Mitch's senses pulsed at Beth's closeness, quickening even more as he gave her a long appraising look.

If it weren't for the fact that Beth had a sixteen-year-old son, Mitch would've guessed she was still in her twenties. Her skin was tanned and freckled, giving her a youthful glow, and her curvaceous figure did nothing to give away her age. She was a blonde-haired, blue-eyed beauty. And those blue eyes of hers were doing everything in their power not to look at him.

Mitch could tell their closeness was disturbing Beth. The gentlemanly thing to do would be to put her at ease. But the way she raised her chin and squinted her eyes, she was all but challenging him to do or say something. He couldn't help himself. He was never one to back down from a challenge. Mitch would like nothing more than to wrap Beth up in his arms and give her an exploratory kiss. But he knew all that would do is land him on his butt in the middle of the highway with nowhere to go. So, instead, he took a step closer and allowed his large frame to tower over her diminutive figure. "So, what do you think of my bedroom?" He grinned. "Inviting, isn't it?"

"Seems kind of cramped," she retorted.

"That's never been a problem for me."

Beth's blood was boiling. She had tried to be polite and accommodating to this guy because of his accident but refused to stand by and let him think she was some desperate, lonely woman he could charm into his bed.

"I'm sure that line works with the kind of women you're used to picking up in bars and strip clubs, but it's not going to work with me. Your type doesn't interest me."

"Oh really? And what exactly is *my* type?" Mitch leaned closer, resting his forearm on the wall behind her.

His actions took what was left of the air in the room and snatched it away. Although Beth was chilled by his forwardness, she wasn't going to back down. She was going to let him know exactly what he could expect from her. If Mitch thought he was going to smooth talk his way into a roadside romp, he was sadly mistaken.

"Look, I won't put up with any crap while you're on my property, do you understand me? You're trespassing at the moment, and even if I allow you to stay, that doesn't mean I want you here. I have myself and my son to look out for. If at any time I think either one of us is in danger, so help me I will shoot first and worry about the consequences later. Do I make myself clear?"

"Completely," Mitch whispered.

She pushed around him and jumped down from the trailer's doorway. She slammed the door so hard, Charlie's head bobbed up from under the hood of the Suburban.

"You okay, Beth?"

She walked right past him. She had no intentions of explaining to her uncle how she'd just been caught snooping or that Mitch had made her feel like a cornered animal waiting for a predator to pounce.

Chapter Five

Mitch tried to catch up with Beth so he could apologize, but her uncle stepped out from under the hood of the Suburban and into his path.

"Is there a problem here, boy?" Charlie asked as a very large wrench slipped in and out of the cloth he was holding. For an old man, he looked pretty menacing.

Mitch watched as Beth disappeared behind the barn. He wanted to go after her, but now he had to contend with her uncle. Mitch decided complete honesty would be his best bet.

"I need to apologize to Beth. I was rude and insulting."

"How rude?" Charlie asked, the wrench moving quicker through the chamois in his hand.

"I may have frightened her. That wasn't my intention, so I need to apologize."

Charlie's gray brows lowered and his jaw clenched tight as he took a step forward and tapped the heavy wrench against Mitch's chest. "You see to it that your apology is sincere. You understand me?"

"Yes, sir." Mitch thought for sure the old man was going to take a swing at him, but instead, Charlie took another step closer.

"Beth is her own woman," the man spat out, fire in his eyes, "and I can't tell her what to do. But, if you cross a line with her—if you hurt Beth in any way or cause her even an ounce of pain—I will drop you like a steer in a roping contest; you understand me, boy?"

"Yes, sir. Please believe me when I say I'm sorry. Beth and I got off on the wrong foot, and I just want to make it right."

"Then I guess you better get to it."

Charlie stepped back, giving Mitch some room to move. As he crossed the yard, the pounding in his head beat in double time, reminding him he was supposed to be taking it easy. He would, but first he wanted to apologize to Beth for his crude behavior.

The sun was fading behind the mountain range on the far side of the barn. When he turned the corner, Mitch was met by a cacophony of squealing, quacking, cackling, and bleating. *Talk about Old MacDonald.* He watched for a minute, entertained by a piglet running in circles, then noticed Beth on the far side of the barn, standing next to the fence, her boot hooked on the bottom rail.

Beth heard Mitch approach but didn't turn around. She was angry and embarrassed. She had over-reacted to his juvenile pick-up lines but to apologize would only send his obviously inflated ego into overdrive.

"Beth, I'm sorry for what I said in the trailer. I didn't mean to scare you. That was not my intention."

"Scare!" She spun around to look at him. "I wasn't scared. I just wanted to set you straight." Beth laughed, to show Mitch she was amused. There was no way she was going to let him know he had frightened her by his forwardness.

"You're here because of unavoidable circumstances. I can't very well turn you out when the doctor says it would be detrimental to your health. You're welcome to stay here for those reasons and those reasons only. I just didn't want you to get the impression I would allow your company under other circumstances." Beth took a deep breath and unhooked her boot from the fence. "Now that we have that understood, I have no problem with you staying on the ranch until the doctor feels it's safe for you to travel. Beth started to walk away, then added, "Just so you know, dinner is at five o'clock; don't be late."

It was five o'clock on the nose when Beth carried a casserole dish of meatloaf to the table and sat down. Shane slouched at the table

JUST AN ACT

clinking his fork repeatedly against his plate.

"Shane, stop doing that."

"Doing what?"

"Hitting your plate with your fork. It's irritating."

"You think everything I do is irritating."

Beth glanced at Mitch, embarrassed her son was being so belligerent. "Shane, that's not true and you know it."

"Whatever."

Again, Beth looked at Mitch. He gave her a slight smile, but she couldn't decide if it was sympathetic or smugness.

"Don't feel as if you have to join us if you're not feeling well," she said, doing nothing to hide her irritation.

"I'm fine. Really."

"Well, you look horrible."

"Gee, thanks. Tell me what you really think."

Beth closed her eyes and counted to three. When she opened them again, she forced a smile. "I'm sorry. Look, it's been a hard day for everyone. I'm going to go ahead and pray for our meal and then shut up."

Who is this woman? Mitch thought as he ate her meatloaf in silence. *She's both exasperating and intriguing. It's obvious she hates having me here, but still, she fixed me dinner and is allowing me—a stranger—to stay on her ranch because she's concerned for my health. Or maybe Shane spilled the beans, and she's afraid I'll sue?*

Shane picked at his meatloaf, wondering when Mitch was going to rat him out. *What is he waiting for? Why did he lie to Mom anyway?* Shane watched Mitch while he ate. He didn't look so good. *What if he dies in the middle of the night? Would the cops somehow blame my mom?* Shane figured the sooner Mitch left, the better off he'd be, but in the meantime, he needed to stay on Mitch's good side.

35

After dinner, Beth washed dishes while Shane and Mitch moved to the den to watch TV. When she was done, Beth went to her office to take care of some business, but was soon distracted by the banter she heard coming from the other room. She crept closer to the den and listened as Mitch and Shane talked sports. Mitch seemed to be holding his own with his opinions regarding baseball, football, and hockey.

The energy Beth heard in her son's voice touched her heart. Lately, Shane had been withdrawn, closing himself off from her and everyone else on the ranch. The older Shane got, the more frustrated he was with the no-nothing town of Triune. He was tired of working the ranch, choosing instead to hang out with the likes of Curtis and Lucas; ever since then, nothing but trouble had followed.

Hearing Shane talk sports with Mitch filled Beth with hope. He sounded like his old self, not the rebellious teen who had emerged in the last few months.

Not wanting to interrupt the connection Mitch was making with Shane, Beth turned to walk away. Then, something in their conversation caught her attention.

"Thanks for not saying anything to my mom."

Beth stopped.

"Well, I can't promise that I won't, but I'd like to know why you did it?"

"It was a jerky thing to do. I know that now. But this lousy town is so boring. There's nothing to do here. I don't have any friends to hang out with because they all live too far away, and I'm tired of taking care of stupid animals all day long."

"So, who were those boys with you?"

"Curtis and Lucas. They're the only friends I have in town, but Mom hates them."

"Can you blame her? If those are the kinds of stunts you pull when you're with them, I would have to side with her."

Beth strained to hear every word. Shane had not been honest with her about what had happened on the highway, and Mitch seemed to be hiding something as well. Though she appreciated Mitch taking her side regarding Shane's choice of friends, she didn't appreciate the fact that he was keeping something from her—something that involved her son.

"You're different, Mitch. You're actually listening to me. My mom treats me like a kid, and Uncle Charlie can only talk about what it was like in the old days growing up on the ranch. My cousin, Travis, is pretty cool, but he's married now and has kids. He doesn't have time for me anymore."

"What about the ranch hands your mother was talking about? How old are they?"

"Brett and Rusty? I don't know. Twenty-three, twenty-four maybe. But they don't like having me around. I cramp their style. Besides, all they're interested in is getting drunk and finding girls that are willing to put out."

"So, you don't think about those kind of things?"

Beth was shocked Mitch was being so forward. She wanted to barge into the room and tell him he had no right to talk to her son about such things, but . . . she did want to hear what Shane had to say.

"Sure, I think about girls and stuff," Shane said, "but what good does it do me? I don't have a girlfriend, and I certainly can't just walk into a bar like they do, buy a girl a beer, and expect her to follow me out to my truck."

"Well, just for the record, any girl who would follow you out to your truck after just one beer isn't the kind of girl you want."

Beth silently sighed with relief, appreciating Mitch's advice—if that's what she could call it.

"So, you're not going to try and make a play for my mom?"

Beth quickly threw her hand over her mouth to muffle her gasp and listened to Mitch choke on whatever it was he was drinking. She held her breath, waiting for him to answer, but he continued to cough and sputter. After clearing his throat, Mitch finally said, "I don't think that would be such a good idea. Your mom seems pretty irritated with me."

"But you think she's hot, right?"

Mitch was silent.

Beth strained.

"Yes. Your mom is very attractive, but I don't think we have much in common. She's being gracious, extending her help and all, but I don't think I should take advantage of her hospitality."

Mitch's answer seemed to suffice Shane, and their conversation quickly turned back to sports. Beth wandered back to her office a little flustered she'd become a topic of discussion along with sports, sex, and drinking. Looking at the clock, she waited another ten minutes before making an appearance in the den. "Shane, I think it's time to call it a night. It's after eleven o'clock, and you promised you would help tomorrow with the fencing on the west end."

Shane begrudgingly got up from the couch.

Mitch quickly extended his hand to him. "It's been nice getting to know you, Shane."

"You too, Mitch," Shane shook his hand. "You're a pretty all-right guy."

Once her son left the room, Beth turned her attention to Mitch. "Did you want to grab some of your things from your trailer before I show you to your room?"

"My room? I thought I was going to sack out in my trailer?"

"Well, since I have to wake you every few hours, it would be easier for me if I didn't have to traipse outside to do it."

"Are you sure? I would hate for you to have nightmares about a maniac or serial killer attacking you in your sleep," he said sarcastically.

"No problem there. I sleep with a twenty-two next to my bed. You're the one who might have nightmares."

Beth's steely gaze let Mitch know she was not someone he wanted to fool with, especially in his current condition. He remembered her earlier warning. 'I will shoot first and worry about the consequences later.' Mitch didn't doubt her for a moment.

Slowly, he got up from the couch, too exhausted to argue. He'd kept it together while talking to Shane—because it was obvious the boy needed some male interaction—but the pounding in his head made it hard for him to focus, especially when Shane questioned him about Beth. When the kid asked him if he was going to make a play for his mom, Mitch had just about lost it. It had taken a minute to compose himself, then he decided to answer as honestly as he could. Fortunately, that satisfied Shane for the moment. Hopefully, they wouldn't have any more conversations like that. Baseball and hockey were subjects he could handle. Talking to a teenage boy about sex and women was not in his wheelhouse.

At the repeated beeping of Beth's alarm, she swung her feet to the ground. She silenced the irritating noise, stood, then wandered down the hall. When Beth pushed opened the door to the guestroom, she felt her pulse quicken.

There, in the glow of moonlight, lay Mitch in a deep slumber, his bare chest moving up and down with every breath. Her grandmother's quilt was neatly folded at the foot of the bed, the warm summer evening making it unnecessary. Beth found herself staring, knowing her attention would go unnoticed by a sleeping Mitch.

To call Mitch handsome would be an understatement. His towering frame and muscular build would get him noticed in any room he entered, but it was his, piercing eyes that captivated her. Beth was afraid to look at him when she spoke because she felt transparent in his gaze. Virile was the word that came to mind when she looked at his rugged jaw and listened to his deep voice, yet his disarming smile gave him a boyish kind of charm.

Beth snapped from her scrutiny and stepped closer to the bed. Her baggy sweatpants and oversized t-shirt were hot and sticky in the summer heat, but knowing she would have to wake Mitch throughout the night, she had chosen something more presentable than her usual camisole and shorts.

"Mitch," she whispered, but he didn't move.

Leaning closer, Beth repeated his name. He stirred but didn't open his eyes. She tried again, raising her voice an octave but only got a groan in response.

"Mitch, wake up." Her words were firmer as she gave his bare arm a shove.

His head lolled to one side but still, his eyes didn't open.

Beth panicked. *What if I can't wake him?*

She sat on the edge of the bed and with both hands firmly placed on his shoulders, she hovered over him and gave him a hearty shake. "Mitch!" she barked.

Mitch's eyes flew open. His body snapped to a sitting position, causing his head to crack against Beth's. They both moaned, grabbing their foreheads. Mitch allowed his head to sink back into the pillows as he swore under his breath.

"I'm sorry." Beth winced.

"What was that for?" Mitch hollered. "The doctor said to wake me up, not beat me up." He rubbed his forehead, mumbling something under his breath. But when his fingers brushed across the bandage, he flinched, repeating a few choice words.

"I tried waking you, but you didn't budge!" Beth shouted as she rubbed her temple. "I was worried something was wrong. Why didn't you tell me you were such a deep sleeper?"

When Mitch brought his hand away from his forehead, Beth saw there was blood on his fingers. Mitch flung the sheets back from his body and stalked to the adjoining bathroom. Beth watched as he flicked on the light and leaned over the pedestal sink. Standing in the doorway, she could see his reflection in the mirror as he examined his blood-soaked bandage.

"Great!" he snapped. "Just great!"

Mitch yanked away the bloody gauze. When he poked at his stitches, Beth stepped next to him and jerked his hand away. "Don't touch it. Your hands aren't clean."

Mitch ignored her, bringing his fingers back up to the open wound.

Exasperated, Beth opened the small closet that held linens, toilet paper, and other supplies, including another first-aid kit. Mitch was still poking at his stitches, causing them to ooze even more.

"Stop touching it and sit down!" she hollered at him.

Mitch flipped down the toilet seat and sat down while Beth pulled several items from the kit and laid them on the edge of the tub. When she turned back around, she realized for the first time Mitch was only wearing a pair of boxer shorts. Heat ignited her cheeks at the awkwardness of their predicament. She could only hope—in his pain—Mitch hadn't noticed her embarrassment.

She tried to focus on the situation at hand. *Stop the bleeding. Bandage it up. Stop the bleeding. Bandage it up.* It was her mantra. But it did little good. No amount of chanting could distract her from noticing Mitch's well-defined abs and strong muscular legs.

Don't you dare embarrass yourself in front of this man! she scolded. But the reprimand worked about as well as her mantra.

Chapter Six

Mitch realized his state of undress bothered Beth, so he grabbed a folded towel from the shelf next to the sink and draped it over his lap. When he looked at Beth, he saw red had crept up from the neck of her shirt and filled her complexion. He fought back the smile that was edging the corner of his lips. The fact that she was embarrassed by his exposure let him know Beth wasn't the rough and rowdy, tough as nails woman she pretended to be.

Mitch snapped from his musings when Beth pressed a piece of gauze to his forehead. "Ouch!" He cursed as he yanked her hand away. "If you're only going to make it worse, just leave it alone."

"Stop being such a baby. I need to stop the bleeding, which means I need to apply pressure."

He let go of her hand, closed his eyes, and braced himself for more pain, only this time Beth was gentler and not as forceful. Mitch tried to relax as she worked on his wound, gritting his teeth when it hurt, but recognizing the fact that she was trying to be as gentle as possible. Beth talked to him with soothing words, letting him know she was almost finished. When he opened his eyes, he was surprised to see her curvaceous figure swaying right in front of his eyes.

The pain magically disappeared.

"Okay, that should do it."

Beth was proud of herself. She'd pulled her act together enough to apply a couple of butterfly bandages to the corner of Mitch's brow where a stitch popped through his skin. Beth was waiting for the glue to dry, when she looked down and realized the whole time she'd been working on Mitch's cut, she had been putting her chest right in his face.

Beth quickly jumped back from Mitch, trying to put distance between them. When her heels caught the side of the tub, Beth lost her balance and knew she was going to end up over the side of it, but at the last second, Mitch reached out a hand and stopped her from tumbling backwards.

Beth sighed with relief, thankful she hadn't ended up in the tub, embarrassing herself even further. Regaining her composure, Beth realized Mitch was still holding her hand. "I think you can let go now," she said.

But he didn't let go. He just looked at her and gave her hand a squeeze. "I'm sorry I snapped at you, Beth. I really do appreciate everything you've done for me."

She didn't know what to say. His tone was soft and his words so sincere. Then, out of the corner of her eye, she saw Shane standing in the middle of the guestroom, looking at them.

"What's going on?" Shane stood, rubbing his eyes, then focused in on their joined hands.

Beth quickly pulled away from Mitch and turned to Shane, wanting to explain, but he didn't give her a chance.

"I knew it!" Shane shouted. "I knew all that talk about sports, and me and my friends was just a load of bull. You don't care about me. All you care about is making time with my mother."

"Shane, stop!" Beth yelled, completely humiliated. But Shane continued.

"You're just like everyone else. All you care about is women and sex. I was stupid to listen to you. I was stupid to think you were different." Shane stormed from the room.

"Shane, that's not true!" Mitch yelled after him. He pushed past Beth and hurried after her son. Beth heard the bedroom door slam and Mitch shouting at Shane to open the door so they could talk.

What next, Lord? She sunk to the edge of the tub, her elbows on her knees, her hands covering her face.

"I'm so sorry, Beth," Mitch said as he walked back into the bathroom and squatted down in front of her. "He had no right talking to you like that."

Beth lifted her face, brushing the wetness from her cheeks. "I don't understand," she sighed. "He was never like this before. He's just so angry all the time."

Walking past Mitch to the adjoining bedroom, Beth caught her reflection in the dresser mirror. She looked like she'd aged years over a matter of minutes.

"I'll give him a minute to cool down," Mitch said. "Then I'll try talking to him.

"No. This is my problem," Beth said as she glanced at the clock on the bedside table. "You need your sleep. I'll be back in a little while to check on you."

Mitch watched as Beth slipped from the room, her shoulders sagging from the weight of her world. He recognized the posture all too well. Many nights he'd seen the same defeat in his own mother. He'd been disrespectful and rebellious as a teenager, and lashed out at his mom much like Shane had just done. Mitch knew what was missing from Shane's life. As hard as Beth tried, she wouldn't be able to give it to him. He needed the same thing Mitch had wanted at his age.

A father.

Chapter Seven

Mitch woke early after a restless night. Though he had tried to get some much needed sleep, every time he closed his eyes, he saw the defeated look on Beth's face after Shane had unloaded on them.

He had tried to apologize to her when she came to check on him throughout the night, but as soon as she knew he was awake, Beth would slip from his room without saying a word.

Shane had overreacted—blown things out of proportion. It was just a misunderstanding. Mitch wanted to set him straight first thing this morning, then apologize to Beth for making a bad situation even worst.

"Can I talk to you for a moment?" Mitch said from where he sat on the front porch swing.

Shane jumped, clearly surprised. "What do you want?" he asked with disdain.

"I'd like to talk about what happened last night."

"There's nothing to talk about. If you want to mess around with my mother you don't need my permission." Shane hurried down the steps and toward the barn.

Mitch caught up with Shane halfway across the yard. He reached for his arm and spun him around. "Don't disrespect your mother like that. She doesn't deserve it. Nothing happened last night. I popped a stitch, and she was bandaging me back up. That's it."

Shane snapped his arm away from Mitch. "Right! I might only be sixteen, but I'm not stupid. I saw the way you were looking at her."

Mitch hung his head. Shane was right. He was attracted to Beth. How could he not be? And it wasn't just because she was a natural beauty. It was her take-no-crap attitude Mitch found intriguing as well. But how could he make Shane believe his interest in him and their conversations from the night before had been for real? He genuinely enjoyed talking with him about sports, movies, and just everyday things.

"Look, Shane, I'm not going to lie to you. You're right. I'm attracted to your mom. But that doesn't mean I didn't enjoy hanging out with you last night."

"Right. I'm sure talking with me was the highlight of your evening. That's why my mom was in your room, and you had your hands all over her."

"It wasn't what it looked like. Besides, I'm only going to be here for a few days; it would be stupid to start something I couldn't finish."

"Come on, are you telling me you've never had a one-night stand before?"

Shane was sticking it to him hard. Mitch took a breath, knowing he needed to be honest with him. "Yes, I've had one-night stands before, but that's not going to happen with your mom. Look, Shane, when I leave here, I'd like to think I made a few friends, not an enemy."

"Whatever."

Shane walked away, leaving Mitch to wonder if he'd gotten through to the kid.

Walking back to the house, Mitch could smell coffee brewing as soon as he hit the porch. When he pushed the screen door open, he saw Beth standing in the kitchen. She looked up at him but quickly turned away.

This is going to be awkward.

He sat at the counter and reached for the cup of coffee she had poured him. "Thanks."

She didn't say a word, she just reached into the refrigerator and pulled out a carton of eggs.

Might as well get this over with.

"Look, Beth, I know last night was awkward, but Shane will get over it."

"Oh, I'm sorry," she said as she plopped the carton of eggs on the counter. "I didn't realize you had experience counseling adolescent boys."

"I don't. But I was one, twenty years ago," he smiled, but her expression stayed cold as ice. "I'm just saying he'll be fine once he's had a chance to cool off and think things over."

"Well, thank you for the psychology lesson, but I think I know my son a little better than you do." She cracked eggs viciously against the side of the stainless steel bowl. "Just keep your opinions and your psychoanalysis to yourself while you're here. I think that would be best for everyone."

"You know what, you're right!"

Mitch decided he'd had enough trying to defuse the situation. Family dynamics weren't his strong suit, so he had no business interfering with whatever was going on here. He got up from the counter and took a step back. "How you deal with your son is your business. So I'm just going to go to my trailer and get out of your way." *And get something stronger to drink than coffee.*

Beth watched as Mitch stalked out the door, slamming the screen door behind him. Growling in frustration, she tossed the fork she'd been using into the sink and dumped the egg mixture down the drain. "I don't get it, God, things were just fine a few days ago. We were our normal dysfunctional selves. Now, this . . . this person shows up, and I'm having battles left and right. Please, just let Uncle Charlie get his truck fixed and get him out of here as soon as possible."

"What was that, Beth?"

She spun around. "Uncle Charlie!" She pulled the dish towel off her shoulder and threw it at him. "You scared me half to death."

"Well, I heard my name mentioned, so I thought you were talking to me." Charlie picked up the towel from the floor and set it on the counter. Grabbing a mug out of the cabinet, he poured himself some coffee and asked, "So, how'd your patient do last night?"

"Great. A real treat. I'll just be glad when he's gone."

"Oh boy. Then you're not going to like what I have to say."

"Why?"

"I called every auto shop I know, and I won't be able to get that windshield until next Wednesday."

"Uncle Charlie, that's a week from now!"

"I'm completely aware of when that is, Beth, but there's nothing I can do about it. As it is, I'm going to have to go pick it up at Tom's. If it hadn't been for his business connections, it would've taken even longer." Charlie removed his hat and rubbed his head, something he did when he was frustrated. "I'm sorry, Beth; that's the best I could do."

She realized how unappreciative she sounded and apologized. "I'm sorry, Uncle Charlie. I didn't mean to snap at you. I just had a miserable night. Between dealing with Mitch, and having a yelling match with Shane, I didn't get much sleep."

"What do you mean 'dealing with Mitch'?" Charlie's stature changed from relaxed to rigid.

"Nothing like that." She assured her uncle, knowing exactly what he was thinking.

He relaxed his shoulders and took a chug of his coffee. "So how is he?"

"Mitch is fine. Well, at least his head is."

"Where is he?"

"I don't know. He grumbled something about going to his trailer."

"Is Shane helping Brett and Rusty today?"

"Yeah, I can only hope that's where he is."

"Is he giving you trouble again? Do you need me to talk to him?"

"No. I need to handle this myself. I just don't know what to do. I trust Curtis and Lucas about as far as I can throw them, but there's no one else for Shane to hang around with. He already hates living here. How do I tell him he can't hang out with the only two boys around?"

The look on his niece's face pained Charlie. She had sacrificed her teenage years for Shane. When she could've been out with her friends, she had done the responsible thing and stayed home with her son. Beth had done everything to give him a stable, loving home, but Shane didn't see it that way. He was blaming her for circumstances out of her control.

"Don't worry too much, Beth. He's a good kid. I'll tell Travis to keep an eye on him. Maybe Brett and Rusty can spend some extra time with him after work."

Beth just shrugged her shoulders, obviously feeling defeated.

"Well, I've got to get some work done today so I better get going. You gonna be okay?" he asked.

"Sure." Beth gave him a timid smile. "It's probably just a phase. Like you said, Shane's a good kid. I just wish there was something more I could do."

It was time for lunch.

Beth hadn't seen Mitch since he'd stormed out at breakfast. *He's probably still in his trailer.* Deciding to do the polite thing, she walked to his trailer and gave the door a knock.

Mitch swung the door open.

"How are you feeling?" she asked as she squinted against the sun.

"Fine."

"I have lunch ready."

"I'm not hungry. I had some crackers a little while ago."

Beth's nose stung. She leaned closer to the doorway and sniffed. His trailer reeked of alcohol. "I see crackers aren't the only thing you had for lunch."

"I had to wash them down with something," he smirked. "Staying hydrated is very important when traveling."

No longer feeling the need to be polite, she said, "I'd appreciate it if you didn't drink while you were on my property."

"Yeah, well, I'd appreciate not being here at all, but there's not much I can do about that right now, is there?"

Beth glared at him. "Fine! If you don't have the willpower to abstain for a few days, that's your problem. Just don't do it around Shane."

"Willpower has nothing to do with it, sweetheart. I'm just doing what I can to make a lousy situation bearable."

Mitch watched Beth turn on her heels and walk away, then heard the screen door slam.

"Just two more days," he mumbled to himself as he plopped down on his sofa bench. Mitch brought the bottle of whiskey up to his lips as he looked out the window at the rolling landscape. He took a long swig, then wiped his mouth. "I can hole up in here for two more days. There's no reason for me to try and make amends or small talk with any of these people. I'll keep my mouth shut, stay out of their business, and then I'll be gone."

Mitch lay around his trailer until late afternoon. When he heard the grind of a truck engine, he looked out the window just in time to see Beth—in her beat-up cowboy hat—drive past his trailer and out of the yard. "Perfect. At least now I can do a little walking around without Attila the Hun watching my every move."

Stepping down from his trailer, Mitch decided to do some snooping, to see if there was somewhere he could hook up his unit. If he was going to stay in his trailer, he would need some water and electricity. He wandered around the perimeter of the house, knowing there had to be a generator somewhere. All houses in the middle of nowhere had generators, or at least he thought so.

When he came up empty, he moved across the large yard to the side of the barn where the pens of farm animals sat in a neat row, bleating, oinking, and other grunting sounds filling the air. He looked at the weathered boards of the barn with its splintered red paint and was instantly reminded of the working set of his first starring role.

The western that had launched his career held many fond

memories for him. It was simpler being part of an ensemble cast. It wasn't until he'd made leading man status that things changed. Changes he didn't like.

Wandering into the barn, it took a minute for Mitch's eyes to adjust. When they did, he saw a row of stalls lining one side of the large structure. A curious Appaloosa immediately stuck its neck out over the stall door. Its head bobbed, ears twitched, and it had a gaze hard as steel. Mitch walked closer and saw the decorative leather strap nailed to the stall door. *Midas.*

"Well, hello, Midas." Mitch extended his hand, but pulled it back just as fast to keep his fingers intact.

The horse snorted as if laughing at him, then turned away. Mitch couldn't believe it. It was like the horse had just told him off and then stuck his rump in his face to boot.

"Cute. Is that something Beth taught you?" Mitch said to the horse.

Just then, motion in the yard drew Mitch's attention. Shane rode into the barn, looking like a rag doll—barely able to sit upright. Mitch took a step back into the shadows and watched as Shane slid from the horse, his legs almost collapsing beneath him. With uneven steps, he guided his mount to one of the empty stalls.

This can't be good.

Mitch watched as Shane fumbled with the buckles on the auburn-colored saddle. With a tug on the skirt and the horn, Shane staggered backwards and crumpled into a heap on the straw-covered floor, the saddle landing on top of his chest.

Mitch stepped inside the stall and lifted the saddle off of Shane. That's when he saw his glossed over eyes and the stupid smirk on his face that could mean only one thing.

"Whatcha been up to, Shane?" Mitch asked in a belittling tone.

Shane looked at him with a dopey grin. "Hammering fences," he said with a slur.

"Looks like you were the one getting hammered." Mitch stuck out his hand and helped him to his feet. When Shane stood within inches of him, he could smell the cheap whiskey on his breath. "Where'd you get the booze?"

"My friends."

"The same friends who convinced you shooting at a passing vehicle was funny?" Mitch asked sarcastically.

"Heck, no. Curtis and Lucas are stupid kids. I was with Brett and Rusty. We were having a really good time today. In fact, they're taking me out tonight."

Shane picked up his tack and stumbled from the stall. He staggered into the tack room, tossed his stuff on a rack and headed for the big double doors.

Mitch debated what he should do as he watched Shane stagger and stumble his way toward the house. *Just let him go. This is none of your business.* Mitch had already been told to butt out, and that's what he should do. Even so, when he saw Shane bite the dust in the yard—landing face down in the dirt—Mitch quickened his steps and helped the kid up.

"Your mother's going to kill you when she sees you like this. You know that, right?"

"That's the beauty of it," Shane said, with the same stupid grin on his face. "She'll never know. I'm gonna be gone before she gets home."

"Gone? Gone where?"

"Out. Brett and Rusty are picking me up."

"The ones that only talk about women and booze? I thought you cramped their style?" Mitch questioned.

"Not anymore. They said it was about time I have some real fun."

Mitch realized by the glint in Shane's eyes he was talking about more than just pranks and dares. "You mean girls?"

Shane leaned in close, whispering in a conspirator's tone. "I mean women. Brett already set it all up. I'm going to have me some Christy tonight," Shane slurred. "She's twenty-two, blonde, and Rusty said she has a thing for younger guys."

Mitch felt a surge of anger. Beth's ranch hands had liquored up her son and were going to push him off the deep end. Shane might not be his responsibility, but he couldn't stand by and do nothing.

"Shane, you can't go with them tonight, and you know it. It's not right."

"What do I care?" Shane took a step back, momentarily losing his balance. When he steadied himself, he locked eyes with Mitch—eyes filled with anger and hatred. "I'm tired of everyone telling me what to do and what not to do. Right or wrong, it doesn't matter."

Shane darted his finger at Mitch while his body swayed. "People only care about right and wrong when it's somebody else doing it. What my mom did was wrong, but no one's preaching to her. What my dad did was wrong, but nobody's making him step up and do the right thing. So you see, it doesn't matter what I do. Right or wrong, it's up to me. It will be my consequences, no one else's. So I'm going to do what I want to do."

Mitch was stunned by Shane's rant but recognized the pain in his voice. The kid was hurting and lashing out. He wanted to hurt his mom because he'd been hurt himself. But Mitch knew it wasn't the answer. He'd been there before. He'd been in Shane's shoes. He'd learned that hurting someone else only made your own pain greater.

Shane moaned as he grabbed for his belly and stumbled, his flush complexion turning a sickening shade of gray. Mitch knew all he could do was get out of the way.

Shane rushed to the scrub brush lining the driveway and dropped to his knees with a thud. He retched with groans so guttural, Mitch was sure the kid's insides were going to end up on the ground.

Coughing at the sour smell of vomit and whiskey, Mitch decided there wasn't much he could do but keep his distance until the heaving stopped. However, even after taking a few steps back, Mitch could still smell alcohol. Then he realized—it was the alcohol on his own breath.

He shook his head in disgust. *I'm no better than he is.*

Though Mitch had learned to control his drinking over the years, he still used alcohol as an anesthetic to life's problems. Instead of working through issues, he walked away and numbed himself to them. Just like he'd done with Beth. He'd avoided talking with her by going to his trailer and grabbing a bottle.

Shane's quiet moan got Mitch's attention. With a sigh, he walked over to where the kid was squatting along the driveway's edge. "Come on, we can't let your mom see you like this." Mitch helped him to his feet and turned him around, but Shane looked out toward the road.

"Wait. Rusty and Brett are expecting me. They'll think I'm some gutless kid if I don't show up."

"Let's not worry about Rusty and Brett right now. In fact, you're probably doing them a favor. If your mother found out what they had planned for you, not only would they be out of jobs, most likely they would be pulling buckshot out of their butts before morning."

Mitch led Shane back to his trailer and helped him inside. He plopped Shane down on his couch then rummaged through his cupboards before pulling out a large stock pot. "Here, if you're going to get sick, you need to get it in the pot. This trailer is brand new, and I don't want to be smelling vomit in the cushions for the next year."

Shane stretched out on the nicely upholstered couch, moaning with every twist and turn.

"So, how were you going to get out of the house without your mom knowing?" Mitch asked the near unconscious teen.

"She always does her errands on Tuesdays. I was just going to leave a note before she got home, telling her I was with Brett and Rusty."

"And you don't think she'd go looking for you?"

"Nah, she trusts them. She doesn't know what they do in their spare time. They act nice and polite around her and Travis. The only one I think might have suspicions about them is Uncle Charlie, but that's because he doesn't trust anyone."

Mitch evaluated the situation and came up with a plan. "Okay, you're still going to write that note. I'll put it on the dining room table where your mom will see it. You'll sober up out here. Then, later tonight, you can slip inside the house like you're getting home from being out with Brett and Rusty."

"But what are they going to think if I don't show up?"

"I don't give a crap what they think!" Mitch snapped. "You

shouldn't either. You should be more worried about your mother finding out about this little episode."

Shane squinted as he looked up at Mitch. "Why are you doing this? What do you care if my mother finds out I've been drinking or that I planned on partying with Brett and Rusty? What business is it of yours?"

"It's not my business, but I have an idea how you feel. I've been down some of these same roads, Shane. Self-destruction is not the answer, and hurting the people who love you won't help either. I'm just trying to save you from making some of the same mistakes I did. You might not care, and you might blow me off tomorrow, but right now, I hope you see that I'm only trying to help. Now, write that note, so I can get it inside before your mother gets back."

Chapter Eight

Shane was finally getting some sleep. He'd lain motionless on Mitch's couch for over an hour, but before that, he'd been pretty miserable. Hot then cold, sick then dizzy. Mitch watched him with both pity and understanding. He knew what it felt like to be a teenage boy growing up without a father. Even though people thought other male figures could fill that role, no one truly understood how a boy felt knowing he'd been deserted by his dad. Mitch didn't know Shane's story, but the results were the same.

Rebellion.

Mitch studied Shane's features while he slept. He was pretty big for being just sixteen, and since Beth was so petite, Mitch could only assume Shane took after his father. Even his sandy-brown hair was several shades darker than Beth's golden-blond.

But Shane wasn't only big, he was built. He had the natural physique of a cowboy—lean in all the right places—but solid like a tree trunk. Mitch wondered how Beth had been able to keep him away from girls for so long. He was a good-looking kid, and would be breaking hearts someday soon.

The popping of gravel in the yard announced Beth was home. Dusk was just beginning to blanket the mountains and the air had finally cooled.

Mitch watched as Beth carried groceries into the house, but it was the flatbed full of wood that caught his attention. He had tinkered as a carpenter before hitting it big. It had been a way of making ends meet, and Mitch enjoyed the work. It had always felt good when he finished a job and saw what he could accomplish with his hands.

Mitch saw Beth walk back to the truck for a second load. He wanted to lend a hand but didn't. He was afraid to cross paths with her and chance being caught in her crosshairs before Shane was back in the house.

He'd never found the generator, so Mitch pulled out some of his camp lanterns and fired them up. The rustling of supplies woke Shane. He moaned and grumbled, then swiveled his feet to the floor. He sat hovering over the pot between his feet.

"Still feeling sick?" Mitch asked in a hushed tone.

"No. My head just feels like it's going to explode."

"Your friends never came by. You think they were just yanking your chain?"

Shane sat back, his head against the window frame. "I was supposed to meet them out on the highway. They probably just kept going."

"You hungry?"

"No way." Shane stretched back out on the couch.

"Your mom pulled up a few minutes ago. Do you think you should just go in and face the music?"

"Why? Have you decided to rat me out?" Instantly, Shane's tone went from quiet to belligerent.

"No. I said you could stay here until you dried out. I'm not going back on my word. I just thought since you've had some time to think about it, you might want to be straight with her."

"She wouldn't understand. She never does."

"You're not even giving her the chance. Beth seems like a pretty reasonable person."

Shane just glared at him.

"Look, Shane, I'm not taking sides if that's what you're thinking. Your mom just seems like the kind of person who would be fair and rational."

"She's only fair when it's convenient for her."

"So, what's the deal with your dad? It's obvious that's what this is all about. What . . . did he leave you guys, and you think your mom is to blame?"

"He didn't leave; she gave him an ultimatum. It was her or the rodeo. She didn't even tell him she was pregnant. He didn't know about me when he left."

"So you think if your father knew about you, he would've stayed?"

"Maybe."

"Have you tried to find him?"

"Not exactly."

"Do you even know who he is?"

Shane turned aside, fresh anger coloring his face. "My mom won't tell me. No one will. She says I'm better off not knowing, that nothing would change, and I'd only get hurt."

"But you think if you confronted him—told him who you were—things would be better?"

"I don't know!" Shane shouted. "But at least I'd have some answers."

"Look, Shane, you can yell all you want, but unless you're ready to face your mother, I'd keep my voice down if I were you."

Shane and Mitch sat in a thick silence while the night sky turned to black. Mitch made sure the shades were drawn, just in case Beth looked their way. It was Shane who finally broke the silence.

"So, what's *your* story?" he asked Mitch in a belligerent tone.

"I was raised by my mother. I didn't know my father either. My mom was the neighborhood barfly so my father could've been just about anyone." Mitch's tone edged on callousness. He had dealt with his pain long ago; now it was just like a scar. The memory hurt, but the physical pain was gone. "My mother was a drunk and wasn't home much. I spent a lot of time on my own."

"You sound okay with it. Doesn't it bother you?" Shane questioned.

"Not as much as it used to. I realized I was only hurting myself by being a vindictive person. It took me a while to straighten out my life, but I finally came to the conclusion that all the time I spent on blame and hatred was a waste. It didn't help. It only made it harder for me to cope."

"Do you still talk with your mom?"

"Yes and no. She suffers from Alzheimer's. Most the time she doesn't even know who I am."

"And you've never tried to find your dad?"

"I was curious for a while. I wanted to know what kind of man he was. If I looked like him, or if we had anything in common. Then I realized I knew all I needed to know. Who you look like or what you do isn't what makes you a man. I know it sounds like a cliché, Shane, but it's what's on the inside that counts. My father used my mother and never looked back. That was the kind of man he was. I don't need to know his name or what he looks like to know I don't want to be anything like him."

Mitch turned to see Shane had fallen back to sleep. He wondered how much Shane had heard and if any of it would sink in. He could only hope he gave Shane something to think about before he allowed bitterness and anger to ruin his life.

Beth saw the note from Shane and sighed. "Well, at least he's not out with Lucas and Curtis." She put down the groceries and went back to the truck for a second load.

Glancing at the Airstream, Beth walked toward the cab of her pickup. She could see light through the drawn shades in the trailer and a shadow of a figure moving around. Beth felt bad for snapping at Mitch earlier in the day, but alcohol was one thing she didn't tolerate. She knew all too well nothing good came from drinking. *So, do I go apologize or let sleeping dogs lie?* Not sure what to do, Beth carried the rest of her groceries into the house, deciding the wood could wait until tomorrow.

While putting away her groceries and then as she fixed dinner, Beth found herself still thinking about Mitch. *What is my problem?* Her thoughts were so confusing and random, she was having a hard time making sense of them.

She replayed the conversation between Mitch and Shane—the one they'd had prior to her son accusing Mitch of making a play for her. Shane had opened up to him and seemed to enjoy having another man to talk to. It had been music to her ears. In that instance, she glimpsed the Shane of old, not the teenager filled with anger and bitterness.

Then why do I feel so much tension between us? Because she pegged Mitch as someone who used his looks to smooth talk women into anything. She couldn't deny he was gorgeous, but she wasn't going to fall for his brand of charm. It only served to antagonize her more.

She tried to put herself in Mitch's situation. He was supposed to be on vacation but ended up in the middle of nowhere at the mercy of strangers. This was obviously not the vacation he'd bargained for. But he still had no right taking it out on her. She was only trying to help.

After a mental debate of who was right and who was wrong, Beth decided she would try again.

When dinner was ready, she dished up a bowl of chili and cut a few pieces of cornbread from the pan. Grabbing a soda from the refrigerator, Beth carefully carried everything out to Mitch's trailer.

She tapped on the door with the toe of her boot since her hands weren't free to knock. When Mitch answered the door, Beth smiled. "I thought you might be hungry."

Mitch just stood there, a twisted look on his face.

"Well, are you hungry or not?" she asked, trying to be polite but irritated that he just stood there staring at her.

This is not good.

Mitch knew he had to get Beth away from his trailer before—

As if on cue, Shane rolled over on the couch, letting out a painful moan.

Mitch looked at Beth and knew by the way she squinted her eyes and furrowed her brow—she'd heard.

"What's going on?" she asked, then tried to climb the first step of the trailer.

"I can explain," Mitch said, putting his hands on Beth's shoulders, keeping her from pushing past him.

"Explain nothing! Who do you have in there?"

Mitch continued to dodge and weave to keep Beth from going any further.

"Look, unless you want this bowl of chili down the front of you, you'd better move out of my way."

Her blue eyes were like fire.

Mitch knew the gig was up, so he stepped back out of the doorway and watched as she climbed up the steps.

"What in the world?"

Chapter Nine

Beth stood in Mitch's trailer trying to process what she was seeing.

Her son was sprawled out on Mitch's couch, a bucket at his side.

"You no good, filthy—" Beth yelled at Mitch as she dropped the food she was holding onto the stovetop, then bent to sit at her son's side. "Shane," Beth shook him slightly. "Shane, what happened?"

Shane woke up looking like he was in some sort of fog.

"He got a hold of some liquor and did a number on himself," Mitch volunteered from where he was standing.

Beth jumped to her feet, turned to Mitch, and gave him a shove. "Didn't I tell you to keep your liquor away from him?" She shoved him again. "How could you do this?" And again. "What kind of person lets a kid get plastered?"

Before Beth could shove him one more time, Mitch grabbed her wrists and stop her. "It wasn't my fault, dammit! And if you would just shut up for one second, I could explain!"

She snapped her wrist free from his hold and hollered back, "Then what's he doing here like that? I can't believe you! All we've done is tried to help you, and this is how you repay us?"

"Help? That's a good one. If it wasn't for your delinquent son, I wouldn't even be here."

"What? No, forget it." Beth moved away from him. "Don't try to change the subject. Just tell me, how did Shane ended up like this? And if he didn't get the liquor from you, then from who?"

"Your ranch hands, that's who!" Mitch stepped forward, putting Beth on the defensive. She took a step back, but Mitch continued to close the space between them until she was backed up against the wall.

"And that's not all they had planned for him," Mitch continued. "Shane came stumbling into the yard while you were gone. He was so drunk he fell off his horse. It seems your hired help had a whole evening lined up for him. Shane was babbling about how he was going to hook up with some girl who was going to show him a really good time. Well, it was obvious to me Shane was in no condition to go anywhere, especially when he was only going to get into more trouble. I made Shane stay home and have been trying to sober him up ever since. If I'm guilty of anything, it's for getting involved where I don't belong. I should have just let Shane go off half-cocked and let you deal with the fallout."

Mitch paced the short hall. When he turned back, Beth saw anger in his eyes. "Look, I'm sorry for getting involved! I'm sorry for interfering with your kid! I'm sorry I met the whole lot of you! Now, if you'll just get your son out of my trailer, I promise you, even if I have to walk, I will be out of here first thing in the morning!"

Beth felt as if she'd just been hit by a ton of bricks. She was trying to digest everything Mitch had spewed at her, but was having a hard time getting past the picture of Shane behaving wildly with some girl.

Tears stung her eyes. All her fight gone. Beth could no longer take the penetrating stare Mitch had fixed on her from the moment of his outburst. She dropped her gaze to the floor and tried to breathe.

Shane stirred on the couch, his eyes trying to focus. Clearly, he was in no shape to walk.

"If you could just help me get Shane to his room, I promise I won't bother you anymore." Her quiet tone echoed the defeat she felt within her heart.

Mitch felt beyond horrible. He'd let Beth have it with both barrels, and now she looked like she was going to fall apart. Everything he'd said was true. But knowing how hurtful the truth could be, he realized he'd shown her no mercy. He wanted to put her in her place and let her know it was her that had the problems, not him. Well, he'd gotten his way, but somehow making himself out to be the better person was a hollow victory.

Getting Shane through the doorway of the trailer and upstairs to his room was slow going. He was conscious enough to know he'd been found out and tried to offer his mom an incoherent apology. He mumbled on for a few minutes before drifting back to sleep.

Mitch and Beth lowered Shane to his bed. Beth pulled the comforter up around his chin and crossed the room to turn on the bathroom light. Then, she stood at the foot of his bed just staring at him.

Beth felt powerless to save Shane. He was her child, but at the moment, it felt like she was looking at a perfect stranger. The teenager lying in front of her was not the little boy she had taught to rope and ride before he could even read. She didn't know what to do. Shane was growing up. He would no longer look to her to calm his fears, chase away bad dreams, or make him feel better when he fell and hurt himself. The pain he was dealing with now was all her fault. It was because of the poor choices she had made when she was a teenager.

Beth sighed and dragged her hand down her face, feeling like she was a hundred years old.

"There's nothing more you can do tonight, Beth. He just needs to sleep it off." Mitch's words were soft. Compassionate.

Beth hadn't realized that Mitch was still standing there. The fact that he was witnessing the breakdown of her family was not easy for her to handle. She felt like a total failure.

Beth walked to the door, turned the light off, and slipped past Mitch into the hallway. She took the stairs slowly, not feeling too steady. When she got as far as the kitchen, Beth sunk to the barstool, laid her head on the counter and cried.

Mitch didn't know what to do. He wanted to comfort Beth, but felt it would be hypocritical of him. After all, he had taken great pleasure in telling her how screwed up her son was. He'd lashed out in anger but now felt he should do something to make things right.

"Beth, I'm sorry I went off on you like that. I'm sure I could've handled the situation better."

"Why should you be sorry?" Beth sat up and swiped at the tears on her cheeks. "I'm the failure. I'm the one pointing a finger at everyone else when I know there's no one to blame but myself."

He watched as she got up from the barstool.

"Thank you for trying to help Shane. Now, if you don't mind, I think I'll go cry myself to sleep." She excused herself and went upstairs.

Mitch knew the last thing Beth needed was to be left alone with the condemnation she was heaping on herself. But he was in no position to argue. Against his better judgment, he left.

Walking to his trailer, Mitch felt like he'd been kicked in the gut. He cleaned up the food Beth had dropped on the stove and straightened up the couch Shane had been sprawled out on. He turned off the lantern and felt his way to the bedroom. He lay on his bed and stared into the blackness of the night, replaying the events of the day. *To think I got away from Hollywood so I could live my life free from drama.* The irony made him laugh. Though he found nothing amusing about Shane's rebellion or Beth's heartbreak, it just reminded him that life equaled drama, no matter where you lived.

Beth curled up in the chair that sat in the corner of Shane's room and watched him sleep. Only one other time in her life had she contemplated leaving the Diamond-J, and that was to follow Shane's father and try to fit into his world. When that didn't work out, she had vowed she would never leave again.

The Diamond-J was the only home Beth knew. Her family had owned the land for over a hundred years, and this is where she thought she belonged. But now she would have to rethink that.

Beth had always thought one day Shane would see the importance of having a heritage; he would choose to continue in the business that had been the backbone of her family for generations. But she was wrong. Keeping Shane here was only making him resent her even more. She had to make a choice, her land or her son. Of course, the choice was obvious, but that wouldn't make her decision any less difficult.

Chapter Ten

Beth wasn't sure what woke her, but when she looked across her son's room, the bathroom door was just swinging closed. Shane was finally awake.

She had debated for hours how she should handle the situation, but still felt at a loss. *It's not even dawn yet. Maybe I should just wait until morning.* Beth stood to leave just as the toilet flushed and the bathroom door creaked open. Shane walked groggily to his bed, sat on the edge, and raked his hands through his disheveled hair.

Beth sat back down. "How are you feeling?" she asked, trying to make her voice sound even, not argumentative.

"Like I just got stampeded." His tone was low and weak.

"Liquor will do that to you."

Shane slowly turned to face her. "Mom, I don't know what to say. I know what I did was wrong, but nothing I can say will make it right. I'm sorry I'm such a screw-up and such a disappointment to you."

Beth moved to sit next to him. She draped her arm around his shoulders and held him tight. "I'd be lying to say I wasn't disappointed, but I love you, Shane. It hurts me to see you so at odds with yourself and with me. I know you're struggling, and I know at times life doesn't seem fair, but we're in this together. We're all we've got."

"I know that, Mom, but that doesn't change anything." His tone wasn't disrespectful, just defeated.

"Maybe it does."

"What do you mean?"

"I need to stop thinking about the past and start looking to the future. I know this isn't the life you want. I just thought one day you would come to love this land like I do. I realize now I was wrong." Beth cleared her throat, trying not to let emotion seep into what she wanted to say. "Tell you what, if you can bear with me through one more summer, I'll make plans to move us to the city."

"What?" Shane looked at her, shocked. "But what about the ranch?"

"I'll talk to Uncle Charlie and Travis, see if they'll buy me out. And if they're not interested, I'll put it on the selling block."

"You know you won't do that," he said, defiantly. "All your talk about history and heritage, and how a Justin has owned this land for over a hundred years. You said you would never sell. No matter what."

"But what about us, Shane? This is not where you want to be. If I don't have someone to pass the land down to, what good is holding on to it? You've got to know that you are more important to me than this land, or the past, or anything else."

"You'd really do it? You'd sell the ranch because of me?"

"No. I'd sell it because of us. I only want to do what's right for us. So, I'm asking you to be patient just a little bit longer. Three months, six months tops. I'll make sure we're moved in time for you to start the winter semester at a real high school. I'll talk to Uncle Charlie about it sometime this week and get the ball rolling. Can you give me that long? Can you promise me no more alcohol or getting into trouble?"

Shane hugged his mom. "I promise, no more drinking or hanging out with Lucas or Curtis, or Brett and Rusty. I'll work really hard to get the ranch in tiptop shape by fall."

Beth got up from the bed and again wiped the tears from her eyes. "Well, you don't need to be worrying about Brett and Rusty. They'll be getting their walking papers today."

"You're going to fire them?" Shane's eyes grew big.

"They're lucky I'm not pressing charges. Giving alcohol to a minor can get them in all kinds of trouble. They'd better be happy it's just their jobs they're losing. And about Mitch—"

JUST AN ACT

"Don't be mad at him, Mom. He was only trying to help."

"Well, I don't appreciate that kind of help. You could have been really sick. What if something terrible had happened to you?"

"But Mom, I wasn't sick; I was drunk. If it wasn't for him, I would've gone out with Brett and Rusty and really gotten myself into trouble."

"And what were you going to do?"

Shane looked at her, then looked away.

"Mitch said you were going to meet a girl. Is that true?"

Shane was silent.

"Do you think that would've been fun? Getting some girl drunk and then taking advantage of her?"

Shane looked at her with shock. "No."

"Good. I would hate to think I raised my son to have such little respect for the opposite sex."

Beth wanted to continue her line of questioning, but could see how uncomfortable Shane was talking about sex with her. She decided to tackle that subject another day.

By the time they got done talking, the sun was up and the day was beginning. Beth was dog-tired, but had a lot to accomplish, starting with giving Brett and Rusty a piece of her mind and giving them the boot as well. As she walked toward the bedroom door, Shane lay back across his bed.

"I know you're not going to feel like it, but I'm going to need you to help Uncle Charlie with the herd. Rusty and Brett were supposed to, but with them gone we're all going to have to work a little harder."

Shane moaned, but agreed.

Beth took a quick shower and dressed for what was going to be a very long day. She smelled coffee as she came down the stairs, and knew Uncle Charlie would hassle her for having to fix it himself.

"I'm in no mood for any harassing, Uncle Charlie."

He took a swig of coffee and nodded in understanding. "Mitch told me you and Shane had a hard night."

"What else did he tell you?" She was agitated Mitch had butted in once again.

"Nothing. He just said you and Shane had a late night, and I should cut you some slack."

"And when did he have a chance to tell you that?"

"He was making coffee and doing the dishes when I came in."

Beth looked at the kitchen and realized the mess she had chosen to ignore the previous night was gone.

"You want to talk about it?" Charlie asked.

"As a matter of fact, I do. I'm firing Brett and Rusty. They took Shane out and got him drunk yesterday. Then, they made arrangements for him to hook up with some girl. I won't tolerate that kind of garbage on my property."

"I hear ya. I knew those boys were up to no good. You want me to do it?"

"No. I have a few things I'd like to say to them myself. Just have them come see me. I'll be working on the tack room. Then you'll have to put the word out for some new hands. If you could just make sure Rusty and Brett have cleared out by tomorrow, I'd appreciate it."

"You sure you don't want me talkin' to them?"

"No. I can handle it."

"How's Shane?" Charlie asked.

"He's pretty torn up. He'll be feeling it for the rest of the day, but he'll be out to help you with the herd. I told him he would have to pick up the slack with Brett and Rusty gone."

"I'm sure he was thrilled about that." Charlie's tone was sarcastic.

"He might not be thrilled, but let's just say we have come to an understanding."

"Okay then." Charlie swilled the last of his coffee. "I'll go tell the delinquents you want to talk to them."

"And no giving them a heads-up. They had their fun watching Shane squirm, so I'm going to do the same to them."

As soon as Charlie was gone, Beth made her way to the wood stacked in the back of her truck. She realized now would not be a good time to take on a new project. Being low staffed, she'd have to put it on hold for another time.

She was headed back for a second load of wood when she saw

Mitch stacking two-by-sixes in the cradle of his arm.

"You don't need to do that," she said in a cool tone.

"I know." He continued to load up his arms and followed her to the work shed.

Beth didn't say anything because her feelings were balancing somewhere between anger and guilt. Mitch was the first to speak after they had carried in the last load.

"How's Shane?"

"He's feeling it, but he'll be fine." She moved toward the door, but Mitch stopped her with a gently placed hand to her forearm.

"How are you?"

"Me? I don't know." She turned to look at him. "I'm sure I owe you an apology for blaming you for Shane's drinking, but I'm still mad that you had intended on keeping it a secret."

"And I owe you an apology for interfering. It's just that, well . . . I see a lot of myself in Shane when I was his age. I kind of know what he's going through. At least I think I have an idea."

"So do I, Mitch, but I thought I could be enough. All I've ever wanted to be is a good mother. I've prayed and loved and encouraged, but it just isn't enough. He doesn't see that everything I've done— I've done for him. To give him a home. A foundation. He only sees me as the person that kept from him the one thing he wanted most— to know his father."

Mitch was about to say something to her, but Beth hurried away before she could burst into tears and make things even worse. It was bad enough she'd bared her soul in front of him. She wasn't going to let him witness her in complete meltdown mode as well. Beth actually felt sorry for Mitch. *Poor guy. What a vacation this has turned out to be for him.*

Thankfully, Mitch was decent enough to go back to his trailer and give Beth some space. She walked over to the work shed to regroup and kill some time while waiting for Brett and Rusty. Laying out the plans for the tack room extension, she went over the checklist to make sure she'd gotten all the needed supplies.

When she saw dust being kicked up in the pasture, Beth pushed her emotions aside. Rusty and Brett would be here any minute, and she had to have her act together. As much as she wanted to give the jerks a piece of her mind—really tighten the screws on them—she decided to keep it short and sweet. She wouldn't waste a single minute more on them than was necessary.

Beth watched as the two ranch hands dismounted and walked toward her. She took a deep breath and reminded herself to stay calm and keep a cool head.

"You wanted to talk to us, boss lady?" Brett said as he removed his hat.

"Yeah, I do. You're fired. Both of you. I want you to clear your stuff out of the bunkhouse and be gone by tomorrow."

They were clearly shocked.

"I don't get it," Rusty said, looking confused.

"What don't you get? You're fired. End of conversation." She stood defiantly, hands firmly on her hips. "Now get off my land."

Brett paced a few steps away and then turned back around. "This is all because of Shane, isn't it?" he shouted. "What did he tell you? Did he blame us? Because it was his fault."

Brett's yelling caused Beth to snap. She charged toward him and jabbed a finger at his chest. "You gave him liquor, you idiot! He's only sixteen! What were you thinking?"

"He wanted it! He asked us to show him a good time, and we did!"

"You stupid punk! If he had asked you to light him on fire, would you have done that, too? He's just a kid. You should feel lucky I'm not having you arrested."

Brett shoved Beth against the wall, shocking her.

"Get your hands off of me," she hollered as she struggled to get free.

"Come on, Brett, what are you doing?" Rusty yanked on Brett's arm, but he just shook him off.

"I'm not going to let some broad talk to me like I'm a piece of trash."

Beth tried to scream, but Brett clamped his hand over her mouth, snapping her head back against the wall. "So, what are you going to do now, boss lady? Now that someone else is calling the shots?"

Beth was terrified. There was no way she had the strength to overpower him.

"Knock it off, Brett," Rusty yelled. "You're only making things worse."

"Let's just say I'm getting my severance pay." Brett pressed his body against Beth's, moved his hand, then crushed his lips against hers. She did the only thing she could do. Beth clamped on to his lip with her teeth and bit down.

Brett pulled away, spitting blood on the ground. "Why you stupid bit—" He stretched out his hand to strike Beth, but his wrist was caught in mid-air.

Mitch spun Brett around and cold-cocked him, knocking him to the floor. Mitch sprawled out on top of Brett, but the kid didn't give up. The two men wrestled and swung at each other.

"You're on your own, Brett." Rusty jumped the rail, got on his horse, and took off.

"Mitch, let him go!" Beth was watching the way Mitch's punches were connecting and was afraid he was going to seriously hurt Brett. "Mitch, come on, let him go!"

Mitch laid one more punch on Brett before stopping. He got to his feet, rested his hands on his knees, and panted. Brett got to his knees, his face dirty and bloody.

"Get out of here, Brett," Beth hollered. "I don't ever want to see you anywhere near my land again."

Brett looked at her with a venomous stare before getting to his feet. Wiping blood from his lips, he staggered to his horse and rode away.

When Beth turned to Mitch, she saw he was spitting blood and wiping his lip with his sleeve.

"Mitch, are you okay?" Beth waited for him to stand up straight, so she could see if he was hurt, or if his stitches were bleeding again. But he immediately turned the question back on her.

"Are *you* okay?" Mitch gently wiped her cheek. "You're bleeding."

"No. That was his."

"But you're okay, right? He didn't do anything . . . I mean, he didn't have the chance to—"

"I'm okay, Mitch, really." She clenched her hands together, trying to hide her shaking. "I admit I wasn't prepared for him to . . . to react like that, but I'm okay."

Mitch wrapped his arm around her shoulders in a protective embrace. She would've pulled away if it wasn't for the fact that her legs were shaking so badly she wasn't sure she could stand on her own. They walked back to the house without saying a word.

Once inside, Mitch led her to the couch and sat opposite her on the coffee table. He looked at her intently and asked, "What happened?"

"When I told them they were fired, Brett went crazy on me."

"Do you think they'll cause any more trouble?"

"No. I don't think so considering I could bring some sizable charges against them. Well, at least against Brett."

"I think you should!" Mitch snapped, blood trickling out of the corner of his mouth. "You can't let that punk get away with that."

"Nothing really happened," she said, even though she felt like she was going to throw-up. "He was just trying to scare me, but he's gone now. That's all that matters." Beth looked at Mitch and could see his lip was beginning to swell.

"You need to get some ice on that." Beth moved toward the kitchen, but Mitch cut her off.

"I'll get the ice. You call Charlie and let him know what happened. Make sure he gets those punks out of here right away."

Beth grabbed her cell phone from its charging pad, and speed dialed Charlie.

"Uncle Charlie, yeah, it's me. No, I'm not checking up on Shane. I just wanted to let you know I talked to Rusty and Brett; they're not too happy about losing their jobs. I just thought it might be wise to make sure they were out of here tonight so we don't have any trouble."

Mitch yanked the phone away from Beth, leaving her speechless.

JUST AN ACT

He put it to his ear and didn't hold back. "Charlie, this is Mitch. Beth is sugar-coating it. I had to pry one of those punks off of her. They're more than trouble; they're dangerous."

Beth lunged for the phone, but Mitch swerved away. He gave a few more answers before handing it back to her. She took it begrudgingly, knowing she was going to have some explaining to do.

"I'm fine, really. No. No, Uncle Charlie, Mitch stopped him before he could do anything. I'm fine. It was no big deal. Okay, okay, I'll explain later. Just make sure they leave."

Beth ended the call, then glared at Mitch while he held a washcloth of ice to his face. "I wish you hadn't said anything to Uncle Charlie. He's an old man and shouldn't be made to worry."

"Well, I thought Charlie should know exactly what he was dealing with."

Mitch dumped the ice cubes in the sink and tossed the washcloth on the counter. "So, what are you going to do now?"

"What do you mean?"

"You're shorthanded."

"Charlie is going to work on getting some new hands, and Shane's agreed to help pick up the slack."

"Really? So you two are on speaking terms?"

"We've worked out an agreement."

"What kind of agreement?"

Beth didn't want to go into it with Mitch. "Look, I know you're just trying to help, but I can handle things. I've been managing this ranch for almost ten years now. I've got things under control."

"You mean how you controlled that guy out there?" Mitch barked.

"Mitch, please, this isn't your—"

He threw up his hands. "Fine, have it your way." As he stalked toward the front door, Mitch asked, "Did Charlie say when he would have the parts for my truck?"

Beth cringed, knowing he wasn't going to like the answer. "Yeah. Wednesday."

"You mean later today?" Mitch took a few more steps.

"No. I mean . . . *next* Wednesday."

Mitch turned around with a look of disbelief. "You're kidding me, right?"

"I'm afraid not. He did all he could, but that was the earliest—"

"Wait a minute! What am I supposed to do for another week?" Mitch sauntered. "This is bull—" Her raised brow dared him to continue. He censored his language but did nothing to lower his voice. "I could've bought a tow truck and been gone by now! But no, you told me Charlie was a car guy, and he would fix it for me. This is ridiculous!"

Beth knew Mitch was disappointed, but this wasn't her fault, and she didn't feel like listening to it. "Then you call someone! See if you can do any better."

"I'd love to, but I don't have a phone."

She left the room, grabbed an old telephone book from her office, and slammed it down on the kitchen counter along with the cordless phone. "Here you go! You find someone else who can help you. I have work to do."

Chapter Eleven

While Mitch took the phone book and disappeared into his trailer, Beth started putting together a list of prospective buyers for the ranch. She'd had interested parties over the years, but never gave them or their offers a second thought. Not once had she entertained the idea of selling the Diamond-J, but that was then. Beth now knew she had to make some changes if what was left of her and Shane's relationship was going to survive.

Out of curiosity, Beth turned to her computer and searched for realtor websites in the Kansas City area. She clicked the first one on the list and started filling in parameters on their search page. Three bedrooms, two bathrooms, price range, lot size. She would only be interested in looking at properties measured by the acre not the foot. Although she knew it was important to move to a neighborhood where Shane could attend a traditional high school and be more involved with high school activities, there was no way she was going to live in a cookie-cutter house with no room to breathe and neighbors so close you could carry on a conversation through an open window.

Beth laughed to herself when the first several listings were over the three-million dollar mark. *Yeah, that's not going to happen.* Though she had filled in a broad dollar amount—just to see what was out there—Beth had no intentions of spending that kind of money. Even though the ranch would sell in the millions, she would need those funds to last her a good long time.

Beth continued to scroll and click, concentrating more on the acreage than the condition of the homes. The house itself was low on her priority list. Granted, she didn't want to live in a falling down fixer-upper, but paint and home repairs didn't scare her. It was land Beth would need if she was going to make the move. As long as she had a place for her horses, room to breathe, and Shane, Beth could make it anywhere. At least that's what she kept telling herself.

But how? How am I going to leave the only home I've ever known?

"Okay, you were right and I was wrong."

The sound of Mitch's voice startled her. Beth spun her chair around to see him standing in the doorway with the telephone book in his hand.

"Would you mind not barging in on me like that!" she huffed.

"I didn't *barge* in. I walked in. You just didn't hear me."

Mitch glanced over her shoulder at her computer screen, but with one quick keystroke, Beth made the page disappear. "So, what did you find out?" she asked, turning back to Mitch.

"I found out that no one in Kansas understands the meaning of urgent, quickly, as soon as possible, or I'll pay through the nose if you hurry."

"So, I take it you didn't have any success?" Beth said sarcastically.

"None whatsoever. You would've thought I was asking for an obscure part for a foreign car. The last time I looked, the Suburban was an American-made vehicle."

Beth folded her arms against her chest and listened to Mitch with mild interest as he listed his frustrations. He did everything from complain about the phone book—stating it was too old—to criticizing the local mechanics, accusing them of being inconsiderate and lazy. "They aren't even taking into consideration the fact that I'm stranded here, and I don't have a week to waste."

"Are you through?" Beth asked, sounding slightly annoyed.

"I'm frustrated, all right!" Mitch snapped.

"Well, if you're done, I have some work to do." Beth brushed past Mitch and walked to the front entryway. Grabbing her cowboy hat off the peg by the door, she settled it on her head, leaving Mitch behind.

Mitch stormed out onto the porch—a rebuttal on his lips—but stopped. Instead, he found himself watching Beth as she strolled across the yard, his eyes focused on the cut of her jeans and the rhythm of her walk. He couldn't help himself. She might be exasperating, but Beth was still a woman . . . and Mitch was still very much a man.

After taking a few minutes to cool off, Mitch walked to the barn and found Beth saddling a beautiful Palomino.

"What are you doing?" he asked.

"I have some things I need to check on."

"You're not going out by yourself, are you?"

Beth gave him a peculiar look. "Yes, do you have a problem with that?"

"As a matter of fact, I do. What if you come across that punk again?"

"I can handle myself."

"You can handle yourself? Like you handled yourself earlier today?"

Beth ignored him and walked to the tack room.

"So, that's your answer to everything," he raised his voice, "to just ignore problems, turn your back, and pretend everything's okay?"

Mitch just about fell over backward when Beth emerged from the tack room—rifle in hand—challenging him with her eyes. He watched as she slid the rifle into the holster on her saddle and led the Palomino from the stall.

Beth stopped, mere inches from him and said, "I know you think I'm some helpless woman who can't take care of herself or her son, but I can handle myself and my business just fine. I'm not blind, stupid, or naive. And since you don't know me, you're just going to have to take my word for it."

Beth's expression was filled with an odd mixture of hurt and intensity as she walked away.

Mitch didn't understand how he kept winding up on the wrong side of Beth's emotions. He didn't mean to insult her; his concern for her safety was genuine. Just thinking about what could've happened if he hadn't been around to pull that punk off of Beth made his blood run cold. Mitch didn't want to see anything else happen to her.

Geez, is that so bad?

He hurried to the yard, hoping to stop Beth before she left. "Wait a minute," Mitch hollered, then jogged to close the distance between them.

Beth was in the saddle and near a gate that led to open pastureland when she stopped. She didn't bother to turn around, so Mitch positioned himself in front of her. He stroked the Palomino's neck and scratched her jowls, waiting for Beth to make eye contact with him. When it was obvious she wasn't going to, he squinted against the sun and sighed. "Look, Beth, I'm sorry. I didn't mean to insult you. Somehow, I keep tripping over my words and saying the wrong things."

Beth looked out over the open land, ignoring Mitch while her horse leaned into his massaging hands.

Well, at least her horse likes me.

Mitch closed one eye—again fighting the sun—as he looked up at Beth. "Are we good?"

There was something in the way Mitch said *we*. Something personal. Beth felt a flutter in her chest as she absorbed the effect his words had on her. "Fine. Apology accepted."

"Then can I ask a favor?" He smiled up at her.

Beth couldn't help but smile back. "You sure are pushy, you know that?"

"I wouldn't call it pushy. I like to think of it as being assertive."

She just rolled her eyes. "What's the favor?"

"Can I ride with you?"

"Why?" Instantly, her frustration returned and she did nothing to hide it. "I told you I can take care of myself."

"I'm not doubting that. I would just feel better knowing you weren't alone if there was any trouble."

"And how am I going to defend both of us when you're falling out of the saddle?"

"Hey, I might be a city boy, but I've had some experience."

"Riding a pony in front of the market for a quarter doesn't count," she quipped.

"Why don't you give me a chance before shutting me down?"

Beth thought for a moment before swinging Pandora back toward the barn. "Fine."

"Great. I'll be right back." He headed toward his trailer.

"Where are you going?" she hollered after him.

"I need to change."

Beth thought he was being ridiculous, but continued to the barn anyway. She dismounted Pandora and loose tied her to a rail. Once in the tack room, Beth gathered up Midas' gear and headed to his stall.

He whinnied and snorted—excited he was going to get a chance to go on a run. Beth took a few moments to love on him and massage his withers before prepping him for his ride.

"Okay, Midas, don't get too excited. You're going to have a beginner on your back; I need you to behave."

"Why do you keep insisting I'm a beginner?"

Beth turned around. Mitch no longer had on the Dockers and polo shirt he'd been wearing. Now he was in faded jeans, a button-down shirt, and the boots she had seen in his closet. He had a beat-up, brown felt cowboy hat pulled down over the bandage on his forehead and a little boy smile on his face. Her eyes traveled over him more than once, not intentionally, but she couldn't help herself. He looked so good . . . so right . . . Beth felt the flutter in her chest again and realized she was staring.

"Wow, look at you. Promise you a pony ride and you turn into Hopalong Cassidy!" She turned her attention back to Midas, trying to sound unimpressed. When she finished, Beth glanced at Mitch while leading Midas from his stall. "So, have you really ridden a horse before?"

"Yes, for about a year."

"Why?"

"I was working on a ranch at the time."

"Really? Doing what?"

"Ranch stuff."

"Stuff like what?"

"Don't you know?" he said with a smirk.

Beth was ready to fire off another question but decided it was useless. It was obvious she wasn't going to get a straight answer.

She watched as Mitch put his foot in the stirrup and hoisted himself into the saddle. Even though Midas was sixteen hands tall, Mitch's motion had been smooth. Experienced.

Swinging up into the saddle next to him, Beth asked, "You ready?" She looked at Mitch from under the brim of her tattered straw cowboy hat.

"Sure, just waiting for you."

Beth guided Pandora to the gate, leaned out of the saddle to unlatch it and swung the gate wide. Midas sauntered through the opening, and Beth latched it once Pandora stepped through to the other side. Mitch waited for her to lead the way, then fell into step beside her.

"So, what are we doing?" Mitch asked as he glanced at the bundle tethered to her saddle.

She looked at him with a raised brow. She had agreed he could ride along but had said nothing about wanting his help.

"When I asked Shane if he, Rusty, and Brett had repaired the fence yesterday, he couldn't remember. We'll be bringing a herd up tomorrow, so I need to make sure the repairs are finished."

Mitch answered with a silent nod.

Midas was beginning to move to the position he liked best. The lead. He quickened his stride and ended up a few paces ahead of Pandora. Beth didn't mind. She enjoyed the opportunity to study Mitch without the chance of being caught.

Again, Beth felt a strange flutter in her chest and was finally willing to identify it for what it was.

Attraction.

There was no sense denying it. The fact was, she found Mitch very attractive.

What wasn't to like? He was tall, chiseled, and incredibly handsome. But since they kept butting heads, she didn't want to give him the satisfaction of knowing he had gotten her attention.

Even so, it wasn't just his good looks Beth found attractive. It was the way Mitch had talked to Shane that first night. He could've easily blown off her son, but he hadn't. He'd taken the time to talk about things Shane was interested in, and had even defended her opinion about Curtis and Lucas when Shane started to grumble. And when she thought about what could've happened if Mitch hadn't talked Shane out of going with Brett and Rusty . . . it was more than she wanted to entertain. In his own way, Mitch was trying to help. For that she was willing to cut him a little slack.

It wasn't long before Midas became more assertive, taking Mitch to a canter. Beth pressed Pandora's sides with her knees—so she could keep up—but her attention was on how well Mitch was handling the change of pace. *He really can ride.* That explained the boots in his closet but not the fact that he had chosen to ruin such an expensive pair.

They rode for over twenty minutes in silence before coming across a large bundle of wire on the ground and the section of fence that was dilapidated and in need of repair. Beth swung out of her saddle and looked at the mess the boys had left behind. Along with the wire, post digger, and tools, there were empty bottles, cigarette butts, and trashy magazines.

She looked at Mitch, feeling humiliated all over again.

He hurried to pick up the magazines, but not before she grabbed one for herself.

She hung her head, mortified.

"Beth, it's natural for boys to be curious about women." He tried consoling her.

"But this isn't natural!" She shook the magazine in her hand. "This is trash! Magazines like these aren't going to teach him anything. They're degrading and disgusting! Is this how he thinks about women? That this is all they're good for?"

"Come on, Beth, you know that's not true." Mitch's tone was

soothing and calm. "Shane has had you as an example his entire life. He knows a real woman is strong, intelligent, and self-confident."

Beth kicked at a bottle, then grabbed some gloves out of one of Pandora's saddlebags and tossed a pair to Mitch. She yanked them on, then began to wrestle carelessly with the spool of barbed wire, catching it on her sleeve and again on her jeans. When a barb caught her on the forehead, she winced. That's when Mitch pulled the spool from her hands.

"Beth!" he raised his voice. "Tearing yourself up with barbed wire is not going to help matters."

She stiffened, ready to fire back, but when she saw compassion in Mitch's eyes, her shoulders slumped. "I'm sorry. You don't deserve this. I'm just so frustrated."

"I can see that."

She took a couple of breaths, trying to regain a modicum of composure. When she raised a gloved hand to her forehead, Mitch promptly pulled it away. "Don't touch it. Your hands aren't clean." He grinned as he used the same warning she had used on him earlier.

He pulled off one of his gloves and gently wiped his thumb across the small dot of blood on her forehead. "It's only a scratch. Just leave it alone and it will dry up on its own."

"Thank you, Dr. Burk." Beth tipped her head.

"You're welcome."

The huskiness in Mitch's voice was her first warning. When he took a step closer—glancing at her lips—that was her second. But, when Beth imagined what it would feel like to have his lips pressed against hers, an electric shock shot through the core of her body, setting off all kinds of alarms. She quickly took a step back and walked over to where one of the posts was leaning at a haphazard angle.

"So, what happened?" Mitch asked.

"What?" *Does he really expect me to explain what just happened between us?*

"The posts? What happened to them?"

Maybe it was just me. Maybe he didn't feel anything at all.

Beth cleared her throat, trying to sound casual even though her head was spinning. "Who knows?" she said as she surveyed the ground. "Cattle like to use the posts to scratch themselves. If one of the posts were loose, it would have gone down, and then the weight pulling the wire would have caused a domino effect. But it could have been any of a number of other things. Ground squirrels digging to close to the post. Rotted wood. Saturated dirt. The herd pressing against the fence." Beth spoke louder the further she moved down the line.

"So, what we really need to do is remove the wire, then get these posts back up and sturdy before reattaching the wire, right?"

"Pretty much," Beth mumbled.

"Okay." Mitch clapped his hands together and rubbed them like he was itching to get started. "Then we need to dig deeper."

Chapter Twelve

Beth and Mitch had been working on the fence line for over an hour. Beth worked her way along the line of twisted barbed wire, pulling it from the downed posts, patching it where needed, while Mitch muscled the post digger into the hard and unforgiving ground. Even though his progress was slow, Beth was impressed with the tireless energy he exerted. It was obvious he wasn't easily intimidated by hard work.

When Beth was done patching the last section of wire, she turned around to see Mitch pulling his sweat-moistened shirt off his back and tossing it on the ground. He then positioned himself to the left of the fourth post and went to work. She watched unnoticed as he moved, his muscles clenching and his body glistening. Beth admired the cut of his torso and the cable-like muscles that flexed across his shoulders and back. His body was as rugged as his masculine good looks. He was the whole package. Physically anyway.

What are you doing? She questioned herself, feeling heat invade her complexion. *You're acting like a hormone-driven adolescent. You know nothing about him, and he'll be gone in a week. So, knock it off!*

Beth walked to where Pandora was ground tied and grabbed her canteen from around the saddle horn. She took a long swig trying to quench the heat spreading throughout her body. Wiping her forearm across her mouth, she inhaled a deep breath and turned back around.

Immediately, she zeroed in on Mitch's abs. Every time he lifted the post digger over his head, his abdomen flexed to show off a well-defined eight-pack.

You're pathetic! You're ogling Mitch like men do the skin

magazines you just labeled disgusting. Get a grip!

Beth took another swig of water while bickering with her conscience, but it was no use. Every time she looked at Mitch all she saw was muscles and bronze. *That does it!*

With her canteen in hand, Beth marched over to where Mitch was working in a steady rhythm. He stopped to rest—his hands leaning on top of the post digger—his chest pulsing at the strenuous work.

"Here." She handed him the canteen. "You know you shouldn't be working this hard. The doc said to take it easy."

"I'm fine. Working outdoors gives me energy." He took a deep breath then exhaled. "Fresh air, the sun on my skin, it feels great."

"Yeah, well, it might feel great, but the sun is stronger than you think. If you don't put your shirt back on, you're going to end up with a nasty sunburn."

Mitch took a couple of good swallows from the canteen before handing it back to her. "I guess you're right," he said, eyeing one side of her face and then the other. "You're already getting a little red."

Beth tried to act casual, knowing good and well her hat offered plenty of protection from the sun. The redness Mitch was referring to had nothing to do with the weather.

Although Mitch took her suggestion and put his shirt back on, he didn't bother to button it. So Beth worked the rest of the time with her head down and her mouth shut.

It took over three hours, but they were finally done. The extra work Mitch put in to dig the holes deeper convinced Beth she wouldn't have problems with this section of fence for some time to come. When the realization of what she was thinking sunk in, she sighed. *Doesn't matter. I won't be here that long.*

Beth watched as Mitch gathered all the tools and equipment into one pile, a perplexed look clouding his features.

"Don't worry about it," she said. "We can't carry it all on horseback. I'll have to drive the truck out here later."

While Beth loaded some of the hand tools into her saddlebag, she watched as Mitch casually rolled together the magazines he confiscated and fastened them to the tie-downs on Midas' saddle. Beth appreciated the gesture. She really did. Even so, it only stood as a reminder of yet another conversation she needed to have with her son. *God, give me the strength and self-control not to wring Shane's neck.* She clasped the buckle on Pandora's saddlebag then leaned her head against the worn leather. *Spoken like a loving mother.*

But I am a loving mother, darn it! That's why I want to blister his butt!

Beth removed her hat to mop the sweat from her brow, then angrily pulled it down over her forehead. She lifted herself onto Pandora's back and watched as Mitch hoisted himself up onto Midas.

"Thanks for your help, Mitch. This would've taken me twice as long, and I never could've dug the holes as deep as you did."

"It was my pleasure. I need to work off the hospitality you've shown me."

"I'm sorry, did you say hospitality or *hostility?*" Beth asked with a chuckle.

"Don't be so hard on yourself, Beth. It's obvious I showed up at a challenging time, and my being here has only compounded your problems. I wish I could do more to help; I can be quite handy, you know."

"That's not necessary, Mitch, but I appreciate the offer."

Beth looked off into the distance, melancholy weighing on her shoulders. She allowed herself to think—for even the briefest moment—what it would be like to have a man in her life. Someone who was willing to share the load, help run the ranch she loved, hold her at the end of a difficult day. It had been a long time since she'd entertained such thoughts, but Mitch reminded her of something she had chosen not to dwell on.

She was lonely. Lonely for—

"So, tell me about yourself, Beth."

Mitch's words interrupted her train of thought. "I'm sorry, what?"

"Tell me about yourself, about the Diamond-J."

"There isn't much to tell that you don't already know. This land is in my blood. I guess I was either blind or naive to think I could raise my son here, and he would love it as much as I do. I didn't realize living so far from town was making Shane miss out on the 'evolution of society' as he puts it. I was always happy here as a kid, so I assumed Shane would be, too."

"What made it so much fun that you didn't go looking for adventure elsewhere? It seems like a lot of hard work, especially for a girl."

Beth ignored the sexist comment, knowing Mitch didn't mean anything by it. "It all seemed like fun back then. The Diamond-J was teeming with activity, and we had at least a dozen ranch hands. I spent most my time with the horses, learning how to rope and ride." Beth smiled, thinking about her younger days. "I guess I was kind of spoiled, being the only girl. The hard work was always being done by someone else."

"What about your mom?"

Beth's heart stuttered, forgetting to beat. It had been a long time since she had talked about her mother, and it took her a minute to speak.

"Beth, I didn't mean—"

"No. It's all right. It's just been a while." She gave him a reassuring smile. "My mom died when I was fourteen. Brain cancer. By the time we knew something was wrong, it was too late. Nothing could be done. My mother died less than six months after being diagnosed. As hard as it was to see her go, it was a relief in the end. The last three months she could barely communicate with us. She was only a shell of the person I knew and loved." Beth paused for a moment before continuing.

"Before my mom got sick, she spent every spare moment outdoors. She embraced ranch life. It was her lifeblood." Beth shrugged. "I guess that's where I get it from. My mother was always working with the horses, taking care of the goats, or feeding the chickens. I remember helping her bottle feed some piglets when the sow died. Gosh . . . I couldn't have been more than four or five. She absolutely loved animals." Beth could feel the wistful memory broaden her smile.

"My mom was beautiful, too, not some country bumpkin. She was crowned rodeo queen four years in a row. She finally stopped entering, convinced my father was rigging it somehow."

Beth laughed to herself, remembering the way her mother always teased her father about that. *Admit it, Jack, you liked being married to a rodeo queen so you paid off those cronies of yours to tip the scales in my favor.*

Jeanette Marie Justin, I did no such thing. You were—and always will be—the prettiest girl in three counties.

"Beth . . ."

She looked over to Mitch riding beside her. "Sorry. I guess I sort of drifted off there for a moment."

"It looked like it was a good memory," Mitch said.

Beth smiled. "It was. Anyway, after retiring her crown, my mom decided to concentrate on her riding. She was a champion barrel racer. My dad said she won every competition she entered, and was better than most men. My mom stopped competing when she was pregnant with me, but never lost her edge. Even when I was a teenager, I remember her challenging the ranch hands at the end of the day. No matter how many men tried, no one could beat her time."

"That must have been fun to watch," Mitch said.

"It was. Though it was even better seeing the way my father beamed with pride whenever he watched my mother ride."

Beth lowered her eyes and noticed the way her teardrops darkened the worn leather of Pandora's saddle. She turned, brushing away the tears from her cheeks with the back of her hand.

"My mother taught me how to rope and ride before she got sick. I remember I was practicing in the rink when my parents got home from the doctor. I knew something was wrong when they didn't come over to watch me ride. My mom was given a death sentence that day. She was never the same after that. Even as strong as she was, I know she gave in to the disease. It was horrible to watch. I told Uncle Charlie, if I ever find out news like that, I'm going to leave Shane a letter telling him how much I love him, then take my shotgun to a quiet place and end it all. There's no way I want my son to watch me deteriorate like that."

"You wouldn't really do that, would you?" Mitch asked, clearly disturbed.

Beth sighed. "No. I like to think I would, but taking my own life wouldn't make it any easier on Shane. Besides, God frowns on it." Beth chuckled, trying to lighten the mood. "Even still, I don't want doctors to go to heroic lengths to prolong my life if something serious happens to me. Both Shane and Uncle Charlie know that."

Mitch glanced over at Beth. "I'm sorry about your mom."

"So am I."

Beth knew by the look on Mitch's face he still had more questions, so she volunteered what she assumed would be next on his mind.

"My dad died ten years ago in October. He'd led a hard life of alcohol and tobacco before he met my mom and came to know the Lord. Even though he had quit his vices, they eventually caught up with him. You can only abuse your body for so long before you end up paying the price."

"He had to be young," Mitch commented.

"Sixty-five. He was actually fourteen years older than my mother when they got married."

"Wow, how did they meet?"

"The rodeo, of course," Beth laughed. "Back then, the rodeo was equivalent to the Academy Awards in these parts. Everyone went, and everyone knew everyone else. Well, except for my mother and her parents. They had just moved to Kansas from Nebraska. The minute my father saw my mother, he said he was 'ready to sell it all and follow her anywhere.' "

Beth beamed with pride as she recounted her parents' story.

"Come to find out, my grandfather had purchased the ranch just the other side of the Diamond-J. My father planned on winning my mom over with his charm and good looks, but she would have none of it." Beth sighed for a moment remembering the rugged man she had loved and lost.

"My father was your typical cowboy. Hard liquor. Chewing tobacco. Rough language. And stubborn as a mule. My mother, on the other hand, came from a Christian home. Her parents were extremely conservative and saw nothing but trouble when Jack Justin cornered their daughter at the rodeo and tried to woo her. My mother admitted to me that even though my dad was completely wrong for her, she was instantly attracted to him. There was something there. A spark. A shudder. She couldn't explain it, but she couldn't ignore it either."

Beth gasped, realizing for the first time she knew exactly what her mother had felt. *No. It couldn't be.*

"Are you all right?" Mitch asked, sounding worried.

She glanced over at Mitch—riding alongside her—a thousand thoughts streaming through her mind. *I'm mistaken. I have to be.*

"I'm fine," Beth said, then quickly refocused on her parents' story.

"My father and mother would meet every day where their property lines intersected. My father was incredibly good-looking, and my mother told me how she had to lean on the fence post just so her knees wouldn't give out. She knew my father was older than her, worldly, and set in his ways, but she also knew nothing was impossible with God. So, my mother decided to evangelize my father instead of date him."

"You're kidding!" Mitch said with a chuckle.

"Nope. She knew he wouldn't last long if he was only looking for a quick roll in the hay, so she was going to put him to the test. That's where it all started for them. Before they got married, my father saw that all his old habits were crutches and not honoring to God. He accepted Jesus as his Savior and became a changed man. My mother knew it was God's doing, because in all their years together, he never wavered in his commitment to her or to God."

"It must have been hard on your Dad when she got sick," Mitch added softly.

"It devastated him. My father always said my mother hung the moon and stars, and she was the light God had used to brighten his world. So, after her death, my father felt lost. His sorrow was so overwhelming he started drinking again. I never once blamed him for wanting to make the hurt go away because I was struggling myself.

"Then, during one of his more sober moments, he realized how disappointed my mother would have been knowing he turned to the bottle instead of the Lord. That was all it took. My father never drank again. And even though he was angry with God for taking my mother away, he did everything he could to comfort me and try to explain that often God's ways are not our ways.

"I think it was therapy for him to have to help me through the loss. Every Scripture he gave me and every prayer he prayed proved to make him stronger, and eventually brought us closer together."

"Sounds like even though you lost your parents at a young age, you have a lifetime of wonderful memories."

"I do, and I'm thankful for that."

"And you still have your aunt and uncle."

"Well, I have Uncle Charlie. I don't really consider Sarah as my aunt. Uncle Charlie remarried five years ago. She and I aren't that close, but she's been great for him."

"So, what about Shane's father, where does he fit in the picture?"

Beth felt like she'd just been doused with a bucket of cold water. She sat up straighter, her back rigid. She had no intentions of discussing Shane's father. Those memories were *not* as pleasant. "He doesn't. End of subject." She pressed Pandora to quicken the pace.

When Mitch caught up to her, he immediately apologized. "I'm sorry, Beth. That's none of my business."

"You're right, so let's just forget it." She looked at Mitch figuring it was his turn to share. "So, what about you? All I know so far is you're Mitch Burk—a man on vacation. You're from New York and California and . . . oh yeah . . . that's all I know." She gave him a curious look with the hint of a smirk.

Mitch should have seen that one coming. Beth had shared an awful lot. It was only natural she would turn the tables on him. *That's okay. She mostly talked about her childhood.* He could do that. It wouldn't be pretty, but he wouldn't have to explain who he really was.

"Well, unfortunately, I don't have any good childhood memories. My mother was the neighborhood tramp, and I never figured out who my father was. I had to fend for myself since the age of seven. If my mother wasn't drunk and angry, she was passed out and useless. Men paraded through my house every night, shocked my mother would do the things she did with a kid in the house but not disgusted enough to leave."

Mitch couldn't believe, after all these years, it still hurt to talk about his mother. It was painful to remember back to a time when he was afraid and alone. He was just a little boy. He should have been playing stickball in the streets, and running through hydrants on hot summer days. Instead, he was cleaning up vomit, and figuring out how to do his own laundry in the kitchen sink.

He looked at Beth and could tell she was trying to disguise her shock, but she wasn't that good of an actress.

Mitch swallowed the emotion clogging his throat and continued. "I learned how to steal at the age of eight, just so I could eat one decent meal a day. My mom was violent and abusive and accused me of ruining her life. She had been a dancer before she got pregnant and blamed me for her non-existent career." Mitch could still remember her rants and the terrible things she said to him.

"I realized at a young age I had no one to rely on but myself. I knew I would need an education if I was ever going to get out of the hellhole I was living in, so I stayed in school. My grades weren't stellar, but passable. Things changed for me right before I turned sixteen."

"What happened?"

"I tried pick-pocketing a man and got caught."

"Were you arrested?"

"No. The man's quote was 'why is a bright kid like you doing such a stupid thing like this?' So I told him. It turned out the guy was pretty well off. He was touched by my story, and offered me a job. The rest, as they say, is history. I got my GED, became an emancipated minor, and moved to California with the guy when his job transferred him there."

"And just like that, you left?"

"Are you kidding me? That was the chance I needed to make something of myself."

"What did your mother say?" Beth asked cautiously.

"When I told her I was moving out, she asked me to leave her enough money for a bottle of booze and a pack of cigarettes."

Beth gasped. "I'm sorry, Mitch. That had to be awful for you."

"No. In fact, it made it easier."

"Easier? How?"

"I remember walking home that day feeling guilty. I was finally getting out of that god-forsaken place, but the thought of leaving my mother behind ate at me. Even though she had done nothing to nurture a relationship between us, she was still my mother. I couldn't ignore her the way she had me all those years. So, I decided no matter what it took, I would send for her later. But when all she cared about was her next bottle of whiskey, I was through. I walked out the door with no intention of ever looking back."

Beth looked hesitant, but asked, "Did you ever see your mother again?"

"Yeah. I went back to the dilapidated apartment I had left five years earlier and found her sitting in the same ratty recliner she always did. The only difference was she no longer had a cigarette dangling from her lips, and she looked like she'd aged twenty years. When my mom barely recognized me, I figured she was either drunk or delusional. When she didn't seem to remember having a son and was confused why I was in her apartment, I had her checked out by a doctor. She was diagnosed with Alzheimer's. The doctor warned me there wasn't much that could be done for her, so I set her up in a convalescent home specializing in the care of Alzheimer's patients. I tried visiting her often enough so she wouldn't forget who I was. That only lasted about two years. Now I am just another stranger who wanders in and out of her life."

Mitch choked on his words. What he wouldn't give for just one good memory from his childhood.

Beth could hear the emotion in Mitch's voice, even though he was trying to mask it with a dry cough. She couldn't even imagine the pain he'd suffered as a child or understand how after all he'd been through, he was still taking care of a woman who was nothing more than the womb who brought him into the world.

Beth was sorry she had dredged up such painful memories for Mitch. And even though she still had a ton of questions, she decided to be extremely cautious before asking anymore questions about his past.

As they neared the gate, Beth unfastened the latch and pushed it wide open. When she looked up, she saw Shane, Charlie, and Travis kicking up dust in the distance.

Oh no!

Looking at her watch, Beth realized it was lunchtime. She and Mitch had ridden at such a slow pace while talking, time had gotten away from her. Now, everyone was riding in for lunch, and she had absolutely nothing prepared.

"Great! I completely forgot about lunch," Beth said as she hurried Pandora into the barn and hooked a lead rope on her bridle.

"Go ahead inside," Mitch said as he led Midas into his stall. "I'll finish out here while you work on lunch." He moved to Pandora's side and reached under her belly for the cinch strap.

"Are you sure you know what you're doing?"

"It's not that hard, Beth. All I have to do is remove her gear and brush her down. It's not brain surgery."

"Are you sure?"

"Well, it's either that or you'll have to explain why lunch isn't ready. Shane already has a bad impression of me. Let's not give him a reason to get the wrong idea about how we spent the morning."

The impact of what Mitch was saying was all the convincing Beth needed. She jogged toward the house already preparing lunch in her mind. However, it was the way Mitch said 'we' that danced among her thoughts, making her heart flutter.

Chapter Thirteen

Lunch was a bit late, but thankfully not enough for anyone to question it. Charlie introduced Travis to Mitch, and then pulled Mitch aside to get what Beth was sure was a more detailed version of what had happened between her and Brett.

When Charlie worked his way into the kitchen at the end of the meal, Beth knew he was checking up on her.

"Mitch told me what happened. Are you sure you're okay?"

"He didn't tell you, you browbeat him into explaining," Beth huffed, wanting to put the whole incident behind her.

"Doesn't matter. I know what I know and if those boys weren't gone already, there would be hell to pay."

"So, you know for sure they're gone?"

"Yeah, as soon as I got off the phone with you, I called Travis. By the time he drove over to the bunkhouse, they had already hitched their beat-up trailer to Rusty's truck and cleared out their belongings. Travis went ahead and paid them in cash for the hours they worked. He didn't want them hanging around causing trouble."

"Great, so Travis knows, too?" Beth swung around to look at Charlie. "You didn't say anything in front of Shane, did you?"

"No. He just thinks all the hoopla is on account of them getting him drunk. Shane has no idea Brett went after you."

"Good. He feels guilty enough. I don't want him feeling any worse."

"Maybe you should tell him what happened. Shane needs to learn that self-destructive behavior usually hurts those around you. He needs to start taking responsibility for his actions."

"I know, Uncle Charlie, but not this time. I have some other matters to discuss with him first."

"I could tell at lunch you weren't happy about something. What else is gnawing at you?"

"When Mitch and I went to do the fencing, we found a bunch of smut magazines along with a lot of empty bottles." Beth hung her head in embarrassment once again.

Charlie pulled her close and offered a hug. "I'm sorry, Beth. Parenting can be a real pain in the butt sometimes, but hang in there. I had my issues with Travis when he was growing up, but look at what a fine, God-fearing man he's turned out to be."

"That does give me some hope." Beth gave him a squeeze before turning her attention back to the dishes.

"It will all work out. You'll see. Sometimes the ruts in the road are just a little bigger than we anticipate." Charlie stopped his counseling but continued to stare at Beth.

"What?" she said with a chuckle, wondering what he was staring at.

"So . . . Mitch helped you with the fence line?" he asked with a smirk.

"Yeah, what of it? He feels the need to help out in exchange for him being allowed to stay here. So I let him help."

"How'd he do? He's kind of a pretty boy to be working with his hands and getting himself dirty. Besides, that wallop to the head looked serious."

"Actually, come to find out, he's worked on a ranch before. He didn't do too bad riding Midas, and he was a huge help with the post digger. We were able to get almost sixty feet of fence done in just a couple of hours. I told him he should be taking it easy, but he seemed to be enjoying himself."

"Then maybe you should offer him a job. You are short-handed, you know?" Charlie's look was devilish.

"Mitch isn't looking for a job. He's on vacation, which means he has a job somewhere else. Besides, he and Shane have already butted heads."

"Maybe that's because Shane doesn't like having someone around who can read him so well. You're a great mom, Beth, but there are times when Shane's got your number and knows how to play you."

Beth bristled. She worked hard at having a good relationship with her son. Only recently had they begun to clash.

"Look, Uncle Charlie," she was wagging her finger, but he didn't let her continue. He backed out of the kitchen, hands up in surrender.

"I'm going; I'm going."

"I'm telling you, Mitch, you look just like him, except your hair is darker."

Mitch felt cornered. He had overheard Shane talking to Travis at lunch about Simon Grey, the actor, and how much he looked like him. Mitch had steered clear of the conversation, but Shane wasn't letting it rest.

"Do you know who I'm talking about, Uncle Charlie?"

"I don't even know *what* you're talking about," Charlie said as he stepped out onto the porch.

"I knew Mitch reminded me of someone, but it wasn't until I saw him in jeans and boots that I realized who he looks like. Remember that show called *Range Riders*? Mitch looks just like the actor Simon Grey."

Charlie turned toward Mitch and stared at him with a slight squint.

"Well, in that case," Mitch said, hoping to diffuse the situation, "I better make sure my agent knows where to send my six-figure paychecks. Oh, and I'll need to catch up on my fan mail. I don't want to keep the ladies waiting. Then I'll call my chauffeur to come pick me up and take me back to my million-dollar home with a view."

Shane rolled his eyes. "I just said you *looked* like him. There's no reason to act like such a jerk."

Charlie reminded Shane and Travis how much work still had to be done, so the three of them walked to their horses and rode off together while Mitch sweated it out on the porch. *That was close. Hopefully, Shane got that out of his system and it doesn't come up again.*

Beth was still busy in the kitchen when Mitch decided it would be a good time to check the Internet and see if anything was being said about his disappearing act. He'd already been gone a couple of weeks. By now, Jerry was probably freaking out and having to come up with some major excuses to explain his absence at previously scheduled appearances.

He walked quietly to Beth's office and rolled the mouse over the desktop to bring the computer out of sleep mode. When he did, Mitch was struck by the fact that the last thing Beth had been looking at was a realtor's site. Listings around Kansas City.

So, that's the deal you made with Shane. You're going to move.

Mitch just shook his head. In the few conversations he'd had with Beth, it was obvious the ranch was her life. The fact she was willing to sacrifice it for her son made Mitch both envious of their bond, and angry Shane was being so selfish.

Stepping back from Beth's computer, Mitch didn't know what to do with the information he had stumbled across. What could he do? It was none of his business. Besides, he would be gone by next week, and had no right interfering.

Then why did he feel so involved?

Mitch slipped from Beth's office and went outside. He stood on the front porch and looked at everything that encompassed Beth's world and liked it.

A lot.

Especially the blue-eyed blonde that made the life of a rancher look anything but boring.

"What are you thinking?"

Beth startled him.

"Nothing. Just enjoying the scenery."

The night had turned out nothing like Beth had expected. Even after exchanging harsh words with Mitch earlier in the day, Shane warmed right back up to him. Mitch had an uncanny way of working past Shane's tough-guy exterior and the walls her son had so skillfully erected in the last few months. By the end of the evening, the two of them were talking and laughing like it was as natural as breathing. It was great to hear Shane having such a good time.

It made what Beth had to do even harder.

Mitch excused himself for the night as Shane took the stairs to his room. Beth went around turning off lights, stalling while praying God would give her the words to say.

"Hey, can we talk?" Beth asked, while standing in the doorway of Shane's room.

He was already in bed but scooted up against the headboard, hands clasped behind his head. "Come on, Mom, I've heard it from you, Uncle Charlie, Travis, even Mitch. I know it was stupid, and I promised I wouldn't do it again."

Beth had to take a breath. Bare-chested with his hands behind his head, Shane no longer looked like a child; he looked like a man. When had her little boy grown up? Wasn't it just yesterday when she scolded him for bringing a piglet into the house, and grounded him for hiding frogs in the bathtub?

Beth consciously cleared her head of all the little boy problems they had already overcome. Tonight she had to be strong enough to address adolescent problems without totally losing it.

Okay, God. Here we go.

"I'm glad you realize messing around with alcohol is stupid, but that's not what I wanted to talk to you about." Beth tossed one of the skin magazines on his bed. "*This* is what I wanted to talk to you about."

Shane sat up even straighter—his mouth gaping open—when he saw what landed on his bedspread.

Beth waited a second, then broke the silence. "Go ahead, Shane, pick it up."

"I don't want to."

"But you did when you were with Rusty and Brett," she said matter-of-factly. Stepping forward, Beth picked up the tattered magazine and started thumbing through it.

Shane's face twisted in what Beth could only hope was total mortification.

"So, is this how you see women?" Beth asked as she took a seat on the corner of his bed and turned the centerfold picture toward him.

"No." Shane immediately looked away.

"Do you think this is how women like to be treated?" Again, she turned the magazine toward Shane and showed him a picture of a scantily-clad woman wrapped in chains.

"No." He didn't even bother to look.

"How would you feel if I decided to pose for one of these magazines?"

Shane's head snapped up; a look of shock like Beth had never seen before darkened his complexion. "That's disgusting!"

"Is it? No more so than you wanting to look at them." Beth was being cool and measured. She wasn't enjoying what she was doing, but she wanted Shane to see the immorality and depravity of what he had done.

"This is filth, Shane! Absolute filth! I understand you are growing up, and that you're curious about women and sex. I would be foolish to think otherwise. But this," she shoved the magazine at him and shook it, "this is warped and demented and unhealthy. If you fantasize about things like this, you will never find a woman who will be able to satisfy your desires. You will ruin your marriage before it even has a chance to succeed."

Shane hung his head. "I don't know what to say, Mom." He swung his feet over the side of the bed and sat alongside her. Digging his elbows into his knees, Shane scrubbed his fingers through his hair and let out a sigh. "I knew it was wrong. Even though Brett and Rusty said women like to be dominated and manhandled, I didn't believe them." He got up and paced his small room. "I'm sorry, Mom, really I am. I don't mean to keep screwing up. I know I'm a huge disappointment to you because I don't want to grow-up like you did, but—"

"Wait a minute, Shane." Beth stood and walked over to where he was leaning against the wall. "You are *not* a disappointment to me. I love you. I will always love you, regardless of where we live, or how much we argue. It's because I love you that I want to guard your heart against things that will hurt you like alcohol and pornography. Don't ever doubt that, Shane, not for one minute."

Beth stepped forward and hugged her son. *Please God, let him hear my heart.* She held on to Shane, almost afraid to let him go. When she did, Shane plopped down on his bed and mumbled, "I guess I better prepare myself for another lecture from Uncle Charlie and Travis."

"I didn't tell Travis, but Uncle Charlie knows, and Mitch. But that's only because he was with me when I found the magazines. He thought I should cut you some slack and chalk it up to curiosity."

Shane shrugged. "I *was* curious, and—"

"And what?"

"And now I know it's wrong."

"Good." Beth turned to leave.

"Mom, does this mean our deal is off?"

She stopped before she got to the doorway. "No. I made a deal. But I've got to tell you, many more issues like this, and I'll have to rethink my end of the bargain. If I'm going to take such a drastic step, I've got to know you're with me, not defying me."

"Thanks, Mom. And I'm really sorry."

Walking to her room, Beth collapsed onto her bed. *Thank you, Lord. Thank you that Shane was receptive and appears to be regretful. Help me, God. Help me to know when to listen and when to come down on him. I don't want to be an ignorant parent, but I don't want to drive him away either.*

Beth continued her talk with God while she ran a hot bath and dumped the magazine in the wastebasket under the sink. When she had sunk into the soothing water, she could feel her body relax, but her mind continued to spin.

Chapter Fourteen

Mitch had been waiting less than five minutes when Shane walked out the door and down the steps.

"Can I talk to you for a minute?" Mitch asked.

Shane dropped his head back from his shoulders. "Why?"

"I think you need to tell your mom how we met."

Shane turned. "Now? Are you kidding me? That would be strike three!"

"But she's going to find out eventually, and I think it would be better if she heard it from you. You know, wipe the slate clean."

"Why? Are you going to tell her if I don't?" Shane lifted his chin defiantly.

Mitch looked away and thought a moment before answering. "Yes. I don't feel right keeping it from her. I covered for you the day of the accident because you kept ranting and raving that your mother was going to kill you. Since I didn't know what your home life was like, I wanted to make sure you weren't in any real danger. However, now I think Beth deserves to know the truth, and you need to take responsibility for your actions."

Shane pushed his boot around in the dirt and took a few moments to respond. "I'll do it tonight, after dinner. That will give me enough time to work up the nerve."

"Okay, but if you don't tell her before tomorrow, I will."

"I said I would, so just get off my case!"

Mitch watched as Shane stalked away. He waited a few minutes then followed him into the barn.

"Look, Shane, I know you're ticked off at me, but I wanted to let you know it looks like I'm going to be around for a few more days."

"So."

"So . . . if there's anything you want to talk about, I promise, I'll be straight with you."

"I don't know what you mean." Shane grabbed his gear and headed to Apollo's stall.

"Just that I was sixteen once, and I know what's going through your mind. So, if you have any questions about women . . . or sex, I'd rather you talk to me then get some perverted idea about it from those magazines."

"Forget it," Shane said as he lobbed the saddle onto Apollo's back.

"Look, I just want to help."

"Right. As long as I spill my guts to my mom before morning. Some help."

"You know, Shane, you brought this on yourself. I'm not out to get you, and neither is your mother. I just thought I would let you know I'll be around if you wanted to talk. That's all. The choice is yours." Mitch started to walk away.

"Mitch . . ." Shane called after him, his tone a little less belligerent. He turned around

"Could you be there . . . when I tell my mom? That way when she goes ballistic you can pull her off me before she beats the tar out of me."

"I don't think she would do that, but, yeah, I'll be there," he assured Shane with a grin.

Mitch climbed the front steps and knocked on the screen door before he pulled it open. Beth had just poured herself a cup of coffee and was making something on the stove.

"So, are you always an early riser or is it because you can't sleep?" she asked.

"I was never one to waste the day," Mitch said as she handed him a mug from the cupboard. "What's on the agenda for today?"

"What do you mean? You're on vacation." Beth gave him a smile.

"Hey, I believe in pulling my own weight."

Beth divvied up scrambled eggs between two plates just as the toaster popped up four slices of wheat bread. "And you were very helpful yesterday, but I don't want you to feel an obligation."

"I *don't* feel an obligation. I just like to be kept busy."

"You're supposed to be resting, per the doctor's instructions. I shouldn't have even let you go out yesterday."

"Sitting around drives me crazy. And since I didn't drop dead last night, I must be okay."

He poured himself a cup of coffee, took the plate she handed him, and walked over to the dining room table. Beth joined him and as soon as she took her seat, bowed her head in prayer.

"Thank you, Lord, for this food, our night of rest, and the strength you're going to give us for another day. Lord, work on Shane's heart. Let Your ways be his ways, and help me to be sensitive to his needs. Thank you for Mitch and the help he's been both on the ranch and with Shane. Provide the help he needs to get him on his way. We give this day to You. Amen."

Mitch was touched Beth mentioned him in her prayer, and a little surprised she had actually admitted he'd been a help.

"That was nice." He smiled at her.

A weak smile creased her face before she put a forkful of eggs in her mouth.

When they were done with breakfast, Mitch asked if he could use Beth's computer.

"Still looking for someone to bail you out of here?" she teased.

"No. I just needed to check a few things."

"Okay. So I have to ask, where's your phone?"

"I don't have one."

"What do you mean, you don't have one? Everyone has a phone. Even though I hate technology and use mine only once in a blue moon, I still have one."

Mitch shrugged. "My contract was up before I left. I didn't feel like renewing it. I figured I'd see how long I could go before I missed it. So far, it's been great. No interruptions. No dinging, ringing, or chiming."

"Huh, we actually have something in common."

Mitch smiled. "So, can I jump on your computer for a few minutes?"

"Sure."

He dismissed himself and wandered down the hall.

While Mitch was busy on her computer, Beth walked to the work shed and went over the sketches she had roughed out for the tack room extension. She was fine-tuning a few measurements when Mitch came up behind her.

"So, what are the plans for?" he asked.

Beth looked over her shoulder and into the most incredible pair of hazel eyes. She turned back around, not wanting to be caught in his stare. "The tack room has seen better days. So, instead of just repairing it, I decided to expand it, but I'm debating if it's even worth the time."

"Why wouldn't it be worth it?"

Now that she was planning on selling the ranch, there were more important things that needed to be done than enlarging the tack room. However, Beth didn't want to explain all that to Mitch. "I just meant I have a list of repairs and other things that need my attention. The tack room can wait until fall."

"Do you mind?" Mitch pointed to the plans.

She scooted over so he could step closer to the work table. Beth watched as he examined the rough sketches and read her doodled notes in the margins.

"Did you draw these plans yourself?" Mitch asked as he continued to study them.

"What gave it away? The pink ink or my chicken scratch math around the edges?"

He laughed. "Actually, they're not bad." Mitch looked at them some more. "Tell you what . . . why don't you let me work on the tack room? That way, you'll be free to work on something else."

"Why?"

"Why not? I use to do carpentry when I was between jobs, and your plans are pretty straight forward."

"You don't have to do that, Mitch. You're supposed to be on vacation, or at the very least resting. Why are you trying so hard to be put to work? Obviously this wasn't your vacation destination, but the least you could do is relax."

"And why are you trying so hard to brush away my help?" He crossed his arms against his chest. "It's like pulling teeth to get you to acknowledge I'm an able-bodied person who could be a real asset to you these next few days." Beth tried to interrupt, but he continued. "Look, I'll have plenty of vacation time left when I leave here, but you'll still have a laundry list of jobs to do. Let me help while I can."

The only thing Mitch was incorrect in assuming is that Beth had *most definitely* noticed how able-bodied he was. That was part of the problem. She felt an attraction for Mitch. No, it was more like an unhealthy distraction. One she had to keep reminding herself was pointless. He would be gone in a few days, and that was just fine with her.

"Okay. You got it." She brushed her hands together and took a step back. "You work on the tack room, and I'll work on something else."

"Perfect!"

"All the tools are here, the footings are already poured, and all the wood is right there." She pointed to the stack in the corner. "You screw up, you replace the wood."

"Deal."

Mitch had been working for hours measuring and cutting wood. With the pieces that would make up the framework done, he turned off the table-saw, lifted the cut boards up onto his shoulder, and carried them out to the side of the barn. After setting them down near the footings, he glanced up at the sun, surprised by its early-morning intensity.

As he was walking away, Mitch heard the animals raising a ruckus from around the side of the barn. He just shook his head and laughed. *Not in a million years. Old MacDonald I am not.*

Returning to the work shed, Mitch pulled down a tool belt from a hook on the wall and loaded up the pockets with all the necessary items: nails, measuring tape, hammer, square, and pencil; then, rolled up Beth's sketches and shoved them under his arm. Back at the footings, he laid out the plans on a work table he'd constructed from an old piece of plywood and two sawhorses, then used a couple of two-by-fours to hold the papers in place. Once Mitch had his bearings, he got to work.

It didn't take long for him to fall into an easy rhythm. Mitch was surprised how good it felt to be swinging a hammer again. The enjoyment he got from working with his hands was one he'd forgotten about. After spending months doing odd jobs around the Hollywood-Burbank area—waiting for his big break—Mitch never thought he would find himself leaning over a sawhorse again. Even so, he felt strangely at home.

What in the world? The animals were once again going crazy. The bleating and cackling were loud, but the squeal of pigs was earsplitting.

Mitch walked around the corner of the barn to see what all the fuss was about, only to find Beth—with mud splattered on her jeans—running around a large holding pen. He laughed out loud at the sight of her chasing a piglet and having little luck catching him. "What are you doing?"

Beth stopped, looking hot, frustrated, and annoyed.

"What does it look like I'm doing?" She pushed her hat back from her face and planted her hands on her hips.

"What's wrong? That little piggy doesn't want to go to market?" Mitch laughed.

"Very funny."

"I thought you were in the house taking care of business."

"No," Beth answered, while the piglet scurried over to the plank of wood separating him from his mother. "I said I had 'other work' to take care of. This is the 'other work.' I needed to replace that board on the pen. When I did, he got out. I've been chasing him for well over twenty minutes, but I can't catch him."

"So, why bother? Look at you. You're covered in mud and who knows what else."

"I don't want him to get out of the pen. The only reason he hasn't escaped already is because he's too busy concentrating on getting back to his mother. He hasn't noticed the numerous places in the fence that he could slip through. Once he does, he's history."

Mitch observed how the piglet stood directly opposite his mother, his snout sticking through the planks to touch hers. "So what's the big deal? He's just standing there. Go pick him up and toss him over the fence."

"Silly me. Why didn't I think of that?" Beth said sarcastically, then snapped, "What do you think I've been trying to do?"

"Oh, come on, Beth, surely you can outrun a little piggy," Mitch said, mockingly.

"If you think it's so easy, you do it," Beth challenged, crossing her arms against her chest.

"Okay. Piece of cake."

Mitch quickly unbuckled the tool belt from around his hips and laid it aside. Hooking his boot on the middle rung of the fence, he vaulted over the top in one easy motion. As he slowly approached the squealing piglet, Mitch hunched down closer to the ground. When he was within a foot of the pig, he stretched out his arms, ready to grab it, but at the last second, the piglet bolted. Mitch lunged forward hoping to corner the animal and almost drilled his head into the fencepost.

Beth laughed hysterically. "What's the matter, Mitch, you're not going to let a little piggy outwit you, are you?"

He ignored her, turned toward the little creature running around screaming his head off, and started chasing him. Mitch ran three laps around the large enclosure before he bent over to catch his breath, a few choice words escaping his lips.

"Uh, uh, uh," Beth teased, "no swearing around the youngins'."

"Okay, let's double team the little runt," Mitch said while panting.

"We'll wait for him to go back to mama. Then, you close in on him. If he gets passed you, I'll back you up."

Beth continued to laugh. "Okay, but I think he's got our number."

Taking a wide stance, Beth bent down and slowly crept forward. She was within inches of the piglet, when just like before, the critter scrambled between her legs. Mitch was at the ready, catching the little guy before he could get away, but the piglet continued to wiggle and squirm in his hands. Struggling to hold on to the runt, Mitch lost his balance and fell backwards in the dirt and muck, the piglet scampering away.

Beth collapsed against the fence in a fit of laughter. "Who's covered in mud now?"

Mitch was not amused. He sat in a pile of who knows what, mud splattered all over his white t-shirt. He was glad he'd taken off the button down he'd been wearing earlier, but that didn't make him any less annoyed. He waited for a moment—counting to ten—trying not to lose his cool, but Beth continued to taunt and tease him, all the while clutching her side in amusement.

"Okay, cowboy," she said as she mockingly rolled up her sleeves. "Let me show you how it's done."

When Beth ran past him to corner the piglet, Mitch didn't stop to think. He just reached out for Beth's ankle, and with a yank, pulled her down beside him. Landing with a splat, the only thing that stopped Beth's face from actually hitting the sludge was her outstretched hands and sheer determination.

"You jerk!" Beth got to her knees, grabbed a handful of compacted straw and muck, and flung it at him.

Mitch turned away just in time, the wad of straw hitting him right between the shoulder blades. When he twisted back around, Beth was getting to her feet. "So, that's how you want to play? Well, bring it on, sister."

Beth tried to run, but was no match for Mitch's long strides. He caught up with her, grabbed her from behind, and pulled Beth back against his chest.

"Let me go!" she hollered between gasps of laughter.

He walked toward the water trough, while Beth kicked and screamed. "Oh, I'll let you go. I just think that temper of yours needs a little cooling off."

"Stop! Stop right now! Don't you dare put me in there!"

"Dare? Did you just dare me?" Mitch panted in amusement. "I *never* refuse a dare."

"Mitch, I swear, if you don't put me down right now I'll—"

"You'll what? The way I see it, you're in no position to be making threats." He took two more strides.

"Okay, okay, truce," she hollered playfully.

"So you give up?" He stepped closer to the galvanized tub.

"No. I called a truce."

"No way! This is not ending in a truce. Give up or you're going in." His tone held no anger, only unadulterated pleasure.

Beth continued to squirm, but wasn't as successful as the squealing piglet. Her laughter quickly turned to panic when Beth realized she was within inches of the tub of cold water. Mitch spun her around and reached for the crook of her knees. Not knowing what else to do, Beth wrapped her hands around his neck and held on for dear life. If she was going in, then he was going in, too.

"I'm giving you one more chance, Beth," Mitch said as he held her in his arms. "All you have to do is admit I won, and I'll let you go."

Punishment was the furthest thing from Beth's mind. Mitch held her against his chest, their faces just inches apart, his eyes trained on hers. She would admit anything if it meant she could feel this way forever.

"Okay," she whispered, her heart beating feverishly. "You win."

The sexy smile that spread across Mitch's face was intoxicating. Though he let go of her knees so she could stand, Mitch still held her dangerously close. Beth felt her feet touch the ground, but did nothing to remove her arms from around his neck. Before Beth knew what

JUST AN ACT

was happening, Mitch leaned down and covered her lips with his. With his hand on the small of Beth's back, Mitch pressed her closer, deepening his kiss. She felt her body react to the warmth of his touch, her lips kissing him back.

Then common sense kicked in.

She quickly took a step back, her arms dropping to her sides. "Why did you do that?"

"Because . . . you wanted me to." His smile was smug and self-assured.

"I wanted you to?" she protested.

"So we agree," he said nonchalantly as he brushed at the straw stuck to his jeans.

"No! We don't!" She grabbed her hat from where it had landed in the straw, unlatched the fence, and stormed away.

Chapter Fifteen

"Me thinks she dost protest too much," Mitch mused under his breath. He recognized the look in Beth's eyes. He'd seen it there a few times before. She was as attracted to him as he was to her. Beth was just too stubborn or too guarded to admit it.

He walked over to where Beth had placed the new board on the pigpen. With a couple of yanks, he freed the board from the stud far enough for the squealing piglet to shimmy through. Mitch pounded the board back in place and smiled at his genius. Of course, he had thought of it from the beginning, but the other proved to be so much more fun.

Mitch wiped the grime from his hands on to the back of his mud soaked jeans. He would need to change before he did anything else; then Mitch would be ready for round two.

Beth opened the backdoor of the house and slipped into the mudroom. Yanking off her boots, she quickly stripped off her muddy jeans and t-shirt and dropped them into the utility sink. Peaking around the door that led into the hallway, Beth listened. She knew no one was home, but had to be absolutely sure before she sprinted to the downstairs bathroom in nothing but her skivvies.

After turning on the shower—making sure the water was the perfect mixture of hot and cold—Beth discarded her underthings and stood under the steaming flood. It took a while for the barnyard stench to disappear and several more minutes to remove the crusted straw tangled in her hair. But no matter how many times she ran a washcloth over her face, Beth could still feel the burning sensation of Mitch's lips pressed to hers. *Why did I kiss him back? Now he's going to think I'm some pathetic, attention-starved woman willing to hook up with the first stranger who comes along.*

Beth was lost in thought when suddenly the shower water turned icy cold. "Oh, come on," she leaned her head against the tile. "Please don't tell me the water heater is going out, too?" Beth stepped out of the shower and towel dried her hair before wrapping it around her body. Scooping up her remaining clothes, she hurried upstairs so she could get dressed. When Beth reached the landing, she froze. Mitch was walking toward her, barefooted, a pair of jeans riding low on his hips, as he roughed a towel through his hair.

"Mitch, what are you doing up here?" She clenched her towel even tighter.

Mitch stood, his gaze transfixed on Beth's glistening shoulders and the waterdrops that ran off the tips of her hair.

"I . . . I don't have running water," he did his best to avert his eyes. "I needed to wash up. I'm . . . sorry. I should have waited outside until you were done." His eyes swept across her again, noticing the flowery apparel she had clutched in her hands.

Without another word, Beth stormed by him and slammed her bedroom door shut.

Beth paced—panicked by the recklessness in her heart. She was falling for a stranger, a man she'd known only a few days. *Who am I kidding . . . a man I don't know at all. Mitch could be a criminal on the run or a grifter looking for an easy score. Mitch might not even be his real name.*

Beth argued with herself as she yanked a brush through her tangled hair. She knew Mitch was none of those things, and trying to blame him for the attraction she felt was the most pitiful form of denial. She was an adult and had to take responsibility for her own heart.

Putting down the hairbrush, Beth walked to the antique dresser on the other side of the room and grabbed a change of clothes. Sitting on the edge of the bed, Beth pulled on a pair of jeans and shimmied them up around her hips. After putting on a sports bra and t-shirt, she walked back to the bathroom, pulled her hair into a ponytail, and looked at her reflection in the mirror. *Is it so wrong to be attracted to a man? Just because I'm a single mom doesn't disqualify me from being a woman.*

She'd told herself for years that she didn't need a man. She had Shane; he was enough. But no matter how many times Beth repeated that little pep talk, one thought always resounded inside her heart.

She was lonely.

Lonely for a man to help her shoulder the responsibility of the ranch. Lonely for someone to help her make financial decisions. *Expand the herd or sell off the land?* Lonely for someone to curl up with at the end of a long hard day? Lonely for someone who would remind her she was a woman.

Glancing at the bedside clock, Beth realized the day was getting away from her. She had to get her mind back on things that mattered. And since Mitch would be gone in a few days, she had to cut him from the list. She wasn't sure what she would say to him, but whatever it was, it would have to be done in private, far from Uncle Charlie's prying ears and Shane's watchful stare.

Mitch, Shane, Charlie, and Travis all gathered at the table for lunch. Beth tried to act natural, but her pulse was beating so rapidly she thought for sure she was going to pass out. She joined in on what conversations she could but finally gave up when her nerves got the better of her. Beth decided she was better off in the kitchen looking busy than sitting with the guys where she was forced to exchange polite glances with Mitch.

When lunch was over, Charlie, Travis, and Shane headed out to work with the cattle while Mitch hung back. He crossed the yard to the barn, but only for the sake of appearances. As soon as the men were out of sight, he headed back to the house. Beth was staring out the kitchen window, but turned when she heard the screen door snap shut.

"Can we talk?" Mitch asked as he walked closer to the kitchen.

"I don't think you're going to like what I have to say," she said, while scouring what looked like an already clean kitchen counter.

"Then I'll start." He stood beside her and leaned back against the counter, crossing his ankles and his arms. "I like you, Beth. And I'd like to stick around a little while longer to see where that takes us."

"And for that same reason, I think it would be best for all of us if you left as planned."

"Why?"

"Because my life is complicated enough right now."

"Maybe you're the one that's complicating things."

"What's that supposed to mean?" She threw down the sponge and planted her fist on her hip.

"You're too analytical. You've probably already come up with a hundred reasons why I should leave. Why don't you just relax and allow things to play out?"

"And what do you mean by 'play out'?"

"You know, play out. Take one day at a time. See where it leads us."

"And if you're lucky, it will lead to my bed, right? We'll share a couple of intimate nights together, then you'll see I was right—that this wasn't such a good idea—and you'll move on."

"So you're afraid of an intimate relationship, is that it?" he asked bluntly.

"That's none of your business."

Beth tried to walk away but he grabbed her, gently but firmly. She looked at his hand, then at him with an icy cold stare.

He let her go.

"Beth, I wouldn't hurt you like that, but I won't lie to you either. A physical relationship is something I would be interested in. But I know you're not the kind of woman to do casual. You have Shane to consider and your faith. I respect that."

"So, why are we talking about this? Do you think if you stay longer, you'll wear me down? You think I'll give in to my needs and throw caution to the wind? You're charming, Mitch, and it's obvious you know how to use that charm to get your way, but I'm not going to allow you that chance. I'm not going to hop into bed with you because you're nice to my son or good with a hammer."

"Actually, I give you more credit than that, but thanks for painting such a vivid picture of who you think I am." Mitch was genuinely insulted by her character assassination. Probably because it hit so close to home.

He paced a few steps away—needing to put a little distance between them— and then turned. "I'll admit it; I'm no Boy Scout. And yes, I've charmed my way into getting what I wanted from a woman on more than one occasion, but I left that world behind."

"This *vacation* . . . this ludicrous *fact-finding mission* I'm on is because I know something is missing in my life. I blame my mother for my crappy childhood and swore I would never end up like her. Once I was successful I thought I'd feel a sense of peace and contentment, but I didn't. So I turned to women, alcohol, even recreational drugs, but I always had this emptiness inside me. Then one morning, as I was sitting in my bedroom: a drink in one hand, a joint in the other, and a woman in my bed I didn't even know, I realized it didn't matter how much money I had or who I pretended to be. Nothing on the outside was going to make me feel whole on the inside."

Beth sighed. "Why are you telling me all this? Do you think if I feel sorry for you, I'll change my mind? Because I won't."

"No. I'm telling you all this because I think you might have what I've been looking for. Your life is full; your faith is real. And the love you have for Shane is . . . is like nothing I've ever seen before. You're whole, Beth. I see it. I sense it. Even with all that's happened in the last few days, it's like you have this internal glue keeping you together. I want that, too. I want a life that is more than just existing.

JUST AN ACT

I want a life worth living, even with its struggles and hardships."

She shrugged as if his words didn't mean a thing. "That's quite a line considering you've only known me a few days."

Mitch backed away, feeling as if he'd been physically punched. He'd been honest with Beth, as honest as he'd ever been with someone, but she thought it was just a line.

It served him right.

Mitch put his hands up in surrender. "I'm sorry I offended you, Beth. That wasn't my intention. I'll leave as soon as Charlie gets my windshield fixed." He headed toward the door. "I'll be working on the tack room. I want to have it framed out before I leave." He walked away hoping she would stop him and at least give him a chance.

Beth's silence hurt more than her words.

Chapter Sixteen

Beth was sickened by what she had done.

Her belligerence—her need to put Mitch in his place to prove she wasn't going to fall for his smooth-talking lines—had just blown-up in her face.

Not one thing Beth had said was godly. Instead, she had been judgmental, cruel, and unbending. Mitch had been touched by her faith, seen a difference in her life, yet Beth had treated him as if he was undeserving of grace or even an ounce of respect.

Cruel, that's what she'd been.

No . . . a hypocrite was more like it.

Beth had really screwed up. There would be no going back. Sure, she would apologize, and Mitch would be polite enough to accept. But when he left the Diamond-J, Mitch would take with him the harsh words she had spewed and probably remember very little of the faith he first saw in her.

Mitch was right. It *was* faith that was missing in his life. But, had she ruined it for him? Would he continue to seek it out? Or, had Beth just decimated any interest Mitch would ever have in God?

Shane watched as Mitch swung a hammer, the force of his swing, burying a nail into the wood.

"You did this all by yourself?" Shane asked.

"Yep."

"Looks pretty good."

Mitch didn't say anything, he just kept drilling nail after nail. Shane got the distinct feeling something was wrong. He watched Mitch for a few more minutes mesmerized by the guy's strength. With only a tank top on, Shane could see Mitch's biceps flex with every swing, his muscles contort with every strike. He also realized it wasn't just strength Mitch was wielding, but anger as well.

"What's wrong?" Shane asked.

"Nothing. Just trying to get this done before I leave."

Shane watched as Mitch finished anchoring a support beam, then asked, "Should I talk with my mom before or after dinner?"

"Doesn't matter to me." Mitch looked at Shane as he swiped his forearm across the beads of perspiration on his brow and reached for another piece of wood. "In fact, you don't have to tell her at all if you don't want to. It makes no difference to me. I had no right butting in between you and your mom." Mitch swung the hammer so hard he buried a three-inch nail with only two blows.

"But I thought you told me—"

"Look, Shane," Mitch interrupted, "why should you take my advice? I'm not a family counselor. In fact, I'm nothing more than an inconvenience and a pain in the . . . your mother's backside. You decide how you want to handle things. It's none of my business."

"Well, geez, I wish you would've said that before I spent all day thinking about it. Now I'm psyched up to tell her."

"Then do it."

"Will you still come with me?"

"Sure, not that I think that will help anything."

"Okay, then I think I want to do it now, before I have something in my stomach. I could barely eat lunch knowing I was going to have to say something. I either want to enjoy dinner or skip it all together. I don't want to gag on it while I'm spilling my guts."

Mitch tossed the hammer aside, removed the tool belt from his hips, and grabbed for his shirt hanging from the end of a two-by-four. "Okay, let's get this over with."

They walked across the yard in silence, Mitch wondering if this was such a good idea. Even though he felt Beth had a right to know—and Shane needed to take responsibility for his actions—he certainly wasn't looking forward to being there for the fireworks.

"Mom, are you here?" Shane shouted as he pushed open the screen door.

"Just a minute," Beth hollered from down the hallway.

The two of them headed into the living room. Mitch plopped down in one of the wing-backed chairs while Shane paced back and forth in front of the fireplace.

When Beth entered the room, she looked at Mitch where he was sitting across the room, then to her son. "What's going on?"

Shane took a deep breath. "I need to tell you something, and I asked Mitch to be here when I did."

"Okay." Beth cautiously took a seat on the couch as she glanced at Mitch one more time, then back to Shane. "What is it?"

Shane's story came out in a rush of words. "I shot at Mitch's truck. That's why he drove off the road. That's how he got hurt." Shane blew out the breath he'd been holding then look at his mom.

Mitch waited for Beth to explode. *Three, two, one . . .*

"You . . . Did . . . What?!"

She didn't disappoint.

"Lucas and Curtis dared me, so I shot at Mitch's windshield."

"You're telling me you used a gun? A real gun?"

Shane nodded, sheepishly.

Beth's head sunk into her hands. Mitch watched her fingers claw through her hair. "What were you thinking?" She looked at Shane. "Or were you even thinking at all?" Beth bolted to her feet and began to pace, her lips a thin line, her shoulders taunt with anger.

Mitch couldn't stand it. When he saw tears forming in her eyes, he intervened.

"Beth, it's my fault you didn't know the truth from the beginning," Mitch blurted out as he stood up. "I covered for Shane, not knowing how you would react. If you want to be mad at someone, you can be mad at me."

Mitch figured he'd be leaving in a few days, so he might as well deflect as much of Beth's wrath away from Shane as possible. The kid would have enough to deal with after he was gone.

Beth turned to him, eyes blazing. "And to think, I was beating myself up for what I said to you earlier, when all along you've been lying to me. I suppose you gave Shane the atta-boy speech when he came home drunk—only playing the part of the Good Samaritan for my benefit. Did you smirk behind my back when you saw him dabbling in pornography, too?"

"Mom, stop!" Shane hollered. "It's my fault. All of it. Mitch told me Lucas and Curtis weren't my friends, and I should find someone better to hang around with. And when I came home drunk, Mitch read me the riot act. Sure he sobered me up, but not without giving me a lecture that rivaled any you've ever given me. He even told me I could talk to him about women, so I wouldn't turn into a pervert."

Mitch grimaced as Shane butchered what he had said. *Great. Now Beth is going to think I called her son a pervert behind her back.*

"Mitch has tried to be my friend," Shane continued. "He was the one who said I needed to come clean. He didn't like the idea of lying to you, and thought I should get everything out in the open. Mitch has been trying to help me, Mom. I've just been too stubborn to see it."

"Where's the gun now?" she asked, her eyes darting between the both of them.

"In the truck. Shoved between the seat cushions," Mitch offered.

He watched as Beth rubbed her hand across her face. First, her mouth, then forehead, and back to her mouth again. She was speechless.

"Say something, Mom. I can't stand it when you don't say anything."

"I don't know what to say, Shane, or even what to do. I . . . I feel like I don't know who you are anymore. Maybe I should just call the police and let them deal with this. Discharging a firearm in public is against the law, Shane."

"I know. I know. Everything I've done lately is stupid. I know that now. Please, Mom, you've got to believe me. I'm really sorry."

Beth could see the pleading in Shane's eyes. Even though he sounded sincere, she doubted her instincts. If his recent behavior was any indication of what he'd been doing in his spare time, Beth's parental intuition was failing miserably.

Looking at her son, picturing him with a gun in his hand, made Beth feel sick to her stomach. Shane was only one stupid step away from doing something irreversible. *He shot at Mitch. He could have hit him. He could have killed him.* The thought of it made her head swim.

"Shane, I need you to go to your room right now. This is a lot for me to absorb, and quite frankly, I have no idea what I'm going to do."

"But Mom—"

"Please, Shane, just do it." Her voice was weak but controlled.

Mitch watched as Beth walked out the front door. *God, I don't know you personally but Beth does, and she's really hurting right about now. Help her deal with all that's on her plate.*

Mitch gave Beth a few minutes to regroup before going to look for her. When he saw her leaning against the back fence—staring at the orange-streaked sky of sunset—he slowly closed the distance between them. As he got closer, Mitch thought he heard Beth mumbling, then realized she was having a conversation with God. He waited until she was done before asking, "Are you okay?"

"No. I'm nowhere near okay. This has to be one of the worse weeks of my life." A flood of uncontrolled tears ran down her face, something Mitch instinctively knew wasn't part of Beth's nature.

When he could stand it no longer, he turned Beth around, pulled her close, and let her cry against his chest.

Feeling she was on the verge of collapse, Beth held on to Mitch for dear life. "I don't understand," she cried. "I've tried so hard, really I have. I've spent hours pleading with God, praying I wouldn't screw things up. I've tried to be a good example for Shane, but I don't think I can handle much more. I just don't have the strength."

"Yes, you do," Mitch whispered as he held her close, gently stroking her hair. "You're just tired. A lot has happened this week. It's like Shane's adolescence exploded on him overnight, giving you no time to slow into it, and me being here—getting under your skin—hasn't helped matters any."

"Mitch, this isn't your fault. I'm the one with her head in the sand. I should have seen the signs earlier. I knew Shane wasn't happy here. It's all my fault."

"Beth you need to let it go for now. Let someone else be the strong one for a change. I have pretty broad shoulders. I think I can handle the mantle for a few minutes."

Her crying slowed and became more controlled. "I know Shane thinks finding his father will change everything, but he doesn't understand." Beth looked up into Mitch's eyes. "When I found out I was pregnant, I told Shane's father, but he didn't care about me or the fact that I was carrying his baby. His only concern was himself and his future in the rodeo. I thought what we had was love, but to him, it was only sex. I was shocked. Devastated. He said he'd only been looking for a good time, and I had made myself more than available. Don't you see? This is my fault. I rebelled when I was young. I turned away from God and went behind my father's back. My dad didn't know what was going on until it was too late. Now I'm reaping my just rewards. I rebelled. Now, Shane is rebelling against me."

Mitch brushed his thumb across her face, wiping the tears from her cheeks.

"I don't know much about God, but I don't think that's how he operates. Beth, you need to tell Shane the truth. He has this idea that his father never knew about him, that you gave the guy an ultimatum and forced him to choose. Why aren't you telling Shane the truth instead of letting him direct his anger toward you?"

Beth was surprised Mitch knew so much, and irritated that he questioned the way she had chosen to handle the situation.

"I have to protect Shane. I would rather he be angry with me, then go off half-cocked looking for a father who didn't give a rip about him. I know my son. The devastation of being rejected would crush Shane. I refuse to put him through that."

"Did you ever talk with his father again, after Shane was born?"

She nodded. "I went to see him when the rodeo came to Wichita."

"What happened?"

"He thought I was there to rekindle old times, to have a little fun. But when I told him about Shane, he was horrified. He figured I would've gotten an abortion before admitting to my father what we'd been doing. He was angry and threatened me not to make trouble for him, or I'd be sorry."

Fresh tears fell quickly from her eyes.

"Beth . . ." Mitch pulled her close. "You need to tell Shane. He needs to stop blaming you."

"But what if Shane goes looking for his father? What if Cole—"

Beth locked eyes with Mitch, horrified she had said Cole's name out loud; a name she hadn't spoken for almost sixteen years. "Please, Mitch, you can't say anything to Shane. You can't let him know his father's name."

"It's none of my business, Beth, but I think you should let him know. You're tearing yourself up and letting Shane abuse you because of his degenerate father."

Beth pulled away. "No! He can't know! Cole threatened me once. If Shane was to show up looking for him, Cole might feel cornered and do something horrible."

"To his own son?"

"His temper, along with his drinking is something I could never predict. I can't risk it. I can't risk Shane ever being around him."

Mitch wrapped her in his arms, and promised he wouldn't interfere.

Chapter Seventeen

Mitch didn't sleep at all that night. One word kept punctuating his thoughts. Hypocrite. Even though he had prodded Shane into telling the truth about the accident, and was encouraging Beth to be honest with Shane regarding his father, Mitch was hiding a secret of his own. He wanted to tell them—really he did—but Beth was already dealing with so much. Discovering she was harboring a celebrity the paparazzi was determined to find was just one more thing she didn't need to worry about.

Why add to her load? I'll be gone soon enough.

The next day came early, and unfortunately, the incredible headache Beth had nursed throughout the night was still thumping behind her eyes. Her head felt like it would explode from the amount of emotion and information it was trying to absorb.

Beth was watching her son turn into a delinquent overnight. Drinking. Dabbling in pornography. Shooting a gun. And those were just the things she was aware of. What if there was more?

And then there was the way Beth had humiliated herself in front of Mitch. *What was I thinking, letting him hold me like that?*

Beth had readily accepted the comfort Mitch had offered, and though he had been a complete gentleman, Beth was angry at herself for allowing them such an intimate moment. She had just finished telling Mitch she wasn't looking for a relationship, and then boom, she falls into his arms.

However, the thought Beth was having the hardest time wrapping her mind around was the fact that Mitch now knew her most guarded secret . . . and there was nothing she could do about it.

Beth's world was quickly spinning out of control.

When she heard the creaks and groans from the old floorboards, Beth knew Shane was up getting ready for work. They had talked long into the night. Shane had done everything in his power to convince Beth he had never played with guns in the past or done anything malicious or violent toward anyone else. He promised there was nothing more he was hiding from her. Nevertheless, she still felt skittish.

Beth had never had any reason to doubt Shane before, but then again, she never would have dreamt her son would have done the things he had in the last few days either. Beth knew she had to be stern with Shane, but what if he bolted? What if he continued his rebellion and took off to find his father?

She pulled a sweatshirt over her t-shirt and shorts and stumbled down the hall feeling older than she'd ever felt before. *Who would have thought raising a son would be more painful than giving birth to him?*

She gently rapped on the his bedroom door. "Shane, you decent?"

"Just a minute."

She waited.

"Okay."

Beth turned the glass knob and stood in the doorway. Shane turned toward her as he buckled his belt.

"Shane, I've got to know when you leave this house, you're not going to do anything rash or impulsive."

"Mom, I told you last night, I'll do whatever it takes to get you to trust me again."

"I want to believe you, Shane, really I do."

Silence filled the room. Beth waited for Shane to say something more, but he just stood there, staring at the floor.

With a sigh, Beth went downstairs to fix breakfast. Shane made his way to the bar and took a seat, quickly eating the eggs and toast

Beth put in front of him, leaving little room for conversation. It was just as well; Beth didn't know if there was anything left to say.

Mitch watched as Shane rode out of the yard. He wanted to talk to him but knew now was not the time. He scaled the porch steps and knocked on the front door. It was early, and he didn't want an awkward run-in with Beth like the one they'd had the previous afternoon. Through the beveled glass, Mitch watched Beth walk toward the door. She opened it and leaned against the frame for balance.

"Good morning," Beth said as their eyes met briefly before she looked away. "There are eggs and toast in the kitchen. Help yourself." She turned around without another word, sounding completely broken. It killed Mitch to see such defeat in her posture.

Breakfast didn't interest him at all. Mitch was more concerned with Beth. He wandered down the hall to her office only to find it empty. He found her in the den sitting on the couch, curled up in the corner, her face expressionless.

"How did it go last night with Shane?"

"I did a lot of yelling, and he did a lot of apologizing."

Mitch sat on the couch next to her in silence.

"I owe you an apology, Mitch," she spoke softly.

"Beth, you don't have—"

"Yes . . . I do. I said some things about you that were unfair. I'm sorry."

"It's okay. I know I didn't make the greatest first impression. I don't blame you for jumping to the wrong conclusions."

"But it was still wrong. You've done nothing but be nice to us. Not only nice, but you've been a big help, too. I never even thanked you for the way you handled Brett. And now I realize you could've made things a lot harder on me if you had decided to involve the police and press charges against Shane. I can't say I understand why you didn't, but thank you."

Mitch relaxed, allowing himself to sink into the comfort of the couch. "Even though we met under adverse circumstances, I could tell Shane was basically a good kid—misguided by his friends, but good. You know, when we drove into the yard that day, his first concern was for you."

"For me?"

"Yeah. Shane told me not to take out my anger on you, that you didn't deserve it. So you see, Beth, your son wants to protect you as much as you want to protect him. That's why Shane lashed out when he thought I was making a move on you. He might not know how to handle himself yet, but Shane doesn't want to see you get hurt. That's an instinct born of love. Right now, he's angry, confused, and making stupid choices, but don't for a minute think that Shane doesn't love you. He's just having a hard time showing it right now."

Beth sat quietly, thankful for Mitch's encouraging words and the chance to see things from his perspective, but it was the tenderness in which he spoke that resonated in her heart. She flashed back to the kiss they had shared, and the way Mitch's arms felt around her when he had held her yesterday. His words, his arms, his ways, they exuded such strength and confidence. These last few days—even though she and Mitch had bickered and butted heads—had been what she always knew was missing from her life. Companionship. Someone to share her day with. Someone to share the load.

After her father died, she had struggled with loneliness. Night after night she had asked God to bring someone special into her life, but as time passed, Beth stopped asking. She had convinced herself singleness was the consequence of her rebellious youth, knowing full well that sin came at a price. Beth wasn't angry at God. After all, it had been her choices and actions that had made her a single mom, not God's discipline.

As the years went on, Beth's faith deepened and her connection with God grew stronger. She acknowledged that God was her partner in life, and He would be there every step of the way. So, Beth focused her energies on the things that were most important to her—Shane and the ranch.

She had raised Shane the best way she knew how, with discipline and faith in God. She taught him right from wrong, praying he would grow up to be nothing like his father. The Diamond-J thrived under her management. Even the years they had faced drought and disease, she always succeeded in turning a profit.

At the end of every day, Beth thanked God for all she had accomplished and asked for strength for another day. Even so, there was still that rare occasion, when Beth would lay awake at night, acutely aware of the physical loneliness she felt. Those were the nights she would talk to God, and ask Him to bring someone special into her life.

But this can't be an answer to those prayers. Mitch isn't even a believer. Why would God bring someone into my life who didn't share my faith?

Beth's mind was immediately filled with the vision she had always had of her mom and dad in their younger days, talking to each other over the fence line, her mom evangelizing the hardened cowboy.

Is that what God was asking her to do? Mitch already admitted to seeing something different in her; something he felt was missing from his life. Could it be that God orchestrated all of this to bring Mitch to Christ? Beth wasn't sure, but immediately felt an overwhelming sense of responsibility. *Please, God, don't make me accountable for just one more person. I'm barely hanging on myself. You need to rethink this one before I screw up someone else's life.*

It was as if God heard her plea and answered immediately within her soul. *Your ways are not my ways.*

"Beth . . . you okay?"

The sound of Mitch's voice snapped her back to reality.

"You kind of zoned out on me for a moment. Are you okay?" Mitch looked concerned.

"I'm fine. There's just so much I don't know, or I don't

understand. I was just kind of debating with God. It says in the Bible that those who hope in the Lord will not grow weary. Well, that's a fractured paraphrase, but still. I passed weary a long time ago. I think God is giving me way more credit than I deserve. I used to think I could rise to any occasion; I've always been a *dig deep* kind of person. But now, I feel like I've been digging for so long, the walls are ready to collapse around me."

"You're just tired. You need to stop putting such pressure on yourself and allow things to play out. Doesn't it say somewhere in the Bible about taking things one day at a time and that worrying is a sin? If you have faith in God like you say you do, let Him carry the ball for a while."

Beth turned to Mitch, holding back the laughter of irony. Mitch was quoting scripture to her. *Okay God, I get it.* All she could think of was the story of Balaam's donkey. Balaam had been so stubborn that God had to use a donkey to speak to him. Not that Beth was comparing Mitch to a donkey, she was just amused at the thought of God using Mitch to preach to her, when she had thought it would be the other way around.

Mitch was right. She was too tired to try to figure things out. *This is all you, God. But I have to ask . . . couldn't you have made Mitch a little less attractive? I could concentrate a whole lot better on evangelizing him if he was short, pudgy, and homely instead of tall, dark, and handsome.*

My ways are not your ways. The verse echoed again.

I know, I know.

"Beth, you're doing it again."

She looked at Mitch, and he returned her look with scrutiny. "Maybe you should lie down. You didn't get a lot of sleep last night, and you keep zoning out."

"No, I'm fine, really." She forced a small smile. Beth knew she wasn't fooling him, but it was the best she could do. "Thank you, Mitch, for everything. I'm sorry it's taken me this long to say anything."

He shifted to the edge of the couch. "Well, I know how you can make it up to me." He smirked.

Here we go. Just when I think he's a decent guy, he's going to ruin it by making a mov—"

"Offer me a job."

"What?" Beth was taken completely off-guard.

"Offer me a job. Let me stay on and help around here. I could finish the tack room, help out Charlie until he finds replacements for those two jerks, and I could help keep an eye on Shane—make sure he's not getting into any more trouble."

"But Mitch, you already have a job."

"Not really."

"What do you mean? You told me you were on vacation."

"Well, vacation sounded better than unemployed. I wasn't lying, exactly. I was employed right up until the time I quit. I just thought it might sound better if you thought you were helping a vacationing businessman, not an unemployed drifter."

Beth raised her brow at his mild deception.

"So, what do you say? You need help, and I need a job. I have my own place to stay and all the time in the world."

"The pays not great," she said matter-of-factly.

"I don't need much."

"The work can be long and tiresome."

"That doesn't bother me."

"Shane was right when he said there's nothing to do in Triune. You'll be bored before you know it."

"I've found ways to entertain myself in the past."

Beth glared. "I won't allow alcohol."

"I figured as much."

Mitch quickly dispensed of every reason Beth gave him for *not* sticking around. She was ready with one more when he stopped her.

"Beth, you can pepper me with all kinds of reasons why I shouldn't stay, but that's not going to change the way I feel. You'll be helping me as much as I'll be helping you. I need some time to evaluate my life." Mitch sighed, looking troubled. "I need a nice, quiet place with limited interruptions and distractions to help me figure out where I go from here. The way I see it, the Diamond-J is the perfect place to do that."

Later, when everyone gathered for lunch, Beth explained that Mitch would be staying to help while they were short-handed. Charlie and Travis were quick to express their approval and appreciation. Though Shane didn't comment, it was obvious he was glad as well.

After lunch, Shane walked to the mailbox at the end of their dirt road, thinking about the weird twist of events that had brought Mitch to the Diamond-J. There was something about him. Shane wasn't sure what it was, but he felt a connection with Mitch. He was easier to talk to than his mom or Uncle Charlie, even Travis. Maybe it was because he was an outsider. Someone who wouldn't always answer him with, 'Did you pray about it?' Or, 'What do you think the Lord would have you to do?' Shane loved God and everything, but the thought of getting some straight answers to some hard questions interested him.

He took the bundle from the mailbox and noticed some activity in the field across from their house. All week he had seen trucks coming and going. If he wasn't mistaken, it looked as if the frame of a house was going up. He didn't get it. He lived in Triune because it was drilled into him that it was his heritage. *Why on earth would someone want to move here? They must be crazy.* He thought as he walked back to the house.

Beth watched as Mitch headed for the tack room, debating whether their arrangement was going to work. She and Mitch had never discussed the kiss they had shared or the sparks that were evident between them. Instead, Beth determined to be the *light* God wanted her to be. She convinced herself the reason Mitch was staying was because the Diamond-J needed the extra help. Beth wouldn't allow her head to hear what her heart was saying.

Chapter Eighteen

A few weeks had passed since Beth agreed to let Mitch stay at the Diamond-J. Charlie had fixed up his Suburban with a new windshield and a few minor adjustments here and there. It still needed a realignment, but that was something Mitch would take care of once he was back on the road. His Airstream sat in the same place in the driveway, but Mitch only used it for sleeping since he ate all his meals in the house with Beth, Shane, and the guys. Beth had even turned over the downstairs bathroom to him, so he didn't have to go to the hassle of hooking up his trailer.

The last few weeks had been like nothing Mitch had ever experienced. Being a part of an active ranch, getting his hands dirty, working hard, even the aches and pains from being in the saddle all day were somehow rewarding. He was finally doing something that mattered. It's what he'd been looking for. Simplicity, quiet—the camaraderie of being with Shane, Charlie, and Travis—all of it felt so right, everything except for the distance Beth had put between them. Though she was always polite during meals, and didn't shy away from talking to him when everyone else was around, Mitch couldn't help but notice she made sure they were never alone together.

Unfortunately, because of that distance, Mitch still had not told Beth and Shane who he really was. He kept waiting for the right time to present itself, but it never came. Or, it did, and Mitch just didn't want to spoil the mood. He was still afraid the moment Beth found out who he really was, his time on the Diamond-J would be over. Something Mitch wasn't ready for yet.

Beth wasn't ignoring Mitch; she was just keeping a healthy distance between them. Though he was at every meal—and in the house each night talking with Shane or watching TV—they had done little talking, just the two of them.

Beth felt the awkwardness between them and sensed Mitch felt it as well. She wasn't sure what to do about it but had decided it would be up to God to open an avenue of dialogue between them. And even if the opportunity never presented itself, Beth wouldn't push it. For the time being, she would just be thankful for the connection Mitch had made with Shane, because the change in her son was the difference between night and day.

Shane and Mitch watched Sports Center every night and talked for hours about different leagues, individual players, and every stat imaginable. Beth was thrilled he had someone who shared his interests in sports, but felt guilty because she realized all that Shane had missed out on. To hear him talk so passionately about the sports he'd never had the opportunity to play, made her feel like a failure as a parent. Beth realized she had to come to grips with the fact that Shane was not the cowboy she had been at his age. For him, his eyes would always be on what lay outside the fence line. Although moving was the last thing Beth wanted to do, she realized it was the chance she would have to take to salvage their relationship before it was too late. The Diamond-J would always be in her heart, but Beth wanted to make sure Shane was always a part of her life.

While Mitch and Shane spent each night in front of the television, Beth perused her computer for house listings in the rural areas surrounding Wichita and Topeka. None of them excited her; nothing would ever compare to the Diamond-J.

Unable to concentrate a minute longer on square footage, lot size, or location, Beth decided to sit on the front porch and appreciate the simplicity of a perfect June evening. Knowing her days were numbered, she wanted to store up as many memories as she could—even if they were little things like the creaks in the rickety porch swing, the stillness of night, or a sky brilliant with stars.

Sitting back in the swing, Beth closed her eyes and inhaled the familiar scent of home.

"Mind if I join you?"

Beth flinched, surprised she hadn't heard Mitch walk out onto the porch. "No. Not at all." Beth opened her eyes and stared off into the distance.

"It's amazing how many stars you can see at night when you're not looking through the lights and smog of the city." Mitch leaned on the rail, his head tilted back as he studied the sky.

"I know. As a little girl, I always thought God favored cowboys. I was sure He put more stars over ranches because He realized how much we enjoyed them."

Mitch's light chuckle made her smile.

"Beth, I've really enjoyed these last few weeks, working with the guys, especially getting to spend time with Shane. But I get the impression you're avoiding me. If it's because I kissed you, I'm sorry."

She was glad they were talking outside where the darkness of the night could mask the heat in her complexion. "I'm not avoiding you. I just thought it was best to let it go for the time being."

Mitch nodded like he understood. He continued to stare up at the sky as he asked his next question. "So . . . if I wanted to kiss you again, would I be met with the same reaction?"

"I don't think it's a good idea, Mitch."

"Why not?"

"Look, there's no easy way to say this without sounding pious or judgmental, but I'm going to say it anyway. The Bible is very clear that believers should not be married to unbelievers."

He laughed. "Beth, I wasn't proposing, I just wanted to know how you would feel if I wanted to spend some time with you."

She turned to him, wanting him to understand the seriousness of the situation. "But what happens if we do spend time together, and it becomes serious? Then what? Do I ignore my feelings for you or the commandments of God? God doesn't want me to be in a position where I have to choose. That's why He warns us about it in advance."

"But you're assuming I don't believe in God."

It was not the reaction she was expecting.

"I believe in God, Beth. I know this whole world didn't just coincidently appear. That would be crazy. There had to be a creator."

"Good. I'm glad you don't buy off on the whole evolution thing, but there's more to it than that. Believing in God as the Creator of the world is one thing, but it's what you believe about Jesus that matters."

"Then explain it to me. Give me a chance to understand it."

Mitch's words were so genuine Beth couldn't help but believe he had a real interest in her faith—but to accept it would be another thing.

"It's kind of late to start such a deep conversation. I think it would be better left to when we have more time."

"Then how about tomorrow?"

"Tomorrow?"

"Yeah. It's Saturday. You could play hooky for one day, right? We could go for a ride. Maybe take lunch with us. There have been some other things I've been meaning to talk to you about anyway."

Beth's first reaction was to say no. It sounded too intimate. How would she explain it to Shane without him getting the wrong impression? *But what if this is God's way of giving me the opportunity to talk to Mitch about faith and forgiveness?*

"You're thinking about it," Mitch prodded her with his killer smile. "Come on, Beth, you've done nothing but work since I got here. You deserve some time off to relax."

"Okay," she conceded, "but I'm viewing this as a Sunday school lesson, not a date." Beth wanted to make sure her intentions were clear.

"That's fine," he answered, showing no resistance to her disclaimer.

Beth felt slightly embarrassed. She assumed Mitch was looking for an excuse to spend time alone with her. *Humph, maybe he really does just want to talk?*

"Let's head out around ten o'clock," he said.

"Okay. I'll make sure and pack us a lunch."

Chapter Nineteen

The next day, Beth met Mitch in the stables where he already had Midas saddled and ready to go. He had even pulled Pandora's tack and had it waiting for Beth next to the mare's stall.

Beth was quiet as they rode out of the yard, still not convinced it was such a good idea. Even if Mitch had the best of intentions, she wasn't sure her motivations were as pure. Beth couldn't deny her attraction for Mitch. It was strong—something she hadn't experienced since Cole. *Yeah, and look how good that turned out.*

Beth scolded herself every time her heart asked the question, *What if?* There was no 'what if?' she told herself repeatedly. Sooner or later, Mitch would get bored and be on his way. Beth had to keep drilling that into her head, because allowing herself to believe anything different would only end in heartache.

"You and Midas sure seem to have hit it off," Beth said as they rode side by side.

"He's a great horse. Shane told me he was your father's. I feel honored you've allowed me to ride him while I've been here."

"I think Midas is enjoying it as much as you are. Shane and I take turns exercising and riding him, but I don't think it's enough. He's liked having you around."

"And what about you? Have you liked having me around?"

"Of course, I have. The change in Shane has been incredible. The time you've spent with him talking sports and sharing his interests, I know has really meant a lot to Shane."

"That wasn't exactly the answer I was looking for." Mitch glanced her way with a mischievous smile.

Beth was trying to ignore how good Mitch looked in his snug-fitting shirt and ragged jeans. She kept reminding herself the only reason she'd agreed to this ride was because God wanted her to go, but the little voice in her head wasn't very convincing.

They had been riding for a little over an hour when Beth veered toward an out-cropping of trees. "I thought that would be a nice place to stop," she said, pointing to the south. "At least we'll have a little shade from the sun."

"Sounds good to me." Mitch smiled as he followed her lead.

After dismounting and tossing Pandora's reins over a low slung branch, Beth untied the blanket roll attached to her saddle and snapped it to its full size.

"Here, I'll do that."

Beth watched as Mitch laid the blanket down where the ground was level and had the least amount of rocks. He then sprawled out on the checkered cloth, resting his hands behind his head, relaxation evidently his goal, as much as eating.

Beth felt far from relaxed. It had been a long time since she'd talked to anyone about faith in God. Though it wasn't always easy, it was instinctive. No, it was more than that, it was a lifeline. She couldn't imagine having to do life without believing in Someone greater than herself. However, she'd grown up watching her mom and dad live out their faith day after day. Seeing is believing. What she saw in her parents was what she wanted in her own life. Mitch didn't have that luxury. From what he had shared, his childhood had been near tragic. He'd never been able to rely on anyone other than himself. Relinquishing control to God would be difficult for someone who'd been on his own for so long.

Okay, God, I agreed to do this, but you've got to give me the right words to say. Don't let me sound uppity, self-righteous, or condemning.

Kneeling on the corner of the blanket, Beth unloaded her knapsack of goodies, along with her old, weathered Bible. After laying everything out between them, Beth sat back on her heels and bowed to pray, but before she could start, Mitch quickly moved to a sitting position and removed his hat.

She couldn't help but smile.

"Thank you, God, for this food, fellowship, and time of rest. Thank you for the positive impact Mitch has had on Shane and the way you answer prayers in the most mysterious ways. Amen."

Mitch took a bite of his sandwich, then asked, "You think I'm an answer to prayer?" His question wasn't prideful, just quizzical.

"I do," Beth answered, between swallows.

"Even if I'm not a Christian?"

"God can use all kinds of situations and people to teach us or show us what He wants from our lives."

"Hum," Mitch nodded, seemingly surprised.

As they ate, a light breeze pulled at Beth's hair, but was little help against the midday sun. Mitch must have felt the heat as well because he removed his button-up cotton shirt and left it in a heap on the blanket.

Beth couldn't help but notice how Mitch's tan had deepened, and his arms seemed to be even more muscular than when he'd arrived. The navy t-shirt he was wearing clung to his corded biceps and outlined the sculpted contours of his shoulders and chest.

Beth turned away, hating herself for being so attracted to Mitch. Every day she found him harder to ignore. However, it wasn't only his good looks. It was his other qualities as well. For one, Mitch had an incredible work ethic. He never shied away from a job or task Uncle Charlie gave him. Hard work was something he definitely wasn't afraid of.

In addition to his work ethic, there was the way Mitch interacted with Shane. There was something between them—some kind of bond. Beth had found them many times talking together in hushed tones on the porch or in the living room after dinner. At first, she was concerned, wondering what was being discussed and if Mitch was the right person to be give her son advice. But, the few snatches of conversation she'd heard or the words Beth had caught in passing had always been positive and carefully measured. She had decided it was God's doing that Mitch was at the Diamond-J, so she turned her concerns into prayers instead of worry.

"You have that look in your eye . . . like you're having an internal debate," Mitch said as he rolled to one elbow and lay staring at Beth.

"I was just wondering what it was you and Shane spend so much time talking about. I mean, I know a lot of it is sports and stuff, but I can't help but wonder what you're talking about when your tone turns quiet."

"Different things. Nothing really to worry about. I mean, he's not talking about running away or suicide or criminal behavior if that's what has you concerned."

"Does he ever talk to you about . . . women?" Beth asked, feeling a bit awkward.

Mitch smiled politely. "Yes. Women have come up on occasion."

"And what did you tell him?"

Mitch didn't answer; he just looked off into the distance. Beth couldn't tell if he was ignoring her question or contemplating what to say.

Either way, it bothered her. She didn't want a carefully formulated answer; she wanted the truth. After all, Shane was her son, and Beth was sure her value system differed from Mitch's when it came to relationships, intimacy, and sex.

She was ready to say something when Mitch turned back to her with an answer. "Without jeopardizing the trust Shane's put in me, let's just say he has a heightened awareness of the opposite sex but nothing unusual for his age."

Beth didn't even know how to respond to that. How did Mitch know what was or wasn't appropriate for Shane's age? Had Shane asked Mitch about his intimate experiences, and if so, was he offering graphic details of his conquests?

Beth was trying hard not to get mad or overreact, but her parental side couldn't simply stand by while Mitch filled Shane's mind with who knows what kind of stories.

"Mitch," she said softly, trying to keep her tone calm—not judgmental. "I know Shane has really latched on to you these last few weeks, and I'm thankful for all the time you've spent with him, but

I'm not sure I feel comfortable knowing you are discussing sex with him."

"Because you're afraid I'm going to say something that doesn't line-up with your way of thinking?"

"It's not just my 'way of thinking,' Mitch. It's my principles and beliefs—beliefs I feel strongly about."

"Then why haven't you taken the time to discuss them with Shane?"

Beth was a little taken back by Mitch's accusation. She hadn't expected to be put on the defensive.

"I *have* told Shane how I feel . . . on occasion. There just haven't been many instances where we've been able to talk about such private issues."

"No, Beth, you haven't told him *how you feel* or *why you feel* the way you do. You've only told Shane what the Bible says, that you believe it, and he needs to obey it. You've given him rules, not reasons."

Beth's temper began to simmer. The reason she had agreed to go on this ride was to help Mitch have a better understanding of God, not for him to point out her deficits in parenting. "You know what, Mitch, this was a bad idea." Shifting her weight, Beth balanced on the balls of her feet and started to gather the food containers scattered on the blanket. "I thought we came out here to talk about you, not me."

Mitch grabbed her hand. "Beth, calm down and let me explain."

Angered by his *you're overreacting* tone, Beth yanked her hand away, losing her balance and dropping everything in her hands. Frustrated, she bit back a few choice words, righted herself, and once again picked up the remnants of their picnic.

"Come on, Beth, just hear me out."

Mitch's tone was soft, more apologetic than patronizing. When Beth chanced a glance in his direction, she expected to find a smirk, but was met with a look of concern. Taking a deep breath, she sat back on her heels and exhaled with a huff. "Fine. Explain."

"Shane's a bright kid, Beth. You have to give him more than do's and don'ts. You need to give him reasons for not drinking or smoking and explain why sex isn't to be taken lightly."

"How?"

"Like you said, tell him how you feel about things, not just what you believe."

"Mitch, you're talking in circles. I told you, I already explained to Shane how I fe—"

"No, you haven't." Mitch cut her off.

"Yes, I have!" she hollered back.

"Then tell me, Beth, why is sex wrong?" Mitch asked bluntly. "Why should Shane believe you over everything he sees on television and in the media? I bet if I scrolled through his iPod right now I would find songs telling him 'to go get some,' 'just have a good time,' 'get it while you can.' If all of society is telling him to set his own boundaries—that it's up to him to decide what's right for him—why should he listen to you?"

"Because TV, movies, and song lyrics don't tell the whole story, dang-it!" Beth pounded her fist on her thigh. "They don't explain how you feel after you've allowed yourself to be used by someone, or how you no longer feel like a whole person because you've given a piece of yourself away. The media portrays sex as an act, not a feeling. They separate the physical from the emotional. Movies sell sex as something to be explored, but seldom do they show the psychological fallout that happens to the person who thought they were in a committed relationship, while the other person was only looking for a good time."

Beth fought to control the tears gathering in her eyes as she remembered the pain she had felt at Cole's betrayal. She glanced at Mitch, but quickly looked away before continuing.

"I've been there. I know what it feels like to be discarded like a piece of trash. What I gave to Shane's dad was an expression of my love—at least I thought it was. But to him, it was only sex. Because of my naivety, I will never be whole again. I will carry that experience into my next relationship. Subliminally, I will make comparisons or have expectations. How fair is that to the other person? Any relationship I might have will always be compared to what I've already experienced—good or bad. People who say it's just an act, not a feeling, are lying. You can't separate the physical from the emotional. The media is selling fantasy, not reality!"

"You're absolutely right!"

Beth was stunned. If she and Mitch were on the same side, why were they arguing? And why had she shared so much with him? Beth turned away but he sat up and shifted his position, forcing her to look at him.

"Beth, you need to tell Shane exactly what you just told me. I'm not saying he won't still be curious, or that he's not going to make his own mistakes, but it's important for him to know you have real reasons—personal reasons why you believe what you do, not 'because the Bible says so.' "

She was completely confused. Beth thought Mitch had wanted to learn more about the Bible, about faith, about what it was to be a Christian, but instead, he was discounting the standards given by God.

"So, you're saying you don't think the Bible's enough? That it's not necessary?"

"I'm not saying that at all. I'm just saying you have to give reasons for why you believe what you do." Mitch got to his feet and began to pace. "It's like you believing God used me to bring help to Shane. It didn't make sense to me at all. But then you explained how God can use any circumstance or any person to help another. I mean, when you think of it, God used Shane's rebellion, so I would eventually wind up here. I thought I was being cursed, getting stuck in the middle of nowhere with a punk kid and a woman ready to blow my head off. It was like a bad episode of the Twilight Zone, but look at all that's happened since then." Mitch squatted down in front of her, forcing her to make eye contact with him.

"Like I told you before, I don't believe in coincidences. I know there's more to life than randomness and chance. Everything happens for a reason. That's what I've been learning, and what I'm trying to tell you. You need to give Shane a reason to believe you, not what he's being told by his friends and the media. You'll have to get pretty personal, and it will probably be uncomfortable, but come on Beth, he's your son. You need to put your pride and inhibitions aside if you want to get through to him."

Beth's shoulders slumped as she let out the breath she'd been holding the whole time Mitch had been lecturing her.

She'd blown it.

Big time.

How could I have been so blind?

Shane had been a curious child. When he was a little boy, he asked her what seemed like a hundred questions a day. Whenever she could, Beth used the Bible to explain to Shane why there were no dinosaurs, why the sun could light up the whole sky, but the moon couldn't, what it meant to be a Christian, and if God loved his Son so much, why did He let Him die? However, she had shied away from the harder question . . . why he didn't have a daddy?

When Shane got older, and the questions turned to alcohol, smoking, and tattoos, she had done the same thing, quoted Scripture or told him to look it up in the Bible. Beth turned his questions into research projects. She'd used the Bible like a dictionary and told Shane to read it for himself. And when he asked about his father, she gave the same answer every time. His father had chosen to leave and there was nothing they could do about it. Beth had never taken the time to sit down and talk with Shane, to explain to him what had really happened between her and Cole, and that they were better off without him.

Without realizing it, somewhere along the line the questions had stopped. Shane no longer looked to Beth for answers.

Because you didn't give him answers, you gave him quotes. Words and sentences, not reasons and explanations.

Beth thought of all the missed opportunities—opportunities where she could've had meaningful conversations with Shane—and chances for her to connect with him during this pivotal time in his life.

Beth felt overwhelmed and humiliated. She thought God had brought Mitch to the Diamond-J so she could show him the errors of his ways and to help get his life in order. How arrogant to think he was the only one in need of help.

Once again, Beth reached for the loose items on the blanket and stuffed them into her knapsack.

"Hey, we're not leaving already, are we?" Mitch questioned as Beth walked to Pandora and tied the sack back on to the mare's saddle.

"Why not? Isn't this what you wanted to tell me?"

"No. Not really. You're the one who brought it up. I actually had some other things I needed to discuss with you."

"I don't know if I can handle much more. Not today."

"Come on, Beth, this is important, and it's taken me this long to work up the courage."

Mitch reached for Beth's hand and led her back to the blanket. She wanted to pull away, afraid this is where things were going to get too personal. Beth's only concession was maybe now that Mitch knew how she felt about relationships he would understand not to toy with her affections.

They each took a seat on the blanket. Mitch hooked his elbows around his pulled up knees and pushed back his hat from his brow. He swallowed hard and steeled himself for what he was about to say.

"Beth, I'm not who I say I am. I mean, I am, but not who you think I am."

"What are you talking about?" Beth looked completely baffled.

"Though my real name *is* Mitch Burk, most people know me as Simon Grey."

"I don't get it," she said with a shrug. "Who's Simon Grey?"

"Me. You see I wasn't exactly on vacation when I had my little accident. It was more like a hiatus."

"What do you mean a hiatus?"

"Beth, I'm an actor."

Her expression changed immediately. "Wait a minute. Simon Grey. He's the AWOL actor who's been all over the Internet. The

Hollywood Hunk who up and disappeared." She sat up straighter and glared. "Is that why you're here?"

"What do you mean?"

"Is this some sort of research project for your next movie or something?"

"No, Beth, I—"

"You set this whole thing up, didn't you?"

"Set what up?"

"This!" She flung her arms out. "You being here in the middle of nowhere. What . . . is it publicity you're after?"

"I—"

"Well, it worked. You're all over the Internet. You have been for weeks. So, what are you going to do next? Leak your whereabouts to the press, so they can swarm all over my property? Are you going to tell them how you've been roughing it out in the middle of the sticks, fixing fences and chasing pigs?" Beth shook her head, tears rimming her eyes. "This was all just a role to you, wasn't it?"

She got up and stormed over to where Pandora stood.

Mitch quickly got to his feet. "Beth, you've got this all wrong and you know it. I didn't plan any of this. Everything just kind of happened. I didn't lie to you. My name *is* Mitch Burk. I just didn't explain about Simon Grey. I figured I'd only be here for a few days so it really didn't matter."

"Well, it does matter! I trusted you!"

Beth reached for the saddle horn and hooked her boot in the stirrup. However, before she could swing up into the saddle, Mitch stopped and pulled her down next to him.

"Okay, you've had your chance, Beth. Now it's mine."

She snapped her arm from his grasp and took a step back.

"The reason I was out in the middle of 'the sticks' as you call it, is because I was running—running from the empty, vacant life I had created for myself. I thought I had arrived. I thought I had gotten what I was looking for in life, but all I got was tired. Tired of people pretending to be my friends, pretending to have my best interest in mind, when all they cared about was furthering their own careers. My publicist doesn't care about me. All she cares about is making sure I'm seen at the right parties, in the right circles, with the right women. My agent thinks I'm crazy. He's convinced if I disappear for any length of time, I'll be forgotten. But that's exactly what I want. I want to forget Simon Grey ever existed. Jerry says he cares about me, about my future, but I think he cares more about the hefty salary he's gotten used to. Jerry sees his meal ticket driving away with no guarantee of coming back, so he's desperate to change my mind. But I'm just a paycheck to him, not a person."

Beth's features softened. He was making headway, so he continued.

"That's why I'm here, Beth. Not because of a movie, or publicity, or anything else. I ended up here because I didn't want to be there. I've stayed because . . ."

He looked at her, hoping Beth could see in his eyes the reason he'd stayed.

"I'm sorry I didn't tell you sooner, but with all you were dealing with, I didn't want to add more chaos to your life. I'm sorry, Beth. What more can I say?"

Mitch shoved his hands in his pockets and waited for Beth to say something. She stroked Pandora's withers, refusing to make eye contact with him.

After a few minutes, she looked at him. Barely. "I don't know what you want me to say, Mitch," she said, before turning and walking away.

He followed after her. "Tell me I can stay. Tell me you're not going to push me away now that I've told you the truth." He fell into step beside Beth and waited for her to say something.

"So, are you really looking for answers or just a way out?" Beth asked, after walking full circle back to where the blanket still lay on the ground.

"What do you mean by that?"

"Well, like you said," she explained, while gathering up the blanket. "You were running *away* from something more than you were running *to* something. If you were just looking for a way out, you found it. You walked away. You dropped off the map. No one knows where you are. Isn't that what you wanted?" She turned, looking directly into his eyes.

"I don't know. That's what I'm still trying to figure out." Mitch wanted to reach for Beth, to tell her he'd found what he was looking for with her, Shane, and the Diamond-J. But didn't. He'd already given her enough to deal with.

"Look, it's getting late." She rolled up the blanket and fastened it to Pandora's saddle. "I think we need to get back."

"But I never got that Sunday school lesson." Mitch smiled, trying to lighten the mood.

"Maybe some other time." Beth swung up into the saddle, clicking her tongue. Pandora took her cue and started for home.

Mitch had no choice but to follow.

They were almost back to the ranch before Beth broke the silence. "You *are* going to tell Shane, right?"

"Yeah," Mitch chuckled. "He's already cornered me twice, telling me how much I look like Simon Grey. It was only a matter of time before he called my bluff."

"I don't get it. I don't think you look anything like the picture I keep seeing on the web."

"That's because Simon Grey has bleached-blonde hair and is clean shaven. I, on the other hand, have brown hair and three-day stubble."

When Beth glanced at him, Mitch was sure he saw the hint of a smile. "What?"

Beth shrugged and quickly turned away. "I didn't say anything."

"You were smiling at something. What . . . you prefer me as a blonde?"

"No. I think you look good just the way you are."

It wasn't a firm admission, but it was something. Something that let Mitch know—even though Beth tried to brush him off as an annoyance—she had feelings for him. She just wasn't willing to acknowledge them.

At least not yet.

Chapter Twenty

Beth slowly brushed Pandora, using the time alone to rethink her conversation with Mitch. It was obvious he was still searching, looking for something he hadn't been able to find in fame or fortune. But Beth didn't feel like she was qualified to tell him how to live his life. Her life had been one struggle after another. She was far from being an expert.

Shane was in the kitchen when Beth finally went inside. She couldn't help but notice the grin on his face.

"Okay, Shane, what have you been up to?"

"What's that supposed to mean?" His tone was defensive but his grin never diminished.

"That grin of yours. You're up to something, and I want to know what it is."

"*I'm* not up to anything. *I'm* not the one who went on a picnic ride with Mitch." The inflection in Shane's voice was as obvious as his smile.

Beth was momentarily speechless.

"You like him, don't you?" Shane's eyebrow bounced as he spoke.

"Shane, stop that. Mitch is a friend. That's all."

"Why is that all? Come on, Mom, I can tell he likes you. Why not loosen up a little bit? You're not getting any younger, you know."

"Well, thank you for that update." Beth good-heartily punched her son in the arm as she pushed past him to pour herself a glass of water from the tap.

"I'm just saying it's been kind of nice having Mitch around. He's pretty cool, don't you think?"

Beth tried to choose her words carefully. "I think Mitch has been a great help these last few weeks. But I also know he has a life he needs to get back to. I've appreciated what he's done, but that's it."

"Mom, you know I love you, right? But you are so full of it." Shane shook his head in mock disappointment while she stood with her mouth hanging open, shocked by her son's declaration. "I've seen the way you look at him when you think no one's watching. There's no sense arguing with me. You think he's hot, and you know it."

"Shane!"

His laughter filled the air and warmed her heart.

"Come on, Mom, as much as you try to act casual around him. I can see you like him. Why won't you just admit it?" He crossed his arms across his chest daring her to deny it.

"Shane, I think you've gotten the wrong idea."

"No I haven't. You're just not being honest with yourself."

Beth's head was spinning. When had Shane become so observant and perceptive?

"Why is it so hard for you to admit it?" He chuckled, his tone low and deep.

Hearing the baritone in Shane's voice, Beth realized, once again, that her son was becoming a young man. "It's a little more complicated than that, Shane," she huffed.

"Only because you're making it complicated."

Beth thought about her conversation with Mitch. His real identity. Her very real commitment to God. To say it was *complicated* was putting it mildly.

"Shane, I admit Mitch is a great guy but—"

"Well, thank you." Mitch emerged from the hallway and leaned against the kitchen bar area, interrupting Beth's train of thought.

"Ahh . . . I was just telling Shane how much I appreciate you. I mean, the work you've done. Around the ranch, that is." Beth tripped over her words, wondering how much of their conversation Mitch had overheard.

"Glad I could help." He smiled at her, then turned to Shane.

"Think we could chat for a few minutes?"

"Sure."

"Beth, do you mind?" Mitch asked.

"No. Not at all. I have some business to take care of anyway." She excused herself, welcoming the interruption and the chance to side-step Shane's interrogation.

Once inside her office, she closed the door with a heavy sigh—her heart pounding out of control. Shane had read her like a book. Beth thought she'd been able to hide her attraction to Mitch, but obviously hadn't done a very good job of it. Even with the revelation regarding his true identity, and the fact that Mitch still hadn't divulged the extent of his *private* conversations with Shane, she couldn't help but be thankful he had decided to stick around on the ranch even after his truck had been repaired.

Though their start had been rocky, Mitch had proven himself to be helpful, compassionate, and caring—especially where Shane was concerned. Beth appreciated the energy Mitch was pouring into her son, even if she had her apprehensions regarding their topics of discussion. And, if she was honest with herself, having Mitch around to talk with over a meal, or at the end of a long hard day of work had been enjoyable as well.

Maybe a little too enjoyable.

Beth squeezed her eyes shut, hating the fact that Mitch affected her this way. She knew God's Word was clear in matters like these. Unequally yoked. The phrase spun around in her head like a paper pinwheel in the wind. But she couldn't discount the Word of God. To ignore Him now because her hormones were on high alert would be jeopardizing the only relationship that had been a constant in her life.

Sitting at her desk, Beth stared at the computer screen. She reached for the mouse, then stopped, bowing her head instead. She wanted to be strong, faithful, and committed to the Lord, but she also wanted to be held, and kissed, and loved by a man. After all, beneath a day of sweat and dirt, and a ratty cowboy hat, was a woman captivated by a man.

No! Stop it! Nothing good can come from this.

Shoving her confused feelings aside, Beth clicked the computer mouse, bringing the screen to life. Checking her e-mails, Beth saw she had a message from the land broker she had contacted after both Uncle Charlie and Travis had declined buying her out.

Beth had painstaking explained why she would be selling the Diamond-J at the end of the summer, and that she was giving them first right of refusal, which they both did. Charlie wanted to keep his parcel of land, but would allow the bulk of the Diamond-J to go on the selling block. He had been realistic in his decision, explaining to Beth he was too old to take on the responsibility of running the entire ranch.

Beth was sure Travis would feel an obligation to keep the Diamond-J in the family, but he had declined, too. Come to find out, Travis had been struggling for some time with the idea of going back to school to finish his engineering degree. Travis had put his education on hold years ago when Charlie had suffered a heart attack. He'd come home to give his father a hand, and before Travis knew it, he and his wife were raising two little girls on their corner of the ranch. Travis enjoyed the outdoors, the hard work, and the time spent with his dad, but felt now would be the right time to make a change.

Beth was very specific with the broker she had chosen to work with. After he agreed to keep the identity of the Diamond-J confidential, she'd signed a contract with him to list the land and bring any offers to her attention that were worth considering. All the pertinent information was available to prospective buyers, but unless an offer was deemed plausible, the identity of the Diamond-J would not be disclosed.

She'd already seen a few offers that were less than she wanted to entertain, but Beth was trying to remain optimistic and patient. A lot could happen in a few months' time.

Distracted momentarily, she glanced out the window and saw her son walking with Mitch. Beth was sure Mitch was telling Shane about his true identity, and hoped Shane took the news well. When she saw him heading for the backdoor, Beth pressed the print button on her computer and walked to meet him.

"Mom, I was right." Shane waltzed in the house with a smile. "Mitch is Simon. I knew it. I tried telling Travis."

"So, you're not upset?"

"Upset? Why would I be upset? Mitch is a star, and he's living here with us. I think it's cool."

Beth couldn't believe how animated Shane was.

"Isn't it something? People from L.A. to New York are looking all over for him, and he's right here, busting his hump shoveling manure."

Beth was glad Mitch's admission hadn't turned Shane against him. Even though she knew it would be easier on her if Mitch just picked up and left, Beth wasn't ready for him to leave.

Not just yet.

Mitch walked through the backdoor, the smile on his face making him look more attractive than usual, if that was even possible.

"I guess I should have told him first. Then maybe you wouldn't have given me such a hard time."

Shane turned to her. "Mom, what did you say?"

"I . . . I was just concerned you were going to feel lied to." Beth stumbled over her words, still caught in the power of Mitch's stare.

"Nah . . . what's the use of being mad? I think it's pretty awesome. I just can't believe Mitch stuck around this long, taking attitude from you."

"Attitude from me?" Beth chuckled defensively. "What about you? If I remember correctly, you were the one reading Mitch the riot act the first night he was here."

Shane opened his mouth to defend himself, but ended up conceding. "Okay, so I was a little ticked off, but that was before, when I thought Mitch was a creep."

"Well, thanks for that vote of confidence, Shane. I'm glad to know I've improved my ranking."

"No problem." Shane playfully slapped Mitch on the back.

"Okay, now that the mutual admiration club has come to order," Beth said sarcastically, but with a smile that was hard to hide, "how about you two go work on the grill while I get things ready for dinner?"

Mitch and Shane joked and teased as they headed toward the backdoor. Beth went to the kitchen and pulled out the steaks that had been marinating in the refrigerator, then put water on to boil for eggs and noodles. She would make her killer macaroni salad along with grilled corn-on-the-cob and seasoned red potatoes.

Beth set the table for the three of them, overwhelmed with the thoughts of domesticity. This is what she wanted, what was missing from her life.

Over the years, she had convinced herself she didn't need companionship, that a relationship would require too much work and energy. Shane and the Diamond-J had always been Beth's priorities and monopolized most of her time. But still, there were those moments . . .

Maybe it wasn't too late for her after all.

Chapter Twenty-One

The barbeque was the perfect way to end the day. Shane assaulted Mitch with questions about Hollywood, acting, stunts, and movie stars, while Beth sat back enjoying the interaction between the two very dynamic men.

Mitch and Shane continued their conversation in the living room while Beth did dishes and cleaned up the kitchen. When she was finished, she turned off the light over the sink and in the dining room. Walking to the stairs, Beth glanced toward the living room, surprised to see Mitch sitting by himself.

"Where'd Shane go?"

"He said he had something to take care of in his room. I think he wanted to give us some time alone together." Mitch smiled, causing Beth to blush.

"I hope you told him that wasn't necessary." She tried to act casual as she took a seat on the opposite side of the room.

"Oh, I don't know. I was thinking a walk would be kind of nice." He looked at her as if asking for permission.

"Mitch . . ."

"Oh, come on. It's just a walk, not a proposal." Mitch got to his feet and extended a hand to help her up.

Beth sighed. "Okay." She allowed Mitch to pull her to her feet, then continued toward the front door. "But only because I need to work off some of that dinner."

Mitch pushed the creaky screen open and allowed her to walk ahead of him. "I don't see any need for you to worry about that."

Beth turned in time to see Mitch's eyes lingering on the fit of her jeans. "That's it." She turned, walking back into the house.

"Come on, Beth," Mitch laughed as he stopped her from walking away. "I've respected your feelings and kept my hands to myself, but that doesn't mean I can't admire the view."

He walked Beth down the steps, his arm casually resting across her shoulders. When she gave him a questioning glance, he pulled his arm back in surrender and shoved his hands in his pockets.

They only walked as far as the fence line on the other side of the barn when Beth stopped. Leaning against the rail, she looked at Mitch. "Tell me again why you're here."

He smiled. "I thought I was helping out."

"No, I know that, but why did you leave Hollywood? After the childhood you had, I would think you'd be enjoying the wealth of your achievements."

Mitch sighed, resting his arms across the rails of the fence.

"The way I see it, I've lived two different lives. Half my life I lived in poverty and neglect, struggling just to survive. Then, my life turned around, and I ended up living in excess, having everything I thought I ever wanted. But nothing changed inside me. I still feel empty, like I'm just not getting it. That's why I left. In some ways, I think I was better off living on the streets, having to struggle for everything. At least then, I was thankful and appreciated everything I could get my hands on."

Beth hung her head, knowing what was missing from Mitch's life—what he was looking for—but felt completely inadequate to tell him. How did she explain that a relationship with Christ is what he was searching for, when her own relationship seemed so fragile? Her life looked dysfunctional and entirely out of control. She was a horrible example of someone who had supposedly put their faith in Christ.

Rude, that's what she'd been. Belligerent and rude. Beth had accused Mitch of making moves on her and getting her son drunk. Not once had she given him the benefit of the doubt. Even when Mitch had come clean about his true identity, Beth blew up at him, refusing to extend him an ounce of grace. Her first instinct was always cynicism and judgment. She was an emotional volcano, constantly on the verge of erupting. Definitely not an attractive example of someone who claimed to have put their faith and trust in God.

"What are you thinking?" Mitch asked with a smile. "I can see the little wheels spinning behind your eyes."

"I know what's missing from your life, Mitch. It's a relationship with Christ. However, I certainly haven't made Christianity look that appealing. My life has been a train wreck since you arrived. So I can only imagine what you must think of the whole faith-in-God-thing."

"You're being too hard on yourself, Beth. Like I said, I do see a difference in your life. I know your faith is being stretched right now, but you haven't given up. I mean, if it were me—and I was battling some of the obstacles I've seen you face in the last few weeks—I would've checked out a long time ago.

"But I've watched you, Beth, when you didn't know I was around. I've seen you talking with God, reading your Bible, praying when you should be screaming. Your faith is a lifeline, and you're holding on to it with all your might."

Beth felt overwhelmed by Mitch's appraisal. He portrayed her as strong and dedicated, neither of which she'd felt in the last few months. "I think you're giving me more credit than I deserve."

"No. I'm telling you what I see. Now, I didn't say you were perfect, and some of your words have been pretty ruthless—even hurtful—but I chalk that up to being human."

For an instant, Beth felt buoyed by Mitch's assessment of her faith, but that feeling of pride was quickly dashed when he pointed out her less than charitable words.

Staring at the dirt—embarrassed by her behavior—Beth felt Mitch's finger gently tip her chin up, forcing her to meet his stare. "I forgive you," he said, his grin playful and kind.

Beth felt that strange flutter again within her heart. She wanted to reach out to Mitch, to feel the strength of his arms around her, to press her lips against his, to feel the warmth of his touch.

Beth involuntarily leaned in closer.

JUST AN ACT

"How do you know God is real?"

Like a splash of cold water, her intimate thoughts were doused by Mitch's question. "What?"

"How is it that God is so real to you?" he asked, his expression serious.

Mitch is asking about salvation. He might know it, but that's what he's asking. Beth was speechless. Did God really trust her to share the Gospel with Mitch? *I'll do it, God, but you need to give me the words to say.*

"It's hard to explain. I mean, it shouldn't be, but I'm not sure how to describe it." Beth took a couple steps away from the rail, trying to decide the best way to answer Mitch's question. She could quote scripture about the presence of God, but somehow didn't think that would suffice. With a deep breath, she stepped back to the rail and looked out over the expanse of the Diamond-J.

"When I was a little girl, I believed in Jesus because my mother told me He loved little children. She explained how He healed a girl who was sick, a man who was blind, and another who couldn't walk. I thought Jesus was magical. He seemed so caring, especially toward the underdog. However, when my mom got sick, the magic stopped. Jesus didn't heal my mother, and because of that, I didn't think He loved me. I no longer saw a caring God, only a taskmaster with a lot of do's and don'ts. I figured if He wasn't going to answer my prayers, then I wasn't going to obey His rules. That's when I began to rebel."

Beth chanced a look at Mitch, his hazel eyes full of warmth. "Let's walk," he said in a low tone.

They strolled in silence, following the rail, while Beth summoned the courage to go on.

"Cole worked for my father as a ranch hand. He'd come by one day, looking for a job. He planned on staying until he had enough money to get on the rodeo circuit. I was only sixteen, Cole was twenty-two. I was immediately smitten by his good looks. He wasn't polished by any stretch of the imagination, but I think it was his rough-around-the-edges allure that piqued my curiosity. Even though I knew Cole would only be with us for a season, I did everything I could to get his attention.

"My mom had taught me how to barrel race, so just like her, I would challenge the hands to improve my time. I knew Cole noticed me, but all he saw was the boss's little girl. He called me sweetie and sweetheart, and treated me like a child, but I wanted him to know I was more than just a little girl. That's when I started hanging out in the stables and around the barn at the end of the day. I snuck out of the house at night so I could flirt and drink with the men. I acted horrible, all for the sake of getting Cole's attention. The younger men fell all over themselves to get me to look their way, so I used them, hoping to make Cole jealous. Unfortunately, my plan worked all too well."

Beth stopped when she realized how far they'd gotten from the house. "We should probably head back." They turned around and retraced their steps to the barn.

"I guess you could've chosen a better way to start a relationship," Mitch said, not a hint of judgement in his tone.

"Believe me, it wasn't a relationship, at least not where Cole was concerned. I was just too stupid to realize I was being used," Beth sighed. "The more I drank, the more attention Cole showed me. I thought my plan was working perfectly. He was affectionate, called me beautiful, and made me feel special. One night, he kissed me in front of the other men, Cole's way of letting them know I belonged to him. After that, we started spending time together alone. That's when things got out of control. Kissing turned to passionate necking and sensual caresses. Then one night, Cole pulled me into one of the stalls and . . ."

Beth choked on her words, remembering that night. She'd drunk too much and was barely coherent. She knew what was going on, and had asked Cole to stop, but he just kept telling her how much he loved her, and that he couldn't wait any longer. Beth didn't want to lose him, so she finally gave in.

"You don't need to tell me any of this, Beth," Mitch whispered. "I have no right to pry into your personal life."

Tears cooled her cheeks. "But it's part of who I am." Beth took a deep cleansing breath, swallowed her emotions, and continued.

"Our relationship was physical from then on. I knew it was wrong, and at times I was frightened, but I was in love with Cole, and would do anything for him. Even lie and deceive my father. I just kept telling myself we would get married, and everything would be all right. Cole and I would follow the rodeo circuit and be together forever. We talked about all the fun we'd have traveling across the country. That is, until I told Cole I was pregnant.

"From that moment on, he treated me like garbage. Cole dumped me and made sure the other men knew I was up for grabs. He humiliated me in front of them, describing me like I was a piece of meat back on the auction block. I was devastated. My world was falling apart. I was sixteen and pregnant, and the man I thought I loved wouldn't even look at me. Knowing I had to do something, I cornered Cole one night and told him I was going to confess to my father everything we had done. He just laughed, called me a tease, and said I got exactly what I deserved. So I threatened him. I was childish enough to think if I accused Cole of rape, he would change his mind and marry me."

"What'd he do?"

"He beat me up."

Mitch stopped in his track. "He what?"

Beth continued walking, forcing Mitch to keep up with her. "I pushed Cole too far, and he snapped. I told him I'd call the police and have him arrested. Cole knew if I did, he would be finished. Since I was a minor, it didn't matter if it was consensual sex or not. He would be arrested for statutory rape, and his career would be over before it even got started. Cole slapped me and shoved me against the wall, ranting that he wasn't going to let some two-bit tramp come between him and his shot at the rodeo. That's when he threatened to kill my father and burn down the ranch if I made trouble for him. He threw two hundred dollars at me, told me to get an abortion, and turned to walk away. I didn't know what to do, so I picked up a shovel and hit him square in the back. Cole wheeled around, grabbed me by the forearms and literally threw me across the stall. When I hit the wall,

I crumpled to the ground. My head was spinning, but Cole wasn't done. He came at me again and kicked me. I curled up into a ball, trying to protect the baby. That's when his boot caught me in the forehead. I blacked out. When I woke up, he was gone."

Beth turned to Mitch, hating the twisted look of pity on his face.

"Beth, I don't know what to say. And I certainly don't know why that son-of-a . . ." Mitch edited himself as he forked his fingers through his hair, sauntering like a caged animal. "Why didn't your father go after Cole? I would've dropped the guy where he stood, and worried about the consequences later. I can't believe your father let him get away. How could he just—"

"I didn't tell him!" Beth shouted, interrupting Mitch's tirade. "At least not right away," she mumbled.

"What?" Mitch looked at her, horrified and angry. "The man nearly killed you, and you didn't tell anyone? Are you kidding me? What were you thinking?"

Mitch's recrimination made her feel stupid, humiliated, and worthy of blame.

The same way she had felt that night.

Beth hurried her steps, wanting to put as much distance between her and Mitch's indignation as possible.

"Beth, I'm sorry," Mitch caught up to her, softening his tone. "I was completely out of line. I had no right talking to you like that."

Beth kept walking.

As she closed the distance between her and the barn, Beth felt Mitch's hand on her elbow. He gave it a gentle squeeze, his way of asking her to stop. She did, but kept her eyes fixed ahead.

"Come on, Beth, I'm sorry. It's just that I . . . I care for you. Imagining you going through something that awful . . . I just kind of lost it for a moment."

Not bothering to look at Mitch, Beth started walking again.

"Tell me what happened," he asked softly. "Please."

Beth took a minute to gather her thoughts, then continued.

"That night—when I came to—I was completely disoriented. I didn't know how much time had passed or if Cole had made good on his threat to hurt my dad. I was bleeding and could barely walk, but I hurried as best as I could to the house. When I heard my Dad and Uncle Charlie talking on the back porch, I fell apart. My dad was okay. That was all that mattered.

"Slowly, I made it upstairs to my room and took a shower, thinking I would be able to hide the cuts and bruises from my dad, but I didn't factor in the pain. The next morning, I couldn't even get out of bed."

Beth involuntarily winced, remembering how she felt that day. Reaching the back of the barn, she leaned against it, thankful for the support. Mitch stood in front of her, hands tucked in his back pockets, waiting for her to continue.

"When I didn't show at breakfast the next morning, my father came looking for me. He stood in the doorway of my bedroom, shocked. He rushed to my bedside and asked me what happened. But I was too afraid to tell him the truth. I was terrified what he might do—and what Cole would do to him in return. Instead, I made up an elaborate story about Pandora. I told him she got spooked while I was in her stall. I said she reared up, knocked me to the ground, and stomped on me. I was pretty sure my father knew I was lying—not that he knew the truth. It's just that I had gotten hurt before, after doing something my father specifically forbade me to do. I always felt the need to prove I was as tough as any guy on the ranch. I think my dad was trying to smoke me out, so, he called my bluff."

"What do you mean?"

"Immediately, my dad started talking about putting Pandora down. He kept saying he didn't want to risk another episode of aggressive behavior. Finally, I burst into tears and told him what happened . . . and everything else I had done."

Beth looked at Mitch. "I will never forget the look on my father's face. He stared at me in utter disbelief. He was devastated. Crushed. Disappointed. When he broke down and cried, it hurt worse than the pain from Cole's beating. The only other time I had seen my father like that was when my mother died. Knowing I had caused him that amount of pain was almost more than I could bear."

"Did he go after Cole?"

"No, but he wanted to. He kept threatening to kill Cole—to hunt him down and make him pay. When Dad talked about involving the police, I became hysterical. I told him I wouldn't be able to handle the humiliation of an interrogation, and if he really loved me—even after everything I had done—he would let me handle things my way. My dad was furious, not understanding why I would want Cole to get away with what he'd done to me, but all I could think about was Cole's threat to kill my father. I couldn't let that happen.

"In the end, my father backed down, but only because he was concerned about my condition. I was in a lot of pain and afraid that I might lose the baby. I agreed to see a doctor, but only if he agreed not to involve the police."

Mitch and Beth walked up the steps of the front porch and took a seat on the swing.

"Beth, I'm so sorry you had to go through all that. I feel honored that you trusted me with your story."

"The reason I told you," Beth turned to Mitch, "is because it was during that time in my life when I started to understand what grace and unconditional love were. My father showed me love without limitations. He never once acted embarrassed when he had to introduce his pregnant, unwed daughter to new buyers, and he always smiled with pride every time he introduced Shane as his grandchild."

Beth smiled to herself at the memory. *I miss you, Dad. I wish you were here right now. You would know what to do.*

"Beth," Mitch put his hand on her knee and squeezed, "are you all right?"

She looked up at him and smiled. "Yeah, I'm fine. Anyway," Beth said as she sat up straighter, "that's when God really got a hold on my life. My father's example of unconditional love helped me better understand the love of God and the relationship He wanted to have with me. So, I rededicated my life to Christ when Shane was just a few months old and promised to raise my son to know the love of the Savior. It wasn't easy, since the church we attended wasn't as forgiving as my father, but I tried to—"

"Wait a minute. What do you mean?"

Beth shrugged. "It was an ultra-conservative church and it didn't appreciate having an unwed, teenage mother in their congregation—as if I was a poster child advocating adultery. The older women treated me like I had the plague, and the younger men leered at me like I was community property. I stuck it out for years, out of respect for my father, but after he was gone, it only worsened. The kicker came one afternoon when Shane and I were driving home from church. He asked me what an adulteress was. That's when I decided I had enough. I wasn't coping very well with the death of my father, and I certainly didn't have the energy to waste on people who didn't know the meaning of grace. I pulled back from everyone. It wasn't easy, and God and I had our fair share of falling outs."

Beth sighed, thinking of all the times she rode out to the open field so she could have a shouting match with God.

"I was pretty angry with God when my father passed away and for how I was treated in the community. I've also had more than a few heated discussions with Him over Shane's rebellion. I keep begging God to reveal Himself to Shane, like He did to me. However, I also understand that choosing to have God in your life is a personal decision everyone has to make for themselves. I can't force Shane to love God or acknowledge who God is. It's something he has to do for himself. Sometimes God lets us have our own way, no matter how self-destructive, so that we can come to the realization that we can't make it on our own power."

Beth looked at Mitch, hoping some of what she was saying was sinking in. "It's not an easy life, but I don't know how I would cope if I didn't have God to rely on at the end of the day."

Mitch sat silently while Beth twisted her hands together in her lap, embarrassed she had told him so much about her past.

"Wow. I didn't mean to dump all that on you. I guess that's why I freaked out when I saw Shane with those magazines. I know what it feels like to do anything to get noticed and then end up being ostracized or used and tossed away. I don't ever want Shane to think it's okay to use a woman or see her as nothing more than an object."

"I don't think you need to worry about that, Beth. He has you as a role model."

"But it isn't enough. Shane is obsessed with the thought of meeting his father."

"Is he still involved with the rodeo?"

Beth looked away, fighting the resentment she felt for Cole. "Oh yeah. In fact, he's touted as the All-American cowboy. He's a three-time champion, married to an ex-rodeo queen, and has two precious little girls. Cole has worked hard to create a wholesome reputation. That's what has me worried. The rodeo community might seem rough around the edges—with their drinking and carousing ways—but behind the booze and the tobacco, lies a conservatism built on loving God and country, respecting others, and doing what is right. If Cole's fans ever learned he had a child out of wedlock—especially with a sixteen-year-old girl—and that he abandoned them, never once trying to make things right, his standing within the rodeo community would be shattered."

Beth twisted her hands in her lap. "If Shane ever found out who his father is and tried to confront him, I don't know what Cole would do. I know what he did the last time he thought his back was up against a wall. I ended up with a split lip, cracked ribs, and a concussion. The only difference now is Cole has even more to lose. If Shane—"

The squeaky hinges on the old screen door interrupted Beth. When she turned around, she saw Shane standing in the doorway, his eyes red with emotion.

"Shane!" Beth jumped to her feet, her mind replaying everything she had said.

"Cole Dempsey is my father?" His words were monotone, like he was having a hard time comprehending them.

"Shane, I can explain."

He looked confused and hurt. "All this time I thought I had some lowlife bum for a father, and that was why you never would tell me who he was. But that's not true. Cole Dempsey is not a bum. I get it now . . . you're not embarrassed of him; you're embarrassed of me."

JUST AN ACT

"Shane, no, that's not tr—"

Shane slammed the screen before Beth could stop him. Watching him run down the hall and out the backdoor, Beth hurried around the side of the porch hoping to stop Shane before he got too far. She stood in the backyard, her eyes searching the darkness for him. That's when she heard Mitch yelling from the front of the house. By the time Beth rounded the corner, she saw Shane riding off on Apollo, bareback, cutting through the field at a breakneck speed. Mitch was already running toward the barn when she caught up with him.

Mitch headed for the tack room, but Beth didn't waste the time. She opened Pandora's stall, threw herself over the mare's back, and bolted out of the barn.

Mitch hurried from the tack room, but Beth was already gone, a fog of dust kicked up in her wake. He wanted to take off after her, but wasn't experienced enough. He could ride without the luxury of a saddle, but not without reins. He quickly pulled the bridle over Midas' forehead, desperate to catch up to Beth and Shane.

Mitch leaned close to Midas' withers as they ran through the open field. It was so dark he could hardly see, forcing him to rely on Midas' instincts to get them where they were going. All Mitch could do was hold on tight as the animal's muscular legs propelled them forward.

When a shrill pierced the darkness, Midas reared up. Mitch tried to hold on, but it was no use. Midas dumped Mitch to the ground, then trotted away.

It took a minute for Mitch to get to his feet and inhale the breath that was knocked from his lungs. He cursed, ready to pummel Midas for letting him down at such a crucial time. He squinted against the darkness, trying to get his bearings and wondering what kind of animal could've made such a blood-curdling cry. When he heard snorting and neighing, Mitch focused in on the sound. He spotted Midas about fifty yards ahead of him, pawing the ground and dipping his head in agitation. Mitch stalked toward the animal hoping Midas wouldn't take off and leave him stranded.

That's when Mitch saw them.
Midas stood watch over Pandora's crumpled body.
Beth pinned to the ground beneath her.

Chapter Twenty-Two

Mitch collapsed alongside Pandora and Beth, not knowing what to do. Pandora grunted in pain and lashed about, the force of the animal's body rolling on top of Beth, trapping her against the rocky ground.

Beth cried out in pain as she tugged on her leg, trying to pull it free. "Mitch, I'm stuck. My leg . . . I think it's broken." Her words were laced with equal parts fear and anguish.

Mitch reached under Beth's arms and pulled, but her pain-filled scream made him want to puke. He changed his tactics, deciding instead to get Pandora to her feet.

The mare was panting hard, snorting and grunting. Mitch pushed at her massive form, but was unable to get the horse on her feet. Not knowing what else to do, Mitch got on the ground alongside Beth and strained to wedge his legs between Pandora and the earthen soil.

"Don't hurt her, Mitch," Beth sobbed as he worked at creating a pocket of space between Pandora's body and Beth's leg.

Finally, he saw Beth inch backwards. With a heart-wrenching wail, she dragged herself free from Pandora's weight.

Beth collapsed against the ground, covering her face, sobbing uncontrollably. Mitch knelt at her side.

"It's going to be okay, Beth. I'm going to go for help."

"But what about Shane? You have to find him."

Mitch looked at her leg, realizing it was a serious break from the way it was twisted and disfigured. "I'll find him, Beth, but right now we need to get you to a hospital."

Swearing under his breath at the helplessness he felt, Mitch looked around at the nothingness that surrounded them. How was he supposed to find Shane, and help Beth and Pandora all at the same time? He brushed Beth's hair back from her face—her skin feeling clammy and cold.

I can't do it all. She needs my help. Shane will just have to fend for himself.

"Beth," Mitch stroked her face, "I have to go get the truck. You need to hang on until I get back. Can you do that?"

She nodded, her eyes closed.

"How do I get a hold of Charlie?"

"He's on speed dial. Number two." Her voice was thin and raspy, not sounding good at all.

"Beth, don't cop out on me. I need you to stay coherent. Do you hear me?"

"Just . . . hurry." Her words were barely intelligible.

Midas had stayed close the whole time, but it took some coaxing for him to leave Pandora and Beth. Mitch heeled the horse, making sure Midas knew he meant business. He didn't have to ask twice. They were back in the yard in no time, Mitch flying from Midas' back before the horse could even come to a stop. Mitch burst into the house and ran for the phone. Pressing two, he waited for someone to answer.

"Charlie, Beth's had an accident."

Mitch tried to explain as quickly as he could what had happened.

"I've got to get Beth to a hospital, but I need you to look for Shane."

"Where is she now?" Charlie asked, panic in his voice.

"In the pasture. I've got to get back to her."

"I'll meet you there."

"Charlie, Pandora looks pretty bad. You might need to bring something to put her out of her pain."

Mitch quickly gathered some blankets and a first-aid kit. In the barn, he grabbed some twine, then went to the toolshed for a few scraps of wood. He threw everything in the back of Beth's pickup and floored it through the open gate.

The truck bucked and barreled across the pasture, Mitch slowing when he realized he wasn't sure how far to drive. When Mitch finally caught sight of Pandora's massive body in his headlights, he came to a stop. After gathering up the stuff he'd thrown into the bed of the truck, Mitch knelt next to Beth's motionless body. "Beth . . . Beth." Mitch shook her shoulder, petrified when she didn't respond.

"I'm okay, Mitch. Just stop shaking me."

He watched as Beth tried to open her eyes, but the effort was obviously more than she could muster. Her teeth were chattering, and since the weather was too hot for chills, Mitch knew she was going into shock. He threw a blanket across Beth's shoulders and chest, tucking it around her before shifting his attention to her broken leg. He gently cut away her jeans until he saw the bloody puncture wound and the exposed break.

After cutting three lengths of twine with his pocket knife, he carefully placed two slivers of framing on either side of Beth's leg. One by one, he slid the twine underneath her leg and tied the boards to form a brace. Beth cried out against the pressure.

"I'm sorry, Beth, but I've got to immobilize your leg as much as possible."

Just then, Charlie's truck roared up next to Beth's. Mitch watched as the old man looked at Pandora's lifeless form, then lowered himself to Beth's side.

"How's she doing?" Charlie asked as he knelt alongside his niece.

"She's holding her own, but she's hurt pretty bad."

"Uncle Charlie, you need to help Pandora," Beth looked at him with glassy eyes.

"I will, Beth, but first we need to take care of you," he said tenderly.

Beth's truck was too small so Mitch carefully carried her to the backseat of Charlie's extended cab. Charlie rattled off directions to the nearest hospital as Mitch jogged around the front of the vehicle and hopped in the driver's seat. As Mitch pulled the door shut, he made eye contact with Charlie, knowing what it was he had to do.

Mitch made sure Beth was as comfortable as possible before wheeling the truck around and slowly maneuvering over the rutted ground. He'd only driven about fifty yards when he heard a shot that echoed through the night.

He glanced in his rearview mirror to see Beth completely out of it, unaware of what was going on. At that moment, Mitch was thankful her pain was so great she hadn't heard the shot that would forever change her world.

Shane was startled by the shot that pierced the night air. He pulled up on Apollo and waited. He told himself it was a trick. His mother was only trying to get his attention, scaring him into coming home.

He turned, heeled Apollo, and kept going. He wasn't going to be so easily manipulated.

Not anymore.

Chapter Twenty-Three

Mitch paced the waiting room for what seemed like hours. Beth had been put on a gurney and rushed through the double doors the minute they got there, leaving him alone with dire thoughts ricocheting around in his head. *What was happening with Beth? Did Charlie find Shane? If so, were they on their way to the hospital? How was he going to tell Beth about Pandora? What was Shane going to do when he saw the results of his actions?*

Exhausted, Mitch finally sat down in one of the blue plastic chairs that lined the waiting room wall. With his elbows on his knees and his head braced between his hands, Mitch did what he knew Beth would do if their roles were reversed.

God, here I am again. I know I've never had much use for you before, but I'm beginning to see things differently now. Even with everything Beth has gone through, she turns to you for help. I don't understand it. If you have the power to change things, why are you allowing this to happen to her? I don't get it, but I see in Beth a peace she says comes from you. Help her God. Help her and Charlie and Sha—

"Mr. Justin?" The nurse approached Mitch.

He didn't bother correcting her. He just got to his feet, anxious to hear how Beth was doing.

"How is she?"

"She's in recovery right now."

"Can I see her? Is she all right? How bad is she? The break looked pretty ba—"

The nurse held up her hand to stop Mitch's barrage of questions.

"The doctor will be out to talk to you in a few moments. He'll be able to better explain the extent of Mrs. Justin's injuries."

Mitch slumped into the chair, his mind hanging on the word *extent*.

He watched the clock on the wall for the next thirty-five minutes. Thirty-five minutes that felt like an eternity. When an older man in green scrubs walked through the same sterile doors Beth had been wheeled through an eternity ago, Mitch stood.

"Mr. Justin?" he asked as he stepped forward.

"No, I'm afraid there's been a misunderstanding. It's *Miss* Justin. I'm Mitch Burk, a family friend." He extended his hand to the doctor, but instead of accepting his handshake, the cantankerous surgeon looked around the empty room and asked, "Is there someone here from her family I can talk to?"

"No. The family sent me." Mitch's tone was sharp. "Her son is missing and Beth's uncle needed to stay behind to look for him. She's single, and her parents are deceased."

When Mitch saw the irritation in the surgeon's expression, he tempered his words. "Please, doctor, I know you have rules, but I need to know how Beth's doing. I wouldn't be here if it wasn't for the fact that I care for her very much."

Mitch waited, figuring the doctor would quote protocols and procedures before walking away, but instead, the man rubbed at his scruffy face and took a seat in one of the waiting room chairs. He looked up at Mitch with a tired sigh but an assuring smile. "Miss Justin is going to be fine."

Mitch tossed his head back in relief, thanked God, then sat down in the chair next to the doctor and asked, "What about her leg? It looked pretty bad."

"The compound fracture to Miss Justin's tibia was serious, but it—along with multiple contusions and other external injuries—was the least of her problems. It was the concussion, cracked ribs, internal bleeding, and ruptured spleen that gave us some trouble."

Mentally, Mitch repeated the list of Beth's injuries, feeling panicked all over again. "But you said she was going to be fine."

"She is," the doctor reiterated. "We were able to stop the bleeding and remove her spleen. The leg has been set and will be in a cast for six weeks or so. It's the concussion that has me concerned. As a precaution, we'll keep Miss Justin for the next few days to make sure there's no swelling or bleeding. Other than that, she's a very lucky woman."

"When can I see her?"

"Once we get Miss Justin situated in a room."

"Is she okay here? I mean, maybe we should move her to a bigger hospital. Not that anything is wrong with this one, but since Beth has a head injury, maybe she would be better off with a specialist."

"Though that is certainly your right, it's not necessary," the doctor stated emphatically. "Miss Justin will be receiving the utmost of care. Our hospital might be small and in the middle of nowhere, but I assure you, our doctors went through medical school just like everyone else."

"I'm sorry," Mitch said apologetically. "I didn't mean to insult you or your staff. I'm just worried about Beth."

"She'll be fine." His words were firm but reassuring. "I'm just taking extra precautions because of her concussion." The doctor walked toward the automatic doors. "Someone will let you know when she's ready for visitors."

Mitch continued to pace, waiting for the opportunity to see for himself that Beth was okay. Fortunately, he didn't have to wait long. A young woman—who looked barely out of her teens—in a white uniform and a badge identifying her as a volunteer, ushered him through the double doors and down the hall. Mitch could feel the girl staring at him as they walked.

When they stopped in front of room one-seventeen, she turned to him and smiled. "You look like Simon Grey, the actor. You know, the one who's been missing."

Mitch chuckled, trying to sound amused. "I know. Ever since he's gone missing, people keep telling me that. It's funny, a couple of months ago, no one said a thing, but now that the guy has pulled a disappearing act, everyone thinks I look just like him."

The girl blushed as she hugged a stack of papers to her chest. "Well, there is a resemblance, but now that I think of it, Simon Grey is taller and his hair is blonde."

Mitch just smiled. "So . . . Beth . . . can I see her?"

"Yes. Of course." The girl still sounded flustered. "She's a little groggy, and kind of in and out, but you can sit with her."

The volunteer continued down the hall, leaving Mitch at the door. He pressed his hand against the cold, stainless steel panel and slowly pushed the door open. Standing in the shadows of the dimly lit room, Mitch looked at Beth and his heart sunk. Even though she was naturally petite, Mitch had never thought of Beth as frail, but that's exactly how she looked now. His eyes stung with unshed tears, and he had to take a deep, even breath to gather himself. He silently repeated, *she's going to be okay. The doctor said she's going to be okay,* as he moved forward and took a seat in the chair next to her bed.

Mitch studied Beth from head to toe, which was easy to do since her cast leg lay on top of the sterile-looking blanket. Her head was wrapped in gauze, and there were abrasions up and down her arms, but even in spite of the bandages and bruises, Beth looked peaceful. It was a stark contrast to the excruciating pain she'd been in earlier when he had carried her into the emergency room.

Mitch wasn't sure how long he sat staring at Beth, watching the sheet move with every breath she took, but soon enough fatigue started to set in. He got up, wandered the room, inspected every gadget and piece of apparatus, then moved to the window and stared out into the midnight sky. With a sigh, he sat back down, extended his legs in front of him, laced his fingers behind his head, and closed his eyes.

Mitch was awakened by the sound of squeaky shoes on the tile floor. Amazed that he'd actually fallen asleep, he looked at his watch realizing he had dozed off over an hour ago. Beth's eyes slowly fluttered open as the nurse poked and prodded her. Mitch could see she was confused and a little disoriented.

"Miss Justin, do you know where you are?" the nurse asked.

It took her minute before she answered. "The hospital."

"And do you know who this handsome gentleman is?" The nurse stepped back so Beth could see Mitch.

She turned her head, looking confused. Mitch waited for it to register. When Beth smiled, he grinned in return, reached for her hand, and gave it a squeeze. "Hey, sleepyhead, how are you feeling?"

"Like a tin can that's been crushed and tossed in the trash." She closed her eyes for a second then opened them again, looking frantic. "Where's Shane? Did you find him?"

"Charlie was looking for him. I'm sure he's found him by now."

"How long ago was that?"

"A while, but Beth, I'm sure he's all right. He was just angry and needed some space."

"Will you call Uncle Charlie and find out? Please. My phone should be around here somewhere." Beth tried sitting up, but winced at the pain.

"Miss Justin, you need to lay still. You just got out of surgery," the nurse admonished.

"But, my phone. I need to find my phone."

Mitch located the bag that had Beth's clothes in it. Sure enough, her phone was still in her pocket, but the screen was shattered. He pressed the button to turn it on—not having much hope—but it lit up right away. After a few minutes of fiddling, Mitch found Charlie's number, but the phone wouldn't dial. Using the hospital's instead, he called Charlie's number, hoping he would have good news.

In the light of the dawning sun, Charlie saw the silhouette of Shane perched on the fence, Apollo grazing nearby. Charlie cursed under his breath, angry Shane had refused to answer his phone all night long.

Shane looked over his shoulder, but only for a second before he turned around, ignoring Charlie all together.

With his blood boiling, Charlie got out of Beth's truck and stalked toward Shane.

"I don't want to hear it, Uncle Charlie," he hollered, without even looking at him. "Mom had no right keeping my father from me all these years. How could she be so selfish? She told me it was for my own good, but that's a lie. She only cares about herself."

Before Shane could react, Charlie pulled him from the fence by the neck of his shirt and pushed him to the ground. "Shut up!" He lunged over his nephew, wagging a shaky finger in his face. "Just shut your mouth before you say something you'll regret. You think you know it all. You don't know nothin'!"

Charlie could see Shane was momentarily stunned, but recovered quick enough. "I know my father is Cole Dempsey!" Shane yelled as he got to his feet. "I know he's a decent guy and would do the right thing if he knew he had a son!"

"Oh really? You think your daddy is a 'decent guy'?" Charlie came at him again, pinning Shane to the fence with his stare and his extended finger.

"Let me tell you how 'decent' he is. He *does* know about you. Your mother went to see him after you were born, told him he had a son. And you know what he said? He told your mother she had better keep her distance and her snot-nose brat away from him. He called her a tramp and accused her of passing herself around like a cheap bottle of hooch. He swore there was no way he was going to get roped into marryin' a girl stupid enough to get pregnant, especially when he might not even be the father."

Shane stared at Charlie. "You're lying. Just like Mom has done all these years."

"Oh, am I? And if I was to say he beat her up and left her unconscious in the barn, would I be lying then?" Charlie waited for that to sink in before he continued.

"Your dad is not the Cole Dempsey you see on TV. Your dad is a selfish, manipulative, and dangerous man. He walked away from you and your mother, never once looking back. Sure, he might have the All-American image now, but that's not the man who kicked your mother when she laid crumpled in a stall and threatened her never to come near him again."

"I don't care what you say," Shane argued back. "I'm going to find Cole Dempsey and tell him who I am. Let's see him deny having a son when I'm standing right in front of his face." Shane's chin was set, his teeth clenched, and his fists in a ball.

"Fine. You do what you want, Shane. But while you've been out here feeling sorry for yourself—thinkin' everyone is against you—your mother's been taken to the hospital with serious injuries. Injuries she got because she was afraid you were going to hurt yourself. And me . . . I had to put a bullet in Pandora because her leg was shattered so bad there was no way of saving her. But you're right. You go find your father. Maybe you can live with him. Then your mother won't have to sell her ranch—her life-blood—something Beth was willing to do because she's so selfish and only cares about herself."

"Wait, what do you mean Mom's in the hospital?" Shane's complexion turned ashen.

"She tried going after you last night, desperate to talk some sense into you. Pandora went down hard on top of your mother, pinning her to the ground. Mitch took her to the hospital in horrible shape." Charlie turned and headed toward the pickup. "But don't you worry about it. I see you have too much on your mind to worry about anyone but yourself."

"Wait a minute," Shane said as he hurried to catch up with Charlie. "How bad is she hurt?"

"Like I said, she was in horrible shape. Her leg was busted up, and her head was bleeding pretty bad. When I got there, she was barely conscious. But don't let that stop you. You go find the most important person in your life."

Charlie's words were harsh and meant to hurt. He climbed into the truck and revved the engine loudly. Shane ran to the window, holding on, not letting Charlie drive away. "That shot last night. That wasn't to get my attention?"

"No. That was me putting down Pandora."

Tears began to well in Shane's eyes as he stared at Charlie. "I thought it was Mom trying to get me to come home, trying to get my attention."

"I wish it had been. I don't know how I'm going to tell her Pandora is gone." He stared at Shane. "But why am I bothering you with all of this? You have more important things on your mind. You go find that father of yours."

Charlie didn't give Shane a chance to say another word or ask any more questions. He turned the truck around and headed for home. Just then, his phone began to ring. He pulled it from his pocket, not recognizing the number. *Let it be Mitch, Lord. I need some good news.*

"Hey, Charlie, it's me."

Mitch had stepped outside of Beth's room to make the call. He used the excuse that he didn't want to be in the way while the nurse was working on her, but the real reason was he wanted to talk to Charlie without Beth overhearing.

"How is she?" Charlie asked.

"She's going to be fine. She's got a lot of stuff going on, but the doctor said Beth is lucky things weren't worse. Did you find Shane?"

"Yeah, I just left him."

"What do you mean, you left him?"

"At the moment, he's being a belligerent, selfish brat, so I left him to deal with his feelings."

"Did you tell him what happened?" Mitch couldn't believe Shane would be unaffected by the news that his mother was in the hospital.

"Yeah, I told him and I could see the look of fear in his eyes, but I wasn't going to baby him. If he's going to continue to make mistakes in life, he's going to have to deal with the consequences."

"What do I tell Beth?" Mitch didn't understand why Charlie wasn't insisting Shane come to the hospital.

Charlie looked in his rearview mirror, seeing the cloud of dust that was following him. A slight smile creased his face. "Tell her, we'll be there as soon as we can. And tell Beth not to worry about Shane. She needs to take care of herself right now."

"So, Shane *is* with you?"

"He will be by the time I reach the yard. Look, Mitch, I'll take care of things on this end. You just make sure Beth is taken care of, got it?"

"What about Pandora?"

"There was nothing I could do for her. Her leg was busted too bad. She couldn't even get up."

"Okay."

Charlie heard Mitch's disheartened sigh, feeling the same way. "I'll see you in a little while."

"Did you talk to Uncle Charlie? Did he find Shane?" Beth asked, the minute Mitch walked back into the room.

"Calm down, Beth. Everything is going to be okay." Mitch took up his position in the chair beside her bed and reached for her hand. "Charlie said they'll be here as soon as they can. Now, just relax and get some sleep."

Beth stared at Mitch, looking weak and still a little out of it. "What aren't you telling me?"

Mitch sighed, scooted his chair closer to her bed, and squeezed Beth's hand. He hadn't wanted to tell her about Pandora, but he knew she needed to know. "Beth . . ." he swallowed, realizing it was going to be even harder than he imagined, "it's Pandora. I'm afraid she didn't make it."

Beth turned away from him and began to cry.

"I'm sorry, Beth. I know how much she meant to you." Mitch didn't have the words to comfort her. Beth's relationship with Pandora was special. Pandora was her companion and friend, a constant in Beth's life when life itself had been cruel and confusing. It was just one more loss Beth would have to endure.

I don't understand you, God. Really, I don't. Mitch thought to himself as he listened to Beth cry herself to sleep.

Mitch watched Beth's slow rhythmic breathing, thankful she was getting some much-needed rest. It had been a long night, and most likely would be a long day. Needing a cup of coffee, Mitch stepped from Beth's room, surprised to see the small hospital buzzing with activity. Mitch yawned as he crossed the corridor to the nurses' station, and smiled at the teenage volunteer behind the counter.

"Can you point me in the direction of the cafeteria?" he asked.

She stared at him like she was looking at a ghost. All of a sudden, Mitch realized he'd taken for granted the anonymity he'd enjoyed on the Diamond-J. Now, out among people again, he was going to have to dodge the questions and the stares.

Mitch quickly explained to the wide-eyed girl that he was constantly being mistaken for some actor fella from Hollywood. Before she could comment, Mitch returned to the safety of Beth's room, realizing he would have to keep a low profile while at the hospital. If he didn't keep to himself, it wouldn't be long before the media would be tipped off, and they would decide to come investigate the *sightings* for themselves.

Chapter Twenty-Four

Mitch stirred in the chair alongside Beth's bed. He turned toward the door to see Charlie and Shane had slipped inside the room. When Mitch looked at Shane, he felt a sudden surge of emotion that took him completely by surprise. He realized his feelings for the boy had grown much deeper than a casual friendship.

Mitch got up from the chair and shook Charlie's hand. Shane took a few steps forward, then stopped near the foot of his mother's bed. Mitch watched as the color in Shane's complexion quickly faded to gray. Putting a hand on the teen's shoulder, Mitch gave it a squeeze.

"She's going to be all right," Mitch tried to reassure him.

Shane twisted his hands together and took deep swallows, obviously struggling with his mom's condition. Mitch could only imagine the guilt Shane was feeling. When the kid's eyes began to water and his shoulders slumped, Mitch instinctively pulled the boy to his side and held him tight.

"It's going to be all right, Shane."

The teenager, full of anger the last time Mitch saw him, crumpled, overcome with emotion. As much as Shane wanted to prove to everyone that he was all grown up, he still had the tenderness of a boy.

"This is all my fault," Shane's voice quivered. "I didn't mean for this to happen. I was just so mad. Mom kept my father from me all this time, and now I find out I knew him all along."

"I know it's hard for you to see your mom in this condition, but Beth needs to know that you're okay." Mitch lowered his tone to a whisper. "You also need to assure her you're not going to take off again while she's in the hospital."

"Hey, don't talk about me like I'm not even here." Beth's voice was a whisper, but everyone turned their attention to where she was trying to scoot herself into an upright position. She winced and let out a meek whimper before she gave up and let her head fall back against the pillow.

"Here, let me help you." Mitch step forward and showed Beth the mattress controls on the bed rail.

"Hi, Mom," Shane said with an unsure voice.

"Shane." She smiled and reached out her hand.

He stepped closer and took it. "I'm so sorry. I didn't mean for this to happen. I wish it was me. I deserve—"

"Shane, stop blaming yourself. It was an accident," Beth assured him.

"But it was my fault."

"No, Shane, it was my fault. I should have told you sooner. I only wanted to protect you, but now I realize I was wrong. You had a right to know. I'm sorry."

Mitch could hear the emotion Beth was trying so hard to control. He watched as Shane looked over the extent of her injuries once more. "Are you sure you're going to be okay, Mom?"

"Yeah. I'm a little busted up, but I'll be fine." She smiled as she glanced from Shane to Uncle Charlie to Mitch.

"I'm going to call Sarah and Travis and let them know you're gonna be okay," Charlie said with a smile and tear-rimmed eyes. "Sarah wouldn't believe me until I saw you for myself. You know how she can be."

After Charlie left, the room grew silent.

Mitch watched as Beth's eyes fluttered shut. Her exhaustion paired with heavy medication was causing her to drift in and out. Mitch watched as Shane stood transfixed along Beth's bedside. He was dusty and disheveled from being out in the pasture all night, and he looked like he was ready to break emotionally.

"Want to get some breakfast?" Mitch whispered to him.

"I'm not hungry."

Shane's hat was pulled down low across his forehead. Mitch was sure he was trying to hide the tears in his eyes, but there was no hiding the emotion in his voice.

"Okay, then go with me, so I can get some coffee. But first, I need to borrow this." Mitch grabbed Shane's hat and pulled it snug on his head. "I need the extra camouflage. One of the nurses is already eyeballing me."

Shane quickly swiped at the tears in his eyes before they walked out into the hall. Charlie was on the phone and waved, signally he would catch up with them in a few minutes. Mitch and Shane walked quietly to the small cafeteria at the end of the main corridor. Mitch grabbed a large foam cup and filled it with steaming black coffee. And even though Shane said he wasn't hungry, he reached for a package of donuts and a carton of orange juice.

Mitch handed Shane a twenty to pay the cashier, so he could duck into a booth without having to make small talk. Shane slid in across from him and twisted the lid off of his juice. He took a swig, and then sat playing with the cellophane on his donuts.

"What are you thinking?" Mitch asked, leaning back further in the booth.

"Nothing."

"Doesn't look like nothing," he persisted.

Shane took a few moments, obviously caught in some sort of internal struggle. "Uncle Charlie told me what happened between my mom and my . . . dad."

"And?" Mitch took a mouthful of coffee.

Shane didn't look at Mitch, he just kept fiddling with his donuts. "I still want to meet him."

Mitch tried to cover his surprise. He took another sip of coffee before asking, "What good do you think that's going to do?"

"I don't know. Probably none. But I've got to find out. I've got to hear it for myself."

Playing with the rim of his coffee cup, Mitch hung his head in disappointment. Even though he'd only known Beth a short time—and couldn't pretend to know everything about her—he knew one thing for sure, Beth loved her son. She loved him fiercely. Her decision to keep Shane's father out of the picture had not been made out of spite or anger. Beth had done it for Shane's protection.

"I know you're angry, Mitch, but you don't understand." Shane pulled and twisted at the plastic ring from around the top of his juice container. "I love my mom, and I don't want to hurt her. But I need to know the truth, and the only way I'm going to know that is if I hear it straight from him."

Mitch understood Shane's need to confront his father. As a child, he had rehearsed over and over again what he would say to his own dad if ever given the opportunity. Unfortunately, Mitch also knew Beth would be crushed if Shane went against her wishes.

"Shane, I'm not going to try to change your mind or tell you how pointless it is to talk to a man who was never there for you. But I am going to ask you to wait before you go after this Dempsey guy. Your mother needs you right now, on the ranch and emotionally. Please don't do anything that's going to interfere with her recovery."

Shane was poised for a rebuttal when Mitch put up his hand to stop him. "Look, I will personally escort you wherever it is you want to go to meet him," Mitch's tone was firm and there was no mistaking his irritation, "but not until your mother has had a chance to get back on her feet. You've waited sixteen years. I don't think another few weeks is going to kill you. Your mother deserves that much."

Shane nodded. "I don't want to hurt my mom, really I don't. This is just something I've got to do. But you're right. I can wait. At least until I can explain it so she understands."

Mitch knew no amount of explaining would help Beth understand, but at least he'd gotten Shane to agree to wait. It was the best he could do for now.

Charlie walked into the cafeteria and joined Mitch and Shane in the booth. "I talked to Travis. He has everything covered at the ranch." Charlie looked from Mitch to Shane and back to Mitch again. "Is there something you're not telling me? Beth *is* going to be okay, right?"

"She's going to be fine, though she might not bounce back as quickly as she'd like. Besides the broken leg, and all her internal injuries, a concussion is nothing to mess around with. The doctor wants to keep her for a few days just to make sure there's no brain swelling."

Mitch saw renewed worry in Shane's eyes, but he wasn't going to sugarcoat it. Shane needed to know his mother was in serious condition because of his poor choices. He needed to know his decisions affected not only himself but those around him. Maybe it would make him think twice before pursuing his father.

"So, what else did I miss?" Charlie asked. "You two looked deep in conversation when I walked in."

"Just talking." Mitch decided to keep the conversation just between the two of them. Charlie would only assault Shane verbally, making him more defiant. Mitch was hoping Shane would have a change of heart.

A change only he could make.

Mitch, Charlie, and Shane visited with Beth throughout the afternoon. She had tried to put on a brave front, but had finally conceded to a stronger dose of pain medication, causing her to drift in and out of their conversations.

When an older nurse came in to check on Beth, she didn't look at all pleased. She turned to Mitch with a slight huff, and said, "Miss Justin really needs her rest. I think she would be a lot more comfortable without having company to entertain." She looked from Mitch, to Charlie, and then smiled at Shane. "Your mom is going to be fine, honey, but her body has been through a traumatic event. It's important that she gets her rest."

The nurse stood like a sentry next to Beth's bed until Mitch got to his feet and turned to Shane. "She's right. We should probably go." He turned back to Beth and brushed his hand across her forehead. When her eyes opened, he hunched over with a smile. "Beth, we're going to go now. You need your rest."

She gave him an anxious look and then turned to Shane, extending her hand to him. "Are you going to be all right?"

Shane stepped forward and squeezed her hand. "Yeah, Mom, I'm going to be fine. You just take care of yourself, okay?"

Beth nodded and waited for Shane to leave the room, then she turned to Mitch. "I'm worried about him, Mitch. Promise me you'll call if Shane acts . . . I don't know . . . weird or . . . off."

"He's going to be fine, Beth, but I'll call you if I have any concerns."

"Wait a minute, I don't have a phone anymore."

"I wrote down your bedside phone number. Don't worry, okay?" They exchanged reassuring smiles before Beth closed her eyes, drifting back to sleep.

Mitch swapped vehicles with Charlie in the hospital parking lot before heading home. Shane was a quiet passenger, which was fine with Mitch. He was exhausted and didn't feel much like talking. Especially if Shane brought up his father again. Mitch didn't trust himself to be civil, so he decided silence would have to do.

As Mitch neared the Diamond-J, he was surprised to see a band of kids walking alongside the road. Slowing down next to the gravel shoulder, Mitch leaned across Shane to peer out the open window.

"Where are you kids headed?"

"Home." One of the older boys answered politely.

"Where's home?" Mitch asked.

The teen pointed to a double-wide trailer and a newly framed house down the road from the Diamond-J.

"My condolences," Shane said in a sarcastic tone.

"Why do you say that?" The older boy chuckled, while Mitch gave Shane an irritated shove.

"Because you'll be bored out of your minds. I thought it was bad enough being born and raised here, but I feel sorry for you. You actually moved here."

"Hey," the teen said smiling, "we like Triune. In fact, Tom and I helped our dad scout out the property." The boy motioned to the teen who was obviously his twin brother. He stepped forward and introduced himself.

"Hi, I'm Tom Carter." He stuck his hand through the window and shook Shane's hand.

"Shane Justin," he said with a sturdy grip, "and this is Mitch."

Introductions were made all around, including a little redhead named Kat. Mitch watched as Shane sat up a little straighter, obviously interested in the girl with the timid smile.

After a few moments of conversation, everyone waved good-bye and said in a casual open-ended way, "see you around."

As Mitch pulled back on the highway, he watched Shane strain to catch another glimpse of the redheaded girl through the side mirror of the truck. Mitch smiled to himself. *Something tells me that won't be the last we see of the Carters.*

Travis was standing in the yard when Mitch pulled in. "Hey, how's Beth doing?" he asked as he removed his hat and wiped the sweat from his brow.

"She's lucky. That's what the doctor is saying," Mitch answered as he got out of the truck. "How are things here?"

"Fine. Everyone's fed and watered. Midas is having a hard time of it though. He senses something is wrong and has been irritated most of the afternoon."

"Where's Pandora?" Shane asked solemnly.

Travis looked at the ground, his hands planted on his waist. "I had Dr. Collins take care of her. I knew Beth wouldn't be home right away, and it wasn't something that could wait. Besides, she didn't need to see that."

Shane nodded. "I'll be in my room," he said to the both of them, before walking toward the house.

"Some lessons are hard to learn in life," Travis said to Mitch as they watched Shane walk away.

"Especially when you're just a kid."

Once in the house, Mitch looked around expecting to see Beth working in the kitchen or walking down the hall from her office. She was the lifeblood of the ranch and without her the place felt empty. When there was a crash upstairs, Mitch decided he'd better go investigate.

Peeking into Shane's room, Mitch watched as he righted the chair in the corner. "You okay?"

"Yeah."

Mitch figured he had kicked it over, venting his anger, frustration, or hurt. He wasn't sure which.

"Okay, well, I need to take a shower, so I'll be downstairs if you need me."

"Fine."

Mitch was ready to say something more but decided against it. He realized Shane needed to work things out for himself, so he turned to leave.

"That's it? You're not going to lecture me or tell me what a horrible person I am?"

Mitch turned back around. "You're not a horrible person, Shane. Besides, what good would that do? You don't need me telling you what to do or how to feel. No one can make up your mind for you, except you. If you're convinced finding a complete stranger is going to change your life for the better, then go for it. My only concern is your mom. She doesn't need that kind of stress right now."

"I told you I would wait until I could make Mom understand why I need to do this . . . or at least until she was feeling better."

"Yeah, that's more like it. I don't care how long you wait, she's never going to understand why you would want to meet the man who threatened her and beat her up." Mitch walked away, knowing if he discussed it with Shane any longer, they would end up in an argument. And right now, he just didn't have the energy.

After his shower, Mitch decided to use Beth's computer to check on some of his accounts and investments. He also e-mailed Jerry to let him know he was okay, but not to expect him back anytime soon. Mitch could only imagine the string of expletives his agent would use when he got that e-mail, but it didn't matter. Mitch was sure he'd found the life he was searching for in the middle of Kansas. Even though he was turning his back on Hollywood, Mitch would be forever grateful for the adventure and the financial benefits stardom would afford him in the future. It might have led to his personal meltdown, but it also led him to the woman who was quickly becoming the most important thing in his life.

When he was done checking his accounts, Mitch began surfing the Internet, clicking from one entertainment website to another. Sure enough, his disappearance was still making headlines. Most sites had him in an undisclosed rehab facility, though none of the tabloids could agree on what addiction he was fighting.

Mitch was clicking through a sports website when an idea struck him. Opening Beth's history file, Mitch looked at sites she'd been frequenting. Several real estate listings filled the column. He clicked on a few of them, tracing Beth's steps through home listings and property investments in the Wichita and Topeka areas when he stumbled across the listing for the Diamond-J. Of course, it wasn't listed as the Diamond-J. It was under the heading of investments and property acquisitions, but the description was undeniably that of Beth's ranch.

All the specifics were listed: working cattle ranch, acreage, number of buildings, heads of cattle, and other particulars, but it did not disclose its exact location. It only gave the realtor's number and stated interested buyers could contact the agent for further information.

Mitch felt his stomach tighten. The thought of Beth selling her family homestead, her heritage, the land she loved, seemed so unfair. He wanted to take Shane by the shoulders and shake some sense into the kid. Someone needed to make Shane see the sacrifice his mom would be making. A decision that could not be taken back after a deal was signed.

Mitch was halfway up the stairs to talk some sense into Shane when he stopped. It wasn't his place to interfere. He needed to recognize where he stood in the situation. Though Mitch's feelings for Beth had long surpassed friendship—and he would like to think she felt the same way—he knew coming between Beth and Shane would be a no win situation. All Mitch could do is hope that somehow, someway, things would begin to turn around.

Chapter Twenty-Five

The next morning, Mitch shuffled in from his trailer and headed for the downstairs bathroom. As he was brushing his teeth, Shane leaned against the doorway.

"Hey, I was thinking I should stick around here and give Travis and Uncle Charlie a hand. Do you think Mom will understand if I don't visit her?"

"As long as that's your reason," Mitch answered, finishing up at the sink and moving past Shane.

"What do you mean by that?"

"You're not avoiding her, are you?"

"No. I just thought I could be a bigger help if I was here." Shane glanced away and shook his head. "It was hard, seeing her in that much pain." His voice cracked with emotion.

Mitch was glad to see Shane wasn't completely unaffected by the seriousness of Beth's condition.

"Yeah, it was, but don't worry," he tried to sound upbeat, "your mom's tough. She's going to be fine."

"She'll understand, right? I mean, Uncle Charlie and Travis can't run the ranch all by themselves."

"I'll make sure she understands." Mitch put a hand on Shane's shoulder and gave it a squeeze. "And I think Charlie and Travis will appreciate the extra help."

When Mitch pulled from the gravel drive an hour later, he glanced across the way to the open field where construction was going on. He turned Beth's truck around and drove down the long rutted road.

"Good afternoon." A man that looked to be in his late forties walked over to where Mitch had come to a stop.

"Your house is shaping up really nice." Mitch got out of the truck, tugged his hat down close to his brow, and shook the man's hand. "I'm Mitch. I'm from the Diamond-J across the way."

"Hank." He answered, his grip firm and strong. "My boys said they met you yesterday, said you have a son about their age."

"Shane's not my son," Mitch clarified.

"Sorry. I guess I just assumed." The man acted sheepish with his blunder. Mitch allowed the comment to pass.

"Actually, it was Tom and Tim I was hoping to talk to, but I guess I should talk to you first."

"About what?"

"We could use some extra help on the Diamond-J. I was wondering if they would be interested in a side job, that is until your ranch is up and running?"

"What finds you needin' help?"

"Well, we had to let a few hands go, and now Beth—she's the proprietor of the ranch—is in the hospital with a busted leg."

Before Mitch could say anymore, Tom came out from around the side of the trailer and walked up to the two men.

"Hi, Mitch, what brings you here?"

"He was seeing if you boys would be interested in picking up some work," his fathered answered.

"Sure." Tom answered almost immediately. Mitch liked the kid's enthusiasm. He was agreeing to work without even knowing what he was being asked to do.

"Well, I wanted to make sure it was okay with your dad first. I didn't want to pull you away from any projects he needs your help with."

"Actually, we're waiting on an inspection before we can do much more to the house. I have a few odd jobs I need to get done, but nothing I can't do on my own," Hank volunteered as Tim walked up to the group.

"What's up?"

"Mitch is looking for some help." Tom filled him in.

"Sure. It would be better than sitting around here waiting for that stupid inspector."

"Okay then." Mitch perked up. "I'm on my way to the hospital, but you can go on over. You'll probably find Shane in the stables. He'll be able to tell you what needs to be done."

"The hospital?" Tim blurted out.

"Shane's mom—the owner of the ranch—had a riding accident. Her horse went down, landing on top of her. Beth was pinned to the ground and got pretty banged up. A busted leg. Broken ribs. A concussion. Her mount was worse, and had to be put down."

"That's quite a list of injuries," Hank said with concern.

"I know," Mitch nodded in agreement. "Thankfully, her doctor feels she'll be home in a few days. It will be slow going for a while, but Beth is a tough lady. She's not going to let this stop her. But I think she'll feel better knowing the ranch isn't being neglected while she's gone."

Mitch heard the emotion in his voice just speaking about Beth, and realized it didn't go unnoticed by the other three men. He dipped his head, but was unable to hide his smile.

"Boys, why don't you go tell your mom where you're going and what you'll be up to."

When Tim and Tom walked away, Mitch sensed a bit of tension coming from the senior Carter.

"Look, Hank, if this is an imposition, I completely understand."

"No," the older man waved his hand like it was no bother, "but, at the risk of sounding judgmental—'cause your business is your own—I would like to better understand the arrangement you have with the boy's mother. I don't mean to pry or come off as condescending. It's just that my wife and I have conservative views regarding relationships. That doesn't mean our boys don't know what goes on in the world, but I would prefer they not be influenced by a lifestyle we don't agree with."

Mitch could tell Hank was choosing his words cautiously, and respected the man for being direct. He'd obviously done a good job raising his family and didn't want the ethics he'd taught his kids to be challenged by a complete stranger.

"It's a long story as to how I ended up on the Diamond-J, but just so you know, I live in my Airstream that's parked in the yard. Though I have deep affection for Beth, she is a strong Christian woman who lives by high standards of her own."

"And how does she feel about you?"

Mitch gave a slight shrug. "I would like to think she feels the same way, but we still have some things to work through."

Hank nodded, but his gaze remained intense.

Mitch shifted uncomfortably.

"I'm sorry for staring. I just can't get over the fact that I feel like I've met you before. You look so familiar. Yet I can't put my finger on it."

"Believe me, I get that all the time." Mitch played it off coolly.

When Mitch walked into Beth's hospital room, she smiled at him, then looked over his shoulder toward the door. Her smile faded.

"If you're looking for Shane, he stayed home. He feels responsible for the work load at the ranch and wanted to do his part," Mitch said as he moved to her bedside and bent to place a tender kiss on her forehead, bandage and all.

Beth blushed at his intimate gesture, then sighed, "He hates me."

"He doesn't hate you," Mitch chuckled as he took a seat next to her bed and placed his hat on the cap of his knee.

"What am I going to do, Mitch? Now that Shane knows about Cole, he's not going to let it rest." Beth's face was strained with concern.

"He's going to have questions he needs answered, but he's a good kid, Beth, and Shane loves you. You've got to believe that." Mitch had no intention of telling Beth about his conversation with Shane. There was no sense worrying her further.

Shane was in the barn when he heard noise in the yard. Shielding his eyes against the sun, he watched as the Carter brothers got off a quad and walked toward him.

"What are you guys doing here?" Shane asked as he shuffled forward.

"Mitch stopped by and asked if we'd be interested in some extra work, so here we are," one of them volunteered. "It's Tom, by the way, in case you forgot," he said as he took a slow look around.

"Why?" Shane asked dumbfounded.

"Why not?" Tim looked at him perplexed and waited for an answer. "Hey, if you don't want the help, that's fine, but—"

"No. It's cool. I just didn't know Mitch talked to you."

"He told us about your mom being in the hospital," Tim commented. "That has to be rough."

"What did he tell you?" Shane had to bite back the belligerence he was feeling.

"That she was thrown from her horse and broke her leg."

"Yeah, she'll be there a few more days." Shane's thoughts turned inward. He kept picturing his mom in the cold, sterile hospital bed, and the pain she was in because of him. It made him feel sick inside.

"So," Tom clapped his hands and rubbed them together with energy, "what can we do?"

In just a few hours' time, Shane, Tim, and Tom had completely mucked out the stables and were almost done laying fresh hay. Uncle Charlie and Travis had come by to check on things and seemed surprised to see Shane hard at work. Shane made introductions all around and listened as Tim and Tom spoke about their new home with enthusiasm and excitement. He didn't get it. They were moving to the boondocks and were actually excited about it when all Shane could think about was getting out.

Even though Shane and the Carters didn't agree on how or where they wanted to live, it was still nice talking with guys his own age. Whenever Shane hung out with Lucas and Curtis, they were always plotting or scheming some stupid plan that would get them into trouble. But Tom and Tim were different. They talked all morning about music, movies, sports, even girls. They debated the pros and cons of baseball's designated hitter and differed in their movie likes and dislikes, but overall Shane felt instant camaraderie with the twins. In fact, the three of them had gotten so caught up talking and working, Shane took a double-take when he looked at his watch; it was almost noon.

"Hey, why don't we go inside and see what I can find for lunch," Shane suggested.

Tim was leaning on his pitchfork as Tom wheeled an empty barrow to the other side of the stable.

"Sounds good to me. I'm not picky," Tom said.

The three of them started toward the house when a swirl of dust kicked up by yet another ATV got their attention. Tim and Tom obviously knew who it was, but Shane strained to figure it out. He was stunned to see the cute redhead come to a stop, step off the quad, and unfasten a milk crate attached to the back of the ATV. She approached the three of them, casually glancing at Shane, as she walked toward Tom.

"Mom had me bring over lunch," she said, before turning to Shane. "She was sorry to hear about your mom's accident and wanted to help out."

"Here, let me take that for you." Shane quickly stepped closer and reached for the crate.

She gave him an appreciative smile.

After a few moments of awkward silence, she moved toward her quad.

"You could stay and join us if you want. That way you can take the crate back when we're done." Shane regretted saying anything the minute the words were out of his mouth. His reason was lame and he'd spoken so fast, it made him sound desperate.

"I can't. Mom is expecting me back home. Besides, Tim or Tom can bring the crate home when they're done." She mounted the quad and started the engine with the push of a button. "But thanks for the invite."

She smiled coyly at him before looping around and heading back down the driveway, Shane watching her all the way.

"I would ask you what you're thinking, but I'm not quite sure I want to know." Tim gave Shane a playful slug to the arm before taking the crate from him and moving toward the house. "After all, she is my sister."

"What are you talking about? I was just being polite."

"Oh, is that what you call it?"

Tim and Tom continued to joke and tease until the three of them were in the house. Shane ignored their comments as he grabbed three sodas from the refrigerator. All he could think about was the way Kat looked as she roared down the driveway.

When the three of them took seats at the dining room table, Shane watched as Tim and Tom bowed in silent prayer. When they were done, Tim turned to Shane and asked, "So, what's your story?"

"What do you mean?"

"Have you lived here your whole life?"

"If you can call it that," Shane said sarcastically as he swigged his soda.

"Why the negativity?"

"What's there to be positive about? I live in the middle of nowhere, with no friends, and nothing to do for fun."

"What about school?"

"Oh yeah, that's fun. I have to leave at six in the morning, ride the bus, go to classes, and turn around and get back on the bus for another hour. The school is so small it doesn't have a football team or a baseball team. And last year, the gym got messed up when a tornado touched down and took off its roof, so we didn't have basketball all year either. I have chores before I leave and chores when I get home. By the time I get done with homework and dinner, it's time to crash. Not exactly what I call fun. But that's okay. This year things are going to be different. If everything goes as planned, we'll be out of here by the end of the year."

"You're moving?"

"Yep," Shane said with a grin, excited it was finally going to happen.

"Is it because of your mom's accident?" Tim asked.

"No. If it was up to her, we would never leave. This is her family's property. The "J" in Diamond-J, stands for Justin. It's been in her family for over a hundred years."

"Then why move?" Tom asked.

"Because it's dumb," Shane said defensively. "She's a woman running a ranch on her own. Well, not completely on her own. Uncle Charlie and Travis help, but they shouldn't have to."

Tim looked at him confused.

"Uncle Charlie is getting too old to ride and rope the herd, even if he won't admit it," Shane explained, "and Travis has a wife and two little girls. They shouldn't be forced to live in a place where the only things to play with are rocks and twigs. They should live in the city where there are parks and Girl Scouts and things like that."

"Don't you think that's their decision to make?" Tom asked.

"Yeah, you're right. Just like I've decided to get out while I can. I want to live a normal life, in a normal neighborhood, getting to do normal things. I want to try out for the football team and hang out with friends. I want to get my own car and be able to drive something besides a tractor or a twenty-year-old pickup truck."

Tim shrugged as if he didn't see the point, but was willing to let it go. "So, what happened to your dad?"

Shane clenched his jaw in anger. "He ditched my mom before I was born." Standing up abruptly, Shane walked to the kitchen and tossed the rest of his lunch in the trash. "I need to check the well on the north side. You guys can come if you want, but don't feel like you have to." Shane slammed the screen door, punctuating the end of their conversation.

Mitch stepped into the hallway to give Beth some privacy. The therapist needed to help her get settled back into bed, and since there was no easy or modest way to do that, he volunteered to step outside.

It had been painful for Mitch to watch Beth grimace her way through the therapy session. With crutches under both arms, she maneuvered awkwardly around the room, trying to get a feel for the crutches. The therapist assured Beth it would get easier with time, but Beth's uneven steps, and the frustrated look on her face, clearly expressed her doubts.

When the door swung open, the therapist stepped outside and smiled at Mitch. "You can go back in now," she said, then stared at him like she had something more to say.

Mitch knew the look all too well.

"Has anyone ever told you, you look like Simon Grey, the actor?"

"Yeah, I get that a lot. Makes me feel sorry for the guy." Mitch tried to defuse her interest with humor.

"Believe me," she smirked at him with a little too much admiration, "you have nothing to be sorry about."

Mitch smiled politely, then quickly disappeared inside Beth's room, wondering how long he would be able to keep up his charade.

Approaching Beth's bed, he saw her eyes were closed and her cheeks were flush from exertion. Mitch tried to be quiet as he moved the chair closer to her bed, but Beth turned toward him and opened her eyes.

"You look beat," he said.

"I feel beat," she sighed, closing her eyes.

Mitch reached for the television controller attached to the bed rail and clicked it on. Then he turned his chair slightly and stretched his legs out in front of him.

"You don't need to stay," Beth said in a near whisper.

"Are you giving me the brush off?" he asked teasingly.

"No. It just seems ridiculous for you to waste your time here."

"Being in the bedroom of a beautiful woman is *never* a waste of time."

Beth looked at him, clearly stunned.

Mitch laughed as he reached for her hand and brought it to his lips. "You're cute when you're speechless, you know that?"

She pulled back her hand and tossed the small tissue box from the bed tray at him, clipping him on the shoulder. "And you can be such a pill."

"Would that be the pill that makes you feel all better?" he said with a bouncing brow and a warm kiss to her reclaimed hand.

"How about the kind of pill that gets stuck at the back of your throat and no matter how hard you try to wash it away, it just stays there and pesters you."

Mitch stood and leaned over the bedrail, brushing back a dampened curl from her forehead—a testimony to Beth's exhaustion. "You do look pretty worn out. Maybe I should go so you can get some rest."

Mitch placed a gentle kiss against Beth's brow and wished her sweet dreams. She closed her eyes, so she wouldn't have to watch him walk away. Beth hadn't wanted him to leave but knew it was for the best. Mitch was getting way too comfortable with her—his tender gestures more and more intimate.

But it wasn't all his fault.

Beth's resilience was weakening, and she found herself craving the feel of his touch. She was allowing her commitment to God to blur and needed to put some distance between Mitch and her before lines were crossed.

A tear trailed down the side of Beth's face, wetting her ear. *God, what am I going to do? I know this feeling, and I know it's wrong. How could you let me fall in love with Mitch—knowing he doesn't know you?*

It might have been only a month since Mitch landed on the Diamond-J, but to Beth it felt like a lifetime. So many things had happened since he arrived. Shane's rebellion, Brett's assault, and Beth's decision to sell a piece of her heart. Mitch had talked her through each situation and had come to Beth's defense when he thought she was in danger.

Beth had done her best to avoid time alone with Mitch after their shared kiss. And had been successful. Even so, there were so many other qualities she appreciated about Mitch, qualities she couldn't help but find attractive. His work ethic was phenomenal. He worked hard from dawn to dusk and did it with such enthusiasm. No task was too difficult or too dirty. Mitch had told her on more than one occasion, he was convinced this is what he was meant to do in life. Even Uncle Charlie and Travis sang Mitch's praises and were beginning to treat him like one of the family.

And then there were Mitch's late-night talks with Shane. They were like a balm to Beth's weary soul. Mitch was connecting with her son on a level deeper than she, Uncle Charlie, or Travis had ever been able to forge. Even though there were times she was nervous about the subject matter of their conversations, Beth came to realize putting her head in the sand would not prevent Shane from growing up. He had the hormones of a teenager and needed answers to questions, no matter how awkward or uncomfortable they were.

She'd had a few freak-out moments when Mitch mentioned some of the topics they had discussed, but he promised Beth he would never encourage Shane to do anything contrary to her conservative beliefs. Of course, Mitch also said he wouldn't shy away from controversial issues. Shane needed to know about sex, STD's, and other subjects that were hot topics among teenagers. Mitch explained to Beth that he'd made lots of mistakes and taken stupid risks when he was young because he hadn't thought through the ramifications of his actions. Now, Mitch could talk to Shane openly and honestly as the voice of experience.

Mitch also reminded Beth that Shane was a good-looking kid. When they move to the city—and he attends a larger high school—Shane would be flooded with every choice, temptation, and proposition imaginable. The current youth culture thought nothing of binge drinking, experimenting with drugs, and sexual exploration. Kids today thought they were invincible. Mitch's goal was to make sure Shane understood the very real consequences that came with recreational drinking, drugs, or sex of any kind.

How could I not be attracted to a man who has invested so much time in Shane and the Diamond-J? They are the two most important things in my life, besides my relationship with God.

And there was the rub.

Once again, Beth was contemplating a relationship with a man because she felt the pangs of desire and attraction. She wanted to believe in the man who had invested hours working her land and talking to her son, even though the tabloids painted a completely different picture of the same man.

Didn't the fiasco with Cole teach you anything? She scolded herself. *Men will do whatever it takes to make you feel special. Sure, Mitch has been good to you while he's been here, and yes, everyone thinks he's a great guy. But you know in your heart of hearts Mitch isn't right for you. You just think he is because you're tired and lonely.*

I can't do this to myself.

Not again.

Chapter Twenty-Six

Mitch left the hospital feeling confused, even a bit disheartened. The way he felt about Beth was more powerful than anything he had ever felt before. It wasn't just passion, though he'd spent many nights lying awake, his mind drifting to places it shouldn't have gone. Even so, it was more than that. Beth was special. Her unique balance between strength and vulnerability fascinated him, but it was witnessing her quiet faith that completely captivated him.

Mitch thought back over his life and how he had always felt alone, never deserving of love. Even after moving to California with Richard, he felt an overwhelming need to be successful in order to pay Richard back for believing in him. Once stardom hit, Mitch convinced himself, he would never be lonely again. He dated beautiful women, attended lavish parties, and traveled to exotic locations. Mitch was living the dream, but deep down inside, he still felt empty. Vacant.

He didn't see that vacancy in Beth. Even with all she'd gone through in life—even in the last month—somehow Beth was still living. Not just surviving, but living. Beth fought for her son, for her ranch, and for everything she believed to be important.

Mitch knew it was Beth's relationship with God that buoyed her, encouraged her to never give up, and calmed her at the end of a rough day. Mitch not only admired the relationship she had, he envied it.

These thoughts continued to swirl through Mitch's mind as he carefully maneuvered undetected through the grocery store.

Mitch was still in a reflective mood when he got home. After carrying the first load of groceries into the house, he headed back to the truck. That's when he saw Shane ride into the yard, Tim and Tom trailing behind him on an ATV.

"Why are you home so early?" Shane asked as he hopped down from Apollo's back. "Is Mom okay?"

"She's a little sore. The physical therapist had her up on crutches today. She was pretty wiped out when I left."

Shane looked dejected, pushing dirt around with the toe of his boot.

"She's going to be fine, Shane. I just figured if I left early, she could get some more rest. So, tell me, what have you guys been up to?"

The three boys filled Mitch in on the work they had gotten done.

"Then you must be hungry. Help me carry these groceries inside, then I'll get started on dinner. You boys are welcome to stay. I've got plenty. That's what happens when you shop on an empty stomach."

"Actually," Shane spoke up, "Mrs. Carter invited me over for dinner, if that's okay with you?"

"Sure, if you want to. I mean, I was going to barbeque some steaks, but I guess we can have them another night."

Mitch couldn't believe how domesticated he sounded. He actually was disappointed Shane wouldn't be spending the evening with him, something he'd grown accustomed to.

"Is something wrong, Mitch?" Shane turned serious. "What aren't you telling me?"

Mitch realized his melancholy mood was worrying Shane.

"No. Nothing's wrong. Everything's fine." Mitch assured him with a smile. "Go ahead to the Carter's. I have some work to do anyway."

"You sure you're okay? You look kind of . . . lost."

Mitch smiled, trying to mask his mood. "No, I'm fine. Just tired, I guess. Go on. Your mom will be glad you're making new friends."

"Do you mind if I take the truck?"

"Does your mom let you drive without a license?"

"I'm just going across the street."

Mitch thought about it for a moment. "Okay, just make sure you bring it back in one piece."

"No problem."

Mitch grabbed the last of the groceries before tossing Shane the keys.

When he was done putting away the refrigerator items, Mitch grabbed a soda, then sat down in front of Beth's computer and did some surfing. He checked the e-mail account he'd set up earlier and saw the inbox loaded with mail from Jerry. Mitch knew he needed to call him; he just wasn't looking forward to the explosion of questions. It didn't matter. Jerry wouldn't be able to change his mind. Mitch knew what he wanted, and no one was going to tell him differently.

He reached for the phone alongside the computer and dialed the number Jerry had included in every e-mail.

"Jerry, it's Mitch."

"Well . . . it's about time!"

Mitch listened as Jerry unloaded on him. He cussed and yelled, asking Mitch numerous questions but not giving him a chance to respond to any of them. Mitch waited for him to lose his head of steam before saying anything.

"Are you done?" Mitch finally asked.

"Yeah, I'm done. Are you done finding yourself? Because I have a hefty contract here from Entertainment Nightly asking for an exclusive when you resurface."

There was no way to cushion this. Mitch just had to say it. "Jerry, I'm not coming back."

"What do you mean you're not coming back?"

"Just what I said. I'm done."

"Simon, come on, you're not done. In fact, your little disappearing act has put your name on the lips of every entertainment show and tabloid reporter from coast to coast."

"I don't care, Jerry. I've found what I'm looking for."

"What are you talking about? Oh, I get it . . . you found a woman, is that it? Bring her along. You'll be able to give her anything she could possibly want. Your stock is through the roof. From here on

JUST AN ACT

out, you're going to be able to write your own ticket."

"Jerry, I'm sorry. I know you're disappointed—and I appreciate everything you've done for me and my career—but this is the end for me."

"No . . . no, I can't accept that. Give yourself a little more time to think this through. Don't call it quits. Not yet. You might be having fun now, but it won't be long before you're itching to be back in front of the camera. Being a nobody isn't going to agree with you."

"You're wrong, Jerry. I'm sorry."

Mitch hung up the phone, even though Jerry was still begging him to reconsider. His agent would be mad for a while, but it wouldn't last, nothing in Hollywood did. Jerry would forget all about Simon Grey the minute a hot new heartthrob walked through his door, looking for representation.

Free.

That's what he was . . . free.

Leaning back in the desk chair, he looked out the office window to the open field. Mitch inhaled the musty scent he'd grown used to after weeks of working the ranch. And when he closed his eyes, he saw Beth with her sassy smile, and her tattered hat pulled low across her forehead.

This is what I want.

Mitch felt transformed. Not only was Hollywood out of the picture, but alcohol was as well. Not since the day after Shane had found them tangled together in the bathroom had Mitch had a drink. A month wasn't a huge record by any stretch of the imagination, but Mitch knew it was going to last. Alcohol was no longer a crutch he needed to lean on, or where he wanted to turn when life got hard. Besides, all Mitch had to do was imagine the disappointment and hurt in Beth's eyes if he went back to drinking. That was enough to keep him sober.

Although Mitch wasn't kidding himself into thinking there still wouldn't be obstacles, hard days, and difficult choices ahead, he was up to the challenge. He wanted to be there for Beth, and for Shane. Mitch wanted to be someone they could count on.

After his time of introspection, Mitch opened his eyes and saw Beth's Bible sitting on the corner of her desk. He picked it up and started thumbing through it. The pages were worn and many of the margins were filled with notes. Mitch took it with him to the kitchen where he grabbed another soda, then moved to the den and sunk down on the couch.

Mitch leafed through the well-worn book, having no idea where to begin. He wasn't completely unfamiliar with the Bible. He knew it didn't read like a novel, so he didn't have to start in the beginning. However, Mitch had no idea how to find the answers to his questions.

Seeing Beth's bookmark, Mitch decided he might as well start there. *The Gospel According to John* was written in bold print. The first page was an introduction, like in a script. It was letting the reader know who the players were, the time frame, setting the scene, even the plot. It was entitled Theological Message. However, it was the first few sentences that grabbed his attention.

John is both the simplest and the most profound of the Gospels. Its language is so pure and simple, that beginning readers are almost always directed to read John first.

Mitch had found his place to start.

It was almost midnight when Shane got home. He glanced at the microwave pizza box sitting on the kitchen counter and noticed lights were still on in the den. When he rounded the corner, Shane saw Mitch sprawled out on the couch, his mother's Bible in his hand.

"What are you doing?" Shane asked inquisitively.

"Figuring a few things out," Mitch answered as he continued to read. Finally, he looked up at Shane. "So, how was dinner?"

"Good."

"And the company?"

Shane leaned against the wall and nodded his approval. "Tim and Tom are okay guys. We have a lot in common."

"What about the rest of the family? I met their dad when I went to ask Tim and Tom about working. He seemed like a pretty straight arrow."

"Yeah, he is, but friendly. His wife is, too. Mrs. Carter assured me I was welcome anytime. She also told me to come and get her if Mom needed help to get situated, or with any chores once she was home."

"That was nice."

"Yeah, like I said, they're real nice people." Shane plopped down in one of the side chairs. "So, what are you doing?" he asked again, looking at his mom's Bible in Mitch's hand.

"I'm looking for answers. I see something in your mom, something different. It's hard to explain, but I know it has to do with her faith. I'm just trying to make some sense of it."

"You're sure it's not just Mom that has you all hot and bothered?"

Mitch smiled. "I'm not going to lie. I have feelings for your mom—deep feelings. But nothing can come of it if I don't get my life straightened out. I'm not going to become just one more battlefield for her to deal with. I know this is important to Beth," Mitch said, holding up her Bible, "and if it's not important to me, we're not going to have common ground. I've been in enough relationships to know two individuals do not make a couple. If you only care about yourself and your own interests, it never lasts. I won't hurt Beth like that. She deserves better."

"So, just ask Mom. I'm sure she'd be willing to help you."

"No, I've got to do this for myself. I don't want her to think the only reason I'm interested in God is to appease her."

"But that's the truth, right? The reason you're looking for answers is so you can get on her good side. You know Mom won't give you the time of day if you're not a Christian. The whole "unequally yoked" thing," Shane said with air quotes. He knew he was being judgmental, but didn't care. He might like Mitch—and appreciated having him around—but Shane wasn't going to stand by and watch as Mitch put the moves on his mom. "So, this is your angle to soften her up? Act interested in God?"

"It's not an angle or an act, Shane. Believe it or not, I respect Beth's commitment to her faith. She's an incredible woman who has experienced some really hard knocks in life. But she doesn't allow obstacles to slow her down. Even though life doesn't play by the rules, Beth doesn't change the way she plays the game. She has a solid foundation, and more guts and strength than I've ever had. Beth's beautiful on the outside, there's no denying that, but it's her inner strength and tenacity that makes her so attractive."

"Whatever," Shane said flippantly.

"Hey!" Mitch snapped at him. "Where is all this hostility coming from?"

"I just don't want to see my mom get hurt."

"Really? This coming from the kid who's willing to sacrifice his relationship with his mom, while he chases after a father who cares nothing about him."

"That's not fair!"

"Fair? You think it's fair that Beth is ready to sell everything she has—to sacrifice her heart and soul—just to make you happy? You're taking her for granted, Shane. I hope you see that before it's too late."

They locked eyes in a stand-off of emotion, but Shane was determined to have the last word.

"I might not have a father, but that doesn't mean I'm looking for one in Cole Dempsey . . . or in you. So, you can keep your little speeches to yourself. I love my mom and I never meant to hurt her. But what I choose to do in the future—with my future—is none of your business."

Mitch listened as Shane took the steps two at a time, punctuating his anger by slamming his bedroom door.

He groaned, letting his head fall back against the couch cushion. *So this is what it's like talking to a teenager.* Mitch hadn't meant to pick a fight with Shane, and he certainly didn't want to live with tension between them. Determined to be the bigger man, Mitch decided to apologize. He climbed the stairs and rapped on Shane's bedroom door.

"Save it, Mitch," Shane yelled from inside.

Mitch pushed the door opened anyway and saw Shane hovering over the bathroom sink, brushing his teeth. He tossed a glance at Mitch, swished water around in his mouth, and spit before turning off the bathroom light. He leaned against the doorjamb, his arms crossed against his chest. "What? Did you have something else to lecture me on?"

"No. I came to apologize. You're right. I'm not your dad; I had no business telling you off like that." Mitch took a step forward and extended his hand. "Truce?"

Shane stared at Mitch's outstretched hand a moment before shaking it silently.

"I'm sorry, Shane. It's just so hard for me to stand back and watch you make some of the same mistakes I did. I'm not trying to tell you what to do; I'm just trying to warn you what *not* to do. Bitterness is a powerful poison, but the only person it eats away at is you. Your father doesn't feel your pain, or your hurt, but that same pain and hurt is tearing you up inside."

When Mitch realized he was lecturing again, he quickly threw up his hands in surrender. "Sorry. I'll stop." Turning toward the hall he said, "I'll be heading to the hospital early tomorrow. Did you want to go?"

"No. Tim and Tom are coming over again. We're getting a lot done, and I would feel better knowing I was getting the ranch in shape."

"Okay. Then I guess I'll see you tomorrow. Goodnight."

Chapter Twenty-Seven

When Mitch heard Shane moving around upstairs, he glanced at his watch and realized time had gotten away from him. "Shoot! How'd that happen?" He finished what he was doing on the computer and hurried to the kitchen.

With Beth in the hospital, Mitch had taken on the chore of making breakfast each morning. He didn't do much. Usually, it was just toast or sometimes eggs, but he knew Beth would appreciate his efforts. It also gave Mitch a chance to catch up with Shane.

But today was different. Mitch had been up before dawn tapping away on Beth's computer. He had tossed and turned all night with an idea that wouldn't let him rest, so he got up early to work on it. Now he was behind schedule.

He had just filled the toaster with four slices of bread when Shane walked into the kitchen.

"Why were you up so early?" Shane asked as he pulled a carton of orange juice from the refrigerator and poured himself a glass.

"I had some fan mail to answer," Mitch teased.

"Very funny." Shane took a seat at the bar just as the toast popped up.

Mitch put two slices of bread on a plate and slid it in front of Shane. He passed Shane the jar of strawberry jam while he opted for plain old butter.

"Should I plan on bringing something home for dinner, or will you be at the Carter's?" It was a dumb question. Every night since Beth ended up in the hospital, Mitch had gotten used to coming home to an empty house, a note on the table telling him Shane was at the

Carter's.

"I'll probably be hanging out with Tim and Tom, but how about picking up some Pop Tarts for breakfast. That way you won't have to slave over a hot toaster."

"Ha-ha. Aren't you quick-witted this morning."

Shane just smiled.

Mitch finished his toast and set his plate in the sink. "I'll see you later," he said as he headed for the door. "Call me if anything comes up."

Shane gave him a nod before Mitch pushed open the screen door and hurried down the front steps. When he looked to his left, he saw Charlie approaching. Walking over to the gate, Mitch dragged it open then closed it behind Hammer as Charlie dismounted.

"Headed to the hospital?" Charlie asked.

"Yeah."

"How's she doing?"

"You know Beth, she thinks everyone is fussing over nothing. I don't think she's willing to admit how serious her injuries were."

"Yeah. Beth's pretty stubborn."

"In more ways than one," Mitch mumbled.

Charlie tipped his hat back. "Something I should know about?"

Mitch shook his head. "No. It's me."

Charlie studied him for a moment, his look thoughtful. "Just give her some space, Mitch. She'll come around."

"What are you talking about?"

"I'm old Mitch, not stupid. I know that look. Of course, the first time I saw it, I wanted to knock it off your face and tell you to get lost. But now that I've gotten to know you a little better, I'm willing to cut you a little slack."

"I appreciate that."

"But . . . if you hurt Beth . . . I promise you, I'll have you hanged, drawn, and quartered."

Mitch chuckled, even though he felt discouraged. "I'm not sure you have anything to worry about. Just about the time I think Beth is ready to admit she has feelings for me, she pulls back. I'm not sure she's going to let me in."

Charlie sighed. "You gotta understand, Mitch, Cole used her in the most despicable way. She was blindsided. Devastated. Her self-esteem was in shambles when he left. She trusted him, above her father, above her faith; then he betrayed her. It's going to be hard for her to trust again. Just give her some time. Let her take things at her own pace. Like I said, she'll come around."

Mitch looked at Charlie and smiled. "Let me get this straight, you're actually *giving* me advice on how to woo your niece?"

The old man scratched the back of his neck and shrugged. "I guess I am."

"Why?"

He looked at Mitch. "Because you're good for her . . . and for Shane." Charlie walked a little closer and put his hand on Mitch's shoulder. He gave it a firm squeeze—a *I have a point to make* squeeze. "Besides, as far as the world's concern, you've disappeared. It will make it easier for me to get rid of your body if you screw up." Charlie just laughed as he tipped his hat and walked Hammer over to the barn.

Mitch knew Charlie was only kidding.

Well . . . he was ninety percent sure.

Mitch left the hospital more excited than he'd been in a long time. After five painstaking days in the hospital, Beth would be released tomorrow. Finally, she would be coming home.

Home where she belonged.

Mitch stopped at the market, the florist, and a few other places before heading to the ranch. He planned on welcoming Beth home in style.

Figuring he would be coming home to an empty house, Mitch was surprised to see a quad by the barn and a light on in the toolshed. Walking toward the shed, he expected to find Shane and one of the Carter boys. But as he got closer, Mitch heard the soft whispers of a female voice.

When Mitch peered around the corner, he saw Shane standing

dangerously close to a girl—the redhead—her hand in his.

"Hu-hum." Mitch cleared his throat to get their attention.

The redhead's back was to the door, but when she heard Mitch, she quickly snatched her hand from Shane's and spun around, her complexion crimson.

"Mitch, hi, I didn't hear you pull up," Shane said.

"I guess not," Mitch raised his brow and smiled.

"Mitch, this is Kat, Tim and Tom's sister. Remember?"

"I remember. Hi Kat, I'm Mitch Burk." He reached forward to shake her hand. She shook it and smiled shyly.

"I was helping Kat make something for her mother's birthday. She got a splinter, so I was just helping her get it out."

Kat voluntarily extended her irritated palm as proof. Mitch looked at Shane with a bit of a smirk, causing Shane to look away.

"Are you done out here?" Mitch asked.

Shane nodded.

"Then why don't you take her project into the house. I'm sure Beth has tweezers somewhere."

The three of them headed inside just as Tim and Tom drove into the yard. The two boys followed after them and joined Kat and Shane at the dining room table while Mitch walked to the kitchen to get the first-aid kit.

"Why are you so red? Are you sick?" Tim asked his sister.

"It's nothing, really," Kat said, clearly embarrassed by all the attention. "I just got a splinter when we were working on the box."

Tim turned her hand over in his. "How'd you do that? I thought Shane was going to do the box for you?"

"I was." Shane tried to defend himself. "But Kat wanted to learn how to use the plane. I was showing her how when she got the splinter."

Mitch extended the first-aid kit to Tim, who was evidently taking charge. "Here, there's some good tweezers in the tray. Since you have this under control, I'm going to grab my groceries." Mitch turned to Shane. "How about giving me a hand?"

Mitch watched as Shane looked at Kat, catching her eye. She gave him a timid smile before he walked away.

As they approached the truck, Shane shook his head. "Are you throwing a party, or what? You have enough groceries here to feed an army."

Mitch looked at the truck, loaded down with bags from the market, a florist, Wal-Mart, and a few other shops. "As a matter-of-fact, your mom gets to come home tomorrow, so I thought I would stock up."

Shane smiled. "That's good, right? I mean she must be doing better if they're letting her come home."

"She's doing much better. The doctor still doesn't know why she was running a fever, but she hasn't had one for a couple days now. She's still moving slow, but that's to be expected."

Shane grabbed a couple of bags. When he turned, Mitch had a hard time controlling his smile.

"What?" Shane asked defensively.

"I didn't say anything," Mitch chuckled.

"No, but you want to." Shane moved around to the side of the truck. "We weren't doing anything wrong, if that's what you're thinking. Like I said, we were working on a shadow box for her mom when Kat got a splinter."

"I didn't say you were doing anything wrong."

"No, but you have that look on your face."

"What look?" Mitch continued to tease.

"That look!" Shane snapped.

Mitch couldn't help but laugh at Shane's exasperation. "Come on, Shane." He kept his voice low as they scaled the porch steps. "I saw the way you were looking at her. You're hooked."

Mitch didn't give Shane a chance to say anything before he swung open the screen door. They carried the groceries into the house, past where Tim was working on Kat's hand. She let out a yelp, and gave her brother a shove. "That hurt!"

"I'm sorry, but I've got to make sure I get a good hold on it. I don't want it to break in two."

Shane hung back while Mitch retrieved the last of the groceries. Kat was standing at the kitchen sink running water over her hand, when Mitch set the last of the bags on the counter. "Did you get it?" he asked.

"Yes, thank you." Her voice was barely above a whisper. She dried her hands and hurried back to the dining room table where Tim was digging through the first-aid kit for the right size bandage.

Mitch put the groceries away while the kids worked on their project. When he was done, he joined them in the dining room and leaned over Shane's shoulder. "So, tell me again what you two are building."

"It's for my mother's birthday," Kat said. "It's the invitation from her and Dad's wedding, and some other little mementos. I'm mounting them in a shadow box."

"What a clever idea." Mitch watched Kat arrange and rearrange the wedding memorabilia on a piece of deep-blue velvet.

"I want it to look just right," she explained as she moved the same four pieces over and over again.

Returning to his own project, Mitch opened cupboard after cupboard looking for some kind of vase or container for the large bundle of flowers sitting in the sink.

"Hey, Shane, do you know if your mom has any vases?"

Shane looked up from the table. "I think she has some in the mudroom cabinet."

Mitch scrounged around in the utility cabinet, finding a few small vases but nothing big enough to hold all the flowers he'd bought. Grumbling his way back to the kitchen, Mitch went through the same cupboards again.

"Didn't you find one in the mudroom?" Shane asked.

"They're all too small. I need something bigger."

"Why don't you make a few different bouquets?" Kat suggested. "You could put them in Miss Justin's bedroom, in the den, even here on the table."

Mitch looked at the girl as she smiled sheepishly, blush once again filling her cheeks. "Would you be willing to give me a hand?"

"Sure." Her eyes brightened along with her smile. "I love flowers."

Kat moved to where the flowers were resting in the sink and unwrapped them. "My goodness, Mr. Burk, you have enough flowers here for four or five bouquets."

"Okay, then let me get some more vases."

"What are these?" Shane asked when Mitch walked back into the kitchen, vases in both hands. Shane held the stack of DVDs from one of the bags and began to list them off. "Two Weeks Notice, You've Got Mail, Maid in Manhattan . . ."

"I got them for your mom. She's going to have a lot of down time; something she's not used to. I thought she might enjoy watching some movies."

Shane continued to flip through the videos as if he was looking for something specific.

"What are you doing?" Mitch asked.

"I'm just seeing if you got anything with Simon Grey in it," Shane said casually.

Mitch threw a dish towel, hitting Shane square in the face. "Why don't you take those to the den? You can go through them later."

Shane looked at him smugly. "Sure thing, Mitch. We can talk about movie choices later." He walked away laughing.

Mitch knew what Shane was doing; he was getting even because he teased him about Kat. Luckily, the Carters didn't pay them any attention.

Kat worked on the flowers in the kitchen while Tim, Tom, and Shane went back to the toolshed to finish the shadow box. Mitch moved around the house, cleaning and straightening, wanting everything to be perfect when Beth came home. Occasionally, he'd catch Kat watching him. She would turn away whenever he looked at her, but she was definitely watching him.

"Done," she said.

Mitch walked over to the kitchen counter where Kat proudly displayed all five vases. Each one was bursting with a wonderful mix of pink roses, yellow tulips, white daisies, and a colorful assortment of wildflowers.

"These look great, Kat."

"Thank you. I had fun doing them, and Miss Justin is going to love them." Kat's eyes traveled from her hands to the flowers and back again. Mitch could tell she felt uncomfortable around him and for the first time, he realized they were alone. Mitch turned to leave but only got as far as the stairs.

"I know who you are."

He stopped and turned around.

"You're Simon Grey."

Mitch started to deny it, but stopped. He chuckled, his hands on his waist, shaking his head. "I guess it was too much for me to think Shane could keep it to himself."

"Shane didn't tell me; I told him."

"*You* told him?" he repeated, sounding confused.

"I commented the other day over dinner how much I thought you looked like Simon Grey. Shane nearly choked. It was all the confirmation I needed."

"So, I guess your whole family knows?"

"Yes . . . but don't worry, we're not going to say anything. We respect your right to privacy." She twisted her hands together, nervously.

"I'm sure you think I'm crazy for wanting to ditch out on life."

"Actually, I think what you've done is quite admirable. Shane told me how you met."

Mitch raised his brow. "He did?"

"Yes. He also told me about a few other jams you got him out of, and that you've spent a lot of time helping Miss Justin around the ranch. Shane thinks a lot of you, Mr. Grey."

"First of all, it's Mitch, and as far as Shane's concerned, I don't think he's too thrilled with me at the moment."

"But I can tell by the way Shane talks about you, he cares what you think. I know he—" Kat was going to say something more when her brothers and Shane walked into the house disagreeing about something. Kat just smiled at Mitch, then joined the boys in the other room.

By the end of the night, Kat had finished her shadow box. Mitch had spent time with the boys debating baseball stats—and sports in general—before excusing himself to Beth's office. He was working at the computer when Shane came in from the porch.

"What time do you think you and Mom will get home tomorrow?" he asked as he leaned against the doorframe.

"I'm hoping not too late," Mitch said. "I want to have enough time to fix her a nice dinner. After almost a week of hospital food, I figured she would appreciate something special."

"Then I'll stay close to the house tomorrow. I want to be here when she gets home."

Mitch was pleased to hear a hint of enthusiasm in Shane's voice. Even though Shane had asked how his mom was doing each night, Mitch had been concerned Shane's excuse for not visiting Beth was really a way to cover his distancing emotions.

"How is she handling losing Pandora?"

"She hasn't talked about it much. I think it will hit her hardest when she's home and Pandora isn't here."

Shane hung his head. "It's going to kill her; I know it. Pandora was the last gift Grandpa gave her before he died. She'll never forgive me."

"You know that's not true, Shane."

He didn't answer; he just turned to walk away.

"Hey, wait a minute there," Mitch stopped him. "We never got a chance to finish our earlier conversation."

"What conversation?"

"Nice try, Romeo," Mitch laughed. "You've been holding out on me."

Shane stood unmoving.

"Come on, Shane, she seems really nice. Why didn't you tell me you and Kat are an item?"

Shane looked ready to deny it, then smiled. "She is nice, isn't she? But I wouldn't say we're an item. We just met."

"Well, she seems pretty lost on you." Mitch leaned back in the desk chair and stretched his hands behind his head. "You're a quick operator. I leave you on your own for less than a week, and boom, you have yourself a girlfriend."

"She's not my girlfriend. We're just friends."

"A friend you're willing to spill your guts to," Mitch added. "From what she told me, you two have spent a lot of time talking."

"Yeah . . . we've done some talking. Kat's a good listener. She doesn't try to fix me. It's been nice talking to someone who can listen without feeling the need to offer an opinion on everything."

"Is talking all you've been doing? You two looked pretty cozy in the shed tonight."

Shane rolled his eyes. "It's a little hard getting *cozy* when her brothers are always around."

"Do they know you're interested?"

"Yeah, and they've already threatened me. They warned me if I as much as *thought* about taking advantage of Kat, they would strip me naked and take a branding iron to . . . well . . . you know."

Mitch laughed. "So, what are you going to do about it?"

"About what?"

"About Kat."

"I don't know," Shane said, kicking the toe of his boot against the doorframe. "The last time I told a girl I liked her, she laughed at me, called me a hick, and said I wasn't worth her time."

"Well, I don't think you have to worry about that. Kat looked smitten when she was talking about you earlier."

"Really?" Shane smiled.

"Of course. You're a good-looking kid and a nice guy. Why wouldn't she be interested?"

Shane just shrugged his shoulders in reply.

"Well," Mitch got up from his chair, "I don't know about you, but I'm beat." He reached for the box sitting on the desk top and waited for Shane to move from the doorway before turning the light off.

"What's in the box?" Shane asked as they climbed the stairs together.

"I bought myself a Bible."

"You're kidding." Shane stopped in his tracks.

"No. Why would you say that?"

"I'm just surprised."

"Then I guess if I told you I found what I was looking for you would be stunned," Mitch continued up the steps.

"What are you saying?" Shane's tone turned serious as he followed.

"I'm saying I'm giving my life over to God. I might not understand all that I need to, but I figure it's a start."

Shane stopped Mitch with an outstretched hand and locked eyes with him. "You're serious."

"Completely. Look, Shane, what are people searching for in life? What do they think will make them happy? Money? Fame? Affluence? I've had all that, and it wasn't the answer. I never felt contentment or peace. The more money I had, the more people latched on to me for a handout. The more fame I got, the more people hounded me—not allowing me any privacy or a moment to myself. Don't you see? The more you have, the more people take. I was no better off in Hollywood than I was in New York. The only difference was I had enough money to hide my emptiness behind expensive cars, trendy nightclubs, and available women."

Shane looked at him in disbelief. "Why? Why do this? What has God ever done for you?"

Mitch was taken back by the bitterness tainting Shane's words. He wanted to address it, but decided not to. Instead, he tried putting into words what he was feeling.

"God brought me here, Shane; I'm convinced of it. He used your rebellion to bring me to the Diamond-J and show me what real living is all about. I realize now that a simple life made up of a hard day's work, quiet evenings, and special people is satisfying and fulfilling. Your mother has shown me how big her God is, and how very real He can be to me, if I let Him. So, you see, God used both you and your mom to show me what was missing in my life."

Mitch could tell by the look on Shane's face, he was completely mystified by what he was hearing.

"You're sure you're not just doing this because of Mom?" Shane asked.

"Yes, I am. But not for the reasons you think." Mitch put a hand on Shane's shoulder—wanting to connect with him—needing Shane to see how serious he was. "When I was at the hospital, I felt helpless to do anything for your mom. All my money, connections, and fame, could do nothing to help her. I realized then the only one who could help Beth was God, so I pleaded with Him to save her. I told Him over and over again how important she was to me, and that He had to do something to help her."

Mitch shrugged, searching for the right words. "I decided it wasn't fair to ask God to deliver or answer my pleas if I didn't have a relationship with Him. That would be like asking a perfect stranger to loan me a hundred bucks, just because I asked him to. If I want God to help me, or answer questions I don't understand, then He needs to be my God, not just Beth's. I realized I needed to have a personal relationship with Him."

Shane looked shocked. Speechless. His eyes welled, and he quickly turned away. Mitch could tell he was doing some soul-searching of his own.

"Look, Shane, I'm not going to pretend I have all the answers, or that I can change my ways overnight, but I want to. I want to be a better man."

Chapter Twenty-Eight

Mitch was working in the kitchen when Shane came down the stairs. "Good morning."

"Mornin'," Shane grumbled as he slumped on the barstool at the counter.

Mitch pushed a plate of pancakes in front of Shane, then dished up a plate for himself. Before digging in, he bowed his head in a short prayer. When he opened his eyes, Shane was staring at him in disbelief.

"Are Tim and Tom coming over?" Mitch asked.

"No. Actually, I'm going to be helping them at their place. They're installing insulation and drywall today. I thought it was only fair I help them out after all the work they've put in over here. But don't worry, I plan on being back by lunch."

"Good, because your mom really misses you. She thinks I'm hiding something from her. She's afraid you're going to take off after your dad, and she won't ever get a chance to explain to you the truth."

"Like I said, I'll be here for lunch. I'll even have it ready if you want."

"Nah, that won't be necessary," Mitch said as he finished his pancakes and put his plate in the sink. "But I'll tell you what you can do. You can clean up these dishes and make sure the flowers have water. I don't want them dying before Beth gets a chance to see them." He took one last swig of coffee before heading out the door.

Beth was asleep when Mitch crept into her room and quietly sat down in the chair alongside the bed. He set the bag he was carrying on the nightstand and studied Beth's features as the morning light filtered through the window shades. "I wonder if you know how beautiful you are?" he whispered, then reached for her hand, stroking it softly with his thumb.

Beth stirred, her eyes fluttering as she tried to focus.

"Good morning, sleepyhead." Mitch smiled as he brought her hand up to his lips and pressed a kiss against her fingers.

"What are you doing here so early?" she asked.

Leaning forward, Mitch shifted his glance from left to right, as if he was doing something underhanded. "I'm breaking you out of this joint."

She laughed. "But the doctor doesn't even make rounds until after ten o'clock."

"No problem; I'll wait." He kissed her hand again and then got up and moved to the window. When he pulled up the blinds, a burst of light brightened the room.

"Good thing I'm already awake," Beth said as she squinted at the harsh rays.

Mitch watched as she pushed herself to a sitting position and finger-combed her disheveled hair. With a sigh, Beth folded back the bed sheets and swiveled her legs over the edge of the bed, slowly lowering her feet to the ground."

"Here, let me help you." He quickly grabbed the crutches that were propped in the corner and handed them to Beth. He followed close by until she'd made it to the bathroom. When she closed the door, Mitch crisscrossed the room aimlessly, anxious to get Beth home.

A young volunteer bounced into the room, way too perky for the early-morning hour. She glanced at the empty bed. "Oops, did we lose a patient?" She laughed at her own joke.

Mitch smiled at the girl's stab at humor. "No, she's in the bathroom."

When the volunteer locked eyes with Mitch, her jaw dropped, and she stared at him in disbelief. "I don't believe it. You're Simon Grey. I would know you anywhere. I've seen all your movies. I can't believe you're here. Everyone in the world is looking for you. Why are you hiding in Kansas? I can't believe you're standing right here in front of me. Can I get your autograph? No, wait, can I get my picture taken with you?"

Mitch felt cornered. There was no use trying to lie his way out of this one. He'd finally come face-to-face with a genuine fan and would not be able to convince her otherwise.

When Beth walked out of the bathroom, she made eye contact with Mitch over the girl's shoulder, a smirk on her face. She hobbled back to the bed and leaned against the rail. "Darcy, this is my foreman. He works for me on the Diamond-J."

Mitch smiled at Beth. She was trying to rescue him, and he loved her for it.

"You have Simon Grey as your foreman?" Darcy squealed, acting like the teenager she was. Beth was about to say something when Mitch stopped her with a raised hand. He removed the tattered cowboy hat he'd gotten in the habit of wearing and twisted it nervously around in his hands.

"You're right, Darcy. I'm Simon Grey."

"I knew it!" she gasped. "Those piercing eyes and that rugged jaw could belong to no one else but Simon Grey."

She must have realized how immature she sounded because she took a step back and covered her flushed cheeks. "Oh my gosh, I'm making a complete fool out of myself in front of Simon Grey."

"No, Darcy, you're not," Mitch said with a sincere smile. "In fact, it's flattering to have someone appreciate the work I've done. But I need to correct you on one important point. I'm not hiding in Kansas; I'm living here."

"I know, but no one knows you're here. Everyone thinks you've fallen off the face of the earth. When they find out you're here, people will—"

"But Darcy, that's just it, I don't want anyone to find out. This isn't a publicity stunt. I left Hollywood because I needed a change in my life. I found what I was looking for, and I don't want anything to spoil it. Especially a media circus."

Beth mentally repeated what Mitch had said. *He found what he was looking for.* What did he mean by that?

Darcy's face fell like a child who'd just found out the truth about Santa Claus. "You mean I can't tell anyone I met you . . . that I was in the same room with you, carrying on a conversation and everything?"

"I know you want to tell your friends, but I'm asking you not to—as a personal favor to me."

She twisted her face in utter disappointment.

"Look, Darcy, I know you're disappointed, but this is very important. Hollywood was killing me. I needed to leave before it was too late. If you can just keep this between us, I promise, I'll make it up to you somehow."

She looked from Mitch to Beth and back again. With a heavy sigh, she said, "I won't tell. I promise. I mean, what kind of fan would I be if I ratted you out to the paparazzi?"

Mitch moved closer to her and reached for her hand. He placed a light kiss on it, before giving it a squeeze. "Thank you."

When he released her hand, she looked at it in awe. "I don't believe it. Simon Grey just kissed my hand." She giggled and blushed all over again, then stared at Mitch like he was a statue.

After a moment of awkward silence, Darcy snapped back to reality. "I'm sorry; I almost forgot why I came in here." She turned to Beth. "Miss Justin, Dr. Cummings wanted you to know he signed your release papers last night. The nurse will be in to check your incision, and the physical therapist will be by shortly to answer any questions you might have. Then you'll be able to leave."

"Thank you, Darcy."

"You're welcome."

She turned to leave, but Mitch was quick to stop her. "Darcy, why don't you give me your phone number. Once we get Beth back on her feet and things calm down, I'll give you a call and see what I can do to make this up to you."

With stars in her eyes, she jotted down her cell phone number on the notepad from Beth's bedside table. When she handed it to Mitch, he gave her one of his killer smiles. Backing out of the room, Darcy stared at Mitch until the door swung shut.

"Do you think she'll be able to keep it to herself?" Beth asked as she stood next to the bed.

"I think so. She seems like a bright girl, and I made it pretty clear how important this is to me."

Beth was fatigued and needed to lie down. As she leaned back into the mattress, Mitch helped lift her legs onto the bed. Beth winced as she tried to get comfortable, while Mitch took a seat alongside her.

When he brushed back a lock of hair from the perspiration on her brow, an electric shock sent tremors through her body. He took her shuddering as a chill and pulled the covers up around her, then closed his hands around hers. Beth looked at him, noticing a difference in his eyes.

"Something's different," Beth sputtered, her words catching in her throat.

"You're right." Mitch agreed with a smile.

"What did you mean when you said you found what you were looking for?" *Please say it's me. Please tell me you're never going to leave.* Beth's heart constricted. *What am I thinking?* She scolded herself. *How can I be disobedient to God and still expect Him to fulfill my selfish desires?* She wanted Mitch. Even if it was wrong, she wanted him to take her in his arms and never let her go.

Mitch was ready to say something, but the shift nurse walked into the room, interrupting them.

"Good morning, Beth. Well, today's the day." She moved around to the far side of the bed and dropped the rail. "Are you ready to go home?"

"More than ready," she answered Nurse Bryant's question, but her eyes never left Mitch.

"Okay then, I just need to check a few things and go over some instructions before you leave."

Mitch let go of her hand and moved from the bed. "I'll just step outside while you do that. Oh, I brought you a change of clothes. They're in the bag." He pointed to the nightstand.

Nurse Bryant smiled at him as he left.

Mitch pulled his hat down low across his brow and leaned against the hallway outside Beth's door. He'd been ready to tell Beth about the change in his life, but felt a sense of relief when they were interrupted. Mitch wanted to tell Beth, but he wanted to do it when they had plenty of time to discuss it. He wanted to make sure she understood the change in him *was* because of her, but *she* wasn't the reason he'd turned to God. She was responsible for pointing him in the right direction, showing him what he needed, what he wanted.

But the decision he'd made was for himself.

An hour later, an orderly wheeled Beth to the patient loading area. Mitch followed along, his hands full with the floral arrangement Charlie and Sarah had sent, and a large plastic bag that held Beth's medications, instructions, release papers, and the clothes she'd been wearing when she'd been brought in. The minute the automatic doors whisked open, Beth let out a satisfying sigh and lifted her face to the sun. She acted like a prisoner finally being set free.

Mitch hurried to where he'd parked Beth's truck in the patient loading area and quickly pushed the hospital bag behind the bench seat before getting in. He held the bouquet next to him as he pulled up to the entrance where Beth was waiting. Shifting the truck into park, he got out just as the orderly offered to help Beth out of her chair. Mitch was at her side in an instant.

"I can do that," he said rather possessively.

The orderly took his cue from Mitch and stepped aside. Mitch bent low to Beth and looped her arms around his neck.

"Mitch, I can walk."

"Just humor me, okay? You'll get your chance to break in those crutches once we're home." Mitch scooped Beth up and lifted her into the truck and watched as she scooted next to the flowers. Mitch made sure she was all in—especially her cast-laden leg—before closing the door. The orderly handed him the crutches, then walked away, rolling the wheelchair back through the hospital entrance.

With the crutches stowed behind the seat, Mitch slid in behind the steering wheel, pinning the flowers between them.

She shifted and sighed, sounding uncomfortable.

"Here, let me put the flowers on the floor," he said as he wedged the basket on the driveshaft between the seat and the underside of the dashboard. "Now you can move closer to me." Mitch smiled.

Beth wrapped her arm around her mid-section and braced herself as she pushed across the worn leather bench and pulled her leg up onto the seat. With her head rested back against Mitch's shoulder, she closed her eyes.

"You all right?"

"Yeah, I just ache." Her words were quiet and winded.

Mitch worried that Beth was pushing it. Maybe it was too soon for her to go home. All he saw was her external injuries—a broken leg, concussion, a few scrapes and bruises—but she'd had internal injuries as well. "Beth, are you sure you should be going home?"

"Dr. Cummings said as long as I take it easy, I'll be fine. I'm just sore."

"But what if you hurt yourself?"

"I'm not going to hurt myself. I just have to work out some of the stiffness." She twisted around so she could look at him and gave a reassuring smile. "I'm going to be fine. I just have to take it slow."

Mitch smiled back at Beth as he carefully reached for her seatbelt and fastened it. "I'm going to hold you to that, you know."

She closed her eyes again. "I'm sure you will."

Mitch had planned on talking to Beth on the way home, to tell her about his decision. But they'd barely cleared the parking lot and pulled out on the highway before her shallow breathing let him know she had drifted off. *That's okay.* He tried to convince himself. *I can wait.* He relaxed behind the wheel, a little disappointed, but focused on the road ahead of him.

Mitch had made the drive every day that week, but this was by far the most enjoyable. Having Beth sitting next to him felt so right.

About twenty minutes down the road Mitch's arm began to tingle and go numb under the pressure of Beth's head. Carefully, he slipped his arm out from behind her and draped it around her shoulders. In her lethargy, Beth nestled closer to him.

Mitch's senses flared and his pulse pounded within his chest. Simon Grey had never shown much control when it came to women. He'd allowed himself the sexual privileges his celebrity status afforded him.

But that was then. This is now.

Simon Grey was a man who had used liquor and women to deaden the emptiness that overwhelmed him. That person no longer existed. Mitch now knew the truth.

He wasn't alone.

God wanted to fill the emptiness Mitch had been trying to mask.

Unfortunately, that didn't change the fact that he was a man.

A man who wanted more than anything to be with Beth.

Not just for a day.

Or a weekend.

But for a lifetime.

Chapter Twenty-Nine

When Mitch passed the Carter house, he gave a couple honks of the horn. He wanted Shane to know they were home earlier than expected.

Beth stirred.

"I'm sorry," she said drowsily, "I didn't mean to fall asleep." Bracing her side, Beth pushed up to a sitting position and let out a long, lingering breath as they drove up to the house.

Mitch watched Beth drink in her surroundings. The Diamond-J was like water to her thirsting soul. It was the very air she breathed. He had no idea how she would live without it.

"Here you go. Home." He reached for her crutches and hurried to open the passenger door.

It was slow going getting Beth to her feet, and she had to hold on to Mitch to steady herself.

"Let me just carry you? It would be a lot eas—"

"No," she said as she tucked the crutches up under her arms. "I need to get used to these things."

She took a few feeble steps while Mitch glanced down the road, hoping to see signs of Shane. *Nothing.* When he turned back to see tears streaming down Beth's face, his heart stopped.

"What is it, Beth? What's wrong?"

She raised her shoulder to dry her tears and looked again at the barn. In an instant, Mitch knew.

"Beth, I'm so sorry." He pulled her close and held on tight. Silently, she cried—her face buried against his chest—her pain both physical and emotional.

Stroking Beth's hair, Mitch searched for something to say, but nothing came. She would need time to process the loss of Pandora, so he just held her close, offering what comfort he could.

After a few moments, Beth pulled away and brushed the tears from her face. She looked toward the barn, then up at him. "I just can't . . ." She swallowed hard. "I can't believe Pandora is gone."

"I know," Mitch said softly. "I know."

With a gently placed hand on the small of her back, he walked alongside Beth as she hobbled up the front steps.

Mitch chanced another look down the driveway, disappointed Shane hadn't made more of an effort to be home and greet his mom. He pulled back the screen, pushed open the door, and stood by as Beth carefully maneuvered through the doorway.

Beth hadn't taken two steps inside when she was greeted with a "Welcome Home" shout from Shane, Uncle Charlie, Sarah, Travis, his wife Cindy, and their two little girls.

The room was decorated with streamers and balloons, and a festive cake sat on the dining room table. Shane stepped forward and carefully wrapped his arms around Beth. "Welcome home, Mom."

Beth started to cry again.

Shane's hug went a long way to give her the assurance she needed, and replace the apprehension she had felt in the hospital. She and Shane had their differences and there were problems they would have to work out, but they would get through it together. His embrace told her so.

Uncle Charlie stepped forward and pressed a light kiss to her cheek. "You damn near scared ten years off my life, and I don't have that many to spare." His eyes were glassy, causing Beth to tear up even more.

Sarah and Cindy were next to give her gentle hugs, then Travis kissed her cheek, looking a little emotional.

Feeling weary and a little unsteady on her crutches, Beth knew she needed to sit down, and when her nieces squeezed against her sides, Beth grimaced slightly and looked to Mitch, who was quick to run interference.

"Okay, I think we need to let Beth sit down," Mitch said as he helped her get situated on the couch, then turned to everyone hovering nearby. "How'd you know we'd be home so early?"

"We didn't," Shane answered. "We were planning on decorating the front porch, the mail box, and the front fence, when all of a sudden we heard you pulling into the yard."

"Well, everything looks wonderful." Beth smiled appreciatively.

"We weren't expecting you until after lunch," Sarah added. "But you can't have cake before you've eaten. Just give Cindy and me a few minutes; we'll whip something up for lunch."

The two women walked to the kitchen while Uncle Charlie, Travis, Shane, and Mitch hovered over her. Heather and Mindy scooted up close to Beth's side and excitedly showed her their new dolls. Beth played along with them while the men talked about the ranch.

"You'd be really impressed, Beth, with the work Shane has done around here. He and the Carter boys have really gotten things in shape this last week." Uncle Charlie put a manly grip on Shane's shoulder, punctuating his pride.

"The Carters? Are those the boys you were telling me about?" she asked Mitch.

"Yeah. They're great guys. Their sister is pretty cool, too. Right Shane?" Mitch gave Shane a nudge.

Beth looked at her son while the men chuckled. "What am I missing here? Shane?"

"It's nothing, Mom. Mitch is just giving me a hard time."

"Okay, who wants chicken salad and who wants turkey?" Cindy asked as she stepped into the room. All attention turned to her, except for Beth's. Her eyes stayed on Shane, wanting to know more, but deciding to wait until they were alone.

Everyone ate lunch together in the dining room. Beth made the effort to sit at the table, propping her leg up on a chair. At first, she enjoyed the lively conversation and comfortable feeling of being home. But when talk turned to what had to be done before selling the ranch, Beth didn't want to listen. She'd been away from the ranch for less than a week, yet it felt like an eternity. What would it be like to leave and never come back?

She lowered her leg to the ground and reached for the crutches leaning against the wall. Conversation stopped, all eyes turning to her.

"Thank you everyone for this wonderful home coming. It was such a nice surprise." She forced a smile, not wanting anyone to know she was struggling. "But I'm feeling a little done-in for the day. If you don't mind, I think I'll go lay down."

Mitch was quick to his feet. "Here, I'll help you."

Beth wanted to refuse, but knew she couldn't navigate the stairs on her own.

Standing at the bottom of the staircase, she looked up, overwhelmed by the task ahead of her.

"Here," Mitch reached for the crutches, "I'll take those."

"No." She held on tight. "I need the practice."

"Not today, you don't."

"Just stand behind me, so I don't fall," Beth said as she traversed the first step.

"Why must you be so stubborn?"

She ignored him as she took the next step.

When Beth reached the upper landing, she was breathing hard, perspiring, her hands shaking as they clutched the crutches.

"Okay, hotshot, you proved you can climb the stairs, now let me help you to your room."

"I can do it on my own," she snapped, hobbling the remaining thirty feet.

When she pushed her bedroom door open, Beth was immediately struck by the scent of flowers. When she saw two bouquets—one on her nightstand and the other on her dresser—she sagged against her crutches, feeling like a heel. Silently, she tottered over to the nightstand and bent down to inhale the floral fragrance.

"I was hoping they would cheer you up."

"They're beautiful."

"But not as beautiful as you."

Beth turned, ready to diffuse Mitch's comment with something humorous or witty, but when she saw the smoky look in his eyes, she could no longer think of anything amusing to say.

He moved closer to her and reached for the crutches as she sunk to the edge of the bed. "You should have seen me in the flower shop. I'm sure I drove the florist crazy. I stood there for over an hour wanting to pick the perfect flower. Finally, I just took a bunch of each."

"Well, I think they're beautiful. All of them."

"But they can't hold a candle to you."

"Oh yeah," she chuckled half-heartedly, "I mean, what man can resist a woman on crutches, sweating like a pig?"

Pushing her pillows against the headboard she leaned back with a heavy sigh.

"Are you kidding? I thought you were gorgeous when you were wallowing with the pigs."

"Very funny." She laughed and winced at the same time as she remembered the day they chased the piglet around the pen.

The day Mitch kissed her.

He sat on the edge of the bed, looking serious. "You okay?"

"All that talk about selling the ranch, I just couldn't handle it anymore."

"I figured that's what was bothering you."

"That, and I don't think I've ever felt so . . . so weak. Even after having Shane, I felt better than I do now."

"That's to be expected. You just had major surgery, and it hasn't even been a full week." He glanced at his watch. "I'm going to get your bag. It's time for some of your medication. Do you want anything else from downstairs?"

"My Bible. Oh shoot!" Beth snapped as Mitch made his way to the door.

"What?"

"I should have checked my e-mail while I was downstairs."

"Well, since you live in the electronic Stone Age and only have a desktop computer, it will have to wait."

"But what if my realtor has been trying to get a hold of me?"

"Like I said, it can wait. Your recovery is what is important right now." He stopped in the doorway. "Anything else?"

She shook her head, then closed her eyes.

Beth's head was pounding. Not so much from the concussion or the exertion, but because her brain was on overload. Selling the ranch, Pandora's death, Shane's change in attitude, and the deepening feelings she had for Mitch, all vied for her attention.

When she opened her eyes, Beth caught a glimpse of the beautiful flowers on the nightstand. Reaching for a pink rose, she gave it a light tug. Inhaling its sweetness lifted her spirits slightly. She'd never had a man buy her flowers before, other than Shane or Uncle Charlie when it was her birthday or Mother's Day.

But this was different.

Everything about Mitch was different.

Mitch returned, juggling her Bible, duffle bag, a glass, and the small plastic pitcher from the hospital room. He set down the pitcher of water and glass on the nightstand, along with her Bible, then reached inside the bag before dropping it on the over-stuffed chair in the corner.

"So, you like your flowers?"

Still holding the delicate stem, Beth inhaled its beautiful sent again. "I love them."

"I'm glad," he answered with a smile as he sat beside her, reading the labels from two different prescriptions and checking his watch. He shuffled a few pills into the palm of his hand and filled the glass with water.

"Here you go." He handed her the glass, then the pills.

She swigged them back with a few swallows of water.

"Go ahead and get some rest. I'll check on you in a little while."

"Is Shane still downstairs?"

"No, he already took off. Why?"

"I just wanted to talk to him, see what he's thinking."

"Beth, you can talk to him this evening. Right now, you need your rest."

"But what's this about someone's sister? Was that just a joke or is Shane really interested in somebody?"

"Beth, you're going to have to ask him."

"But I'm asking you. I'm gone for less than a week, and a girl magically appears. Is this something I should be worried about?"

"You have nothing to worry about, okay? Kat is Tim and Tom's sister. Shane's been spending a lot of time at their house while I've been at the hospital with you. I think he's had dinner over there every night this week. They're a really nice family, Beth. Believe me, you have nothing to worry about."

She frowned at him, wanting more information.

"Don't give me that look," Mitch scolded. "If there's anything more you want to know, you're going to have to ask Shane." He leaned forward and placed a kiss on her forehead before moving toward the door. He gave her a quick backwards glance, winked, then disappeared down the hall.

Chapter Thirty

Beth slept for two hours and lay awake for another. She wanted to fall back to sleep, but her mind was working overtime. Though Beth had been able to push most everything to the back burner of her brain, the one thing that continued to monopolize her thoughts was Mitch.

She was in love with him.

There was no denying it.

What Beth was completely and utterly at a loss about was what she was going to do next.

What am I to do, Lord? I know this isn't what you want for me; it can't be. But then why did you allow Mitch to come? Why did you allow him to invade every part of my thinking, my feelings, my senses?

With a bit of a chip on her shoulder, Beth's questions turned into a one-sided argument. *Okay, God, I can't continue to pretend I don't have feelings for Mitch or brush off the feelings I see in his eyes. I'm admitting I'm too weak. I want to be with him. I want to have someone tangible in my life. If that's not what you want, then you're going to have to put a stop to it, because I'm not strong enough.*

Beth punctuated her internal conversation by jutting out her chin in defiance. *But . . . one thing I'm sure of . . . if I stay up here all night, I'll drive myself crazy.*

Once on her feet, Beth tried to move quietly down the hall, knowing if Mitch heard she was up, he'd try to convince her to stay in bed.

When she got to the stairs, Beth sat down on the top step, deciding it would be easier to scoot on her butt rather than maneuver with her crutches. Sliding the crutches a few steps ahead of her, Beth inched down, one step at a time. She was more than halfway there when she gave her crutches too big of a nudge, sending them clattering to the hardwood floor at the bottom of the stairs.

Before she could do or say anything, Beth heard a crash in the kitchen and watched as Mitch hurried around the corner. Grabbing the banister, he was ready to sprint up the stairs, but caught himself before careening right into her.

"Beth? What the—"

He knelt next to her, the look of terror in his eyes as they darted up and down her body, his hands following suit.

"I'm okay, Mitch. I'm okay. I didn't fall. I'm fine."

She kept repeating herself, trying to make him understand. Finally, she grabbed his hands and brought them to a stop. "I'm fine."

"What happened?" His words were sharp and breathless.

"I was scooting down the stairs when my crutches—"

"Wait. You were what?"

Beth watched his concern turn to anger.

"Why in the world didn't you just yell for me? I would've helped you. Do you realize you nearly gave me a heart attack?"

"Mitch, I'm sorry." She reached out for his shoulder, but he quickly got to his feet. He was angry. Angrier than she had ever seen him before.

"Sorry!?" He looked at her with growing fury as he began to pace. "Dammit, Beth! I thought you fell down the entire flight of stairs!" The veins in his neck bulged as he raked his fingers through his hair.

Beth looked away, knowing he had every right to be upset with her. She'd scared him half-to-death. But more than that, Beth was afraid God was answering her prayer. If she wasn't strong enough to resist her feelings for Mitch, God would change Mitch's feelings for her.

Tears welled in her eyes.

"Beth . . . don't cry. I didn't mean to yell. It's just that you scared me out of my wits."

"I know and I'm sorry. I just got tired of sitting by myself. I had enough of that in the hospital. I just wanted to come downstairs so I wouldn't feel so alone." *So I could be with you.*

"Here, let me help you." His tone softened.

Mitch retrieved the crutches from the floor and helped Beth over to the kitchen breakfast bar.

"What's all this?" she asked—waving to the pans and bowls filling the countertop—while she dried her tears.

"This is your surprise welcome home dinner." Mitch moved to the kitchen. "Surprise!" he said mockingly, before bending down and picking up the bowl that had gone crashing to the floor.

Beth felt horrible. Not only had she scared Mitch to death, she'd ruined his surprise as well. "Boy, I'm batting a thousand, aren't I?"

"That's okay." Mitch offered her a conciliatory smile. "I think I might be in over my head."

"What are you making?"

"Well, I wanted your first dinner home to be special—something you wouldn't make for yourself. So, if everything turns out right, we'll be having chicken cordon bleu, shrimp scampi, baked potatoes, Caesar salad, and of course, we already have our dessert."

Beth raised her brow in surprise, while looking at the countertop covered in ingredients. "This looks like quite an undertaking."

He shrugged. "Like I said, I wanted it to be special."

"Mind if I watch?" she asked, propping herself up on one of the barstools.

"Not at all. You can even offer me some guidance, if you want to."

"Oh no," she chuckled, raising her hands off the counter. "This is your doing. I wouldn't think of butting in."

"Okay then," he postured, trying to look confident. "Prepare to be amazed."

Beth had never needed to show such self-control in her life. Even though she had stifled more than one chuckle, she was sure her amusement was evident in her eyes.

By the time Mitch was done with the chicken, there was egg and flour everywhere. One piece even had to be rinsed off and re-stuffed after it squirted out of Mitch's hands during the battering stage, landing on the kitchen floor.

It was all Beth could do not to laugh out loud.

When it came to cooking the shrimp, Mitch was doing fairly well. That is, until he set out to impress her. Trying to be suave, Mitch attempted to turn the shrimp with a quick flip of his wrist, like chefs do on TV. Unfortunately, most of the shrimp landed on the stovetop instead of in the pan. Beth had to bite her lip to keep from laughing, while Mitch plucked the little pink bodies from the range top and tossed them back in the pan.

In between mini-catastrophes, Mitch moved back and forth to the dining room. He had found her table linens, good china, and crystal goblets, and was setting the table. When Beth realized it was only set for two, she asked, "Isn't Shane eating with us?"

Mitch walked over to the breakfast bar, standing dangerously close, then reached for her hand.

"I was hoping we could have dinner . . . just the two of us."

With Mitch stroking the back of her hand, Beth had a hard time concentrating. Finally, she asked again. "But what about Shane?"

"He's been eating at the Carter's. I figured one more night wouldn't bother him. Besides, it allows him to spend more time with Kat."

"There's that name again," Beth said, momentarily distracted. "When am I going to get a chance to meet this girl?"

"Do you really want to spend the evening talking about Kat?" Mitch moved closer, brushing her hair back from her shoulder, allowing his thumb to brush against her cheek.

Beth's heart was ready to surrender, to give in to what she was feeling. The way Mitch looked at her—the way he made her feel—there was no place she'd rather be than in his arms, his lips telling her how much he wanted her.

But as quickly as Beth's emotions had risen to near volatile heights, her conscience punctured her swelling heart, sending it speeding back to earth. She didn't know what to do or what to say.

Mitch tucked his finger under her chin, forcing her to look at him. "In case you missed it, Beth, I'm trying to court you."

She smiled at the old-fashioned term and swallowed back her emotions. *What are you doing to me, God? This is so not fair!*

"Beth, I know you have apprehensions about me . . . about us, but we can make this work. I know we can."

"How Mitch? We're so different. We come from two completely different worlds. You drove away from your issues—your demons—but I can't. I have to be responsible; I have to think about what's best for Shane."

"What about me?" he asked.

Beth could hear the emotion in Mitch's voice, and it nearly broke her heart.

"Don't you have any feelings for me, Beth?"

"Mitch, that's not fair. Of course, I have feelings for you." She wanted to reach for him—hold him close—but knew that would make things even worse.

"Okay, then, we both admit having feelings for each other. Can't we just go from there and see what happens?"

She was about to say something, when the timer on the stove went off. "Hold that thought," he said as he gently laid a finger across her lips. "Let's enjoy a nice dinner. Then we'll talk about us."

Beth looked around at all the work Mitch had put in to make the night special. It wouldn't be fair to ruin it. "Well, it does smell awfully good," she agreed with a smile.

"Great!" he said, with a quick kiss to her lips.

"Hey! That wasn't . . ." Beth tried scolding him, but it was no use. Mitch hurried to the kitchen, turned off the timer, and pulled several dishes from the oven, while Beth's lips burned from the sensation of his kiss.

Turning to the dining room, she sighed, noticing for the first time how the descending sun bathed the room with a soft romantic glow.

The mood was perfect.

Maybe too perfect for what they needed to discuss.

Beth moved toward the dining room, her bones and muscles aching with every step. Glancing at the clock, she realized it was time for her medication, but the bottles were upstairs on the nightstand.

She hated to ask Mitch to get them, not wanting to admit she was hurting. Instead, she decided to ignore the pain, at least until they were done with dinner.

The floral bouquet at the center of the table scented the already charged atmosphere, however, Mitch didn't stop there. He lit several candles throughout the dining room and turned off the remaining house lights. When he set Beth's dinner salad and main course in front of her, she couldn't help but smile at the little pink pansies decorating the rim of the plate.

"Everything looks perfect, Mitch," she acknowledged as he put his plate down then walked back to the kitchen.

"You had your doubts?" he teased, returning with a bottle of sparkling cider.

"Not doubts. Concerns maybe," she kidded.

"Oh, let me get your medicine. It's just about that time." He ran up the stairs and back down again, putting the bottles alongside her fluted glass. He finally took a seat, surveying his own masterpiece. Squaring his shoulders, he sat a little taller, obviously pleased with the outcome. "Not bad for a city boy, huh?"

"Not bad at all," she said softly, with her eyes trained on him.

"I figured you wouldn't object to a nice bottle of wine to celebrate," he said as he reached for her glass and poured the bubbly apple cider, "but you can't drink alcohol while you're on such heavy medication."

"That's okay. I never developed much of a taste for wine. I cook with sherry on occasion, but I never wanted to put that temptation in front of Shane."

"Well," he said, while filling his own glass, "here's hoping this apple orchard had a good year."

He sipped from his glass, then reached across the table for her hand. "Do you mind if I say grace tonight?"

Beth was befuddled, stumbling slightly over her words. "No . . . sure . . . not at all."

Mitch bowed his head. "God, I'm new at this. But I don't think I need fancy words or a script to tell you how I feel. I think you already know." He squeezed Beth's hand, flooding her heart with warmth.

"Thank you for watching over Beth. I know she still hurts, but I also know it could have been a lot worse. Help Shane with the struggles he's feeling, and show him what really matters in life. And thank you God, for leading me to the Diamond-J. I never did believe in coincidences. I now know my reason for being here was to find You . . . and something else I've been searching for, for a long while. Thanks for this food. I sure hope it tastes good. Amen."

Mitch let go of her hand and raised his eyes. She couldn't help but stare at him, not sure she'd heard him right. "I don't understand," was all she could say.

"Well, I've had a lot of time to myself lately," he said as he cut his chicken and put a piece into his mouth. "In the evenings, after you kicked me out of your hospital room and Shane was at the Carter's, I took the time to do some reading." He swallowed, then speared two shrimp.

"Okay . . ." Beth sat completely still. Confused. No longer interested in food.

Mitch head-nodded at her plate. "If you can't eat and listen at the same time, I'm going to stop talking." He shoved a forkful of potatoes into his mouth and waited for her to follow suit. She quickly cut a slice of chicken and raised it to her lips, but only to appease him. Eating was the last thing on her mind.

"If I didn't know better, I would've thought you marked your Bible just for me."

"My Bible? What do you mean?"

"The first night I picked it up, I had no idea where to start, so I turned to where your bookmark was. It was in the book of John. And right there, in bold letters, it said it was the book for beginning readers."

Beth couldn't believe it. Mitch had read her Bible while she was in the hospital. He'd searched for answers on his own and—from the looks of it, from the words he'd spoken—he found them.

"You're not eating again," he teased.

She pierced a shrimp and shoved it into her mouth, anything to keep him talking. But Mitch seemed perfectly content to finish his meal, knowing he was keeping her in suspense.

But she needed him to cut to the chase.

"What are you saying, Mitch?"

He leaned closer and looked at her with eyes deeper than any ocean. "I'm saying, God used a bullet through my windshield, a rebellious teen, and a firecracker of a ranch owner to show me what was missing in my life." He smiled as he teased, but then turned serious. "I asked God to fill the void."

She played with the napkin on her lap, not saying a word.

"Beth, did you hear me?"

"I heard you." Her tone was soft.

"Okay," he slouched back in his chair. "This isn't quite the reaction I was expecting."

"I'm not sure what to say." Doubt swirled inside her. "I mean, there's more to it than just telling God you're willing to try His way for a while. It's a personal commitment, a life-long commitment."

"What are you saying, Beth?" Mitch bristled. "You don't think I'm capable of making that kind of decision on my own?"

"No. I'm just saying you have to make it for the right reason, for yourself, not for anyone else."

"I did make this decision for myself." His jaw tightened slightly.

"So, I have nothing to do with it?"

"Yes. You have everything to do with it, but not the way you're thinking."

Mitch took a deep breath. He had expected Beth to push back, just not as blunt as she had. But that was all right. He was prepared. He moved around to her side of the table and crouched alongside her chair. He took her hand in his and tried to explain. "Beth, to say this has nothing to do with you would be wrong."

She looked away, clearly disappointed.

"But, it's not what you think." He tugged on her hand, wanting her to look him in the eye. "I didn't make this decision to impress you or get you to let your guard down around me. I did it because I know it's right. I've tried all my life to fill the emptiness inside me with people and things. Since my mother never loved me, I figured that's what was missing. So, I dated women—had relationships—looking for the tangible love I had never felt. But now I realize why the emptiness felt so deep, so hollow. It was a place intended only for God. And now that God's there, the love I feel for other people will only be richer . . . fuller . . . without fear of abandonment."

Tears welled in Beth's eyes. "But you realize just because you've given your life to God doesn't mean life's going to be perfect. He's not a fairy-godfather. The world can still do a number on you."

"I'm aware of that, Beth. I mean, not only have you shown me what real faith is, you've shown it to me under some pretty difficult circumstances. You showed me faith is not what I see on TV when a televangelist tells people the reason they're sick, or poor, or unemployed is because they don't have enough faith. You showed me faith is what you hold on to when life is coming at you a hundred miles an hour—dishing out the worst it has to offer. You made faith real to me. Something I could wrap my arms around."

She arched her brow.

"I didn't mean it like that." He couldn't help but chuckle at his poor choice of words. "Am I getting through to you, Beth? Have I shown you I'm not just some dumb Hollywood actor trying to land his next movie role? I know what's been missing from my life. Now that I have it, I have no intention of going back to what I left behind. Life has never felt more real to me than it does now. God brought us together, Beth. I'm convinced of that."

Mitch got up from where he'd crouched down beside her, stretching his back as he stood. Her eyes never left his. "Look, I didn't mean to tell you over dinner and ruin all this," he said, pointing to their uneaten feast. "I had wanted to tell you on the way home, but you were tired and needed your rest. So, let's not talk anymore about it right now, okay? Let's finish our dinner and have some cake, then you can ask me all the questions piling up behind those beautiful blue eyes of yours."

Chapter Thirty-One

It was all Beth could do to eat dinner and not pepper Mitch with questions. They talked about little things, but her mind was spinning at Mitch's revelation. *Is he sincere, God? Does he know what a salvation commitment is? Is it right of me to question his decision?*

Mitch interrupted her inner debate when he got up and started clearing the dishes.

"Everything tasted wonderful, Mitch. I can't remember the last time I had such an amazing dinner."

"It *was* pretty good, wasn't it?" he said proudly as he reached across for her plate and silverware and stacked them in the kitchen.

Beth slowly lowered her propped leg, feeling stiffness in her hip. Reaching for the crutches, she carefully got to her feet, then looked at the mess in the kitchen that needed to be cleaned up.

"Don't even think about it." Mitch stopped her from taking another step. "I can handle this. You just go into the living room and relax."

"Relax? I'm tired of relaxing," she said, feeling a bit frustrated. "I thought we were going to talk?"

"We will. When I get done cleaning up this mess."

"Fine. I need to check my e-mails anyway. Beth moved to her office while Mitch ran water in the sink and stacked the pots and pans on the drainboard.

When Mitch was done getting the kitchen back in order, he sat down in the living room with a cup of coffee, waiting for Beth to finish what she was doing.

After draining his cup dry, Mitch looked at his watch, wondering what was taking Beth so long. Standing, he was going to check on her when he heard the thump of her crutches on the hardwood floors. When she reached the living room, the look on her face was shadowed with sadness.

"Beth, what's wrong?"

"An offer has been made on the ranch," she said with a stunned, monotone voice.

"Really?" He sat down on the edge of the coffee table.

Beth leaned against the bookshelf.

Mitch didn't know what to say. Beth looked heartbroken. He leaned forward, resting his forearms on his knees.

"You don't have to do this, Beth. You just have to make Shane see how important this place is to you."

"More important than him?" she shot back. "I made my son a promise. If I turn my back on that, he'll think I'm just like his father, choosing something else over him. I can't do that to Shane."

"Beth . . ." Mitch moved to her side and wrapped his arms around her. "It'll work out. You'll see."

Mitch waited for Beth to resist. Instead, he felt her sag against him, overwhelmed with emotion.

"God knows what you're going through, Beth," he whispered in her ear as he stroked her hair. "He knows the decisions you have to make. He's not going to hang you out to dry."

"I know. I'm just so tired."

Mitch could hear the catch in her voice as she spoke into his chest.

"This whole last year seems like it's been one battle after another. I don't have any fight left in me."

"Sure you do," Mitch encouraged. "Like you said, you're just tired. You need a few days of rest to get your strength back. I'm sure you'll be in fightin' form in no time."

She pulled away enough to wipe at the tears wetting the front of his shirt. "I hate feeling like this."

"Oh, I don't know, you feel pretty good to me."

Mitch was only teasing, trying to lighten the mood, but when Beth looked up at him, her eyes revealed what she was feeling.

Instinctively, Mitch's natural impulses took over.

Beth knew what was happening, but did nothing to stop it.

She watched as Mitch leaned closer, waiting for his lips to touch hers. His kiss was soft and gentle not asking more than she was willing to give. Beth accepted his kiss eagerly, and returned his affection willingly.

Feeling embarrassed and confused, Beth pulled away, needing to take a step back, but Mitch held her close

"Why are you doing this to me, Mitch? You realize you're one of my problems, right?" She nervously played with a button on his shirt.

Tipping her chin up, so she had to look at him, Mitch grinned when their eyes met. "I don't see a problem."

"I'm serious." She playfully slapped his chest. "I'm scared. If you haven't already figured it out, I have a hard time trusting people. I can't handle giving my heart away, only to watch you drive off when you decide you've made a horrible mistake."

"I wouldn't do that to you, Beth." Mitch reached up and pushed a wayward strand of hair behind her ear. "I have a responsibility now. Not just to you, but to God. I've got a lot to learn, but I know one thing God requires of me. My word. I'm here for you, Beth. This is where I belong."

The rest of their evening was spent quietly sitting together on the couch, Mitch explaining to Beth all he'd been learning, and Beth listening with amazement. She could only imagine this is how her mother must have felt when her own father had made a one hundred and eighty degree turn in his life.

Thank you, God.

Thank you for bringing Mitch to the Diamond-J.

Chapter Thirty-Two

Voices caused Beth to stir. When she opened her eyes, she saw the questioning look on Shane's face, then realized why. There she was, nestled close to Mitch on the couch, his arm wrapped around her.

Beth's complexion heated as she slowly pushed herself to a sitting position.

"Don't get up on my account. I'm headed to bed," Shane said, then turned to Mitch and teased, "do you always have that effect on women?"

Mitch shrugged his shoulders. "What can I say? It's a gift."

Beth rubbed the sleep from her eyes, trying to focus. "Don't go, Shane. We haven't talked for almost a week. I want to know about this Kat person, how you're doing, what you're thinking. I'm worried about you."

Shane's heart constricted. It had been easy for him to push the accident from his mind when his mother was in the hospital. But now that she was home, he saw the way she hobbled around the house, and the strained look that creased her face whenever she moved. The reality of what he'd done and what it cost her hit him full force.

"Shane, come sit down for a minute."

"But Mom, it's late. I need to—"

"Please, Shane." Her voice was soft, but firm.

As Shane conceded and crossed the living room, Mitch slipped out from behind Beth and got to his feet.

"I've got some e-mailing to do." Mitch stroked Beth's arm. "Just let me know when you're ready to go upstairs."

Shane watched her nod with a smile before Mitch walked away.

"Mom, it's late. Can't this wait until morning?"

"I just need to know what you're thinking."

"I'm not going to run off if that's what you're worried about."

She looked at him, clear through to his soul. "I never meant to hurt you, Shane. I only wanted to protect you. I thought I could love you enough to make it all right."

Dropping down into the chair, Shane twisted his hands over and over again, leaning forward, staring at the floor. "Why didn't you just tell me the truth?"

"How, Shane?" Her voice cracked. "How was I supposed to tell a little boy that his father didn't care enough to stick around? What I told you was true. He did choose the rodeo. That's what he wanted to do."

"But you said he didn't know about me. Why did you lie?"

"Because I knew firsthand how painful it was to feel abandoned and tossed aside. I didn't want you to feel the same way."

"So you lied to me." His words were emphatic.

"I thought I was protecting you. And . . . I was afraid of what you might think of me."

His eyes met hers, seeing how difficult this was for her.

"Shane, what happened between your father and I . . . what he did was wrong, but . . . what I did was wrong, too."

"I don't understand."

"I was sleeping with him, Shane. What happened wasn't a one-time thing. I was drinking, sneaking out at night, doing things I'm not proud of. I got what I asked for. I just wasn't prepared for the consequences."

Shane let his mother's admission sink in. She was taking the blame, even though Shane knew the rest of the story. She was still trying to protect him from the truth. Slowly, his eyes came up to meet hers. "Uncle Charlie said he beat you up."

She nodded slowly. "He was angry with me. I tried blackmailing him into staying. I thought we could make it work if he would only try. I didn't want to believe what we were doing meant nothing to him. I thought I was in love. But to Cole, it was just sex—a good time before he left for the rodeo."

Shane was trying to digest what his mom was saying. It was hard to picture her the way she was describing herself. Sex. Drinking. Rebellion. He never imagined her being anything other than his mom. All his life, she'd lived by rules—was disciplined. The things she was saying just didn't fit.

"Shane, after you were born, I went to see Cole. I thought if he knew he had a beautiful son he'd reconsider, but he didn't. Cole was riding high on the rodeo circuit. Rookie of the Year. He thought I was going to cause him trouble, so he threatened me. Cole told me if I made a scene or tried to ruin his reputation, I'd be sorry. It crushed me to think he hated me that much. It was the final straw. I decided then and there your father would never be a part of your life. He was a horrible, self-centered, angry man. We didn't need him, or at least, I thought we didn't."

Shane got up and took a few strides across the room, raking his fingers through his hair.

"You don't believe me?" she questioned.

"It's just hard to match that image with the one I see on TV."

"No. You're right." Her words were sharp. "He's the All-American cowboy. He has his championships, his trophy bride, his perfect little family. What's not to like? He's made quite the life for himself. Why believe me?"

"Mom, I didn't say I didn't believe you. It's just . . . hard."

"Shane, I realize I can't stop you from contacting him. I'm just asking you to think about it before you do. And please, when you do, I want to know about it."

He stood still, contemplating his mom's request. When he heard her sigh, he turned and looked at her, and saw her eyes were closed.

"You're tired, Mom. You need to get your rest."

She extended her hand to him with a smile. He stepped forward and took it. She gave it a squeeze. "You still didn't tell me about Kat."

"You'll like her, Mom. She's a barrel racer. Just like you."

"Well, then tell me about her."

Shane let go of her hand and took a seat on the coffee table. "There's really nothing to tell. We've talked a few times, went on a couple of short walks."

"Does she like you?"

"I guess," he dipped his head, embarrassed and excited all at once.

"Really? Are you going to bring her around so I can meet her?"

"Probably. But I don't want you to make a big deal about it."

"Okay." She smiled. "Now, why don't you give me a hand?"

By the time Beth reached the bottom of the stairs, Mitch was at her side. Glancing up, she looked at what seemed to be an insurmountable task.

"What do you say we forego with the crutches? You're tired and I don't think I have the patience to watch you hobble up them."

Feeling worn out both physically and emotionally, Beth was more than willing to concede.

In one easy motion, Mitch scooped her up into his arms. Even through her exhaustion Beth's heart fluttered at the feel of Mitch's strength, the musky scent of his shirt, and the warmth of his body against hers.

It scared her.

It had been a long time since she'd felt this way about a man.

From the minute Mitch had shown up, she'd pushed her attraction for him aside, struggling to be obedient, telling herself Mitch would eventually leave and she couldn't allow herself to be hurt again.

And now . . . now it seemed too good to be true.

Beth's mind raced. She didn't want to doubt Mitch, or the decision he'd made. But how could she be sure his belief was genuine? What if he was only acting, or saying what he thought she wanted to hear? What would happen if she trusted him and found out too late it wasn't real? Was she ignoring her doubt because she wanted so much for it to be true?

Mitch gently set her down on the bed. "What's that look for?" he asked, pushing her hair back over her shoulder.

"Nothing, I'm just tired." She closed her eyes.

Mitch sensed a change in Beth's mood. Just an hour ago, she'd snuggled with him in the living room, relaxing and enjoying easy conversation, but now she seemed distant.

Maybe she was thinking again about selling the ranch.

Mitch wondered, but decided not to probe. Beth needed her rest and from the slight pinch in her expression, he could tell she needed medicine as well.

"I'm going to turn off the lights and lock up. I'll be back with your medicine in a minute. Can I get you anything else?"

"No. I'm fine."

Mitch was back in just a few minutes, a glass of water and medicine in hand. He sat on the edge of the bed hoping to see a difference in Beth's disposition. There wasn't one.

Swallowing her medicine with a swig of water, Beth rubbed her temples and stretched her neck from side to side.

"Just so you know, I moved in down the hall while you were gone. I thought it was for the best."

"What do you mean?"

"I was having a hard time reading Shane and wanted to be able to keep an eye on him. But now that you're home, I'll move my things back to my trailer in the morning."

"You don't have to do that, Mitch."

"But I think I should. For appearance sake."

"Appearances? To who?" She chuckled slightly. "Need I remind you, the first night you were here, you stayed in that very same room?"

"But that was different."

"How?"

"Well, I was a hostile patient then, annoyed by my circumstances, while you begrudgingly played the part of Florence Nightingale."

"And now?"

He reached forward and gently caressed her cheek. "Well, I would like to think things are different between us now."

His touch seized her, jolting Beth's heart into a frenzied thumping. "Maybe things have changed between us, but that doesn't mean my principles are going to take a backseat to any relationship we might establish."

Her words were clipped and rigid. She was putting up defenses, pushing him away because she was afraid of her own weaknesses.

"I didn't mean to suggest you would. I just meant that I wouldn't want anyone to get the wrong impression by me being here."

Beth could hear the edge in Mitch's words and see the hurt in his eyes. *Why did I say that? Why am I trying to pick a fight with him?*

"Like I said, I'll move my things out in the morning." Mitch got up and walked to the doorway. "But if you need anything tonight, just holler." He winked at her before turning off the overhead light and disappearing down the hall.

Beth stared at the ceiling, looking at the soft shadows cast by the bedside lamp. Her heart was still racing as she clenched the sheet against her chest, scolding herself for being so rude.

I don't know what to do, God. I want to believe Mitch with all my heart, but is that just wishful thinking? It can't be that simple. How can he be off-limits one day and the next be approved by You? Should I wait? Shouldn't I see if his commitment is real before I give in to the feelings I've squashed for the last few weeks?

Show me God.

Show me what to do.

Chapter Thirty-Three

Beth had a fitful night with very little sleep.

Her thoughts ping-ponged from her feelings for Mitch to Shane's melancholy, from the offer placed on the ranch to the realization Pandora was gone. One moment Beth was convincing herself a change of scenery is what she needed, that selling the ranch was the right thing to do. But quickly, she would change her mind, knowing comfort and familiarity is what she craved.

It wasn't even dawn when she heard the water pipes rattling in the old house and eased her eyes open. Glancing at her bedside clock, she moaned. *It's not even five o'clock yet.* Beth listened for signs of life and thought she heard footsteps in the hall. Then all was quiet.

Beth lay awake for a while longer until she heard the familiar sounds of Shane's morning routine. Easing to the side of the bed, Beth looked at herself, still wearing the clothes she'd worn home from the hospital. She wanted nothing more than to soak in a hot, luxurious bath, and wash away the stiffness in her joints and the aches in her muscles, but that would have to wait. A sponge bath was all Beth was allowed, at least for a few more weeks.

Stumbling and inching her way to the dresser, Beth pulled out a change of clothes, then used one crutch to hobble to the bathroom. Tossing her clothes on the vanity, she closed the door, then looked at herself in the mirror and groaned.

What a mess.

By the time Beth was done wrestling with her clothes, and using what little make-up she owned to make herself look presentable, the house was quiet. She took her medicine with the water left from the night before and stuck a few pills in the pocket of her sweatpants for later. When she reached the landing of the stairs, Beth took the easy way out and shimmied down the steps. She was just righting herself at the bottom when Mitch walked in.

"Hey," he hurried from the front door to where she was standing. "I was just coming to see if you needed some help." Mitch looked her up and down, then smiled appreciatively. "Wow, you look great."

"You mean for a woman on crutches wearing baggy sweatpants and an old tank top."

"No. I mean great. Period."

His smile warmed her. Beth couldn't discount Mitch's compliment completely. She had intentionally tried harder with the few make-up tricks she knew to cover the dark circles under her eyes and give color to her pale complexion. And the hot pink tank top helped her black sweatpants look a little less frumpy.

"I thought you had already left for the day," she said.

"No, not yet. I wanted to make sure you'd be okay on your own before I headed out."

"I'll be fine."

"Yeah, but now I'm not so sure I want to leave." He moved closer, stroking her arms with a devilish smile.

"Ranch work getting too hard for you?" she challenged.

"No way."

"Then I suggest you get out there and earn your keep. You've been slacking off for the last week."

He laughed. "What are you going to do?"

"Take care of business." Beth looked away, not wanting him to see the struggle she was feeling.

"Beth, the offer can wait. You don't need to respond right away."

"It's not going to get any easier the longer I delay it. At the very least, I need to see what the realtor has to say about the offer he sent me."

"But don't make any hard decisions until you've had a chance to think about it. If the buyer is really interested, he'll wait."

"I know, but I have to decide soon. I promised Shane he'd be able to start at a new school by the second semester, but I don't even know where we're going to move yet. I can't keep putting it off. I've got to start making some decisions."

"Shane will understand. Besides, he did have something to do with this little setback of yours."

"I know, but I still have to hold up my end of the bargain."

"But don't push it. Your health is what's important right now."

Beth heard the concern in his voice and smiled. "I won't push it."

"Good. I'll see you at lunch," he said quietly. "But don't worry about making it. I'll take care of it when I get back."

"I'm not an invalid, Mitch. I think I can handle making a few sandwiches."

"Okay. Then I guess I'll see you later." Mitch placed a tender kiss to her forehead and walked away, the screen door creaking behind him.

Beth waited and watched as Mitch left the yard. When she knew he was gone, she made her way to the mudroom and slipped on one of her riding boots.

Slowly, Beth made her way to the barn, concentrating with every step as she crossed the uneven ground and loose gravel. When she walked into the straw-littered building, she had to take a few deep breaths before she could go on. With timid steps, Beth approached Pandora's stall—not wanting to see it vacant—not wanting to acknowledge her loss. Her hand shook as she raised the latch and swung the gate open. Standing in the hollowness of Pandora's stall, Beth cried. She leaned against the worn slats of the stable and allowed herself to grieve for her companion, her confidant, her closest friend.

It took over an hour for Beth to make her way back to the house. Once there, she splashed some water on her face and went to her office so she could bury her grief in her work.

Starting with the stack of mail heaped on her desk, she sorted everything into three piles. Junk. Personal. Bills. Pulling out her checkbook, Beth worked on the stack of bills, glad that nothing was overdue. Next, she ordered needed supplies, then quickly looked through the junk pile before throwing the advertisements away.

Once everything was cleared off her desk, Beth saw the calendar notation for Monday. She had an order for forty heifers. Then, the following week, she had a pick-up of another hundred.

Beth panicked.

Rifling through her contracts, she refreshed herself with the agreements that had been drawn up. Noticing Arnold Porter was listed several times on her phone messages, Beth decided she'd better give him a call.

"Mr. Porter, it's Beth Justin. Sorry it's taken me so long to return your call. Oh, you heard about that. Yeah, it was a nasty fall, but I'm doing better now. I was just calling to make sure we were still on for Monday? I am, if you are. Okay, I guess I'll see you then."

Beth hung up the phone, feeling uncertain. It was already Saturday. They only had one day to round up forty head—that would meet the criteria of the contract—and get them into the holding pen.

Instinctively, Beth reached for the phone, needing to let Uncle Charlie know what they were up against. She punched in three numbers then hung up. *This isn't his fault. I'm not going to stress him out needlessly.*

Beth decided she would wait and talk to him at lunch, to see if they had enough time to fill the order. If not, she would just have to call Porter back and ask for an extension.

Beth continued working, paying no attention to the time when she heard a knock at the front door. Reaching for her crutches, she heard a soft "Hello" coming from the other room.

"Just a minute," Beth yelled, annoyed someone would just let themselves in. Trying to hurry, she tripped, nearly sending herself to the floor. Muttering under her breath, Beth made her way down the hall, craning her neck to see who was in the entryway. When she saw a woman with a stock pot in her hands and a young girl at her side, she immediately knew who they were.

Both women hurried to introduce themselves, their words jumbling together. Two additional attempts at introductions went much the same way, making everyone laugh.

"I'm sorry," the woman with the stock pot and oven mitts smiled, "you must be Beth."

"Yes. And that pot must be heavy." Beth chuckled, no longer feeling irritated.

"As a matter of fact, it is." She hurried to the kitchen and set the pot on the range. "Forgive us for letting ourselves in. Mitch told us it would be okay, but I know how forward it must have looked." Before Beth had a chance to respond, the woman pulled off the oven mitts she was wearing and extended her hand. "I'm Janis Carter and this is my daughter, Katherine."

The petite redhead put down the bag she was holding and shook Beth's hand. "It's nice to meet you, Miss Justin. You can call me Kat."

"It's nice to meet you both. Mitch has told me how kind your entire family has been to Shane while I was in the hospital."

Janis looked at Beth's crutches, then back to her. "We were sure sorry to hear about your accident."

"Thank you."

The three of them stood in an awkward silence before Kat asked, "How do you like your flowers?"

Beth glanced at the bouquet on the dining room table. "They're beautiful, and Mitch put them everywhere—in my bedroom, my office, the den." Beth noticed the look of pride on Kat's face, and it clicked. "Did you have something to do with them?"

"Sort of," Kat smiled, "but it was Mr. Grey's idea to buy them."

Beth was stunned when Kat called Mitch by his stage name. The girl continued to rattle on about the flowers while Beth tried to maintain her composure.

"Once Mr. Grey got the flowers home, he wasn't sure what to do with them. Since he had bought so many, I suggested using more than one vase. That way, he could put them throughout the house. He liked the idea, so he let me do the arranging."

"Well, you did a wonderful job."

"Thank you."

Beth leaned further on her crutches.

"You should be sitting down," Mrs. Carter said. "We didn't come to tire you out. We came to bring lunch."

"You didn't have to do that. I'm getting around pretty well."

"Yes, but I know how my boys eat. I wouldn't wish that on anyone." She laughed. "Besides, it gave me a chance to meet you."

Beth smiled. "Then why don't we take a seat in the den?" She led them to the other room and carefully lowered herself to the couch. Mrs. Carter sat on the other end of the couch while Kat took a seat in one of the side chairs.

"So, what brings you to Triune?"

Chapter Thirty-Four

Beth and Janis enjoyed easy conversation while Kat quietly sat by, adding a comment here and there.

Beth found out the Carter household consisted of five children, Kat being the only girl. Besides Tim and Tom, there was Nate, who was twelve and Dan, who was nine.

The Carters were cattle ranchers, just like Beth. The reason for their move was because they needed more land. Tim and Tom planned to continue in the family business, and eventually wanted to build their own homes. Start their own families.

It tugged at Beth's heart to hear Janis tell how her boys worked side-by-side with their dad, and that they were actually excited with the prospect of taking over the whole operation.

It was what Beth had wanted for Shane.

Unfortunately, it was her dream, not his.

Beth couldn't help but wonder if things would've turned out differently if Shane had learned about ranch life from a man—from his father. Beth's dad had died when Shane was only six, back when Shane looked at farm animals as pets, not chores. Uncle Charlie and Travis had tried to fill that gap, but it just wasn't the same.

Shane had missed out on that bond between a son and a dad, the hero worship a boy has for his father. The *I want to grow up to be just like you, dad,* that every father hopes to hear.

Beth had tried her best to be a good example, to nurture in Shane a love for the land and pride in a hard day's work, but with time, he just became more quarrelsome and distant. On some small scale, Beth even wondered if Shane was embarrassed by her. She certainly wasn't like the other moms she met on parent/teacher nights. Somehow, she always ended up in the corner of the room where the men were talking about feed prices and weather conditions, while the other moms got together for coffee once a week so they could organize fundraisers and talk about the latest guys voted off *The Bachelorette*.

However, the combative attitude reached full force when Shane put two and two together and realized how valuable the herd and the land were, but only if Beth sold it. That's when the real trouble began. Shane resented her for making him work so hard, while giving him a pitiful allowance. He resented the fact that they could be living in comfort, but instead, they busted their butts every day, only to wake up and do it all over again the next day. Shane didn't understand why Beth wanted to continue to do backbreaking chores when she could live a simpler life.

He didn't understand that Beth's lifeblood came from the land. She knew nothing else and had no desire to see what it was she was supposedly missing out on.

A rumble in the yard jarred Beth from her thoughts. She looked at Janis, realizing she had zoned out. "Sorry, I guess this medicine is messing with my mind," Beth lied.

"No problem," Janis said as she got up from the couch, "but since the cavalry is here, I'd better get that spaghetti heated up." She and Kat walked to the kitchen, Beth a few paces behind.

With boisterous conversations, nine men—men and boys that is—burst through Beth's front door and rambled into the dining room. She was stunned, not knowing what was going on.

"Lunch will be ready in just a minute, fellas," Janis said. "Let me just make sure it's warm."

Kat pulled paper plates and napkins from the bag she'd been carrying and started putting them around the table while the men and boys continued to banter and talk.

"Did you all wash up?" Janis asked.

"Yes, ma'am." The boys answered back in unison as they removed their hats and hung them on the back of their chairs.

Mitch moved to Beth's side and pressed a kiss to her cheek. Before she could reprimand him, he rested his hand on the small of her back and made the introductions.

"Beth, this is Hank, Tim, Tom, Nate, and Dan. Guys, this is Beth, the owner of the Diamond-J."

The Carter men immediately stood, tipping their heads slightly.

"I don't understand," Beth mumbled.

Uncle Charlie groused good-naturedly. "You didn't expect me and Travis to bring in the forty head by ourselves, did ya? I'm getting too old to be chasing them steer, and Shane never did learn how to rope that good. And Mitch here . . ." Charlie pointed to him, while the rest of the men erupted in laughter.

"Okay," Mitch threw up his hands in surrender. "It's not as easy as it looks."

"But how did you know about the contract?" Beth interrupted their teasing.

"Mom, it was written on your calendar, plain as day. All I had to do is look at the contract to know what Mr. Porter was expecting. I might not know how to rope, but I can read a contract. Mr. Porter had left a few messages, so I called him back to confirm his delivery would be ready on Monday."

"That's how he knew about my accident?" she stammered.

"You talked to him?" Shane asked.

"Yes, I called him this morning, but he didn't say anything about talking to you."

Shane was going to say something more, but was easily distracted when Kat leaned over the table to set two plates of garlic bread on the table.

"Okay, it's nice and hot," Janis said as she set the large pot on a hot plate in the middle of the table.

Before the men could dig in, Mitch asked Hank if he would like to do the honors of saying grace.

The man stood, bowed his head, and began.

"Our eternal Father in heaven, we come before you with thanksgiving, and praise. We want to thank you, Lord, for the protective hand You placed on Beth. Though tragedy could not be averted, we acknowledge Your mercy on this child of Yours. We pray You will encourage her in the days ahead as she weathers the healing process. We also want to praise You for Your guiding hand in bringing Mitch to the Diamond-J. What seemed to be pure chance, You have shown to be of Your design. God, I pray You will grow in Mitch the seed that You've planted. May we all be used to encourage this new brother of ours. And Lord, I thank You for the diligence of Shane, stepping in on his mother's behalf, seeing to the commitments of the Diamond-J. What a blessing it is for us as parents when our children show such signs of maturity. Bless this food we're about to eat. Allow it to nourish us as we work alongside our brothers and sisters in Christ. We give You all the glory and honor and praise. Amen."

Mitch grabbed the office chair from the other room and pulled it up to the table. Beth sat alongside him like a fly on the wall, listening as the men bantered back and forth.

Kat and Janis dished up their plates last and took a seat at the kitchen bar. But every so often, Beth would catch Shane exchanging glances with Kat, Kat smiling in return.

Beth closed her eyes, enjoying the sounds, the conversations, the laughter. It was reminiscent of her childhood when the ranch bustled with activity, everyone sharing around the dinner table, feeding off the energy of a hard day's work and loving it.

Those were the best years of Beth's life.

Then her mother had died, and everything changed.

The house no longer buzzed. It was quiet and empty, just a place for people to gather and eat. Her father's grief was difficult to navigate, so Beth spent a lot of time on her own—or with Pandora. Then, angry with God—and wanting to get even—Beth rebelled against everything she'd ever been taught. She drank, smoked, and flirted, thinking she was punishing God, when in fact, she was only punishing herself.

That next year, Beth's childhood came to an abrupt end with the birth of Shane.

JUST AN ACT

After that, each year brought a trial of its own. Rustlers. Drought. Fire. Even though Beth knew things would eventually get better, somehow, she became satisfied with just making it through. Beth had given up on joy, deciding she didn't deserve it.

Oh, for the days of innocence.

"Beth, are you alright?" Mitch whispered next to her ear.

She opened her eyes to see concern etched on his face. "I'm fine."

"You must be awfully tired if you can sleep sitting up."

"I wasn't sleeping; I was remembering." She smiled, but could see he was still concerned. She reached for his hand and gave it a squeeze. "I'm fine, really." She pushed her memories behind and pulled herself into the present.

When lunch was over, the men excused themselves from the table, grabbed their hats, and thanked Janis for a wonderful meal. Shane was the first to leave, Kat following him out the door. Beth watched as Janis exchanged a glance with her husband. Beth was relieved to see a smile on the woman's face. No hint of disapproval.

Mitch gave Beth's hand a squeeze. She could see the mischief in his eyes as he leaned forward to kiss her. She turned, only allowing his lips to brush her cheek. His newfound boldness in showing his affection needed to be tempered.

He chuckled. "Message received. I'll try to mind my manners, but I'll warn you, it's getting tough."

Janis started to clear the table of paper plates and wadded up napkins, gathering them up in a trash bag she brought with her.

"Janis, please, let me do that. You've done so much already."

"Nonsense. That's what I love about paper plates, easy clean-up. What kind of neighbor would I be to bring over all this food and leave you with the mess?"

"Believe me, I certainly wouldn't have complained."

Beth leaned on the bar as Janis moved about the kitchen. Beth pointed to the cupboard that held plastic containers for leftovers and watched as Janis dished out the remaining spaghetti.

"I'm sure it hasn't escaped your attention that Kat is sweet on Shane," Janis said, while rinsing out her stock pot.

"I think the feeling is mutual."

"How do you feel about that?" Janis asked.

"I'm not sure. I was going to ask you the same thing."

"Well, it would be naive of me to ignore it, especially now."

"What do you mean by that?" Beth felt a hint of defensiveness.

"Well, Kat has never been allowed to date before. We have a no dating rule. Sixteen is the magic number."

"And Kat isn't sixteen yet?"

"She turned sixteen last month."

Beth understood. "So, you never had to worry about her before now."

"Exactly. But now, with Shane so close, I—"

"Janis," Beth interrupted, "if Shane's done anything inappropriate, I want to know."

"Oh, Beth, goodness no, that's not what I'm getting at. Shane has been nothing but a complete gentleman. He's very respectful of our rules. Most the time he and Kat hang out with the other boys. They have taken a few walks just the two of them, and I think I might've seen them holding hands the other night, but that's all. I just thought we should probably have some ground rules. You know as well as I do, how quickly these things can get out of hand."

Just then, Kat walked back into the house, silencing both women. Beth couldn't tell if Janis was being sincere or if her comment about *things getting out of hand* was a jab at her being a teen mom. Not only did Beth feel judged, but she felt guilty as well.

"Can I help with anything, Mom?"

"No. I think we have everything cleaned up here."

"Kat, you could do me a favor," Beth said, wanting another moment alone with Janis.

"Sure."

"My flowers upstairs could use some water. Would you mind watering them for me? They're so beautiful. I want them to last as long as possible."

"Of course."

"There's a watering can in the mudroom. My room is the on the right."

Janis and Beth waited for her to climb the stairs.

Beth was quick on the defense. "Janis, just because I had a child out of wedlock doesn't mean I would want my son to fall into the same trap as I did. I admit I made a mess of things when I was a teenager, but don't judge Shane by my mistakes. If you would rather Shane not see Kat, just say so."

Kat came bouncing down the steps before Janis could say anything. But it was clear to Beth, the woman had something more to say.

"Kat, why don't you wait for me in the car. Beth has a private matter to discuss with me."

"Okay." Kat quietly walked away.

When the screen door squeaked shut, Janis turned to Beth. "Beth, please, I wasn't judging you."

"Weren't you? I mean, isn't it obvious I let *things get out of hand* in my own life?"

"So did I." Janis' words were quick and to the point.

"What?"

"I wasn't judging you, Beth; I was judging me."

"I don't understand."

"I was already pregnant with Tim and Tom when Hank and I got married."

Beth's shoulders slumped, relieved she wasn't in for a battle.

"We knew better, but we convinced ourselves we had everything under control. We were raised in the church and knew right from wrong. We even shunned our closest friends when they found themselves in the same situation. Somehow, Dan and I thought we were above it all, that temptation wasn't a problem for us. Well, one night we came crashing down from the pedestals we put ourselves on and ended up getting pregnant."

"Do Tim and Tom know?"

"Yes, and so does Kat. We'll tell Nate and Dan when we feel it's appropriate. So you see, I wasn't pointing fingers at you. I don't know your situation. I just know how easily emotions can get out of hand.

Sexual temptation is a strong force to contend with."

Beth hung her head. "I'm sorry I lashed out at you like that. I guess I was feeling a little defensive. I've really tried to raise Shane with godly standards. Sometimes I just feel like a hypocrite, telling him to do as I say and not as I did."

"I understand, Beth." Janis laid a reassuring hand on her shoulder. "It's a humbling thing having to admit to your kids, not only did you mess up, but you expect more from them then you could even manage yourself."

"Have you had any problems with Tim or Tom?"

"Tim was involved with a girl for a while. He knew we didn't approve of her, but continued to see her anyway. It put a strain on our relationship, but we made it through okay. When she finally showed her true colors, Tim realized why it was we didn't like her."

"Wow! With everything Shane has told me, I wouldn't have figured you had those kinds of issues."

Janis laughed. "It's called praying without ceasing. I tell you, Beth, it isn't our power, but the Lord's. I can't tell you how many times Hank had to hold me back from lashing out at that girl. He had to keep reminding me God cares about Tim even more than I do. We can't always make decisions for our kids, but we can certainly pray that God intervenes."

Beth smiled at Janis' candidness. It was refreshing to talk to another mom, something she'd never been able to do before.

"It's going to be okay, Beth. Who knows, this thing between Shane and Kat could blow over tomorrow. I just wanted to make sure we both kept our eyes open to the situation."

By the time Janis and Kat left, Beth was pretty worn out. She was overdue for medicine and was beginning to feel the negative effects. Reaching into the pocket of her sweats, she pulled out the tiny pills and hobbled over to the kitchen sink.

Wanting to be rested when Mitch and Shane came home, Beth decided to lie down for a while. As she got comfortable on the couch, she was reminded of Hank's prayer. His words of thanksgiving and blessings permeated her thinking as she drifted off to sleep.

Chapter Thirty-Five

Beth was still in the fuzziness of sleep when she heard low voices and muffled footsteps. She willed her eyes open, but saw no one. Light thumping upstairs told her Shane and Mitch must be home.

Pushing herself to a sitting position, Beth listened to the sound of running water vibrating the pipes overhead. Mitch came galloping down the steps, walking right past the den.

"Hey!" Beth yelled.

He stepped back in view with a smile.

"Hi, sleepyhead, I'm just taking some things to my trailer. I'll be right back."

Beth leaned back against the couch and closed her eyes. She listened to the squeak of the screen door opening and the slam of it shutting. Three times it opened and three times it slammed shut. Finally, Mitch plopped down on the couch next to her.

"How are you feeling?"

"Pretty good," she said as she rubbed her eyes. "I guess I kind of crashed after lunch."

"That's good. You need your rest." He set a package on her lap. "Here, this came today."

"What is it?"

"Your replacement phone."

"Oh, thanks." She'd hardly missed it since she hadn't been out and about on her own.

"So . . . what do you think of the Carters?" Mitch asked.

"They seem like a really nice family."

"Did you get a chance to talk to Kat and Janis after we left?"

"A little." Beth didn't share what they had talked about, but did have a question for Mitch. "Did you tell the Carters who you are? Because Kat called you Mr. Grey earlier today. I didn't say anything. I guess I was too stunned."

"I didn't tell them; she figured it out for herself. Her family knows. I've fielded a few questions, but they haven't hounded me. I think they realize if I wanted to talk about it, I would do it on my own."

"Are you worried?"

"About them telling the press or something? Nah. They're not that kind of people."

"So what were you doing just now?" Beth asked, wondering why he made so many trips outside.

"Just putting my things back in my trailer."

"You didn't have to do that. I don't have a problem with you staying in the guestroom."

"Well, I do. Tim and Tom have been spending a lot of time here, Kat as well. I don't want them getting the wrong impression."

Beth was ready with a rebuttal, but Mitch pressed a finger to her lips. "Uh, uh, uh, I've already moved my things. End of discussion." He slung his arm over the back of the couch. "Now, tell me about your day."

Beth swallowed hard, trying not to let her emotions show. "I walked out to the barn . . . said good-bye to Pandora." A silent tear ran down her cheek.

Mitch reached for her hand, squeezing it and caressing her fingers with his calloused thumb. "I'm sorry, Beth. I wish we could've done more. Charlie was torn up about it. But he knew he had no choice. He didn't want Pandora to suffer."

"I don't blame him. It's just hard to believe she's gone. I know you must think it's silly, being so attached to an animal, but—"

"I don't think it's silly at all." Gently, Mitch stroked her arm, comforting her as more tears fell. After a few moments, Mitch whispered, "Are you going to be okay?"

Sniffling, she nodded.

"Then I'm going to take a shower." He kissed the top of her head, then stood. "I'll work on dinner when I'm done."

"Janis put the leftover spaghetti in the refrigerator. I'm sure there's plenty for the three of us."

"Correction. The two of us. It's Saturday night and Shane's taking Kat to the movies."

"How? He doesn't even have a license."

"Tim and Tom are tagging along. Shane's giving them the grand tour of the town; then they're all going to see a movie."

Beth sighed in relief. At least she didn't have to worry about Shane and Kat being alone together. Not that she thought Shane would try anything inappropriate. Then again, Beth never thought she'd find him looking at pornography or shooting a gun at a passing vehicle either.

After Mitch disappeared upstairs, Beth awkwardly moved from the couch to her office. She needed to do something—anything—before she went stir crazy.

"Hey, Mom," Shane ducked into her office. "I'm going to town with Tim, Tom, and Kat. I don't know what time I'll be back." He moved to leave.

"Stop!" Beth barked, halting his steps. She waited for him to make eye contact with her, then asked, "Is this a date?"

"Yeah, right," Shane huffed. "It can't be much of a date with her brothers along."

Beth looked at him—wanting more information—but decided to let it go. "Call if you're going to be later than midnight."

"Okay," he said with a quick smile; then he was gone.

Beth turned back to her computer and checked her e-mails. She automatically dumped the advertisements that worked their way through her filters, then clicked on the new e-mail from her realtor.

The offer is solid. The client is looking for investment property. Let me know how you want to proceed.

How *did* she want to proceed? She wanted to tell the broker she was no longer interested in selling, and was taking the Diamond-J off the market. But she couldn't do that. She'd made a promise.

Beth stared at the screen—for who knows how long—but couldn't bring herself to respond.

"Interesting reading?"

"Mitch!" Beth jumped.

He laughed. "I'm sorry. I didn't mean to startle you."

"I didn't hear you come in." She rubbed at her side.

"Of course not. You had your face glued to your monitor."

"It's an e-mail from my realtor. I asked him about the offer."

"And . . ."

"I don't feel good about it. I don't know what it is, but it just doesn't seem right."

"Then pass on it. Tell your realtor you're not willing to make any concessions. Period. Leave it in God's hands. If He wants you to sell, He'll make the perfect deal happen. That is, unless you've changed your mind about selling?"

"Changed my mind?" Beth snapped, getting to her feet and limping past him. "I can't change my mind. This isn't about me, Mitch; this is about Shane." She stutter-stepped toward the kitchen. "I made him a promise, and I have no intentions of going back on it, especially after today. He really proved himself—researching the Porter contract—making sure the delivery was ready. I can tell he's trying. I have to do the same."

She shuffled around the kitchen, pulling out the leftovers from the refrigerator.

Mitch started to say something when Beth gave him a look that said, *drop it*. She poured the leftover spaghetti into a pan and stirred it as it simmered. Mitch moved in behind her, slipping his hands around her waist, resting his chin on her shoulder.

Beth nearly melted at his touch.

She should scold him, but didn't. She was enjoying it too much.

Her heart was pounding with such intensity, Beth was sure Mitch could feel it, too. Then, when he pressed his lips to the base of her neck, her heart raced into an even faster rhythm.

"Beth," he whispered.

"Uh huh," she sighed, feeling like Jell-O in his arms.

"I love you."

Her heart stopped all together.

Beth quickly reminded herself to keep breathing. *Say something, do something.* But what could she say? What could she do?

Smoke rose from the skillet, the smell of burning spaghetti doing nothing to break the trance she was in. Finally, Mitch reached for the dial and clicked off the stove top, then turned her around to face him. He gently cupped her face in his hands and locked eyes with her.

"Did you hear me, Beth? I said I love you."

Tears ran down her cheeks. "And I want to love you too, Mitch, but I'm not sure we can make this work."

"Why not?" he whispered.

"Because when I sell the ranch, Shane and I will be moving to the city. Then what are you going to do?"

"I'll go with you." He smoothed his hands against her hair, stroking her back with reassurance.

"Oh really? And what are you going to do when people figure out who you are? You're a celebrity. You're Simon Grey. You might be able to disappear in the middle of nowhere, but you can't disappear in the middle of a bustling city. You'll be hounded all over again. What are you going to do then when the pressure gets to be too much? Run?"

"No. As long as I have you and Shane, I'll have no reason to run. Sure, it might be hard in the beginning. But as soon as people figure out I'm just a regular guy, they'll leave us alone."

"How can you be so sure?"

"I can't. But it won't matter. God's not going to let anything happen to us. He worked way too hard to bring us together. He's not going to let anyone or anything screw this up. Trust me, Beth. Please. I know we can make this work."

With eyes moist with emotion, Mitch reached for her hands, brought them up to his lips, and kissed them. "I love you, Beth. And I promise, I will never do anything to hurt you. You or Shane."

She looked into his misty eyes and saw the determination of his words. Beth knew—right then and there—she could trust Mitch to make everything all right.

Tears continued to run the length of her cheeks as she reached up and stroked his face. He leaned into her caress, holding her hands with his own. "I love you, Mitch. I've tried fighting my feelings for you, but it's no use. You've turned my world upside down. From the moment Shane drove that beat-up Suburban of yours into the yard, I was sure you were trouble. But, I guess God had something else in mind."

Mitch barely waited for Beth to finish her proclamation before carefully wrapping her in his arms and pressing a fervent kiss to her lips.

Beth returned his kiss, a kiss full of love. Even though she was scared, she was trusting both God and Mitch not to break her heart again.

Chapter Thirty-Six

After dinner, Mitch followed Beth into her office where she was looking at prospective houses online. She wanted something near the city, but not in the center of town. A place close enough for Shane to be involved with all the activities a large high school had to offer, but in an area where she could still have a little land and stables for Midas and Apollo.

She scrolled through listings with determination while Mitch did everything he could to distract her, doing little to hide his affection.

"Come on, Mitch." She scrunched up her shoulders and laughed, bringing his nuzzling to a stop. "I'm trying to get something done here."

"So am I," he said with a roguish growl.

"Mitch, I'm serious. I need to start looking at homes. I need to find a location Shane will be happy with, but somewhere I won't feel claustrophobic." She studied the computer screen, scrolling from one house to another.

"You know, you could be going to all this trouble only to find out Shane has changed his mind about moving."

"You mean because of Kat?" Beth turned and asked. "You really think his feelings could be that serious after only a week?"

"I don't know about his feelings for Kat, but he was pretty serious when we were rounding up cattle today. He was all business. Shane acted like a foreman in charge, making sure every steer we roped met the contract specifications. He even butted heads with Charlie a few times. Maybe the reason Shane never showed an interest in the operations' side of the ranch before was because he didn't think he was needed."

"But I always encouraged Shane to ride along whenever we were rounding up cattle. He just blew me off."

Mitch just shrugged. "Well, maybe he wanted to do more than just ride along; maybe Shane wanted to be involved with the decision-making process. I mean, why would he bother to show an interest, if you and Charlie could do it without him?"

Beth stared blankly at her lap.

"Don't get upset, Beth. I just think you should talk to Shane before making any serious decisions."

After mulling it over, Beth e-mailed her realtor to decline the offer. She explained she'd had a minor setback and needed to extend the timeline of the sale. There was no reason her injuries should cause a delay, but Beth used the excuse to give herself more time.

Just in case Mitch was right about Shane.

Moving to the den, Beth and Mitch got comfortable in front of the TV, deciding to watch one of the movies he had purchased. With his arm draped across her shoulders and her head resting against his chest, Beth enjoyed the skillful banter between Sandra Bullock and Hugh Grant.

But, the more she watched the movie, the more Beth wondered about Mitch's former life as Simon Grey.

"Did you ever date Sandra Bullock?" Beth blurted out, while Sandra's screen character defended her beloved community center.

"What?" Mitch laughed.

"Just asking."

"Come on, Beth."

"Hey," she poked him with her elbow, "I told you my sordid past. I think it's only fair I know about yours."

Mitch sighed. "Sandy was married when I knew her."

"Well, she wasn't always married."

He gave her shoulder a squeeze. "No. I never dated Sandra Bullock."

Beth watched the movie for a few more minutes and then asked, "Do you know Hugh Grant?"

Mitch rested his head back against the couch cushions and chuckled. "I shared a few red carpets with him—and we exchanged pleasantries at a party once—but were we friends? No."

Beth looked up at him, amazed.

"What?"

"I can't believe you're so casual about it."

"Well, what do you want me to say?"

"I don't know."

Beth turned quiet while random thoughts occupied her mind. She conjured up images of Mitch with Hollywood starlets and want-to-be pop stars. She looked at her rumpled tank top and baggy sweats and wondered. *What does he see in me? I wear jeans, muddy boots, and have callouses on my hands. There's no way I can compare with the women he's been with. I don't even own an evening gown.* Beth looked at her unglamorous hands, subconsciously smoothed her hair back from her face, and straightened the hem of her shirt.

"What are you doing?" Mitch asked as she fidgeted.

"Nothing." She quickly tucked her hands—with chewed fingernails and cracked cuticles—under her legs, embarrassed.

Beth turned her attention back to the movie, but it didn't take long before she was thinking again about the lifestyle Mitch must have experienced as a leading man in Hollywood.

Feelings of inferiority poked at her conscience.

"So, did you date anyone I would know?" She asked, trying to sound nonchalant.

"Is that what this is all about?" Mitch turned to her, clearly amused.

Beth felt the flush of embarrassment creep up her neck and heat her face. "Never mind, it was just a question." She crossed her arms tersely against her chest, wincing at the self-inflicted discomfort, then stared at the television, not wanting to see the smile on Mitch's face.

"Beth, come on. Tell me what you're thinking."

"It's nothing. Let's just watch the movie."

"But, Beth . . ."

"I said it was nothing. Just forget it."

Concentrating on the dialogue in the movie, Beth realized she and Mitch were not unlike the main characters—two people from completely different backgrounds. One struggled to live life with purpose, while the other lived a charmed existence.

Mitch reached for the remote and clicked the TV off.

"Hey, I was watching that," Beth protested.

"No, you weren't."

"Yes, I was. Sandra Bullock was coming to the conclusion that she and Hugh Grant were two different people from opposite walks of life. She realized one rarely changed the other."

"So you don't think I can change, is that it?"

Mitch had obviously gotten the subliminal parallel Beth was making.

"What do you think I'm going to do, Beth? Play ranch hand for a few months, allow myself to fall deeper in love with you, then wake up one morning and decide to call it quits? I don't have commitment phobias, Beth, but maybe you do."

"I just don't get it." She shifted so she could look directly at him. "What do you see in me? In this?" Beth gestured toward the blackened sky outside the window. "I have blisters on my hands, and nails that have never seen the inside of a salon. My skin has freckles from spending too much time in the sun, and my idea of dressing up is making sure my jeans have a crease in them and my boots don't have straw stuck to the heel. How do you expect me to compete with the women you've been with?"

"I don't. Why would you even think that?"

"Because you're used to so much better, that's why. When the tabloids finally catch up with you, they're going to have a field day. They'll say you've gone crazy and call me a hick that doesn't know the difference between an evening gown and a nightgown."

"Is that what you're worried about? What people will say?"

"Of course, I'm worried about what people will say. Aren't you?"

"If I was worried about what people say or what they think, I wouldn't be here in the first place. I would've continued to do what was expected of me. In fact, the way I was going, I probably would've ended up in a rehab facility or driven my fully loaded sports car into a tree. Don't you get it, Beth? I'm not looking to replace my lifestyle; I want to improve it. And now that I've found what was missing, I have no intentions of falling back into the same traps I was in before."

Mitch reached for her hands and held them tight. "I love you," he said emphatically. "I love the callous' on your hands and the way you look in blue jeans," he grinned. "I love the freckles across your nose and the way you tip your hat back from your eyes when you get angry."

Beth tried to pull her hands away, embarrassed Mitch read her so easily, but he held her hands even tighter.

"I love you, Beth. I love everything about you. Even though you're bossy, stubborn, and can be a real pain in the butt when someone challenges you, the fire you get in your eyes when you're hell-bent on getting your way is as intoxicating as your smile."

He leaned in closer, bracing his hands against the arm of the couch, pinning Beth to it. "You are the most incredible woman I've ever met. I want nothing more than to work by your side all day and love you all night.

"I want to marry you, Beth."

Beth swallowed hard, not believing her ears. *Did he just say that? Did Mitch just say he wants to marry me?* She looked into his eyes, not knowing what to say, how to respond. "Mitch, I . . . I don't know—"

Mitch stopped her by pressing a finger to her lips, which was good, because she couldn't string two words together anyway.

"Beth, I didn't mean to spring that on you. I know you're not ready for that kind of commitment, so I'm not going to put you on the spot. But I want you to know, I'm willing to wait, because you're everything I've ever wanted."

Before she could say anything, Mitch claimed her lips with a passion and a fire Beth had never felt before.

Hours later, Beth lay awake, unable to rein in the thoughts running through her mind. She and Mitch had decided to call it a night after his impassioned speech and their very intimate kiss. Beth was shocked with his straightforwardness in telling her he wanted to get married. Of course, Beth knew she wanted the same thing, but saying it out loud made it sound so real.

When she heard creaking on the steps, Beth glanced at the clock. Midnight. She listened as Shane walked quietly down the hall to his room. Now that he was home, Beth figured she would finally be able to fall asleep, but her thoughts continued to hold her captive.

She could feel herself smiling and thought it ironic.

Pandora is gone, the ranch is up for sale, and I have a cast on my leg. Not only am I terrified Shane is going to do something reckless like confront Cole, but now I find out he has a girlfriend, creating a completely different list of concerns.

What business do I have smiling? I should be pacing the floors or better yet, in a loony bin mumbling to myself.

But Beth realized why she was smiling. Even though everything in her life was completely out of control, she felt a twinge of hope.

She was learning to trust again.

But it went further than that.

She was in love.

In love with a man who wanted to love her back.

Chapter Thirty-Seven

Beth was up early the next morning feeling alive and invigorated. She carefully scooted down the stairs with her crutches, the smell of fresh-brewed coffee luring her into the kitchen. Expecting to see Mitch, Beth was surprised he wasn't there.

"Hum?"

Hobbling to the front door, Beth watched as the sun was just beginning to rise—the morning sky still a creamy shade of grey—then peered out at Mitch's Airstream. *No lights.* She looked at her stocking feet knowing she should put on her boot, but brushed it off. Carefully maneuvering the porch steps, Beth crossed the yard to the stables.

"Mitch," she called out, thinking he might be feeding the horses. *Nothing.* Gimping around the corner, Beth looked to see if he was with the pigs or the chickens, but he wasn't there either. Glancing at the open field, Beth wondered. *Maybe he went for an early ride?*

The steer in the holding pen caught Beth's eye, so she worked her way over to the fence. Inspecting the small herd, she was impressed by the job the men had done.

Beth stood for a few moments reflecting on her life as a rancher. It was all she'd ever known. *How am I ever going to give this up?* Maybe she would have a talk with Shane—like Mitch suggested—and see if he was having second thoughts.

"What are you doing out here?"

Beth gasped, startled that Mitch had been able to sneak up on her so easily. Once she'd caught her breath, she turned. "I was looking for you. Where were you?"

Mitch pushed his hat back, then leaned forward and stole a morning kiss before answering. "At the Carter's."

"The Carter's? What were you doing there so early?"

"Talking with Hank."

"About what?"

"Things," he said casually. "I have questions about the Bible, so Hank's helping me understand it better."

"Why didn't you ask me?" Beth didn't mean for her voice to sound so bristly, she just felt slighted he didn't ask her.

Mitch shrugged. "I guess I didn't think much about it. I had asked Hank to explain a couple of things to me while you were in the hospital, so he offered to meet with me each morning—to help me out. I thought it sounded like a good idea."

"Oh." Beth realized what Hank was doing. He was mentoring Mitch, 'encouraging this new brother' as he had said in his prayer over lunch the previous day.

"Does that bother you?" Mitch asked.

"No, I'm just surprised, is all." Beth smiled. "So, what do you have on your agenda for the rest of today?"

"Today is Sunday, a day of rest," Mitch stated, like he was a child reciting a Sunday school lesson, "and I plan on doing just that."

"Oh . . . well, I see you learned the most important lesson from the Bible first," she teased.

"You've got that right." Mitch stretched out his legs with a groan. "Besides, I need some down time. I thought I had gotten used to being in the saddle, but rounding up cattle and cutting them off when they get spooked is a lot different than riding fence, repairing posts, and checking water supplies. My legs are killing me." He rubbed his hands against his back pockets.

"Are you sure it's only your legs that are bothering you?" Beth teased as she glanced behind him.

"None of your business." He grinned. "Unless you're volunteering to rub out the kinks?"

Beth laughed. "Not me. You're just going to have to cowboy up and tough it out on your own."

"I wouldn't get too sassy if I were you. I might be sore, but you're disabled. You avoided the water trough once." He glanced toward the galvanized tub. "But that sassiness of yours is going to get you into trouble."

"You wouldn't!" Beth lifted her chin, calling his bluff.

"Wouldn't I? You look pretty confident for someone who has gotten herself into a predicament before."

"Maybe that's because I know when you're bluffing, and you wouldn't do anything to hurt me."

"Um, um, um, there's that sass I was talking about."

Exchanging a playful kiss, they headed toward the house, climbing the steps slowly, chuckling at each other's aches and pains.

Shane was just coming down the stairs when they walked in.

"Hey, how was the movie last night?" Beth asked.

He shrugged. "It was good. Well, the movie was lame, but we still had a good time. We went bowling afterwards." Shane's eyes brightened. "Kat and I buried Tim and Tom."

Beth couldn't help but smile. The look on her son's face was the happiest she had seen him in ages. She hated to squash his good mood, but Beth really wanted to talk to him about the move.

"So . . . do you have any plans for today?"

"Actually, I'm heading over to the Carter's later, after I get my chores done and eat some breakfast. They invited me to have Sunday devotions with them and then lunch. But I don't have to go if you need me here."

"No, that's all right. You go ahead." Beth forced a smile. "But how about we have dinner together?"

"Why?" Shane's bright eyes darkened with concern. "Is something wrong?"

"No, nothing's wrong. It's just that I've been home for three days and haven't gotten to spend any time with you."

"But nothing's wrong, right?" he asked again.

"Nothing's wrong," Beth assured him for a second time.

"Okay, I'll make sure I'm home for dinner," Shane said as he headed toward the front door.

"I'm making pancakes for breakfast." Beth called after him. "So don't take too long."

"Are you going to talk to him about selling?" Mitch asked.

"I'm going to try."

Once in the kitchen, Beth propped her crutches in the corner, choosing to shuffle and hop from countertop to stovetop. It was ironic, the one complaint she'd always had about her house was the fact that the kitchen was so tight. But she definitely appreciated that now because everything she needed was just a few steps away.

After assembling the few ingredients she needed for pancakes, Beth hopped to the refrigerator and pulled out a slab of bacon. Mitch maneuvered around her, trying to be helpful by getting down a mixing bowl and corralling the eggs that were rolling around on the countertop. But in such tight quarters, he was only proving to get in the way.

"I can do this, Mitch, really. It makes me feel useful. But, if you want to be a help, you can get down the pancake pooper from that cupboard." She pointed above the sink.

"The what?" he laughed.

"It's a contraption for pouring pancakes."

When he reached to open the cupboard, Beth saw him wince. "Hey, are you all right?"

"Yeah, just a little stiff."

"It's right there," she said, pointing at the far corner of the cupboard. "It's that white funnel thingy with the little spring-loaded whatchamacallit in the middle of it."

He chuckled. "Are those the technical terms?" Reaching for it, he winced again. Once he had it in his hands, Mitch played with it for a second before handing it to her.

"Thank you. Now, I would appreciate it if you became an interested observer so I can get this done."

"Okay, but if those eggs roll off the counter, don't expect me to clean up the mess."

Mitch massaged his shoulder as he walked away.

"You really are sore, aren't you?" Beth asked, no longer teasing.

"My shoulder is killing me," he admitted, while kneading the taunt muscles around his neck and shoulder. "I really jacked up my arm trying to learn how to rope. I knew it was getting sore, but I didn't realize it was this bad."

"Here," Beth reached inside the freezer and pulled out an ice compress. "Put this on it for a while." She handed it to Mitch and watched as he carefully laid it across his shoulder. "After breakfast, I'll rub some liniment on it. It smells terrible, but works great."

Beth watched as Mitch gingerly took a seat on one of the barstools, reminding her it wasn't only his shoulder that was hurting. She felt horrible he was in pain, but when Mitch grimaced as he sat down, she couldn't help but smirk.

"You're enjoying this, aren't you?" Mitch asked as he tried to get comfortable.

"I'm sorry." Beth laid a hand on his forearm while trying to suppress a giggle. "I didn't mean to laugh. It's just that you look so cute when you're not trying to be all macho."

"Cute! Yeah, that's what I was going for when I was busting my butt—literally— trying to prove to Shane and Charlie that I can do more than just act."

"Is that why you did it? You were trying to earn their approval?"

Mitch dipped his head sheepishly.

"Awe, that's sweet," Beth said as she hobbled around the counter to his side. "You really are courting me."

Mitch swiveled his barstool toward her and pulled her close. "And what if I am?" His smile was captivating. Penetrating.

"Then I'd say you're doing a good job of it." Beth smiled as she brushed her hand against the stubble along his jaw.

Hearing the screen door slam shut, Beth moved away from Mitch, not wanting another awkward scene with Shane. She limped back around the side of the counter and reached for the eggs that were sitting next to the stove. Cracking them on the edge of the mixing bowl, she glanced up at Shane when he stopped at the kitchen bar.

"I'm gonna take a shower before I go to the Carter's."

"Okay, I'll have breakfast ready when you come down."

Beth realized even the simplest task—like mixing pancake batter—was more difficult than usual because of her cracked ribs. After carefully filling her little white contraption, she started plopping the pancake batter onto the griddle while pushing the sizzling bacon around in the pan. She grabbed the bottle of syrup from the refrigerator and stuck it in a pan of simmering water.

Beth could feel Mitch watching her out of the corner of her eye as she balanced on one leg and worked the griddle. Stacking the pancakes on the plate in the middle of the stovetop, she chanced a glance at Mitch, but was unable to discern the expression on his face.

"What's that look for?" she asked.

"What look? I was just enjoying the view," he answered with a sly grin.

Beth felt her cheeks heat up, hating once again that Mitch could make her blush so easily. The amusement in his eyes told her he enjoyed it far too much.

"Well then, I guess I'm just going to have to ignore you."

She continued to stack pancakes on the warming plate while the bacon drained on a pile of paper towels. Taking a can of orange juice concentrate from the freezer, Beth set it in the sink and ran hot water over it. After placing three sets of silverware on the counter, Beth reached for the plates in the overhead cupboard, but not before folding her arm across her midsection for extra support.

"Here, let me set the table." Mitch stood with a groan.

"I've got it, gimpy. You stay put."

"Wow, name calling. Where's the love?"

Beth giggled as she positioned one crutch under her arm and plates and utensils in the other, then limped toward the dining room and assembled three place settings. She moved back to the kitchen to flip the last few pancakes and take the remaining strips of bacon from the pan.

She was just finishing up with the orange juice when Shane came bounding down the stairs, the scent of musk immediately permeating the room. Beth recognized the scent that was distinctly Mitch's. When she made eye contact with Mitch, he quickly shook his head, stopping the question on the tip of her tongue.

"Smells great, Mom," Shane said with enthusiasm as he took the pitcher of orange juice from her, and sat it on the table. "What's with the ice pack, old man?"

"Wow, more name calling. Like mother, like son."

Shane laughed as Mitch slipped the ice pack to the counter, then carried the plate of bacon to the dining room table. When Beth reached for the warm plate of pancakes, Mitch stopped her.

"I'll get that." Using a kitchen towel as a potholder, he carried the heated plate to the table, setting it on the lazy Susan. He then grabbed the butter from the counter and their coffee cups. Beth removed the bottle of syrup from the stove top, toweled it off, and hobbled to the table. Mitch pulled out her chair and waited until she was seated, before sitting down next to her.

"Shane, why don't you say grace?"

Shane tipped his head down and began. "Heavenly Father, thank you for this food, for friends, and for good times. Help Mom heal quickly. Amen." He raised his head, then immediately forked a stack of pancakes.

Though his prayer was short and sweet, it made Beth smile. Not because of his request on her behalf, but because he'd thanked God for 'good times.' She couldn't recall the last time Shane had been so positive.

She shared a smile with Mitch before dishing up her breakfast.

"The Carters seem like a really nice family," Beth said casually as Shane wolfed down his breakfast.

He nodded his head before taking a large gulp of orange juice.

"I mean, Janis told me they moved to Triune so Tim and Tom could eventually expand the family business. They must really enjoy what they do."

Mitch glanced at Beth with a smirk, obviously understanding the subliminal message she was trying to send.

"Hank told me what he had in mind," Mitch chimed in. "He figures the extra land will more than triple their stock and their work load. Once he gets it all set up, he'll put the word out for full-time hands. Sounds like it's going to be a pretty lucrative venture."

"Reminds me of the Diamond-J in years gone by," Beth mused, hoping Shane would see the potential of what it was they were walking away from.

She and Mitch continued to talk about the cattle business and how the Diamond-J still had the capabilities of running a large operation, but Shane didn't take the bait.

He devoured his breakfast, took one last swig of orange juice, then stood. Hurrying around the table, Shane grabbed his hat from the coat rack by the door and said, "I'll be home for dinner."

The screen door slammed shut behind him, punctuating the end of their non-existent conversation.

"It was a good try, Beth, but I doubt he heard a thing you were saying. His mind's not exactly on ranching at the moment."

"Wasn't that your cologne he was wearing?" she asked as Mitch bit into his last strip of bacon.

"Yeah. He asked if he could use it. I was flattered."

"So, what else has he asked you?" Beth wondered how personal Shane had gotten with his questions.

"We've had a few conversations."

Her jaw dropped, but before she could say anything, Mitch stopped her with a raised hand. "It was completely harmless. He just had a few questions."

Beth refrained from peppering Mitch with the questions running through her head. "I guess I can only pray some of the enthusiasm the Carters have for ranching will rub off on him."

"It could happen. Tim and Tom are pretty excited about their plans. For once, Shane is hearing from someone his own age about the cattle business. And the Carters are all about family, and the importance of leaving a legacy for generations to come."

Beth sighed, finishing the last of her breakfast. *If there's a way, God, change Shane's heart before it's too late.*

Mitch stood and started clearing the table of dishes. Wincing when he extended his reach, Beth remembered the discomfort he was in.

"I'll get that liniment. The sooner you have it on, the better you will feel."

She positioned both of her crutches under her arms and started for the steps.

"Let me get it," Mitch offered. "There's no sense in you going up and down the stairs any more than you have to."

"I can do it myself. Besides, if I'm going to be on these things for another few weeks," Beth waved her crutches in the air, "I might as well get used to them. You can't run up and down the stairs for me all day long."

Mitch mumbled something about stubbornness and being pigheaded, but Beth ignored him, taking the steps one at a time.

Several minutes later, Beth returned, breathing heavy, with a sheen of perspiration on her face and shoulders. Gimping over to the dining room, she pulled the cold cream style jar from her pocket and set it on the table.

Mitch dried his hands on a kitchen towel while shaking his head. "Why must you be so stubborn?"

"I thought you said you found my stubbornness 'intoxicating'?" She swiped her forearm across her brow with a hint of a smile.

Mitch laughed as he crossed the room. "No, I said I found your stubbornness to be a 'pain in the butt.'"

"Oh, is that what you said? Somehow I thought you were more poetic than that."

He moved to her side, running his finger the length of her arm, causing a tremor to travel through her body. "But I do find your smile intoxicating." He leaned down, kissing her before she could say anything to deflect his compliment.

Enjoying his kiss far more than she should, Beth took a step back, putting some distance between them. "Take your shirt off."

"Excuse me?" Mitch mischievously arched his brow.

"Your shirt, take it off, so I can put some liniment on your shoulder."

"Wow, for a moment there, I thought you had lost all control."

"You wish." She slapped his chest, playfully.

Reaching over his head for the tail of his V-neck t-shirt, Mitch groaned. Dragging it over his head, he pulled his arms free of the sleeves and tossed the shirt on the table.

Beth didn't know where to look. Her pulse raced at the sight of Mitch's muscular form. The time he'd put in on the ranch made his already chiseled body even more defined.

Reaching for a dining room chair, Mitch flipped it around and straddled the seat. Folding his arms along the back of the chair, caused every muscle across his back to flex.

Beth gathered her composure and reached for the jar of liniment. She stood behind Mitch, trying to keep her mind on his sore muscles instead of his lean body. The minute she unscrewed the cap, the rank odor caused her eyes to water.

"What the heck is in that stuff?" Mitch turned around, his nose twisted in disgust.

"I'm not completely sure. I know it has comfrey and rue bitterroot, witch hazel, and cayenne." Beth ran her fingertips through the amber-looking gel, then smeared it across Mitch's right shoulder. He immediately turned his head away, trying to get his nose as far from his shoulder as possible.

"It's actually a horse liniment. We use it—"

"A what?" Mitch shot from the chair, nearly knocking Beth off balance.

"Relax." She tried hiding her amusement as she pushed him down on the chair. "We use it all the time."

"Okay, so you know it has no short-term effects. But how do you know it won't cause some horrible skin condition or some grotesque growth twenty years from now?"

Beth laughed at his over-reaction. "Uncle Charlie has been using it for years and hasn't developed any strange growths or tumors."

Begrudgingly, Mitch let her continue. "Okay, but I'm warning you, if I find out this is some sort of trick, I *will* retaliate."

"Just relax," she chuckled. "Once you get use to the smell, it actually feels pretty good."

Working the warming gel into Mitch's shoulder, Beth felt the moment his muscles relaxed. His involuntary sigh spoke of the effects the soothing liniment had on his sore muscles.

Massaging his shoulder firmly to help the salve penetrate deep beneath his skin, Beth kneaded the muscles from Mitch's neck to the bulge of his bicep.

"I'll round up cattle every day if this is what I can look forward to at night," Mitch spoke between moans and groans of appreciation. "How 'bout working a little of your magic over here?" Mitch said, pointing to his trapezius and lat muscles.

"Okay, just let me pull up a chair and sit down."

"That's okay, Beth. I don't want you to exert all your energy on me." He began to stand up.

"Would you sit down!" She pressed on his shoulders until he was back in the chair. "Boy . . . you're not a very patient patient, are you?"

"Hey, I could sit here all day. I just don't want you overdoing it."

"Let me worry about that, okay?"

Beth ran her fingers through the gel and smoothed it on to Mitch's back. She rubbed, massaged, and kneaded his muscles, allowing her ministrations to work from one side of his back to the other. Beth's fingers traveled from Mitch's shoulders and neck to his lower back. Her strokes were slow and methodical, doing what she could to release the tension she felt in his knotted muscles.

Soon, Beth realized she was enjoying herself a little too much, her mind traveling to places it should not go.

Beth knew she should stop.

Then why didn't she?

Chapter Thirty-Eight

Mitch was lost in the feel of Beth's touch.

Her fingers worked wonders on his tight muscles, but it was her smooth, methodical strokes that were wreaking havoc on his hormones.

It wasn't the first time Mitch had experienced strong physical feelings for Beth, and it certainly wouldn't be the last. But there was something in her touch that told him Beth was feeling the same thing. It was a feeling he wanted to pursue.

Mitch rose from the chair and turned to face Beth. He reached for her hand, and without a word, she put her hand in his, and stood. Slowly, Mitch stroked her arms, squeezing her elbows, pulling her closer. He brushed his thumb across her lips before bending to taste them for himself.

Beth wrapped her arms around Mitch's neck, and pressed her body against his. The kiss they shared started out slow and refined but quickly escalated to sensual and searching. She could feel the heat of Mitch's skin against her shirt as her fingers caressed the fringe of his hair. Mitch's hands moved up and down her spine, holding her close, eliminating any room between them. Beth felt his labored breathing, her own chest rising and falling in rapid motion. When Mitch deepened their kiss, Beth lost all sense of balance. She clung to him, needing his strength to keep her from falling. That's when she saw flashes of light dance across her closed eyelids.

Warning lights.

With a gasp, Beth pulled away from Mitch, almost stumbling backwards. Mitch reached out for her, but she quickly turned toward the dining room table and began to fumble with the jar of liniment. Too embarrassed to look at Mitch, she kept her head down while trying to get her labored breathing back to normal.

"Beth . . ."

"I need to wash my hands."

She moved around him, hobbling on her cast, reaching for the kitchen counter for balance. Turning the tap water on hot, she briskly rubbed her hands together. *What's gotten into you, Beth? Have you totally lost your mind? You're acting like an oversexed teenager.* Mitch walked up behind her. She felt his presence but didn't know what to do or what to say.

"Beth, we didn't do anything wrong."

"Of course, we didn't. Why would you say that?" Her voice cracked as she continued to scrub her hands. *It's what I was thinking that has me praying for forgiveness.*

"Because you're acting like we did."

"I am not. I just needed to wash this stuff off my hands."

Mitch moved closer. "So, you're saying you didn't feel what I felt?"

Beth didn't answer, she just kept washing hands that were already clean.

Mitch reached around her, turned off the faucet, then gently turned her to face him. "Beth, look at me."

She was too embarrassed.

Placing his finger under her chin, Mitch brought her eyes up to meet his. "We *are* human, Beth."

"Then why were we acting like such animals?"

She was overreacting and knew it. Even though their kiss had turned sensual, they hadn't crossed a line physically.

"I'm sorry, Beth. I shouldn't have let things get so heated."

"I'm the one who should be sorry." She grabbed for the dishtowel and fervently dried her hands. "You're used to taking things to the next level. You were just following your instincts. To you, this was standard procedure. In fact, you've shown a lot of self-control waiting for me to drop my guard. But I know better, Mitch. I shouldn't have let things get out of hand."

Mitch couldn't remember feeling more insulted. Beth thought he was manipulating her, and it angered him. After all this time, after all they had shared, he couldn't believe Beth thought he was capable of something so calloused.

Letting go of her, Mitch walked back to the dining room table and picked up his shirt. "Don't believe the rumors, Beth. I'm not as virile as you give me credit for."

He pulled his shirt over his head, yanking down the hem. "I didn't bed half the women the rag magazines linked me with. Believe it or not, I do have a basic understanding of what morals are. I would've thought you could see that by now." He headed for the door.

"Mitch, I didn't mean—"

"Didn't mean what?" He turned, anger squaring his jaw. "To trivialize my feelings for you? To assume my goal was to get you into bed? To think the only kind of relationship I'm capable of is sexual?" He shook his head in disgust. "I know I'm not perfect, but I thought I'd shown you a glimpse of the man I want to become. I guess I have a lot to learn about Christians. I thought forgiveness and letting go of the past was essential. I know God forgives me and sees me as someone new. I guess it was too much to think you would, too." He pushed the screen door open and let it slam behind him.

Beth stood with her mouth hanging open, tears stinging her eyes. *What did I just do? How could I say those things to him?* She realized the anger she felt at herself, she'd just poured out on Mitch. *How could a day that started so good take such an ugly turn?*

Chapter Thirty-Nine

Beth found Mitch in his trailer. He didn't bother to look at her when she opened the door or even when she struggled to hoist herself up onto the suspended metal step. He just laid on the couch, his left arm behind his head, his sore arm on his chest. With his eyes fixed on the ceiling, he ignored her completely.

With a heavy sigh, she closed the door and sat down next to his feet.

"Mitch, I'm sorry I said those things."

He didn't acknowledge her. He just kept his eyes trained on the ceiling.

"Mitch, please, I didn't mean to make you out to be . . . I mean, I know you're trying to change, and that you're not like that anymore."

"Like what?" He looked at her, his eyes challenging her to explain.

Beth swallowed hard and prayed she wouldn't put her foot in her mouth again. "Like the man I've read about in tabloids and entertainment magazines."

"How would you know what they say? You don't even read those magazines."

She hung her head feeling ashamed by what she'd done.

"You looked them up on the Internet, didn't you?" Mitch pushed himself to a sitting position, his back against the wall. "Beth, look at me."

She did, tears running down her cheeks. "I'm sorry. I did it out of curiosity, after you told me who you were."

"So, you think you know who I am because of what you read in those magazines?"

"No." She shook her head as she reached for his hand. "I know who you are because of what you've told me . . . because of what you've shared with me."

"I'm sorry, Mitch. I didn't mean to make you sound like an opportunist or a lowlife. I was trying to say I understand it's going to be hard for you to have a relationship without sex. Not because you can't, but because you had nothing stopping you in the past. A celibate relationship is something new for you.

"I wasn't blaming you. I was trying to apologize for my own weakness, for letting things get out of control. I didn't mean to tease you or get you all worked up. I'm the one who's the lowlife." She hung her head in embarrassment.

"I'm the one who crossed the line."

Mitch closed his eyes and took a deep breath. Though he was still hurt, Beth's heartfelt apology softened his anger. "Come here." He tugged her hand; she scooted closer. Cradling her neck in his hand, he drew her closer still and placed a tender kiss on her lips, then pressed his forehead against hers.

"You're not a lowlife."

"I feel like a lowlife," she mumbled.

"Well, you're not. I understand what you were trying to say in that backward explanation of yours. Well, sort of," he said, with quiet laughter. "I at least know you didn't mean to hurt me."

"I really didn't. I guess it's just that I feel so inferior. I was trying—"

"Inferior? Inferior how?"

She pulled away, fiddling with her hands. "You know what I mean."

"No, I don't."

She rolled her eyes. "Inferior. The way I dress. The way I act. The way I look. How I live. Come on, Mitch, you've had the cream of the crop when it comes to women. I'm still having a hard time understanding why you would settle for someone like me."

"Beth, we've been over this before. I'm not settling. You're more beautiful than any woman I've ever been with."

"How can you say that?"

"Because it's true."

She looked away.

"Beth, listen to me. I've had physical encounters with women, but never relationships. I've woken up in the morning, a woman in my bed, talking on her cell phone with the man she was meeting later that night. I had another woman tell me she was disappointed with my performance and said I fell short of the hype. They used me as much as I used them.

"The only relationship I ever found myself emotionally involved, was with my co-star in the first film I was cast as a romantic lead. I fell head-over-heels for her, and her with me. Or so I thought. We were an item the entire time we were filming. Then, after the red carpet premiere, she gave me my walking papers. To her, our relationship was just a publicity stunt, something to boost box office sales on a movie that was sure to tank.

"I didn't trust anyone after that. To me, all my co-stars felt like painted shells—beautiful on the outside, empty on the inside. I refused to open up to anyone. Sex and alcohol became ways to release tension, not build relationships.

"So you see, you are the most beautiful woman I've ever been with. You're as beautiful on the inside as you are on the outside."

"Right, I'm beautiful," Beth said sarcastically. "These aren't beauty marks, Mitch." She held up her hand for him to see. "These are calluses."

He took her hand in his and kissed the toughened skin. "I find them beautiful. You know what else I find beautiful? The way your hair looks when you let it down at the end of the day and it falls over your shoulders." Mitch pulled the band that held her golden hair in a ponytail until it fell free from its grasp.

"And your neck." He brushed the back of his knuckles down the slender slope of her neck.

"And the way your cheekbones look when you blush." He caressed them as well.

"And the way your jeans hug all the right places, and the sassy look you get on your face when you plant your hands on your hips. But above everything else, I love the way your eyes tell me your desire for me is as deep as my desire for you. That's why I love you, Beth. Because I know I'm going to be loved in return."

Beth's eyes watered with emotion.

"So, do you believe me when I say you're the most beautiful woman I've ever known?"

"Yes," she whispered, then leaned forward to place a tender kiss to his lips.

"Then marry me."

Beth stared at him, clearly shocked.

"Come on, Beth, let's get married." Mitch waited with anticipation for her answer.

"No." Beth said firmly before getting to her feet.

"What do you mean, no?"

She fiddled with the handle of the Airstream, and carefully stepped down the stairs. "Just what I said. No."

It took a minute for Mitch to react. When he did, he jumped from where he was lying and hurried after her. "Beth . . ." he reached for her elbow, careful not to let her stumble, "why not?"

"Because I'm not ready for that." She turned around to face him. "I have enough changes going on right now. With selling the ranch, Shane, this," she pointed to her cast. "I can't get married with a cast on my leg."

"Is that it? Is that all that's keeping you from saying yes?"

"Mitch, I don't want to rush into anything. I need to think of Shane."

A light breeze swept Beth's loosened hair across her face. Mitch pulled the wayward strands back and looped them behind her ear. "That's okay. I'll wait as long as you need. I'm not going anywhere."

Chapter Forty

Beth and Mitch spent the rest of the day relaxing, watching movies, and just being quiet together. Though his proposal was all she could think about, Beth didn't bring it up. Thankfully, Mitch chose to give her some space.

"I have some work to get done," Beth said as she scooted to the edge of the couch. "E-mails, bills, things like that." Carefully, she got to her feet and scrunched the crutches under her arms.

"Then I'm going to catch up on Sports Center." Mitch reached for the remote. "Shane keeps peppering me with sports trivia, trying to trip me up. So, while he spends time with the Carters, I think I'll load up with some ammunition of my own."

Beth had been scrolling through house listings near Topeka for at least twenty minutes when Mitch called to her from the other room.

"Hey, Beth, you might want to hear this."

Beth groaned, reached for the crutches, and headed for the other room. "What?"

"Just watch."

She turned toward the television as the theme music brought the show back from commercial. The two commentators bantered back and forth about the latest news in baseball and their predictions for the World Series.

"What am I watching for?"

"You'll see."

Beth waited a few seconds longer when all a sudden, a picture of Cole Dempsey appeared over one of the commentator's shoulders.

Her eyes were transfixed to the screen.

"In the world of rodeo, a major player has shocked his fans," the reporter announced. "Three-time All-Around Champion, Cole Dempsey, has been arrested for assault with a deadly weapon. Though details of the altercation are still unfolding, it seems an argument broke out between Dempsey and Daniel Brewer—the foreman of his Oklahoma ranch. Early reports say shots were fired. Though Dempsey says it was simply a misunderstanding, Daniel Brewer is telling a different story. Released on one hundred thousand dollars bail, Dempsey will be arraigned later this week."

"This just isn't Dempsey's year," the other commentator added with a cavalier smile. "Out for the season with a back injury, and separated from his wife of thirteen years, it seems Dempsey has more to worry about than riding a rank bull."

Both commentators chuckled and then moved on to the next headline.

Stunned, Beth slumped to the arm of the chair, speechless.

"I guess Mr. Dempsey is finally getting what he deserves," Mitch said with the same cavalier attitude as the broadcasters.

Beth didn't acknowledge him. All she could think about was the effect it would have on Shane.

"Beth, are you all right?"

It took a moment before she could answer. "I was just wondering how Shane is going to react."

"Hopefully, it will be just the thing to side-line his plans to meet him."

"Meet him?" Beth snapped around to look at Mitch. "What do you mean, meet him?" When Mitch cringed, her stomach plummeted.

"Okay, Beth, now don't get upset."

"Then tell me what you're talking about." She had to work to control her tone.

Mitch pushed himself forward, resting his elbows on his knees. "Shane plans on confronting Dempsey. He wants to tell him who he is."

"When? Where? And you were going to keep this from me?"

"Beth, relax."

"Relax! How am I supposed to relax?" She bit her lip, trying to control her anger. "How do I know Shane hasn't already done something stupid like contact Cole . . . or make arrangements to meet him somewhere?"

"Shane hasn't made any arrangements."

"How do you know? How can you be so sure?"

"Because I told Shane I would take him."

Beth blinked back her surprise, trying to comprehend the fact that not only did Mitch know about Shane's plans, he was actually going to help him.

"I can't believe you!"

"Beth, please, let me explain."

"Explain what? Explain how you've gone behind my back and made plans with Shane? Plans you know I wouldn't agree with. Why would you do that? I told you how I feel about Cole. I told you what he did to me, what he could do to Shane. I can't believe you would encourage him. What were you—"

"Beth!" Mitch shouted as he sprang to his feet. "Are you going to give me a chance to explain, or are you just going to keep ranting?"

Beth clutched her fists, angry Mitch would yell at her like that. She crossed her arms over her chest, ignored the pain, and silently stared at him, giving Mitch the chance he wanted to explain. Though it wouldn't matter. No explanation would be good enough.

"I did it to protect Shane." Mitch's voice was more controlled as he tried to explain. "When you were in the hospital, Shane told me he still wanted to meet his dad—that it was something he had to do. I asked him not to say or do anything right away, to give you some time to recuperate. I promised Shane, if he just gave you a little time to recover, I would personally take him wherever he needed to go to meet the guy."

"Mitch, how could you?"

"Because I could tell I wasn't going to talk Shane out of meeting Dempsey, and I didn't want him to do something stupid, like talk Tim or Tom into taking him somewhere. I figured if Dempsey is the loose cannon you say he is, it wouldn't be safe for Shane to go alone or with another kid. Dempsey thought he was a big man pushing a woman around. I figured he wouldn't try to pull that kind of garbage with Shane if I was standing right there."

The more Mitch talked the more possessive he sounded, like he was protecting his own son.

"I'm sorry, Beth. I thought I was doing the right thing keeping the lines of communication open with Shane. Don't get me wrong, I'm not taking his side. Meeting Dempsey is not going to fill the emptiness Shane's feeling, but he won't know that until he learns it for himself."

Beth didn't say anything. She was still trying to digest everything Mitch had said.

"Beth . . ." He moved closer. "Beth, say something."

"I . . . I don't know what to say."

"Well, at least tell me you understand why I agreed to help Shane. I didn't do it to hurt you, and I didn't purposely keep it from you. I just thought you needed a little more time to recover before you had to deal with this."

Mitch reached for her hand, squeezing it to get her attention. She looked up at him, feeling like she was going to come unglued. "I guess I was only fooling myself into thinking Shane would give up on something he's talked about his entire life."

"Well, like I said, maybe this will change his mind."

"And if it doesn't?" Beth looked at Mitch as if he had the power to make the whole situation go away.

"Then we'll cross that bridge when we get there."

Mitch pulled her close, wrapping his arms around her. Beth sunk into the comfort of his embrace, wanting to draw from the strength he was offering.

"Beth, I'm here for you and Shane. You've got to believe that."

She wanted to. She really did. But every time she turned around, she felt as if another part of her world was unraveling.

Help me God. I don't think I can handle much more.

Chapter Forty-One

Beth worked at the stove while trying to figure out what she was going to say to Shane. She had planned on talking to him about moving, or the possibility of not moving. But now, Beth needed to talk to him about his father before he heard the reports for himself. She wasn't sure how to approach either subject, so she continued to rehearse in her mind different ways she could casually work them into an average dinner conversation.

"Smells good," Mitch inhaled deeply as he leaned over the stove and the simmering strips of steak.

"Fajitas are Shane's favorite."

"Lucky me." He smiled.

Beth could tell Mitch was just trying to lighten the mood.

"What can I do to help?"

"You can grate the cheese while I make the guacamole."

They worked together in silence. Beth found it comforting.

When Shane walked through the door, it took only a second for him to figure out what was for dinner.

"Wow, fajitas. What's the occasion?" Shane said as he approached the kitchen counter, leaning over the bar and stealing a piece of sautéed steak.

"No occasion," Beth answered quickly, forcing herself to smile. "It just sounded good to me, and I knew you'd be in favor of it."

"You got that right." He reached across the counter for another piece of meat but Beth swatted his hand out of the way.

"That's enough," she said playfully. "Why don't you do something constructive like setting the table?"

Once everything was on the table, and the three of them took their place, Beth asked Mitch if he would like to say grace. He looked at her with surprise, but nodded in agreement before bowing his head.

His prayer was short and to the point, asking God to see to Beth's healing and for direction regarding the future. He thanked God for their food and for bringing him to the Diamond-J before he uttered a quick amen.

Shane dug in right away, filling his soft tortilla with sizzling strips of steak and grilled sweet peppers. Mitch made his own masterpiece, but Beth wasn't as enthusiastic about the meal as they were.

Taking a large swallow of soda, Beth sat up straight and readied herself to breech one of the two subjects she knew they needed to discuss.

"Shane, I wanted to talk to you about the selling of the ranch." He looked at her, his mouth stuffed to capacity, waiting for her to say something further. "I want you to know a promise is a promise, and I have every intention of following through with my end of the bargain. It's just that . . . well, I mean with my accident and all . . . not that it won't still happen . . ."

Shane swallowed hard, and cleared his throat. "You're telling me we won't be moving in the fall, is that it?" he asked matter-of-factly.

"I don't see how we can. July is almost gone and most escrows take at least thirty days. I haven't even found a place for us to move yet. And even when I do, by the time I get all the details squared away and start all the paperwork . . . I'm just afraid—"

"Mom, I understand," Shane cut in.

She looked at him, surprised by his casual demeanor. "You're not mad?"

"How can I be mad? It's my fault. If it wasn't for me, you wouldn't be laid up with a bum leg."

"But I promised you could start the new semester in a new school."

"I can stick it out a little while longer."

His laid back tone left her speechless.

"Does Kat have anything to do with your willingness to rough it a little while longer?" Mitch teased.

"Maybe." Shane answered with a grin before rolling another tortilla and stuffing the end into his mouth.

The sense of relief Beth felt was short lived. Though she was thrilled Shane was understanding about the move, she wasn't so sure he would be as docile when it came to the next topic of discussion.

Beth forked a strip of steak and pushed it around in the dollop of guacamole on her plate. She hated to ruin the good mood, but knew she had to finish what she started.

"Shane, there was something else I wanted to talk to you about."

He rolled his eyes playfully and swallowed his mouthful. "Come on, Mom, you're not going to give me the third degree about Kat, are you?"

"No . . . no, that's not it." She stuttered, not knowing how to approach the subject.

"Then what?"

"I want to talk to you about . . . your father."

There. I said it.

Shane sat up a little straighter, his shoulders stiff. "What about him?"

"I know you plan on contacting him. And I know you think if you—"

Shane jumped to his feet and stared at Mitch. "Way to go, Mitch. You just couldn't keep your mouth shut, could you?"

"Shane, don't blame Mitch. It's not like he volunteered the information." Beth tried to calm her son, or at least deflect his anger away from Mitch.

"Right. Let me see . . ." Shane over-exaggerated his pondering of time. "He waited a whole ten days before telling you!"

Shane stormed toward the front door.

"Your father's been arrested," Beth blurted out.

Shane stopped in his tracks, then turned around, shocked and confused. "How do you know that?"

Beth hobbled toward Shane. "It was on ESPN earlier today. He had an argument with someone on his ranch. A gun was involved."

"Is he in jail?"

"No, he's out on bond, but that's not the point." Beth brushed aside the details from the report to get to the heart of the matter. "This proves he hasn't changed. Cole is still a violent man and I don't want you to have anything to do with him."

"Well, if he's not in jail, then it can't be that bad. The cops wouldn't let him go if there was proof he did something wrong."

Beth couldn't believe Shane was actually defending Cole.

"Shane, there's more. He's out of competition because of an injury, and his wife is leaving him. His picture-perfect life is crumbling. If you contact him and pressure him into facing his responsibilities he's liable to lose it all together. I just don't want you to get caught up in all that."

"Well, it's too late. I've already contacted him."

Shane's words were like a bucket of ice water tossed in her face. The shock of his statement rendered her speechless.

Mitch moved from the dining room table to the entryway. "But Shane, I thought I told you I would take you to meet him when it was time. You promised me you would wait until your mom was doing better."

"To meet him, yes, but I didn't say I would wait to contact him."

Beth could see the anger burning behind Mitch's stoic expression. She knew he felt lied to and was ready to explode, but she shook him off, then turned to Shane. "When did you contact him?"

"A few days ago."

"How?" Beth continued.

"I e-mailed his website."

"What did you say?"

"I told him who I was, and that I knew he was my father. I explained I wasn't trying to make trouble for him. I just wanted him to acknowledge who I was."

"Did he answer back?"

"Yes."

Beth couldn't believe it. She never suspected Cole would admit to knowing who Shane was. "What did he say?"

"That he understood there was a possibility he could be my father."

"A possibility!" Beth shouted. "What did he mean by that?"

Shane shifted his eyes to the hardwood floor. Beth could feel his avoidance, so she asked again.

"What did Cole tell you?"

"It doesn't matter. You told me what happened and I believe you. The point is, I let him know I was interested in meeting him, and he didn't completely shut me down."

"Cole agreed to meet you?"

"Not yet. But he didn't say no either."

"Well, with the trouble he's in now, I wouldn't bank on hearing from him anytime soon. Cole only looks out for himself."

"Maybe, but at least I have a way to communicate with him."

"What for? He admitted to you there was a *possibility* he was your father, yet he never sought you out. He ignored the very fact that you were born! Does that sound like someone who wants to be your father? He's a self-centered, self-righteous, son-of-a—"

"Beth!" Mitch shouted, before she lost complete control.

She looked at the challenge in her son's eyes, desperate to make him understand. "Shane, I just don't want to see you get hurt."

"Maybe he's changed. It has been sixteen years. Maybe he's different?"

"He was just arrested for assault!" Beth shouted, her adrenaline spiking once again. "People like that don't change!"

"Well, I'm willing to take that chance."

Beth panicked. For the first time, she realized why she was so afraid of Shane meeting Cole. It wasn't just fear that he would get hurt; Beth was afraid she would lose Shane altogether. She was terrified Cole would pretend to be the iconic father Shane had always wanted. He would brainwash Shane into believing he was a stand-up guy.

Cole was a master manipulator. He would convince Shane she was guilty of keeping them apart all these years. Then she would have to compete for Shane's love. And she would lose. Cole would turn

Shane against her.

Defeat seized Beth as tears slid down her cheeks.

"Mom, don't cry. You're making too big a deal out of this," Shane said softly. "We've e-mailed a couple of times—that's it. Like you said, if he's in trouble with the law, he'll probably be busy for a while. All I wanted to do was open the lines of communication between us, and that's what I did. Now I have to wait and see where it goes from here."

Shane hugged her carefully. "I love you, Mom. Nothing is going to change that."

She held on to him tighter than usual, ignoring the pain, clinging to him, not wanting to let him go. "Be careful, Shane. Don't let him hurt you like he hurt me."

"I won't."

Shane released his hold on her, leaving the three of them in an awkward silence.

"Aah . . . I told Kat I would see her after dinner, but I can call her if you'd rather I stay home?"

"No. You go on. I don't want to ruin the rest of your evening."

"Are you sure? I mean, I'll stay if you still want to talk about all this. I wasn't hiding it from you, I promise. I had every intention of telling you. I was just waiting until you were stronger, like Mitch and I had agreed." Shane made eye contact with Mitch. "I didn't go back on my word."

"There's really nothing more to say," Beth said. "You know how I feel about Cole, but I can't stop you from talking to him. Just be careful."

"I will; I promise."

Once the front door shut, Beth sagged against her crutches.

"You okay?" Mitch asked.

"I don't know," she whispered as she made her way to the couch, sinking into the cushions with the weight of her emotions.

JUST AN ACT

Mitch watched Beth lie down on the couch and close her eyes. He wanted to go to her and promise everything would be all right but knew she needed time to process all that was said. Instead, Mitch quietly cleaned up the dinner that had been interrupted.

God, protect Shane. Don't let him get hurt. And help Beth deal with everything without stressing her health.

Mitch didn't know what else to say. This prayer thing was new to him, but he was sure God was listening.

That was all that mattered.

Chapter Forty-Two

Weeks had gone by since Beth found out Shane was in contact with his father. She showed great self-control not to bring it up or ask if they were still talking. Since Shane hadn't said anything lately, she could only hope that the e-mails had stopped.

Then, one day over lunch, Shane announced that the charges against Cole had been dropped, confirming what Beth had feared. Shane was still communicating with his dad. She listened as Shane explained the misunderstanding that had led to Cole's arrest, cringing when she heard acceptance in Shane's tone.

Night after night, Beth prayed for Cole: that he would reconcile with his wife, and be healthy enough to compete again. She didn't do it because she cared about Cole, she did it because Beth was convinced if he had his *perfect* life back, he would forget all about Shane. Beth felt guilty knowing her prayers were diametrically opposed to her son's. Even so, she would rather live with guilt than have to stand by and watch Shane fall for Cole's lies and get hurt in the process.

In the meantime, Beth watched as Shane and Mitch's relationship continued to grow, something she thanked God for every single day. She had worried Shane would put distance between him and Mitch now that Cole was in the picture, but that hadn't happened. Each night, before they came in for dinner, Mitch would take Shane driving out on the highway, so he could practice for his driver's test. Then, when Shane came home after spending the evening with Kat, he and Mitch would talk on the porch before going to bed.

At times, Beth couldn't help but worry, knowing they were talking about girls, dating, and relationships. She knew Mitch would probably be more open and honest than she wanted, but Beth was confident he would never say anything contrary to her beliefs.

Shane was not only growing on the relationship front, but he was stepping up around the ranch as well. The Diamond-J was bustling with activity as more of the herd was being moved and shipped out to buyers. Shane was proving what Beth always knew, ranching was in his blood. Deep down inside Shane was a Justin. He sat tall in the saddle, barked orders when needed, and when he checked with her regarding orders and deadlines, Shane sounded like a seasoned hand who'd been ranching his entire life.

When Beth watched him walk the fence line each night, hand in hand with Kat—the picture of contentment—she couldn't help but pray that Shane would change his mind about moving before it was too late.

And then there was Mitch.

Beth's heart raced just thinking about him.

Working alongside Uncle Charlie, Travis, and Shane, Mitch had become a full-fledged cowboy and was loving every moment of it. Every day he came in for lunch, covered in dust and sweat, but somehow, Mitch made it look oh so sexy. He would kiss her cheek before washing up, making her blush for everyone to see. Beth scolded him every time, but loved that he did it anyway. Even with the loss of Pandora and breaking her leg, having Mitch in her life made Beth the happiest she'd been in a very long time.

Still, she had moments of doubt. Late at night, when Beth was alone, her insecurities liked to play a game of twenty questions. *What if Shane decided to go live with Cole? And Mitch decided to go back to Hollywood? What would she do then?*

Beth couldn't answer the questions, because she really didn't know what she would do. Shane was her life, and Mitch held her heart. Without either one of them, Beth wasn't sure where she would be, and hoped she would never have to find out.

With dinner almost done, Beth stood in the kitchen waiting for the oven timer to go off. Mitch was taking a shower, and Shane had gone to the Carter's to pick up Kat for dinner. With no one around, Beth grabbed a butter knife from the drawer and slid it up and down inside her cast, desperate for relief.

"What are you doing?"

Beth yelped, startled by Mitch's appearance, but didn't stop what she was doing. "Sneaking up on a woman with a knife in her hand is a dangerous thing to do."

"I didn't sneak," Mitch laughed.

"I can't stand this itching any longer. It's driving me crazy."

"Come on, you only have one more week."

"Well, it won't be soon enough for me." Beth tossed the knife in the sink, just as the timer dinged. Lowering the door, she allowed the aroma of pot roast to fill the kitchen.

"Here, let me get that."

Mitch stepped toward the oven, grabbed the pot holders off the counter, and reached for the roasting pan. With an oven mitt, Beth plucked the foil-covered potatoes from the oven, and placed them on a serving plate.

Mitch removed the lid, exposing the succulent meat, glistening with juices. "Smells wonderful, Beth."

"Thanks. Can you slice it for me?"

"Sure." Mitch pulled a carving knife from the drawer. "I thought Kat was coming over for dinner tonight."

"She is. Shane went to get her."

"That explains why he skipped the driving lesson."

"Yep. He came in, took a shower, then left."

"Has he said any more about his dad?"

"I know they're still e-mailing," Beth said with a chip on her shoulder, "but Cole must be giving him the brush-off. If he had been serious about getting to know Shane, he would've made an attempt to meet him by now."

"Is that what you want?"

"Of course not!" She quickly lowered her voice before continuing. "Shane's only going to get hurt."

The screen door squeaked open, announcing Shane and Kat.

"Hi, Kat."

"Hello, Miss Justin, Mr. Gr—, I mean . . . Mr. Burk."

"Come on now, Kat, we've been over this. It's Beth and Mitch."

"Yes ma'am," she said with a smile.

Mitch carried everything to the table while Beth poured the drinks. After everyone took a seat, Mitch said grace.

They talked about everyday things: the continued progress on the Carter ranch, the herd, Beth getting her cast off. Easy conversation.

As the meal progressed, Shane and Kat whispered among themselves. It was clear Shane was trying to get Kat to say something, but she was reticent. Finally, Shane spoke up, even though Kat tried to hush him.

"Mom, Kat wants to ask a favor, but she's afraid to."

"I'm not afraid." She pushed Shane's shoulder, annoyed. "I just didn't think this would be a good time, with your leg in a cast and losing Pandora."

Beth's heart tightened slightly at the mention of Pandora, but smiled at Kat. "It's all right. What's the favor?"

"Well, I'm entered in the rodeo. Barrel Racing. Shane told me how good you were, so I was wondering if maybe you could give me a few pointers?"

Beth was flattered. "Sure. I mean, I haven't done it for years, but I can certainly watch your technique and give you my opinion."

"That would be great."

"What's your time?"

"I haven't been able to break eighteen seconds. My closest was eighteen-three."

"That's really good," Beth said, remembering how excited she'd been as a teenager when she'd finally broken twenty seconds.

"Yeah, but the girl who beat me last year posted a seventeen-eight."

"So you placed second last year?"

"I've placed second for the last three years," Kat said with defeat.

"Yeah, but not this year. This year you're going to nail the competition," Shane said with enthusiasm.

Kat just smiled.

After dinner, Mitch excused himself to Beth's office while she and Kat talked about the mechanics of barrel racing.

Jerry had sent him a dozen e-mails, each one sounding more urgent than the previous one. Mitch figured it was time he found out what was going on.

"Jerry, it's Mitch."

"Where have you been? I've been trying to reach you for over a week!"

"Calm down. What's got you so worked up?" Mitch asked, irritated with Jerry's tone.

"I'll tell you what's up! If you don't get back here quick, you're going to lose everything!"

"What are you talking about?" Mitch ignored his dramatics.

"Your contract with Lexmar Studios."

"What contract?"

"The one you signed when you were cast in *Here We Go.*"

"Jerry, what are you talking about?"

"In exchange for a larger paycheck up front, you agreed to do the sequel to *Here We Go,* in the event the studio decided to make one."

Mitch dragged his hand down his face, vaguely remembering the deal. "But that movie was a bomb. Why on earth would the studio want to do a sequel, now?"

"Are you kidding me? The chance to do the movie that brings Simon Grey out of hiding? They're all over it. They've got a gold mine, and they know it. Mitch, they're threatening to sue if I don't deliver you by September 1st."

"Can they do that? I mean, is there some sort of buyout clause?"

"No way. They're not budging. Either you show up or they're going to bankrupt you and blackball me. I won't even be able to sign a deal for a toothpaste commercial in this town." Jerry sighed, "I'm sorry, Mitch. I didn't see this coming. Unfortunately, we have no viable options."

Jerry genuinely sounded apologetic and concerned.

Mitch thought for a minute, then asked, "Did Kara sign on for the project?"

"Yep."

Mitch's stomach tightened. *How am I going to explain this to Beth?* "You're sure there aren't any loopholes or extensions we can use, anything to give us some time to sort this out?"

"Nothing. If you had a project on the calendar, we could claim a conflict in scheduling. But since you have nothing, they've got you cornered."

"And this isn't a scheme of yours to drag me back to Hollywood?"

"I wouldn't do that to you, Mitch. Granted, I was pretty ticked off when you left me high and dry, but I've had a few weeks to come to terms with it. I'm not lying. This is the real deal."

Mitch massaged his brow. "Okay, Jerry, I guess I don't have a choice. I'll be in touch."

"Two weeks, Mitch, that's all you have."

"Set up an appointment for the first of September. I'll be there."

Mitch ended the call and sank back into the office chair.

"Be where?"

Mitch spun around to see Beth leaning against the doorframe.

"Who were you talking to?"

"My agent."

"And . . ."

"I have to do another film."

Beth stood up straighter. "I don't understand. I thought you said that part of your life was over? That you were done with acting?"

"I did. I was. But there's this contract I signed years ago. With all the publicity surrounding my disappearance, Lexmar Studios has decided this is the perfect time to collect. If I don't show up by September 1st, they're going to take me to court. Jerry said they'll bankrupt me before they give in." Mitch looked at Beth, willing her to understand.

"Who's Kara?"

Chapter Forty-Three

"It's her, isn't it?" Beth whispered, not wanting it to be true. When Mitch sighed, it was all the answer she needed.

Kara was the actress Mitch had fallen in love with.

She walked away.

"Beth, wait," Mitch called after her, but she kept going, not stopping until she was on the porch. Clinging to the front post, Beth closed her eyes, wanting to scream.

Mitch was going to leave.

She had known all along it was too good to be true, too much to hope for. Once again, Beth let a man in. Now he was going to break her heart.

She was sitting on the swing when the screen door creaked open. Mitch took a seat next to her and reached for her hand. She pulled away.

"Beth, I have to do this. If I don't, it will ruin Jerry. I can't do that to him. He's been too good to me. I just can't leave him holding the bag."

"So go," she said belligerently, then pushed to her feet.

Mitch caught Beth's arm and pulled her down on his lap. She tensed, wanting to pull away. Mitch had promised he would stay. And now he was leaving, just like Cole had sixteen years ago.

Mitch framed her face with his calloused hands and pressed his lips to hers. Beth sensed the assurance he was trying to give, but her wounded heart would not be tricked again. When Beth's hot tears wet their lips, she broke their connection.

"I won't go. It's not worth losing you. Nothing I have is worth that."

"But you said it yourself, if you don't go, your agent will be ruined."

"Jerry is a big boy. He'll have to work this out for himself."

"But what about you? You'll lose everything."

"I don't care about *everything*. I care about you."

Mitch brushed away her tears with the back of his hand. Beth looked into his eyes; unshed tears pooled against her lashes. "I'm afraid I'm going to lose you."

He pulled her close. "You're not going to lose me, Beth. That could never happen."

"But you loved her once. How do you know you won't fall in love with her again?"

"He stroked Beth's hair as he whispered next to her ear. "Because I love you."

Mitch hated the insecurity he saw in Beth's eyes. He wanted to assure her his heart belonged to her—and her alone.

"Beth," he sat back, holding her hand, "marry me. Then I can take you with me, and introduce you as my wife." Mitch looked at her, excited with possibilities. "It will be fun. I'll show you around Hollywood and Malibu. And we can drive up to San Francisco when I get a few days off. It could be our honeymoon."

"Oh sure, because I have nothing else to do." Beth looked at him with a furrowed brow. "It's not like I have a ranch to run and a child to raise. Oh yeah, and a house to buy and a ranch to sell. Sure, I'll just run away to your fantasy world and leave reality behind."

Mitch felt deflated. He hadn't been thinking. Of course, he couldn't expect Beth to drop everything and follow him to Hollywood. It's just that he wanted Beth with him. He didn't want to leave her any more than she wanted to see him go, but he had to do this. Just this one time. And then he'd be back and wouldn't take no for an answer. Mitch was determined to make her, Mrs. Mitchell Samuel Burk.

Chapter Forty-Four

"Oh my gosh, I can't believe how good it feels to have that cast off," Beth said, stroking her hand up and down her leg.

Mitch watched, enjoying the scenery a little too much. He reached for the air conditioner and turned it on high.

Beth laughed. "Why Mr. Burk, I do believe you're blushing."

"What do you expect when you put on a show like that?"

Slapping his shoulder, Beth pouted. "I wasn't putting on a show! It just feels so good to be rid of that cast."

Taking off her seatbelt, she slid across the bench seat and pulled the center belt across her lap. Laying her head against his arm, Beth snuggled close.

"Will you be back by Thanksgiving?" Beth asked, her tone changing from playful to somber.

They had talked very little about Hollywood in the last week, not wanting to spoil what time they had left. After explaining everything to Shane, Uncle Charlie, and Travis, Mitch had spoken to Hank Carter, needing the man's prayer support.

"I don't think we'll be done with filming by then." Mitch reached over, laying his hand on her knee, giving it a squeeze. "But there's always production breaks for the holidays. So, I'll be able to come home."

"What do you think will happen once you're back in Hollywood?"

"What do you mean?"

"You've been AWOL for months. What are you going to tell people when they ask where you've been?"

"I'd like to tell them about us." Mitch leaned down and gave her a quick kiss on the forehead, then focused back on the highway.

"That would be a story," Beth said with a mocking laugh. "I can see the cover of People magazine now. "Leading Man Dates Ranch Hand." "

"I said, I would like to tell them about us . . . but I'm not going to."

"Oh." She sat up straighter, putting a little distance between them.

"Now, Beth, don't look at me like that." He reached for the hand she'd withdrawn from his arm and pulled her close to him. "The reason I'm *not* going to tell anyone where I've been is for your own protection. If the press found out about the Diamond-J, reporters would be bothering you night and day. It would be a circus, and I don't want that to happen while I'm gone."

She was quiet for a few minutes then asked, "So, what *are* you going to tell them?"

Mitch thought for a moment. "I'll tell them I found a nice piece of property to live on, and I plan on going back to it when I'm done filming."

"So, you're not even going to mention that you've been spending time with someone?"

"I can't, Beth. The press are like bloodhounds. If they thought for one minute I was involved with a woman, they'd stop at nothing to find out who you are."

Mitch watched as Beth sat in silence, playing with the buttons on the front of her blouse, staring out the windshield.

"What are you thinking?" he asked as he glanced from the road.

"Nothing," she mumbled under her breath.

"Beth, I can tell you're thinking something. What is it?"

She fiddled some more with her buttons.

"Beth . . ."

"It's nothing." Beth gave Mitch a reassuring smile and rested her head back against his arm. She struggled with the idea that Mitch might be embarrassed of her or the way she lived. But she quickly put it out of her head. He loved her. She knew he did. She wasn't going to let her insecurities ruin the few days they had left together.

When they got home, Beth stepped out of the truck, but didn't walk toward the house. She just stared at the barn, lost in thought.

Mitch came around to her side of the truck and slipped his hand around her waist. "You okay?"

"Yeah, it's just that I've never gone this long without riding. Even when I was pregnant with Shane, I rode until the time I delivered. And now, now I don't have Pandora. And well, I guess I feel a little lost." *Especially since I know I'm going to lose you, too.*

"Come on, Beth," Mitch pulled her closer and started toward the house. "You shouldn't be overdoing it anyway."

Beth conceded and walked with him into the house. Her leg felt weak, but not as weak as her heart.

She wandered into the kitchen, opened the refrigerator and looked inside. Swinging the door closed, she opened the freezer. After moving things around, she closed the door and leaned against the counter with a sigh.

"We should have done some grocery shopping while we were in town. There's nothing to eat."

"Oh, come on," Mitch moved next to her and opened the freezer. We have plenty of things. "I could barbeque some steaks?"

"It would take too long."

"Then how about some hamburgers? I could do them in a skillet."

"Nah, I'm not in the mood for burgers."

"I could fry some chicken?"

Beth wrinkled her nose and shrugged her shoulders.

Mitch swooped in from behind and wrapped his arms around her. "Then what do you want, Beth?" He nuzzled her neck. "Maybe we should skip dinner altogether and find something else to do." His devilish tone told her exactly what he had in mind.

"Oh, shoot!" Mitch took a quick step back.

"What?"

"I was supposed to help Hank with something when we got home." Mitch quickly crossed to the front door. "We can figure out

JUST AN ACT

dinner when I get back." The screen door slammed shut before Beth even had a chance to answer him.

Beth stood alone in silence, stunned by Mitch's quick departure.

So much for finding something else to do.

She sighed, grabbed a soda from the refrigerator, then took a seat in front of her computer, a decision weighing heavy on her mind.

Though Beth hadn't yet told Shane or Mitch, her realtor had contacted her a few days ago with an amazing proposition, one too good to ignore.

A prospective buyer—with an offer above the asking price—had spoken with Beth's realtor at length. He was extremely interested in the property and was prepared to put down a twenty thousand dollar, non-refundable deposit if Beth was willing to take the property off the market for a few months. The potential buyer was in the middle of liquidating some assets and for tax purposes, would prefer to sign a deal closer to the end of the year. He had even included a clause stating Beth could cancel the agreement at any time if she decided not to sell. The only stipulation: he would be given *first right of refusal*, if she put the property back on the market within the next three years.

Beth had told her realtor, she wanted to sleep on it, but it would be ludicrous to pass up such an amazing offer. Beth would have a twenty thousand dollar advance to start making plans if Shane was still dead set on moving, but it also gave her an extension of time, in case Shane had a change of heart. It was a win-win.

But she still had two days to decide.

Beth was clicking from listing to listing when she heard Mitch calling from the yard. Walking slowly toward the front door, Beth had only made it as far as the dining room when Mitch called her again.

"I'm coming!" she yelled, irritated he was being so impatient.

When Beth pushed open the screen door she couldn't believe what she saw. Mitch stood in the yard, holding the reins of a gorgeous white Arabian mare.

Beth was speechless as she descended the steps.

Walking forward, her mouth gaping with amazement, Beth

reached for the regal looking mare, stroking the animal's sturdy jaw.

"Hey, sweetheart," Beth cooed as she slowly moved around the horse, caressing her withers. "You're beautiful," she whispered, emotion muddying her words.

"Do you like her?" Mitch asked softly.

With tears streaking down her face, Beth answered, "She's incredible."

"I thought you could name her Althea."

Beth looked at Mitch inquisitively.

"To stay with the Greek mythology theme. It means *healing*."

Beth brushed away her tears as she continued to stroke the magnificent creature. "She's beautiful, Mitch. Where did you find her? How did you get her here?"

"Hank helped. He has a friend who breeds Arabians. Shane and I picked her out online, and Hank went down to Douglas and brought her up yesterday."

Beth was completely enraptured. Slowly, she glided her hand down the mare's neck and shoulder, then squatted to examine her muscular leg all the way to her fetlock. When Beth stood, she ran her fingers through the horse's mane, massaged her jowls, and stared into deep chestnut eyes. "She's amazing."

"I know nothing can replace Pandora, but I was thinking a good distraction might help you work through your loss."

"Thank you," Beth whispered, even though words seemed so inadequate in exchange for such a gift.

Circling around the mare, Mitch handed Beth the reins. "Do you feel up to a ride?"

"Absolutely!"

Beth threw her arms around Mitch's neck, hugging him tight, never wanting to let go. "I love you, Mitch. I don't deserve you, but I'm so thankful God brought you into my life."

Mitch drew back enough so he could look into her eyes. "It's me that doesn't deserve you. But if you'll have me, I'll spend the rest of my life loving you the way you deserve to be loved."

Mitch kissed Beth thoroughly, passionately. But, when the

spirited mare whinnied and pulled on the reins in Beth's hand, Mitch stepped back and laughed. "Great, another feisty female to contend with."

Beth slapped Mitch's arm. "I'm not feisty. Strong-willed, maybe."

He laughed again. "Fine. Then why doesn't *Miss Strong-willed* go get her boots on, so we can take your new ride for a ride?"

Beth gave him a peck on the cheek. "I'll be right back."

Chapter Forty-Five

When Beth entered the barn, Mitch was standing next to Midas' stall, Midas and the mare muzzle to muzzle.

"So, what do you think, Midas?" Beth asked as she walked over to the patriarch of the stables. As if on cue, he snorted and bobbed his head. Mitch and Beth laughed at Midas' supposed approval. "I'm surprised. He's usually more territorial than this."

Mitch handed the reins to Beth, then stroked Midas with approval. "Actually, they had their first meet and greet yesterday. Hank said it was a good idea to let them get acquainted with each other before finalizing the deal. They took to each other like long lost friends. Hank said it was pretty remarkable behavior."

"Well, if you're okay with her, I guess she can stay." Beth rubbed Midas's forehead and smiled. "What did you call her again?" Beth asked Mitch.

"Althea. Since your horses have names from mythology, I did some research online. Do you like it?"

"Yes, very much so," Beth turned to the mare. "What do you think, Althea? Do you like it?" The mare looked at her with expressive eyes, then winked. "Okay, Althea it is."

Beth followed Mitch to the tack room and reached for the saddle she had used for as long as she could remember. But somehow, it didn't seem right. It didn't belong to Beth; it belonged to Pandora.

When Mitch left, Beth pulled an old cutting saddle from the bottom rung of the saddle tree. Placing it on the saddle stand, she wiped it down, then carried it, a blanket, and a bridle, out to where Althea was tethered.

JUST AN ACT

"Are you sure you can handle that, Beth?" Mitch asked as he looked up from tightening Midas' girth strap.

"Of course, I can," she said, tossing the blanket over Althea's back. I broke my leg, not my arm. If there ever comes a time when I can't saddle my own horse, that will be the day I hang up my hat and stow my boots."

"Well, I can assure you, that's not going to happen on my watch," Mitch said firmly.

But, by the time Beth was done saddling Althea, she was winded. Frustrated, she wiped the perspiration from her forehead, then strained to push her left boot into the stirrup. Althea had to be at least sixteen hands tall, taller than Beth was used to—making it harder for her to get the leverage she needed. Afraid to bounce on her weakened right leg, Beth gripped the skirt of the saddle and tried to muscle her way up onto Althea's back.

"Need a hand?" Mitch asked rhetorically since he didn't wait for her to answer. Settling his hands on the back pockets of Beth's jeans, he gave her the boost she needed. Carefully, she swung her right leg over the saddle and cautiously seated herself, not knowing if the mare would be skittish with an unfamiliar rider. Althea took a few steps to one side, and dipped her head to slacken the reins in Beth's hands, then stood completely still waiting for a command.

Mitch, astride Midas, pulled up alongside Beth.

"Thanks for the hand up."

"Believe me, it was my pleasure," Mitch answered, grinning mischievously.

Beth cocked her head and raised her brow. "Here I thought you were being a gentleman. Come to find out you were just being a man," she teased.

"Guilty as charged," Mitch smiled.

"You're not even going to try to deny it?"

"What's to deny? Confession is good for the soul, and I confess I have a hard time keeping my hands off of you."

Beth laughed openly. "Your honesty is going to get you into trouble."

"Then what do you have in mind for my punishment?"

Beth's insides ignited like a spark to a flame. Though Mitch's words were teasing, the look in his eyes went beyond playful. She wanted to say something—offer a snappy comeback—but her mind couldn't think that fast. Instead, she just shook her head and nudged Althea forward toward the pasture.

"Beth, do you mind if we ride over to the Carter's? Shane is there, and I know Hank would appreciate seeing how well you and Althea are getting along."

"Sure. Lead the way."

After carefully crossing the highway, Beth and Mitch headed down the Carter's driveway. A large trailer was on one side of the dirt road, along with several portable stalls, horses, some chickens, a few vehicles, and stacks of building equipment. The shell of an expansive ranch-style home sat on a small knoll to their left.

"Wow, they've really gotten a lot done, haven't they?"

"Yeah, and they're doing it all themselves. Besides the plumbing and electrical, Hank and the boys have done the rest. Shane has even been giving them a hand."

Beth was surprised it was so quiet. With five kids, she figured there would be more activity in the yard. "It doesn't look like anyone's home, Mitch. Maybe we should come back another time."

"They're probably inside." Mitch dismounted Midas and flipped the reins over the crossbar of a sawhorse. "Come on, I want to show you something." Mitch headed toward the unfinished house instead of the trailer.

Beth hesitated as she carefully slid from Althea's saddle. "Mitch, that's rude. We can't just walk around like we own the place."

But he continued to walked up the makeshift steps in front of the framed out doorway. "It's no big deal. Come on."

Begrudgingly, Beth tied off Althea's reins and navigated the precarious steps. Walking inside the house, Beth looked around the main room. The interior was almost done, making it easy to envision the finished product.

"Wow, this room is huge."

"They have five kids, what do you expect?"

Mitch disappeared into another room while Beth admired the massive fireplace and the view from the roughed-out bay window.

"Mitch, where'd you go?" Beth raised her voice slightly.

"I'm in here."

Beth walked into the other room where Mitch stood alongside a beautifully set table for two. Candles were everywhere, and a drop cloth strung across the window, gave the room a romantic glow. For the second time in less than an hour, Beth was stunned and amazed. "What's all this?"

Mitch walked over to her and slipped his arms around her waist. "I wanted to surprise you with a nice dinner before I have to leave. The Carters volunteered their place and even prepared the meal."

With the mention of Mitch's departure, Beth wilted, afraid something would prevent him from coming back.

Something or someone.

"Come on, Beth, don't look like that."

"Okay," she whispered, forcing a smile, not wanting to ruin Mitch's surprise.

"Knock, knock."

They turned to see Janis standing in the doorway with a tray.

"Dinner is ready, if you are?" She smiled.

"Thank you, Janis," Beth said. "This is all so beautiful."

"Beth's right. You really outdid yourself."

"Well, Kat helped. We just wanted it to be special for the both of you."

Mitch pulled out Beth's chair, before taking a seat across the small, café-style table. Janis handed Mitch a bottle of champagne, then set two impeccably prepared salads on the linen tablecloth. "I'll be back in a few minutes with the main course." Janis smiled, before slipping out of the room.

Reaching across the table, Mitch held out his hand. Beth laid her fingers against his palm, feeling the warmth of his touch. They both bowed their heads as Mitch led them in prayer.

"Thank you, Lord, for leading me to the Diamond-J and allowing me to find love. Be with Beth and Shane in the months to come. Help Beth with the land and the herd, and protect Shane as he looks for answers. Please help the time go by fast. Thanks. Amen." Mitch smiled sheepishly. "That wasn't very eloquent, but I meant it."

"It was perfect." Beth gave him a reassuring smile.

When Mitch reached to pour her some champagne, she held up her hand to stop him.

"It's all right, Beth." Mitch turned the bottle, so she could read the label. "It's non-alcoholic. I wasn't sure if you would still be on pain meds, and I didn't want to chance it." He filled her glass, then his, before they delved into their salads.

Beth pushed the spinach leaves around on her plate, wishing her anxious feelings could be so easily pushed aside. She took a few bites, trying not to concentrate on the fact that Mitch would be leaving. But, the thought of him being so close to someone he once loved was twisting her stomach into knots.

"Has your agent told you any more about the movie?"

Mitch stopped with his fork halfway to his mouth. "Let's not talk about the movie, okay?"

"Sure . . . of course . . . that was stupid of me." Beth absentmindedly pierced the dried cranberries from her salad one at a time until the tine of the fork was full, before remembering cranberries gave her a rash. As stealthily as possible, Beth tried to slide them off—using the lip of the plate for leverage—but their sticky little bodies clung to the fork. Applying a little more force, the cranberries finally gave way, but not before she almost upended her plate. Dropping her fork, Beth steadied the plate, then caught the glass that had been bumped in the process, while Mitch reached out to stop the candlestick from tipping over.

"Sorry," she was quick to apologize for the mini-maelstrom. "I just remembered I shouldn't have cranberries." She smiled, picked up the fork that had landed on her lap, then quickly stabbed a spinach leaf and shoved it into her mouth.

Try as she might, Beth couldn't stop thinking about Mitch leaving. Every breath felt like her last, every bite she took fought with her stomach. Scenarios between Mitch and Kara Kensington raced through her mind, each more scandalous than the last.

"Okay, Beth, what do you want to know?" Mitch leaned back in his chair, wiping his mouth on the napkin from his lap.

"No, you're right. I don't want to ruin the evening."

"Well, it's obvious you're a bundle of nerves and won't be able to enjoy dinner if you have a bunch of unanswered questions. So, go ahead, what is it you want to know?"

She twisted her napkin and laid it alongside her plate. "What will the movie be about? I mean, *Here We Go*, ended with your characters marrying different people."

Mitch looked at her, his stare asking the question.

"Fine! I watched it on Netflix, okay?"

He cleared his throat. "It's set ten years later. Our characters bump into each other at a friend's funeral. They're both divorced."

"And let me guess, they have all kinds of quirky encounters and realize they are still madly in love with each other?"

Mitch sighed, "That *is* why they call it a romantic comedy."

Beth heard the hint of irritation in Mitch's voice and hated that she was responsible for putting it there. She leaned forward to apologize when Janis walked in, carrying a tray loaded with food.

Mitch stood and helped her with the plates. Beth moved her salad out of the way, making room for the main course. Mitch picked up her salad plate and stacked it with his own, before putting it on the tray Janis was holding. He grabbed the basket of rolls and placed them on the side of the table.

"This looks wonderful, Janis," Mitch commented.

"Well, I can't take all the credit. Hank did the steaks."

"It looks delicious," Beth added, even though her appetite was nonexistent.

Janis smiled. "I'll be back later with some dessert." They both watched as she walked away, then Mitch turned to Beth.

"It's just a movie, Beth, a character I'm playing."

"But I don't understand? How do you kiss someone . . . *be* with someone, and not let it affect you?"

"Because you have cameramen, crew members, and gaffers hovering over you and a director making you redo the same scene a dozen times; just because he can. There are hot lights that make you feel like you're melting, a make-up person constantly dabbing at your face, and a hairstylist messing with your hair non-stop. Believe me, no matter how romantic a scene looks, the filming is anything but romantic. In fact, at times, it can be downright embarrassing."

"Then how did you fall in love with her if you were so *unaffected* by it all?" Beth was unable to quell the sarcasm in her tone.

"Because we spent time together off the set. But Beth, that's not going to happen this time. You have nothing to worry about. Kara dropped me like a bad habit as soon as the movie was released, and I haven't talked to her since."

"But you had feelings for her when she broke it off, right? I mean, you said you were in love with her."

"That was a long time ago. Everything has changed since then. I have you now. And all I'm going to be doing while I'm gone is counting down the days until I'm back here. This is my home, Beth, with you and Shane. Please say you trust me."

She looked at Mitch's dark, penetrating eyes—eyes that held promise and understanding. "I trust you," Beth said firmly, "but that doesn't mean I'm not going to hate every minute you're gone."

"Then I guess I can start looking forward to my welcome home party."

Mitch's seductive look tempered Beth's belligerence, causing her skin to flush and her heart to flutter. He laughed, knowing the effect he had on her. "Now that we have that out of the way, we really should eat this wonderful dinner Janis prepared for us, or we're going to hurt her feelings."

Beth agreed, picking up her fork and cutting into her steak.

The remainder of their meal was eaten with less tension and a little more enjoyment. Janis served chocolate fondue for dessert, and Mitch insisted they feed each other the dipped fruit and shortbread. They laughed as they recovered lost pieces of fruit from the bottom of the pot and *apologized* when their aim didn't quite hit its mark.

JUST AN ACT

It was just the distraction Beth needed to get her mind off the fact that Mitch would be leaving in only two short days.

When they finished their meal, they thanked Janis, then strolled to where someone had stabled their horses. When they got closer to the make-shift stalls, Beth saw the silhouette of Shane and Kat leaning against the upper rail.

"So, Mom, what do you think of her?" Shane asked as he stroked Althea's muzzle.

"She's beautiful. Thank you."

"It was Mitch's idea. I just helped him find the right horse. I know she can't replace Pandora, but . . ." Shane looked at her, the weight of guilt still evident in his eyes.

"She's amazing," Beth interrupted, giving Shane a hug, then quickly brushed the tear from her cheek. "Dinner was great, too." Beth turned to Kat, wanting to change the subject.

"My mom was excited to help. She loves cooking and is a romantic at heart."

Shane drew Althea out of the stall and handed Beth the reins while Mitch led Midas.

"Can you give me a leg up, Shane?"

Shane laced his fingers together and cradled Beth's left foot. With a little lift, she was up and in the saddle.

"I'll be home a little later," Shane said as Mitch and Beth readied themselves to leave.

"You know," Mitch looked at Shane, "if we get two hours of driving in tonight and three more tomorrow, I could still take you to get your license before I leave."

"But I thought you had to be back by the first?" Shane answered.

"I do, but my meeting isn't until three-thirty in the afternoon. A flight from here to L.A. will only take a couple of hours. Besides, I promised I would help you get your license. So don't be too late, okay?"

"Okay."

As they rode up the driveway, the turmoil Mitch had felt all through dinner continued to stir inside him. He had put on a brave front, wanting to quiet Beth's fears, but inside, the pain was real.

"Mitch, did you hear me?"

He turned, not realizing Beth had said something.

"I'm sorry, babe. I was just going through a to-do list in my head. *No sense freaking her out with my insecurities.* "What did you say?"

"I was thanking you for realizing how important it is to Shane to get his license."

"Hey, I remember what it was like to be a teenager. Besides, I promised him."

Mitch looked at Beth, momentarily speechless. The glow from the moonlight framed her face and danced off her golden hair, making her appear almost angelic. She took his breath away.

Beth was everything he had ever wanted.

That's when something inside Mitch snapped. It was then that he realized leaving Beth would be the biggest mistake he ever made.

"I'm not going," he said abruptly.

"What?"

"I'm not going back to Hollywood. It's not worth it." He cantered ahead, dismounted Midas, and disappeared inside the barn.

"What are you talking about?" Beth asked, when she marched Althea into the barn seconds later. "You have to go."

"No, I don't."

"*Yes*, you do," Beth said insistently. "This is ridiculous . . . I've been ridiculous." She hurried Althea into her stall, then walked to where Mitch was pulling his tack from Midas' back. "I'm sorry, Mitch. I've made this harder on you than I should have. I've behaved like a spoiled brat. You have to go. I'm not going to let you lose everything on account of me."

"I don't care anymore, Beth. It doesn't matter to me." He turned and pulled her close. "That is, as long as you're willing to marry an unemployed, bankrupt actor?"

"No, Mitch. You're going to Hollywood and getting this over with. Then you're coming back here." Her look was stoic. "It's only a few months, not a lifetime. And that's what we'll have after all this is over."

She wrapped her arms around his neck and smiled. "I love you, Mitch. A few months apart won't change that."

Chapter Forty-Six

Beth watched as the small prop plane idled on the seldom used airfield. Hank, a licensed pilot, volunteered to fly Mitch back to California—an offer Mitch jumped at.

"You're sure that thing is safe?"

"Yes, Beth, it's safe. Better yet, no one will expect me to be on it."

Beth couldn't believe the steps Mitch had taken not to be found out. The frenzy his disappearance had created was magnified now that he was returning. It didn't help that Jerry had confirmed *Here We Go Again* would be Simon Grey's final film.

So, in place of the private jet the studio had offered, Mitch would be arriving in a small prop plane. Instead of landing at LAX or Burbank, Hank would be using an undisclosed municipal airport nearby.

"And Hank knows how to land at a city airport? This isn't crop-dusting, Mitch. He's going to be in crowded airspace. Are you sure he can handle it?"

"Beth, do you think Janis would allow her husband to jeopardize his life, just so I could avoid the paparazzi?"

"But I would feel better if it had more than one engine, or it was newer." She looked at the single-engine plane with its faded paint job and tiny windows.

"Beth, everything is going to be fine."

Mitch was right; she was being ridiculous. After all, the only reason he was taking such precautions was because he didn't trust a private charter not to leak his arrival to the press. And he certainly didn't want his point of origin to be discovered. Kansas wasn't that big. All it would take is for one person to mention that someone resembling Simon Grey was spotted—with a woman—at a small Kansas hospital. The media bloodhounds would do the rest, stopping at nothing until the Diamond-J and Beth were exposed.

"So, your agent's going to meet you where?"

"Hawthorne. It's a small city south of Los Angeles. The airport is busy for its size, but that will work to our benefit."

"And you don't think Jerry will notify the press?"

"No. I was very firm with him. I explained—in no uncertain terms—that the only reason I was coming back was out of respect for him. I also warned, if even one photographer or reporter was at the airport when I arrived, I would turn around and leave. Jerry's not an idiot. He's already getting the publicity he wants. He's not going to blow it by doing something stupid."

Beth stared out at the nothingness that made up the old airstrip.

Mitch wrapped his arms around her waist and waited for her to look at him. "You're sure you won't come with me?"

"We've been over this, Mitch. I just can't pick up and leave, you know that!" Her words came out sharper than she intended, but this wasn't the first time she'd had to tell Mitch no. He had asked her numerous times to make the trip with him, and each time Beth reminded him that she had a responsibility to Shane and the ranch.

"Okay, but you'll think about what I said? As soon as I get back, I want to get married. I don't want to wait any longer."

"I'll think about it. But it will depend on what I've decided to do about the ranch, and of course, I have Shane to consider. And then there's—"

"No. No more excuses, Beth. Come on, why won't you just say yes so I can leave here with a smile on my face?"

Mitch pulled Beth against his chest and held her tight. She rested her cheek against his beating heart, feeling as if her own was being ripped in two. She hated the jealousy that continued to smolder inside her. Envisioning Mitch with Kara Kensington was an ongoing movie playing exclusively in her mind. The woman was gorgeous and someone Mitch had been in love with. He would be spending long days and late nights with her. There would be love scenes and romantic settings. Beth was sure they would reminisce about their past relationship.

What if it's too much for Mitch? What if Kara tells him she wants him back and he discovers he still has feelings for her? What then?

"What are you thinking?" Mitch asked.

She was silent.

"Beth . . ."

Looking up at him, Beth's eyes asked what her heart couldn't speak.

"I don't have feelings for Kara. I told you that."

"How can you be so sure, Mitch? What if one look at her is all it takes to rekindle the feelings you once had? What if she decides to pick up where you two left off and doesn't take no for an answer? What then?"

"That's not going to happen. I'm going to spend every waking moment thinking about you. And you can bet you will be in my dreams as well." He bounced his brow teasingly.

Beth didn't want to be teased or cajoled. She wanted Mitch to stay but knew he couldn't.

Hank waved to him from beside the plane, his pre-flight check completed.

"You'd better go," Beth sighed.

"I'll call every night. I promise."

"Don't make promises you can't keep." Realizing that sounded a little harsh, Beth tried to explain. "Mitch, you're going to be crazy busy all day long and probably working late each night. With the time difference, you'll end up calling me in the middle of the night, which will freak me out. Late-night phone calls usually mean bad news. Just call when you can."

Mitch bent down, pressing his lips to hers, his kiss passionate and consuming. Beth could feel the assurance he was trying to give her. She deepened their kiss—wanting to give him a taste of what he was leaving behind—praying it would be enough to make him want to

JUST AN ACT

come back to her.

Beth pulled away first, quickly swiping an errant tear, trying to stay in control. But when Mitch framed her face with his sturdy hands, rivulets of tears washed down her cheeks. With calloused thumbs, Mitch brushed them away. "I love you, Beth. You know that, right?"

Nodding, she swallowed hard to compose herself. "I love you, too."

Beth watched as the plane taxied down the runway, then disappeared from sight. Walking back to the truck, she did what she could to hide her twisted emotions.

Shane sat behind the wheel, excited to drive them home with his newly issued license. Opening the passenger door, Beth slid in, and with a forced smile, she turned to Shane. "Home, James."

"Yes, ma'am!" Shane smiled as he put the truck in gear and headed back toward the main highway. Not wanting to talk, Beth reached for the radio dial, then stared out the window as she listened to her favorite country singers croon about love lost and love stolen. She finally turned it off, hating the songs she usually sang along with.

"Why are you so worried?" Shane asked.

"I'm not worried. I just hate the thought of Mitch being gone for so long."

"It will go by fast. You'll see."

"I'm glad you feel that way. I guess that means I won't have to hear you moan and groan about how long it is until Christmas vacation or how long and boring school is."

"Well, I wouldn't go that far. But you'll see, Thanksgiving will be here before you know it."

Beth sat curled up on the couch, the house dark except for the glow from the television. She tried convincing herself the only reason she was waiting up was to say good night to Shane. But Beth knew the real reason; she wanted to watch the eleven o'clock news.

She sat through the headlines, sports, and local news before the anchor and co-anchor turned to entertainment reporter Gina Nunez, sitting at the end of the desk, a screenshot of Lexmar Studios over her right shoulder.

"Gina, what do you have for us tonight?"

"Well, Bob, Hollywood's buzzing with the return of Simon Grey." She smiled at him and co-anchor Connie Jones, then turned toward the camera. "After a self-induced sabbatical, Simon Grey is back. And might I say, looking better than ever. Though he's not talking about his disappearing act, it looks to me like he's been working on his tan and his physique."

Beth twisted in her seat, irritated by the woman's lecherous smile.

"Seen here with Agent Jerry Cleveland, reporters caught up with Simon Grey leaving the offices of Lexmar Studios." The camera cut to footage of Mitch walking down the stairs of an ultra-modern office building.

Beth sighed softly. Mitch was wearing the light-blue polo he'd been wearing earlier when they held each other at the airstrip. He looked so good it hurt.

Mitch smiled politely as a reporter asked him questions and photographers snapped pictures.

"So, Simon, it looks like you've been enjoying a little R & R—a little sun, a little conditioning—but why all the secrecy?"

"No secret. I just wanted to get away for a little while." Mitch flashed one of his debonair smiles.

"And what about you and Kara Kensington?"

Beth sat up straighter.

"Kara and I are friends. It will be fun working with her again."

Beth felt her stomach tighten.

"Well, from what I remember, you two had more than just *fun* the last time you worked together." The reporter smiled and returned the mike to under Mitch's chin. He just laughed, waved, and continued down the stairs.

Why did Mitch avoid the question? Why didn't he just tell the reporter he was seeing someone else?

Beth knew why. Mitch already told her if she didn't come with him, he wasn't going to tell people about them. He didn't want to give the press more reasons to snoop around or figure out where he'd been. The clip faded, and the camera cut back to the entertainment reporter at the desk. "That's about it for today, Bob. Simon Grey and Kara Kensington start filming *Here We Go Again* tomorrow."

Beth got up and switched off the television. Feeling frustrated, she walked to the kitchen and opened the refrigerator. Grabbing a bottle of water, she slammed the door shut.

"Wow, what's eating you?"

She spun around to see Shane standing there.

"What? Oh, nothing." She swigged her water, trying to hide her irritation.

"Are you sure? You look like you're upset about something."

"No, I'm just tired."

"Were you waiting up for me? You didn't have to do that. I told you I would be home before midnight."

"No. I was just going to bed myself. Goodnight, Shane." Beth headed upstairs.

"Goodnight, Mom, and don't worry; he'll be home soon."

She turned to see a smirk on Shane's face. Beth didn't bother with a reply, she just continued upstairs.

Lying in bed, Beth wished she hadn't told Mitch not to call. It didn't matter how late it was. Hearing his voice would've made her feel so much better.

The next day, after a restless night with little sleep, Beth was bound and determined to work off her morose feelings. She did her best to hide her irritability at breakfast, but Shane saw right through the bright conversation and benign questions she asked about the new school year.

When Shane left for school, Beth headed to the barn. Althea greeted her with a whinny, which eased her sour disposition, but only slightly. Stroking Althea's muzzle, Beth relived the day Mitch presented her with the beautiful mare. *I thought you could name her Althea. To stay with the Greek mythology theme. It means healing.*

Instantly, Beth's heart ached, thinking about how many miles stood between them.

Knock it off! Stop feeling sorry for yourself.

Beth took Althea for a long ride, using the time alone to survey the ranch. Memories washed over her as she approached the small outcropping of trees she and her parents had planted when she was only a girl. Every year, on the first day of spring, they would ride out as a family and have a picnic by the saplings. The last time the three of them had been here, was the year her mother had told Beth about the cancer. Pausing for a moment, she looked up at the large trees that now shaded her. *Where has the time gone?*

After her ride, Beth concentrated her efforts on the stables. Though it was Shane's job to muck the stalls and lay fresh hay, she was in the mood for labor-intensive work—wanting to be kept as busy as possible.

With perspiration glistening on her bare arms and dust from the hay clinging to her black tank top, Beth took a moment to rest. Glancing at her watch, she was surprised to see it was already one o'clock. Swiping her forearm across her sweaty brow, Beth decided to grab a late lunch.

Before climbing the front steps, Beth patted off the extra dust she was wearing, then washed her face and hands in the downstairs bathroom. Though nothing really sounded good, she pushed leftovers around on the refrigerator shelves, hoping something would jump out at her. Opting for something easy, she grabbed deli meat, cheese, and some mayo, along with a plump peach. After assembling a sandwich and slicing the piece of fruit, Beth ate the simple lunch half-heartedly, hating how loud the silence was that surrounded her.

When she had finished her lackluster meal, Beth headed back outside to the smaller pens alongside the barn where she was greeted with a sing-song of bleating and oinking.

Once again, Beth set a strenuous pace, working up a sweat. Hard work was always her source of therapy when dealing with frustration and anxiety. Today was no different.

After another hour, Beth stopped her shoveling and leaned on the wooden handle. Taking pressure off her right leg, she slowly stretched it out and groaned. She was over doing it and knew it.

Re-injuring yourself will get you nowhere.

Though she listened to her conscience and slowed her pace, Beth still put in another hour of work.

Finally willing to call it a day, Beth stowed the wheelbarrow in the barn and headed toward the house. She was moving noticeably slower, favoring her weak leg.

In the kitchen, Beth filled a large glass with water and nearly drained it without taking a breath. Letting out a satisfying gasp, Beth held the cold glass against her forehead. Even though she was covered in dirt, with sweat trailing down her neck and her clothes clinging to her body like a second skin, Beth felt refreshed. Hard work and a sense of accomplishment always made her feel that way.

Drinking the last swig of water, Beth looked at the clock on the wall. *Three o'clock. Shane won't be home for another hour or so.* Slowly, she climbed the stairs.

Twenty minutes later, Beth stepped out of a steaming shower—feeling human again. She tossed her head forward, wrapped her wet hair in a towel, pulled another around her body, then hurried to her room. After drying off, Beth pulled on a pair of pastel plaid boxer shorts and a flimsy camisole. Her sleep attire wasn't exactly appropriate for the middle of the day, but she would change after she dried her hair.

When the screen door slap shut downstairs, Beth quickly looked at her bedside clock. *Shane's early? Great! Now what?* Bending forward, Beth untwisted the towel from around her head and gave her hair a brisk shake. *Please, God, don't let Shane be in some kind of trouble.* Flipping her hair back, she looked at herself in the full-length mirror, then pulled on another camisole over the one she was already wearing.

Not wanting to assume the worst, Beth tried to keep her tone even. "I thought you were going to be late?" She yelled from the top of the steps. "Didn't you say you and Kat were—"

"Hello, Beth."

She stopped abruptly halfway down the stairs.

Clutching the banister for support—and to hide the tremors racing through her body—Beth knew she should say something, but was too stunned to speak.

"It's been a long time." Cole stepped forward, removing his trademark straw hat. "But I must say, you are looking better than ever."

Chapter Forty-Seven

"Cole, what are you doing here?" Beth's words were sharp, filled with animosity.

"Nice to see you too, Beth."

Cole walked into the living room and made himself at home on the couch.

"I asked you a question!" She followed him.

"I came to see my son."

Cole's words dug at Beth's heart. "A little late for that, don't you think?"

"Not according to Shane. You forget, he's the one who contacted me."

"I'll ask you again. What are you doing here?"

Cole was slow to answer, his eyes wandering over Beth like she was there for his pleasure. "Like I said, I'm here to see my son."

"Why? Why after all these years? I gave you a chance to see him, to be a part of his life. But as I recall, you wanted nothing to do with me or *my* son."

"That was a long time ago."

"Sixteen years to be exact."

"Hey, before you get all bent out of shape, Shane's the one who invited me." Cole stretched his arms across the back of the couch and tossed his feet up on the coffee table.

"He knows you're here?" Beth was shocked Shane had invited Cole without telling her.

"Not exactly."

Beth wanted to slap the smile off his face.

"Shane asked if we could get together—to meet and talk. I had some extra time on my calendar, so I decided to make the drive out."

"This extra time you're talking about, is that because you're out on bail, or because you're off the circuit and your rodeo-queen wife threw your butt out of the house?"

His jaw tightened and his face turned red, but Cole just grinned. "Keeping tabs on me, Beth? I'm flattered."

"It's not hard when your face is plastered across the evening news. Assault, jail, divorce—doesn't sound like you've changed at all."

Beth watched his fists clench. She was playing with fire, knowing Cole had a hair trigger, but refused to back down. "I want you to leave," Beth said, sounding stronger than she felt. "You're not welcome here. Now or ever."

"But that's where you're wrong, Beth," Cole sprung to his feet and crossed the room to where she was standing. "I *am* welcome here, because *my* son invited me here."

"And I'm telling you I don't want you here."

Cole looked at Beth, his stare dropping to the neckline of her camisole, then back to her eyes; his lascivious grin made her skin crawl.

"Is that because you're afraid of me, Beth, or because you can't trust yourself around me?" He took a step closer. "As I remember, you threw yourself at me when you were just a young girl. How much harder will it be for you to keep your hands off me now that you're a woman?" He moved closer still.

Beth's hand came across his face faster than he could react. She took a step back, but Cole quickly grabbed her arm and yanked her close. "Don't ever do that again, do you understand?" His eyes were like ice. "I *will* play dirty if I have to. Either you can be hospitable to me and let me visit with Shane here, or I can convince him to come to my ranch, so we can make up for lost time."

"He would never go with you!" she shouted, yanking her arm free.

"Oh, really? Are you sure about that, Beth? The father he's always wanted to know comes to him on bended knee—apologizing for all the time they've lost—and you don't think Shane would jump at the chance to spend quality time with me on my ranch?"

Cole's threat was clear. If Beth didn't allow him to stay, he would use everything in his power to pull Shane away from her.

"You know how persuasive I can be, Beth. My charms always worked on you. I have no doubt they will work on Shane. Besides, maybe you and I can pick up where we left off." He ran a finger down her arm, causing her to shudder at his touch. "We were pretty good together."

Beth backed away just as she heard gravel pop in the driveway. When she looked at Cole, his smile was confident and smug.

"Will you do me the pleasure of introducing me to my son?"

Beth's emotions raced out of control.

The warning Cole gave her was clear. If she tried to come between him and Shane, she would lose. A debate between what Beth knew and what she feared spun in her head. Beth knew Shane loved her, but he was still angry she'd kept him from his father. Angry enough to leave?

Her insecurities raged. She couldn't lose Shane.

She wouldn't lose Shane.

Cole might be controlling, but he also had a temper that always got the better of him. If Shane saw that, he would know everything Beth had said was true. *Please God, let Cole show his true colors, but please, please, don't let him hurt Shane.*

Beth moved out onto the porch as Shane walked toward the house.

"How was school?"

"Great." He laughed. "Some kid started a fire in the chemistry lab so sixth period was cancelled."

Beth stood in front of the door until Shane climbed the steps. "There's someone here to see you." Beth made sure the animosity she was feeling did not tinge her words.

She opened the screen door and let Shane walk in ahead of her. Cole stepped forward, his hat in his hand, the picture of humility.

"Shane, this is Cole Dempsey." She couldn't bring herself to say he was his father. "Cole, this is Shane."

Cole stuck his hand out to Shane and waited for him to grab it.

Slowly, Shane extended his hand to his father. "I'm sorry, son; I never should've waited this long."

Shane dropped his father's hand, clearly not knowing what to do next.

The three of them stood in awkward silence for what seemed like an eternity. Beth refused to make it easy for Cole. If he wanted to have a relationship with Shane, he was going to have to work hard for it.

"I guess I'm at a loss for words," Cole stuttered. "I was expecting a boy . . . but you're a man."

Shane pulled his shoulders back with pride. Beth glared at Cole, not believing the sincerity he was trying to project.

"I didn't think you would come," Shane finally spoke.

"Well, like I was telling your mom," he shot Beth a glance, "I found a little time in my schedule, and I thought this was important."

"Why didn't you think it was important before I contacted you? It's not like you didn't know where to find me for the last sixteen years."

Beth wanted to pump her fist in the air. *Yes!* Shane wasn't going to be won over so easily.

Cole hung his head and sheepishly fingered the rim of his hat. "I'm sorry, son. I'm not going to try and make excuses for myself. I'm no angel. I'm sure your mom has told you that much."

Cole chanced another look at Beth, a sly smile on his face even though his words sounded genuine. But it didn't fool Beth. It was the smooth-as-silk voice she knew all too well. She realized what Cole was doing. Instead of trying to defend himself in front of Shane, he was going to confess to his short comings and make himself look like a penitent father.

"I know I've made mistakes—big mistakes. But I would like to try building a relationship with you."

"You mean *start* a relationship with me."

That's right, Shane. Stick it to him!

Beth watched as Cole's jaw tightened, but he kept his cool as he placed his hat back on his head. "Maybe I misunderstood your e-mails, Shane. I got the impression you wanted to get to know me. But now that I'm here, I get the feeling you've had a change of heart. I guess I'll just see my way out."

Cole walked past Shane toward the door.

"Wait," Shane called after him.

Cole turned back around.

"I haven't had a change of heart. I want to get to know you, but only if you want to be here. I don't want charity or pity. I'm looking for more than that. So, if you're ready to man up, I'd like to spend some time with you."

Cole smiled and for the second time, extended his hand to Shane. "Then I guess as long as your mom doesn't mind, you have yourself a houseguest for a little while."

Shane reached for Cole's hand, but as soon as their hands touched, Cole pulled Shane into a manly embrace.

"Wait a minute," Beth interrupted, "you can't stay here."

"Why not, Beth? I'm prepared to earn my keep. From what Shane's told me, you could use some help getting your place in shape. I hear you're finally going to sell the Diamond-J. Brave move."

"I don't need your help," she bristled.

"Well, if you prefer, I can stay in the Airstream you have out in the yard."

"No!" Beth snapped. There was no way she was going to allow him to stay in Mitch's trailer.

"Well," Cole turned to Shane, "you could always come to my place. I thought this would be easier, with you being in school and all, but if your mom is opposed to me being here, I guess we'll have to make other arrangements."

Shane turned to Beth, looking for approval. What could she do? Say no and have Cole persuade Shane to go to his place?

"Fine. He can stay." She cringed at the thought of having Cole around.

Cole grinned at her. And in true cowboy fashion, tipped his hat.

Chapter Forty-Eight

Beth went upstairs to change into something more suitable, then to the kitchen to start on dinner. *I can't believe I'm doing this. I can't believe I'm making dinner for Cole.* She pulled hamburger meat from the freezer and tossed it in the microwave to defrost, while Shane helped Cole upstairs with his bags. A minute later, Shane appeared at the kitchen bar.

"Are you all right with this, Mom? I didn't mean to put you on the spot."

"I just can't believe you invited him here without telling me." She pulled a jar of spaghetti sauce from the pantry cupboard, trying to whisper, but her volume grew with every syllable.

"I didn't think he'd come. I mean . . . well . . . I didn't think he'd try . . . Okay, maybe I didn't think, period!" Shane looked pale and completely overwhelmed. "I'm sorry, Mom. I know this has to be hard for you. I'll ask him to leave." Shane stepped away, but Beth stopped him.

"No, Shane. I know how important this is to you. He can stay. But please," she pled, "please be careful."

"Mom," he moaned.

"Shane, I mean it. I know Cole. He's charming and smooth and very manipulative."

"I'm not a woman, Mom. None of that stuff is going to work on me."

"Give me a little more credit than that, Shane. Cole's manipulation didn't just work on me. He fooled Grandpa and Uncle Charlie. Don't think he won't manipulate you, too."

She heard Cole coming down the stairs as the microwave beeped.

"I can't believe this place looks the same," Cole said. "What memories it brings back."

"Really? More like nightmares." Beth knew both Shane and Cole heard her, but neither chose to comment.

"How long before dinner, Beth?"

"Excuse me? I'm not at your beck and call. It will be ready when it's ready."

Cole put up his hands in defense. "Hey, I was just wondering if Shane and I had time for a ride before dinner."

Beth looked at her son, nodding slightly.

"I guess we could go for a short ride, but I need to call Kat first." Shane disappeared outside, leaving Cole and Beth in the kitchen alone.

Beth continued to work on dinner. She slapped down a frying pan on the stove and haphazardly tossed the pound of ground beef in it. After running water in a large pot, she would've slammed it down too, but knew she would just end up with a stovetop full of water. She sat it down carefully, then turned the burners on high.

Pretending Cole wasn't watching her, she reached for a soda in the refrigerator, not bothering to offer him one.

"So, where's this boyfriend Shane was telling me about?"

Beth had just taken a swig of soda when Cole posed his question. Shocked, she inhaled the carbonated liquid. Coughing and sputtering, Beth hung her head over the sink. She couldn't breathe. Her coughing turned to violent choking.

"Are you okay?" Cole gently patted her on the back.

Even in her discomfort, Beth didn't want Cole anywhere near her. She pushed him away, while trying to catch her breath, but all she could do is gasp.

"Little breaths, Beth. Try taking little breaths."

She bent over, her hands on her knees, catching half a breath . . . then another. Her panic began to subside. She was still coughing, but with each breath, she could feel the slightest bit of relief. Finally, Beth stood up straight, tears streaming down her face.

"You gonna be all right?" Cole asked.

"Yeah." Her answer was quick. Hoarse. "Just give me some space."

As Cole turned to walk away, Shane came in from outside. When his eyes met Beth's, he reacted. Shane went straight for Cole, shoving him into the refrigerator. "What did you do to her?"

Cole was obviously stunned. He was a big guy, yet Shane had knocked him back on his heels.

When Shane came at him again, Cole was ready, blocking his assault, stopping his forward motion.

"You son-of-a—"

"Shane!" Beth cut him off. "I'm fine. Cole didn't do anything. I was choking, that's all."

Shane looked at her, then Cole, then back to her again. Beth reached for the dial on the stove, turning off the meat that was spitting and splattering,

"I swallowed wrong and was choking. Cole was just trying to help."

Shane turned to Cole again, his face red, looking embarrassed. "I'm sorry. I thought you were—"

"Hey, no reason to apologize. You thought your mom was in trouble. You were right to defend her. She's lucky to have you around."

"You okay, Mom?" Shane's attention was back on Beth, while she reignited the flame under the frying pan.

"Yeah." She cleared her throat some more. "I'm sorry I scared you."

"Beth, why don't you sit down for a moment and catch your breath? Dinner can wait."

"I'm fine!" she snapped at Cole, refusing to be coddled. "Just leave me alone so I can finish."

Cole turned to Shane. "So, is your lady friend going to join us for dinner?"

"Kat?" Shane shook his head. "No, I wasn't inviting her. I just wanted to let her know I wouldn't be over tonight."

"Did you still want to take that ride?" Cole asked.

Shane didn't answer Cole. He turned to Beth instead. "Are you going to be okay, Mom?"

"I'm fine."

"So what do you say, Shane, just a short ride, so we can have some one-on-one time?" Cole asked.

"Actually," Beth butted in—deciding she didn't want Shane to be alone with Cole for *any* length of time. "I don't think you'll have time for a ride. Why don't you just go out on the porch or sit in the living room if you want to talk? I'll call you when dinner is ready."

"Fine with me," Cole answered as he moved toward the front door.

Of course he chooses outside where I can't hear what he's saying.

When Shane started to follow, Beth grabbed his hand. When he turned to face her, she whispered. "Don't believe everything he tells you."

Shane nodded, then walked outside.

Please, God, don't let Cole brainwash Shane. Beth prayed fervently as she pushed the hamburger meat around in the skillet. *Help him see through Cole's deceptiveness. Don't let him get hurt.*

Beth was in a quandary, knowing one of two things would happen. Either Shane would get sucked in by Cole's manipulation—believing his father to be the iconic figure he knew from TV and magazines—or he would see Cole for the lying, self-centered person he was and feel rejected all over again. Both would have disastrous results.

This is bigger than me, God. I don't know what to do. If I make Cole leave, Shane will accuse me of sabotaging his chance to have a relationship with his father. But if I allow Cole to stay, I'm opening Shane up to who knows what kind of heartache?

Then Beth thought about Mitch and the reaction he would have to Cole's arrival. *He'll come completely unglued.* There's no way Mitch would stay in Hollywood if he knew Cole was at the Diamond-J. Imagining Mitch going toe-to-toe with Cole—knowing their exchange would most likely escalate from verbal to physical—Beth decided it was in everyone's best interest not to tell Mitch about Shane's unexpected houseguest.

No! I just want all of this to be over. Mitch needs to get the movie done as soon as possible so he can come home for good. Besides, Cole's attention span is about the size of a gnat. He'll get bored and restless, then leave. He'll make Shane all kinds of empty promises about e-mailing and visiting. But after a while, he'll lose interest. Shane will become just another discarded hobby to Cole. Then, it will be up to me to pick up the pieces.

Beth continued her one-sided debate while making dinner. She had just about convinced herself everything would be fine, when Cole's threatening words came back to haunt her. *I'll play dirty if I have to.*

A chill ran through her, dashing Beth's confidence, causing her heart to race once more. Taking a deep breath, she walked to the screen door and pushed it open wide. "Dinner's ready."

Both Shane and Cole stood, brushed the dirt from the back of their jeans, then followed her into the house. Cole walked to the bathroom to wash up while Shane turned on the spigot in the kitchen.

"So . . . what did you two talk about?" Beth asked.

Shane shrugged. "Just stuff."

"Stuff? What do you mean, stuff?"

"You know . . . stuff. What I like? What I don't like? What's my favorite sport? If I have any hobbies? How long I'd been seeing Kat?"

"Did he tell you about his arrest?"

"No, I didn't."

Both Shane and Beth turned to see Cole standing by the kitchen bar.

"I figured I would tell Shane about it while the three of us ate. I know it might not make for the most pleasant dinner conversation, but I knew you would want to hear for yourself what happened."

Beth felt like a child caught doing something wrong. She avoided Cole's stare, grabbed the basket of bread from the counter, and walked to the table. "There are drinks in the refrigerator. Take your pick."

After the three of them sat down, Beth asked Shane to say grace. She didn't trust herself to say anything nice, not even in prayer.

"Thank you, Lord, for this food, and . . ." Shane paused, obviously having a hard time knowing what to say, "and thank you for bringing Cole here. I know we have a lot to talk about, some of it not so good, but I've prayed for this day all my life; now it's finally here. Thank you for that. Amen."

Cole acted like he was genuinely touched.

Beth felt like she was going to be sick.

The silence as they ate was deafening; the only noise was the tinny sound of silverware scraping against china. Beth pushed pasta around on her plate, her appetite nonexistent, but Cole had no problem reaching for seconds. Shane glanced at each of them, like he was going to say something, but shoveled a forkful of noodles into his mouth instead.

Finally, it was Cole who broke the ice.

"Beth, I know you're concerned about my arrest, so I guess I might as well tell you what really happened."

"That's where you're wrong!" she snapped, using her fork as a pointer. "I'm not *concerned* about you at all. Not your life, your career, or the trouble you're still getting into. But . . . I think Shane deserves to know what kind of man his father is."

Beth glared at Cole—cocking a brow in challenge. If Cole wanted to play hardball with his idle threats, she would dish it right back at him.

Cole stared at her for a moment, letting Beth know he was on to her little game, then turned to Shane—softening his demeanor. "It's true. I shot at my foreman. But I wasn't trying to hurt him. I was just persuading him to come clean with me."

"What did he do?" Shane asked.

"He slept with my wife," Cole said nonchalantly, before taking a swig of his soda.

Beth dropped her fork, causing it to clank against her plate before skittering off the table and onto the hardwood floor. When she bent to pick it up, she caught Cole's stare, a smug expression on his face.

"Surprised?" Cole asked as she righted herself.

"No. Why would I be surprised? It's none of my business."

"Because you assumed *she* left me. At least that's the spin the media put on it." Cole pushed back from the table, shaking his head.

"They're trying to make me out as a hot-tempered jackass. Just because I don't appreciate them sticking their cameras in my face after a crappy ride, they're trying to paint me as a sore loser with anger issues. The media wants people to think I'm spiraling—losing my temper, my ranking, my wife. But things aren't always what they seem."

He looked at Beth with an intimidating stare, but she refused to give in.

"As for my marriage," Cole continued, "I'm divorcing Cynthia because she's been cheating on me. I pulled a gun on Daniel because he had the audacity to lie to my face, even though I have pictures of him and Cynthia in bed together—my bed to be exact," Cole clarified.

"And let's not forget my 'sagging career,' as the media has labeled it. A bull named Dirt Devil is to blame for that. Unfortunately, he belly-rolled one way, while I went the other. I'm out for the season. Doctor's orders."

Cole looked at Shane, then Beth. "So, there you go. The tabloids diffused in less than sixty seconds." He settled his elbows back on the table, then continued to eat his dinner.

Once again, they sat in silence.

Beth watched Shane, not liking the way he looked at Cole. She saw a twinge of admiration in his eyes. Something Cole clearly did not deserve.

But Beth had to give him credit. Cole was still the smooth-talker he'd been sixteen years ago. He'd gotten the upper hand by laying everything out in the open, proving he had nothing to hide. But he wasn't fooling Beth. He might be divorcing his wife because she was cheating on him, but that didn't mean Cole had been a Boy Scout his entire marriage. She'd bet any amount of money, he had one-night stands lined up in every town on the rodeo circuit. And as for his supposed righteous indignation that spurred Cole to pull a gun on his foreman, Beth would wager a fifth of scotch had more to do with the way he handled the situation than his desire to strong-arm a confession out of his wife's lover.

Beth got up from the table, clearing her plate and silverware, having barely made a dent in her dinner.

"So, that's your secret for staying in such great shape," Cole said, smiling as his eyes slowly traveled over her figure. "You only play with your food instead of eating it."

Beth ignored him.

Walking to the kitchen, she rinsed her dish and silverware before putting them in the dishwasher. While Cole and Shane continued to eat, she worked in the kitchen, storing leftovers, cleaning pots and pans, and wiping down countertops.

While standing at the sink, Beth realized she was favoring her weak leg. The heavy workload she'd put herself through earlier in the day was taking its toll. She would have to be more careful.

When Beth walked back to the dining room table, Cole pushed himself away with a satisfied sigh.

"It was delicious, Beth. But then you always knew your way around the kitchen."

Once again, she ignored his compliment, while gathering the bread basket, butter plate, and her empty glass.

Shane stood and carried the rest of the dishes from the table to the kitchen. Leaning close to Beth, he asked, "You all right, Mom? You're limping."

"I'm just a little sore. I guess I overdid it today."

"What were you doing?"

"I cleaned out the stalls and the pens."

"Why'd you do that?"

"I was trying to keep myself busy."

Shane paused for a moment, then lowered his voice. "Have you heard from Mitch?"

"No. But I told him not to feel like he had to call. Mitch is an adult. There's no reason for him to check in with me every day." Beth hadn't intended for her tone to sound so defensive, but it did.

"So what do you think he'll say when he finds out Cole is here?"

Beth began scrubbing the stove top. "I'm not going to tell him."

Cole got up from the dining room table and stretched. "Excuse me while I go see a man about a horse." He smiled at Beth, knowing she hated the euphemism. Her father had used the phrase once when she was a little girl. Since she loved horses so much, she begged him to let her go with him. It was one of her father's favorite stories to share. Unfortunately, Cole was one of the people he told.

After Cole disappeared down the hall, and the bathroom door shut, Shane turned to her. "Why aren't you going to tell Mitch about Cole?"

She shook her head. "There's no point. Besides, Cole's not going to be here that long."

"I still think Mitch would want to know."

She turned to Shane feeling a little frazzled. "Yeah, well, I'll decide what I'm telling Mitch. And, while we're on the subject, why did you feel the need to tell Cole I was seeing someone?"

"What?"

"Cole asked about my *boyfriend*."

Shane looked at her, and then to his hands. "Because I didn't want him bothering you."

When Beth heard the protectiveness in Shane's words, she softened her tone. "But you didn't tell him who Mitch was, did you?"

"No."

Cole stood in the hallway, listening as Shane and Beth whispered back and forth. *So who is this Mitch guy?*

When Cole turned the corner, both Beth and Shane stopped their conversation and looked at him. Tossing the dishrag in the sink, Beth said, "Well, I'm sure you two want to talk, and I have some work to do. Shane, don't neglect your homework."

Beth slipped by Cole on her way to her office.

Shane walked to the living room and plopped down in one of the side chairs. Cole sat down opposite him, sinking into the comfort of the worn and supple leather. As his eyes wandered around the room, Cole remembered the good times he had spent on the Diamond-J. Even though he had severed all ties to the ranch, Beth, and her father, he couldn't erase the memories.

I doubt Beth's memories are that good.

Cole couldn't say that he blamed her.

He'd been violent and belligerent the last few months he lived at the Diamond-J. Unfortunately, with his drinking out of control, Beth had taken the brunt of his aggression. He was unhappy with himself, hating the life of a ranch hand—someone always telling him what to do. Cole had known then that the rodeo was his only ticket out, and had made sure nothing and no one stood in his way.

Cole remembered the night Beth told him she was pregnant. He thought it was a joke—a trap—her way of keeping him on the ranch. When he found out she was telling the truth, he saw his dreams of the rodeo circuit going up in smoke. The night Beth gave him an ultimatum—threatening to tell her father she'd been raped—Cole went berserk. He'd already had way too much to drink, and her attempt at controlling him pushed him over the edge.

The next day, when Cole realized what he'd done, he'd gathered up his things and left. It had been the coward's thing to do, but Cole wasn't about to let an oversexed teenage girl ruin his life.

For months after that, Cole kept an eye out for Jack Justin—expecting him to show up at one of the local rodeos with a shotgun in hand. When he didn't, Cole figured Beth had gone through with the abortion, leaving him in the clear.

Once his rodeo career took off, Cole never looked back. When Beth confronted him over a year later, he was shocked to find out she'd had the kid. But he wouldn't be deterred. He was on his way to the top. Just because she ruined her life by saddling herself with a kid didn't give Beth the right to ruin his. She'd made her mistake. She would have to live with it.

Cole stared across the room at Shane . . . his son; the *mistake* he had tried to ignore for over sixteen years. His conscience gnawed at him. Cole hadn't expected to feel a connection to Shane, but staring at the spitting image of his younger self definitely played with his mind.

But it was seeing Beth again that had done him in. Cole never would've imagined, after all these years, that he would still have feelings for Beth. Her sassiness—her fire—was just as enticing now as it had been when she was a teenager. The only difference ... Beth was no longer a girl. She was a woman.

A very beautiful woman.

I just might have to change my tactics.

Chapter Forty-Nine

Beth finished taking care of her monthly bills, caught up on some bookkeeping, then began the nightly ritual of surfing the web for a home. She poured over picture after picture, wanting to find a house with a small parcel of land, but a city address. Something Shane wouldn't consider the boondocks.

She glanced at the clock in the bottom corner of the computer screen, surprised how late it was. Closing her eyes, she rolled her head from side to side, rubbing the back of her neck. Stretching out her right leg, Beth massaged the stiffness that had been building all evening.

"Is that the leg you broke?"

Beth gasped loudly, laying her hand against her racing heart. "You scared me half to death." She turned to see Cole standing in the doorway, leaning against the frame. His twinkling blue eyes and incredible smile reminded her of Shane. For the first time, Beth realized how much Shane looked like his father. Amazing how she had blocked that out until now.

Cole still had enough charisma and charm to fill a room, but Beth wasn't fooled. She knew the dark side of his personality. The ugly, painful, self-serving side that had battered her body and crushed her heart. She would not be taken in by his charm or allure again.

"What are you still doing up, Cole?" Beth's words were cold as she turned back to her computer and keyed on the screen saver.

"I was hoping we could carry on a civil conversation."

"Well, I guess that depends on what you consider civil. Were you going to threaten me again?" She stood, crossing her arms against her chest.

"I'm sorry, Beth." Cole hung his head and twisted his large calloused, hands together. "I didn't mean to say those things to you this afternoon. I don't know what came over me."

"Nothing came over you, Cole. It's who you are. You're a bully. Someone who enjoys intimating other people and putting them in their place. Well, it won't work on me anymore. I'm no longer a frightened teenager watching her dreams crumble into a million pieces. I'm an adult now. A mom. A ranch owner. A businesswoman. I've lived a hard life, but I have a wonderful son to show for it. You don't deserve to have a relationship with Shane. He's too good for you. But I won't get in the way if that's what he wants. I can only pray he sees the Cole I know, not the iconic façade you so cleverly hide behind."

Beth waited for Cole to blow-up. She had incited him on purpose, wanting him to lash out at her just to prove to Shane the kind of person he was. But Cole just stood there. She was waiting for him to say something, when the phone rang.

She reached for it without taking her eyes off Cole. "Hello." Her tone was direct.

"Hey, it's me. Is everything all right?"

The sound of Mitch's voice startled her. Turning around, she clutched the receiver close to her ear and whispered. "I'm sorry. I just have a lot on my mind." She softened her tone. "I miss you already."

"I miss you, too. I know it's late there, but I had to call. I'm sorry I didn't call last night, but it was absolute chaos here. By the time I got home, it was well after midnight."

"I know. I saw the report—" Beth caught herself, forgetting Cole was standing right behind her. When she turned to say something to him, Cole was gone. Stepping into the hallway, Beth saw his shadowy figure climbing the stairs.

"What's that, Beth? You're cutting out."

"No, I'm here." She closed the door softly and curled up in her office chair. "I saw the reporters following you when you were leaving the Lexmar offices. It looked pretty chaotic."

"It was crazy. I can't live like this anymore. I'm ready to come home."

"Really?" Beth's heart flip-flopped. "Are you serious?"

"Yeah, I'm serious. I just wish I could. This town has gotten even crazier since I've been gone. November can't come soon enough for me."

Beth's shoulders slumped. She realized Mitch wasn't saying he was coming home. He was just blowing off steam.

"Look, Beth, I'm exhausted, and I have an early call in the morning. I just wanted to be able to hear your voice before I went to bed."

"So, you start shooting tomorrow?" Beth asked. "They sure are moving fast."

"Actually, we started shooting last night, but that still isn't fast enough for me."

"What?" Beth was confused. "What do you mean by that?"

"The sooner we start, the sooner I get to come home."

"Oh."

"Beth, what's wrong? What aren't you telling me?"

"Nothing's wrong. I'm just tired. I overdid it today. Now I'm paying the price." Beth closed her eyes and gritted her teeth. She felt guilty not telling Mitch about Cole. She knew he would want to know. But what good would it do? Like he said, he couldn't come home even if he wanted to.

"Why are you working so hard? The doctor told you to take it easy for the first few weeks."

"I don't have time to *take it easy*. Or did you forget I have a ranch to run?" The minute her words were out, Beth regretted them. "I'm sorry, Mitch. I didn't mean to snap at you. I'm just a little overwhelmed right now."

He sighed. She could hear his exhaustion. "I'm sorry, Beth. I hate this. I hate being so far away—knowing you're working yourself to death."

"It's not that bad. Really. It's just my way of keeping my mind occupied while you're gone."

"You're sure?"

"I'm sure. I just miss you."

"I miss you, too." Mitch's words were punctuated with a yawn.

"You're tired. You better get some rest."

"Can I call you tomorrow?"

"No matter how late," Beth clarified.

When Beth hung up, she felt horrible. She knew she shouldn't keep Cole's unannounced appearance from Mitch. But why worry him?

Cole will be gone in a day or two. Then life can get back to normal.

Cole hurried upstairs for the second time. He only heard bits and pieces of Beth's conversation through the closed door, but what he could make out had definitely piqued his curiosity.

Who is Beth seeing? And how serious is their relationship?

She hadn't told him about Cole's arrival, which could mean one of two things. Either their relationship *isn't* that serious so there is no reason to tell him, or *it is* that serious and she's afraid to tell him.

Cole smiled to himself as he quietly closed his bedroom door.

I made you fall in love with me once before, Beth. I'm sure I can do it again.

Chapter Fifty

The next morning, Beth was already dishing up breakfast when Cole appeared downstairs.

"Good morning," he said politely.

"Morning." Beth didn't bother looking up; she just continued pushing scrambled eggs onto three different plates.

When Shane came in from outdoors, he headed straight for the kitchen counter. "Mom, can you wrap mine in a tortilla? I'm running late." He turned to Cole. "Good morning."

"Late? You don't need to leave for another hour," Beth said.

"No, I need to leave right now. Kat has an early class today."

"Oh."

While Shane ran upstairs, Beth pulled a tortilla from the refrigerator and threw it in the microwave. Waiting for the beep, she quickly assembled a breakfast burrito of eggs, hash browns, and a shot of salsa. Beth rolled it up and stuck it in a paper towel just as Shane came thundering down the stairs.

Handing him the makeshift breakfast, Shane grabbed it and smiled. "Thanks, Mom." He turned toward the front door, but stopped. He looked at Cole, then stepped in front of Beth and lowered his voice to a mumble. "Are you going to be okay with him here?"

"I'll be fine," she whispered, appreciative of Shane's concern.

Giving her a peck on the cheek, Shane said, "Love you, Mom." As he hurried toward the front door, he yelled over his shoulder. "See you after school, Cole."

Then he was gone.

"Wow," Cole turned to Beth. "I don't remember you ever being that enthusiastic about school."

"It's not school Shane's excited about. It's his passenger."

"Ah, yes, young love." Cole looked at Beth with a cocky grin. "You remember what that was like, don't you?"

She snapped her eyes up to meet his. "Actually, I don't. I learned long ago what you and I shared was far from love."

"Oh, come on, Beth. It wasn't all bad." He smiled, his gaze traveling from her eyes, to the snaps on the front of her shirt, then back up again. "We shared some pretty good moments together. You can't tell me you don't remember what it was like to—"

"You know what, Cole," she said, putting her hand up. "You can stop right there. This is not going to turn into some stroll down memory lane. You're here to see Shane, not me."

"That's not exactly true," he sighed. "I still care about you, Beth. I always have."

She laughed, finding his attempt at sincerity a joke. "That's a crock! You never cared about anyone but yourself."

"You're partly right, Beth. The old Cole Dempsey only cared about himself, but I've changed. I've grown up, too."

"Oh, so is that why the first conversation we shared after fifteen years turned into a threat? Or did you forget you told me you would play dirty and try to take Shane away from me?"

Cole hung his head. "Come on, Beth, I didn't mean to say those things. I just panicked when it seemed like you weren't going to give me a chance to meet my son. I overreacted and I'm sorry."

"Whatever." Beth bristled, hating to hear Cole refer to Shane as his son. She pushed a plate of eggs and hash browns in front of him. "I have things I need to get done." She walked away from the kitchen leaving Cole and her appetite behind.

Walking to the barn, Beth had to will her breathing to slow down before she hyperventilated. Cole hadn't even been on her property twenty-four hours, and he was already pushing all the right buttons. *Really, God? You don't think I have enough on my plate? You have to throw Cole into the mix?*

When Beth entered the barn, she saw Althea and smiled. "Hey, pretty girl," she cooed, stepping into the stall. "You feel like going on a ride?" Beth patted her new partner. Picking up a curry comb, she stroked Althea's strong, elegant neck and taunt withers. Beth caressed the mare's silken coat as a ruckus of thoughts vied for her attention.

Where do I start, Lord? I feel guilty that I didn't tell Mitch about Cole, and angry that Cole had the audacity to say he still has feelings for me. And now that Shane is interested in Kat, should I still plan on putting the ranch up for sale? Or should I pull back since he seems to have had a change of heart? Would his change of heart last if he and Kat stopped seeing each other?

Beth wanted to scream. Her life was in such upheaval. Nothing was as it should be. Mitch was gone. Cole was here. Shane finally got his wish, a face-to-face with his father. But who was having to deal with Cole? She was.

Beth tossed the curry comb into the bucket and turned to Althea. "How about we go take some water samples?" she asked, as if she would receive a reply. "I need some time to think."

After getting Althea's tack, Beth bridled the mare, then led her from the stall. Feeling a little stiff from the day before, she took a minute to massage her right leg.

"Should you really be riding if you're not feeling one hundred percent?" Cole asked as he walked through the big barn doors.

Beth straightened up. "I'll be fine." She grabbed the saddle blanket and slung it over Althea's back. "That's the beauty of riding a horse; they do all the work."

"Funny, Beth. You know what I mean."

Ignoring Cole, she reached for the saddle, but Cole beat her to it. Hoisting the heavy equipment onto Althea's back, he centered it on the blanket.

"Can I come with you?"

"Believe it or not, Cole, I'm used to doing things all on my own. I don't need your help, or you following me around everywhere I go." Beth reached for the girth buckle and cinched the strap.

"I didn't say you did, but I would still like to go for a ride. I mean, what else am I going to do until Shane comes home? Come on, Beth, show me what you've done with the place."

Beth looked at Cole, ready to tell him what he could do with his supposed interest, but thought better of it. If he was with her, she could keep an eye on him and prevent him from poking around where he didn't belong.

"Suit yourself."

Cole headed toward the tack room. "What equipment should I use?"

Beth had to think a moment. She really didn't want him riding Midas, but didn't feel comfortable letting him ride Apollo without Shane's permission. "Use the equipment on the top rung. You can ride Midas."

Cole walked out, his arms full of equipment. "The tack room looks nice. Who did that?"

"A friend," Beth answered, without offering the explanation she knew he wanted.

When Cole led Midas from his stall, he nickered and tossed his head about, being his normal ornery self. Cole saddled him quickly, then mounted.

"So, I guess your 'friend' is a little taller than I am?"

Beth didn't bother to acknowledge Cole's question with an answer. She just watched as he dismounted Midas and adjusted the stirrups by an inch or two.

Leading Althea over to the side of her stall, Beth took the bucket of grooming supplies, dumped them on the floor, then flipped over the bucket so she could use it as a step stool. Carefully, she swung her right leg over Althea's back and slowly stretched it out before sitting down. She then turned around to see Cole mount Midas in one fluid motion.

Beth walked Althea out of the barn and to the gate. Unlatching it, she waited for Cole and Midas, then refastened the bolt. Beth didn't tell Cole where they were going or what they were doing; she just rode south, figuring he would follow.

"I was sorry to hear about Pandora. That couldn't have been easy."

"Yeah, well, I've had to deal with a lot of things that haven't been easy, but you wouldn't know about that."

"You know, Beth, you haven't cornered the market on hard knocks."

"Look, I said you could come along. I didn't say anything about small talk."

"Fine."

They rode in silence for another twenty minutes before Cole asked, "So, why are you selling the ranch?"

"That's none of your business."

"Shane told me the deal you two made about moving to the city."

"Then why'd you ask?"

"Guess I wanted to hear your side of it."

"Who said anything about there being sides?"

"Come on, Beth, this land is in your blood. There's no way you would willingly leave it, let alone sell it."

"What good is it to hold on to land when the next generation isn't interested?"

"Hard to believe he's my son."

Beth turned in her saddle and glared at Cole, not the least bit amused. "What's that supposed to mean? If you doubt Shane is your son, why are you here?"

"That's not what I said. I just meant I love ranch life and the outdoors so much, it's hard to believe it skipped a generation." Cole looked at her with intensity. "I knew the minute I laid eyes on Shane, he was my son. I also knew the minute I laid eyes on you what a foolish mistake I made sixteen years ago."

Completely caught off guard, Beth looked at Cole with a mixture of sadness and hate. "Yeah, well, some mistakes can't be fixed."

Beth slipped from Althea's back, then reached in her saddlebag for an empty water vial. Though Cole dismounted, he didn't follow her. Beth gathered the sample, then walked back to Althea. After putting the sample in her bag, Beth pushed her foot into the stirrup and tried to mount, but failed miserably.

The horse's extra height and Beth's weakened leg were proving to be difficult obstacles. She tried again, bouncing lightly on her sore leg, but it was no use. She couldn't get the momentum she needed.

"Here, let me give you a hand." Cole stepped alongside Beth, laced his fingers together, then bent down to give her a leg up.

Beth looked at him with a sneer as she hung on to the horn and the roll of the saddle. "Are you kidding me?"

"I'm not propositioning you, Beth. It's just a leg up."

Looking at him with eyes that said *drop dead*, Beth lifted her leg anyway, knowing she needed his help.

Effortlessly, Cole lifted her into the saddle. He stroked Althea's neck while Beth adjusted herself. When she looked down at him, he was smiling at her with one eye closed, squinting against the sun, his hat pushed back on his forehead. Beth knew Cole was waiting for a thank you.

You can wait all you want, Beth thought to herself as she led Althea away.

While she gathered more water samples, Cole tried to engage Beth in conversation. She gave short answers—mostly yes's and no's. She did it to tick him off, knowing he hated to be ignored. From the tightness in his jaw and the set of his shoulders, she could tell she was succeeding.

When they reached the pond on the far side of the property, Beth dismounted and stood for a minute, a flood of memories washed over her. She had taught Shane how to swim here, just like her mother had taught her before that. How many generations of Justin's had done the very same thing? And now it would come to an end.

"What are you doing?" Cole asked, as he walked up alongside her.

"Just thinking," Beth replied as she bent to get the water sample.

"Do you remember the night you snuck out and we came down here?" Cole asked as he skipped a rock across the surface.

"I came down here a lot." Beth twisted the lid on tight and hurried to put the sample in her saddlebag. She knew exactly what Cole was getting at but didn't want to talk about it.

"You *know* what I'm talking about, Beth," he said in a smooth, sultry tone, then moved from the water's edge to stand dangerously close to her. "We snuck down here to go swimming . . . which led to skinny dipping . . . then to other things."

Beth fumbled with the buckle of the saddlebag, feeling her heart race and her face heat with embarrassment.

He laughed. "So, you *do* remember?" Cole said, obviously seeing the change in her complexion.

"Yes, I remember." She turned to him, wanting Cole to see the pain and anger in her eyes. "I remember it as well as the night you beat me up and left me unconscious in the barn."

Cole turned away and stepped back to the bank of the pond, then settled his eyes on somewhere across the expanse.

"Oh, I guess you don't remember that. Well, let me refresh your memory. I told you I was pregnant. You tossed two hundred dollars at me and told me to get rid of *it*. Later, when I foolishly thought I could threaten you, you used me as a punching bag and—"

"I remember!" Cole shouted, then quickly softened his tone. "Believe me, Beth, I remember. I've tried to forget about that horrible night. Just like I've tried to forget about everything else I gave up when I left the Diamond-J, but believe me, it haunts me as much as it haunts you."

"Oh really," Beth stomped to where Cole was standing—the pain in her leg nothing compared to the pain in her heart. She stood behind him, waiting for Cole to turn around and looked at her, but he didn't budge. "I guess I can see how your life has been one tragedy after another. It must have been awful to be named Rookie of the Year and touted as the next Ty Murray. Oh, and then it was probably pure agony when you won your first world title and married the rodeo queen. And then things must have really gotten hard when you won your second and third world titles, and added two little girls to your list of accomplishments. Yeah, I can see how what you did to *me* was so difficult on *you*."

Cole swung around, eyes glassy and red. He grabbed Beth by the shoulders, startling her. "Beth, I'm so sorry," his eyes pled for understanding. "You've got to believe me. I was young and selfish and only thinking about my future. But now . . . now I know how wrong I was. I've got everything I thought I ever wanted, but never the satisfaction I was looking for. Now I know why. The minute I saw you again, I realized why happiness has eluded me. It was here all the time. Where I should have been . . . with you and Shane."

Beth was stunned by the look of torment in his eyes. Her heart clenched, making it difficult to breathe. Cole took a step toward her, leaving no room between them. Beth watched, still speechless as he lowered his head, his eyes settling on her lips. He was only a breath away when she turned her head.

"What do you think you're doing?" She took a step back.

"I thought . . . maybe we could . . ."

"Well, you thought wrong. I'm not part of the deal. You're here for Shane, not—"

With the sound of approaching hooves, Beth and Cole turned to see Charlie headed their way.

Great. Just what I need. Beth hurried to Althea's side, but was unable to hoist herself into the saddle.

Cole moved to give her a leg up, but Beth slapped his hands away. "I don't need your help, Cole. Now or ever. I've gotten along just fine all these years without you. So has Shane."

"If that was true, he wouldn't have gone to all the trouble of finding me. It's clear Shane wants something more than what you've given him, and I'm it. So, like it or not, Beth, I'm not going anywhere."

Cole's words cut her to the quick, sending a surge of panic through her veins. But Beth refused to let Cole have the upper hand. *I will not lose my son to the likes of you.* "Then let me make myself perfectly clear, just so there aren't any further misunderstandings. You are here to see Shane. And since I know how important this is to him, I'm not going to stand in your way. But, if you think I want you here, you're sadly mistaken. I will be cordial and pleasant; I won't slander you in front of Shane. But don't confuse that with anything more than tolerance. I am confident—with enough time—Shane will see you for the person you really are."

Beth finished her lecture just as Charlie pulled Hammer to a stop. When she looked up, there was no mistaking the shock on her Uncle's face.

"What in the—"

"Hi, Charlie. It's been a long time." Cole grinned as he tipped his hat.

"Not long enough," Charlie groused as he swung out of the saddle and moved himself between her and Cole.

"What's he doing here, Beth?"

"He's here to see Shane."

"And you're all right with that?"

"It's important to Shane," she answered somberly.

Charlie looked at Cole, then back to Beth. "I don't like it." He shook his head in agitation. "I don't like it one bit! He was no good when he was younger, and you can bet he's up to no good now." Charlie turned to Cole, jabbing a finger in his face. "I blamed myself for years because of the hurt you caused Beth. I knew you were trouble, and I should have thrown your sorry butt off this ranch long before you got your hands on her. That's my cross to bear. But I'll be damned if I stand by and let you hurt her again."

"I really don't see how this is any of your business. Beth's a big girl and can make her own decisions. She doesn't need you to run interfer—"

Charlie lunged at Cole, grabbed him by the collar, and pushed him back against Midas' sturdy hindquarters. The horse snorted his disapproval but stayed in place, as solid as a cement wall.

"Beth and Shane are my business! You hear me, boy? So keep that smart mouth of yours shut." Charlie gave him another shove. "I swore if I ever laid eyes on you again, I would kill you for what you did to Beth."

"Uncle Charlie, it's okay." Beth pulled Charlie off of Cole. He took a step back, his hands flexing at his sides.

Cole straightened his collar and brushed at his sleeves. "That's not a very Christian-like attitude, Charlie. What happened to forgive and forget?"

Charlie sprung at Cole again, only stopping when Beth stood between them. With her hands in the center of his chest, she pushed her uncle back a couple of steps.

"I want you out of here. Do you hear me?" Charlie yelled. "This is Justin land and you're not welcome!"

"Uncle Charlie, I already told Cole he could stay."

He looked at Beth like he'd been betrayed. "Why? He has no right being here."

"He's Shane's father."

"No! A father is someone who takes care of you your whole life, is there for you always, no matter what. Cole's no father." Charlie turned to face him, his face beet red with emotion. "You're nothing more than a two-bit hood who took advantage of Beth when she was just a girl. Biologically you're Shane's father, but you'll never be anything more than a deadbeat dad."

"Well, Shane doesn't see it that way. So, as long as *my* son wants me here, this is where I'm going to stay."

Charlie turned back to Beth, his words muffled, "Does Mitch know he's here?"

She glanced over Charlie's shoulder, seeing the curious look on Cole's face. "No, I don't want him to know," she whispered.

"But Beth, he would want to know what's going on. He's worried about you. Mitch called me first thing this morning and told me you were working too hard. He wants me to hire more help." He shot a look at Cole. "Real help."

"It's my decision to let Cole stay. If Shane wants to get to know his father, I want him to do it where I can keep an eye on the situation. This is the way it has to be."

Charlie's expression was one of futility. "I just don't like it. I trust Cole about as far as I can spit."

"It's going to be okay, Uncle Charlie. I can handle this."

"Beth, people like Cole don't change. He's a self-centered, manipulative, son-of-"

"You're right," she whispered, "and the sooner Shane sees that side of Cole the better. Don't worry, Uncle Charlie, I know what I am doing."

"Do you? You thought you knew what you were doing sixteen

years ago and look where it got you."

His words were like a punch in the gut. "You're right, Uncle Charlie, but I'm not that naive little girl anymore. I'm an adult and I have to handle this my way. If Mitch needs to know, I will be the one to tell him, not you or Travis."

"Fine. You do what you see fit. But I don't have to like it." Charlie looked at Cole. "Don't think you're pulling something over on me. People like you seldom change. So help me, as I live and breathe, if you do anything to hurt my family, I will come after you."

Chapter Fifty-One

Once Uncle Charlie left, Cole wasted no time asking Beth about Mitch.

"So, who's this Mitch guy?"

She turned away, ignoring him.

"Come on, Beth. Who is this guy? I mean, if I was him, I would certainly make my presence known if some man started hanging out with my woman—especially a man she had a history with."

"First of all, we're not *hanging* out. Secondly, Mitch was called away on business."

"Thirdly," Cole needled, "maybe it has to do with the fact that you didn't tell him I was here. Why do you suppose that is, Beth?"

"Because I see no reason to bother him with something so inconsequential. Besides, you're here to see Shane, not me."

"Shane might be the reason I came, but like I said before, seeing you has shown me what's been missing in my life."

"Well, you'll excuse me if I don't share your sentiment."

"Come on, Beth. It wasn't all bad."

Cole smiled his trademark smile, the one that used to turn her knees into Jell-O. Beth looked away, not understanding how someone she hated for so long could still have that effect on her.

He started laughing, angering her even more.

"What's so funny?" she snapped.

"I was just remembering the night you got drunk, and Troy challenged you to get in the pen with that crazy bull your dad had. What was his name again?"

Beth hung her head in horror, remembering all too well what a fool she'd made of herself that night, all for the sake of getting Cole to notice her. Cyclone had been their stud bull and Beth—in her inebriated state—was convinced she could ride him.

"Cyclone! That was his name!" Cole laughed some more. "You were so bent on showing all of us how tough you were, you nearly got yourself killed."

Beth didn't remember much about the infamous ride or the way Cyclone had thrown her to the ground. However, she did remember the way Cole had silently carried her upstairs to her bedroom, right past her father's door. He had laid Beth on the bed and kissed her for the first time.

Beth flushed at the memory.

"See," he chuckled, "it wasn't all bad."

"You took advantage of me."

"Maybe I did," Cole grinned. "But you seemed to enjoy it."

"I thought I was in love," she snapped. "I thought *we* were in love."

"Maybe I was, but just too afraid to admit it."

"No!" She would not allow him to patronize her. "It wasn't love I saw in your eyes when I confronted you in Wichita. It was anger and resentment. You didn't care about me, or that you had a son. All you cared about was Cole Dempsey. So don't think you can convince me now that you always had feelings for me, because I'm not buying it."

Beth heeled Althea to a faster pace, hating that Cole had gotten under her skin. With tears stinging her eyes, Beth rode into the yard and swung out of the saddle. When she set her right leg on the ground, she felt it give slightly. She held on to Althea for support, feeling weak. *Don't let him do this to you. He's manipulating you, just like Uncle Charlie said he would. Don't give him that kind of control.* Beth continued her internal pep talk as she limped to Althea's stall.

She heard Cole walk Midas into the barn, but moved so her back was to him. She quickly brushed Althea and put the tack away before heading for the house.

Dragging herself upstairs, Beth had one goal—pain medication. She filled a glass of water in the bathroom then walked to the night stand. She grimaced as she sat on the edge of the bed, reading the label. *Take with food. Drowsiness may occur. Do not drive or operate heavy machinery—*

The phone rang, making her jump. Beth reached for the cordless next to her bed.

"Hello."

"Hey, babe."

Beth sighed with relief. "Mitch, it's so good to hear your voice."

"Is it? You sound exhausted. Is something wrong?"

Hearing the slam of the screen door downstairs reminded Beth exactly what was wrong. *Tell him. He deserves to know.* "I . . . I guess I'm just a little tired." She cringed, knowing she'd blown her chance yet again. "I took a long ride today to get some water samples. I'm pretty stiff."

"Well, just so you know, I called Charlie this morning and asked him to check in on you. I told him you were overdoing it. He's going to see if he can scrounge up some extra help while I'm gone."

"That's not necessary, Mitch. You forget, I ran the ranch just fine before you got here."

"You also had those two twits working for you. I know you, Beth. You're going to push yourself too hard. In fact, it sounds like you already have."

"It's no big deal. I'm just a little sore. The doctor said to expect that for a while. I have to recondition my muscles, but I can't do that just sitting around."

"Okay. Riding is one thing, but riding alone is something else altogether. Something could've happened to you."

"Come on, Mitch, stop worrying. I'm fine. What about you? How are things going there?" Beth quickly changed the subject, not about to admit she wasn't alone.

"Slow."

Beth's shoulders slumped. "What do you mean slow?"

"The director wants to re-shoot the scenes we did last night. He takes the term perfectionist to a whole new level. And this script, it's so ridiculous. Even Kara thinks we're riding a sinking ship."

Just hearing Mitch speak the woman's name made Beth bristle. "Then why did she agree to do it? It's not like she couldn't get work somewhere else."

"Because of the hype. The buzz right now is so—"

"Mitch . . . I can barely hear you. You sound like you're talking in a tunnel."

Beth walked over to the window as if that would somehow make their connection clearer. Turning back around, she gasped. Cole stood in the doorway watching her.

"Beth, what's wrong?"

She eyed Cole. "Nothing. Everything's fine."

Cole arched his brow, smugly.

"Okay, Beth, I've got to go. They're ready for me on the set. But, please promise me you'll take it easy. Let Shane, Charlie, and Travis do the strenuous work. I want you in one piece when I get home. I love you, babe. I'll talk to you soon."

"I love—" The connection dropped before Beth could finish. Slamming the phone back in the dock, she asked, "What do you want, Cole?"

"It's already two o'clock. I thought I would make us some lunch. I just wanted to see if that was okay with you."

"I'm not hungry." Beth grabbed the water glass and took the pain pill she'd been holding in her hand.

"You're not going to get your strength back if you don't eat."

"And I don't need a nursemaid telling me what to do." She brushed past him and headed downstairs, trying to put some distance between them.

Cole eyed the medicine bottle on Beth's nightstand. He walked over, picked up the bottle, and read the label.

Then smiled.

Chapter Fifty-Two

Though she wasn't hungry, Beth knew she needed to eat something to offset the pain medication. Grabbing a yogurt and a banana from the refrigerator, she then headed down the hall to her office. The minute Beth sat down, she realized she'd left the water samples in her saddlebag. Frustrated, Beth dragged herself through the house and out the front door, mumbling to herself the entire way.

Cole was in the kitchen fixing himself a sandwich when she came back in. "I found some steaks in the freezer. I thought I could barbeque them tonight. That is, if you don't mind?"

"Fine," she grumbled as she continued to her office.

Beth readied the water samples in the kit, then cringed at the idea of having to walk it all the way out to the main road. She toyed with the idea of letting Shane mail it tomorrow, but knew she needed to get it in the mail today.

The walk back from the mailbox wasn't nearly as painful as the walk out. *Thank God for pain medication.*

Climbing the steps of the porch, Beth plopped down on the swing, intending on resting for just a minute or two. But the easy sway of the old wooden swing was hypnotic and soothing. Feeling herself being lulled to sleep, she tried fighting it, knowing she had other things to get done, but her eyes wouldn't cooperate.

When Cole stepped out on the porch, he laughed softly. Beth was slumped in the swing, her head and shoulder leaning against one of the sturdy chains suspending it. Gently, Cole slid her legs to the porch and took a seat beside her. He stared at Beth as she slept, remembering what it had felt like being with her—wondering if he'd get the chance to feel that way again.

When he brushed the back of his fingers against her cheek, she stirred. Moving closer, Beth snuggled against his side. Cole looped his arm across the back of the swing, grinning with satisfaction.

Beth had always been a lightweight when it came to medicine. Obviously, she still was. Passed out, unaware of her actions, Cole soaked up the attention. He liked the way she felt warm and soft against his side. He dropped his arm down around Beth, stroking her shoulder, pressing her closer. She stretched her arm across his midsection, and sighed.

"I'm glad you're home, Mitch," she whispered. "Promise me you'll stay."

A flare of jealousy heated Cole's face, but he stroked her still. *Don't worry, I don't plan on leaving.*

He'd been enjoying Beth's insensible state for several minutes when he saw a cloud of dust rolling down the driveway.

Shane was home.

Cole smiled, wanting his son to see them in such close proximity. He waited until Shane pulled past the Airstream. When he did a double take, Cole knew Shane had seen enough.

"Beth, Shane's home." He nudged her to an upright position and slid to the other side of the swing. "Beth."

Beth willed her eyes open, her head feeling like mush. She blinked repeatedly, trying to shake the cobwebs from her mind. When she was finally able to focus, Beth looked at Cole, immediately feeling irritated.

"What are you doing here?"

"Watching you sleep," he chuckled. "You went to mail the water samples, remember?"

Beth did remember that, but not much else.

"When you didn't come back in the house, I got worried. I found you sitting here, not doing much of anything. We were talking about the ranch, and you were catching me up on Charlie and Travis, when you started drifting off. It's obvious you're overworking yourself, Beth. It's midday, and you fell asleep in the middle of a conversation."

When Shane climbed the steps, Beth immediately got the impression something was wrong. "Shane, is everything all right?"

"You tell me." His words were directed at her, but his eyes zoned in on Cole.

"What do you mean by that?" Beth stretched, still trying to shake the heaviness she felt in her limbs.

"What are you doing out here?" Shane asked.

"Uh . . . Cole and I were just getting caught up." Beth had to take Cole's word for it since she didn't remember a thing they were talking about.

"Really, is that what you call it?"

"Shane, what's wrong?"

"Never mind." He swung open the screen door and stormed away.

Beth wanted to go after him, but when she stood, she lost her balance and fell back onto the swing.

"Beth, let him go."

"Why? Something is obviously wrong." She tried standing again, this time her legs were a little steadier.

"Maybe he had an argument with his girlfriend. Just give him some space. If you follow him around, pumping him for information every time he's agitated, he'll start blocking you out."

Beth didn't appreciate Cole giving her parental advice, but she had to admit, he was probably right. If she forced Shane to share his feelings every minute of the day, he would stop talking to her all together. *Adolescence. It certainly isn't for the faint of heart.*

She massaged her forehead, still feeling disoriented.

"Look, Beth, you're tired. Why don't you go upstairs and lie down for a little while? I'll try to strike up a conversation with Shane and see if I can find out what's bothering him."

Beth contemplated Cole's suggestion. It was true. She was exhausted. With the added fatigue from her leg and the last few sleepless nights, she was wiped out. But did she really trust Cole to talk to Shane about personal issues?

"Go on, Beth. Get some sleep. And don't worry about dinner. I'll take care of that, too."

"I'll be awake long before dinner," Beth insisted as she walked toward the screen door. It was only three o'clock. She would lay down for a half-hour, forty-five minutes. Max.

"I don't need you taking care of anything."

Cole waited downstairs for Shane, figuring he was a teenage boy and would head to the refrigerator before long.

It only took ten minutes to prove his theory right.

"Shane, can we talk for a minute?" Cole asked as he took a seat at the counter.

"Sure. Maybe you can explain why I saw you with your hands all over my mother?" He slammed the refrigerator and opened the soda can in his hand.

"It wasn't what it looked like, Shane."

"Then tell me how it was."

"Your mom's just a little emotional right now. She had feelings for me at one time, and I think me being here is a little confusing for her. That, along with the pain she's in, and the argument she had with her boyfriend, I just think—"

"What argument?"

Cole hung his head, trying to look the picture of sincerity. "It's not my place to say anything. I just think Beth got her feelings hurt, something to do with the woman he's working with. But Shane, you can't say anything. If Beth knew I overheard her crying, she would probab—"

"She was crying?"

"Well, yes, but again, that could've been from the pain she's in. Look Shane, I shouldn't have said anything. I just wanted to explain why I was comforting her. Beth needed a shoulder to cry on. Even though I'm sure I wasn't her first choice, I was here and available. Please don't bring it up. It will only upset Beth to think we were talking about her. You know how stubborn your mom can be."

"That's for sure." Shane took a gulp of his soda.

"So, tell me about this girlfriend of yours. She must be something special." Cole worked his magic to change the subject and get Shane to lower his defenses, while inwardly he added an invisible mark in his win column.

Chapter Fifty-Three

Beth awoke feeling disoriented and foggy. Glancing at her alarm clock, she sat up abruptly. "Three hours? I've been asleep three hours?"

Smelling the unmistakable scent of mesquite, Beth vaguely remembered Cole saying something about dinner. Closing her eyes, she tried to remember what else they had talked about, but her mind was a blank, except for the dream she'd had of Mitch coming home and holding her close.

Walking downstairs, Beth moved with a little more fluidity. Although the medication had really knocked her for a loop, at least it had worked. Following the scent to the back porch, Beth saw Cole flipping steaks on the barbeque while Shane sat on the stoop, talking sports.

This is the way it should have been.

If Cole hadn't been so selfish and his actions so painful, we could've had this all along.

Beth shook off the thought because it was too late to go back.

When she pushed open the screen door, Cole smiled at her, looking more charming than he had a right to.

"Well, look who's awake," he winked, as he rolled corn on the cob back and forth across the grill.

"You feeling okay, Mom?" Shane asked as she took a seat beside him on the back steps.

"Now I am." She smiled. "How about you?" Beth asked, hoping Shane would share what had been bothering him earlier.

"I'm fine."

"Did you want to invite Kat over for dinner?"

"No. That's okay. She understands it's important I spend time with Cole."

When the phone rang, Shane darted off the steps to answer it.

Beth turned to Cole. "So, what all have you two been talking about?"

"My career, my ranch in Oklahoma, the finals, my family. Shane just realized he's a half-brother to my two girls."

"How old are they?"

"Nicole is nine and Ariel is seven."

"Mom, it's Mitch." Shane opened the screen door and passed her the phone.

She got to her feet and walked back inside.

"Mitch, I wasn't expecting you to call again."

"I know. But I felt bad that our earlier call was cut short."

"That's okay. I understand," Beth said quietly as she leaned against the wall, hugging the phone to her ear.

"Beth, is there something wrong with Shane? He sounded like he was ticked off about something."

"I know. He came home from school with his nose out of joint, but I don't know why. I think he might've had a disagreement with Kat." *Or he's having a hard time dealing with his mixed emotions regarding his father.* "How are things there?"

"Not bad."

It wasn't what Beth wanted to hear, but she pushed down her frustration and listened as Mitch explained what he'd been doing for the last few hours.

"Beth, are you sure you can't come out here? Even for just a weekend? I miss you so much, it's driving me crazy."

She glanced out the backdoor where Shane and Cole were talking. She didn't trust leaving Shane alone with Cole for any given amount of time. He was too persuasive, too manipulative.

"I can't, Mitch. I just don't feel comfortable leaving Shane."

"I'm sure the Carters would be willing to keep an eye on him, and even help out around the ranch."

JUST AN ACT

Tell him. Tell him Cole is here. "Mitch, I need to tell you—" Static crackled in Beth's ear. "Mitch, are you there?"

"Beth . . . Beth, I can't hear you. If you can hear me, I love you, and I'll try to call again tomorrow."

Beth answered Mitch even though it was obvious he couldn't hear her. She ended the call with a push of a button feeling more frustrated than ever.

Cole walked through the backdoor carrying a platter of steaks and corn on the cob. "Dinner is ready."

"I'm not hungry. You two go ahead."

Shane watched as his mom walked upstairs, wondering what was going on between her and Mitch.

"Come on, Shane, give her some space."

With a final glance upstairs, he followed Cole to the dining room and began setting the table. Yet, he couldn't stop thinking about Mitch and what he must've said to upset his mom.

It wasn't fair.

She already had enough to deal with without Mitch piling it on.

After everything was on the table, Cole took the chair across from Shane. "When you say grace, why don't you say a prayer for your mom. It looks like she could use it."

Shane nodded before bowing his head.

Dinner started out quiet—both Cole and Shane eating more than talking. Then, out of the blue, Cole looked at Shane and shook his head.

"What?" Shane asked defensively.

"You really want to move to the city?"

"Oh man, don't you start on me, too. I've already heard it from everyone—Mom, Uncle Charlie, even my friends across the street."

"I just find it hard to believe that you would rather live in the city with wall-to-wall people and bumper-to-bumper traffic. I mean, ranching is in your blood."

"That's what Mom always says, but I've never felt attached to the land like she does." Shane pierced a piece of steak, then held it up to examine it. "But, moving the herd . . . that was pretty fun."

Cole grinned. "It felt good, didn't it? Measuring them up, filling an order, shipping them off, knowing someone just paid top dollar for the beef you raised."

A smile creased Shane's face. "It definitely gave me a new perspective."

"Well, what do you know? There might be hope for you yet."

Cole leaned back in his chair and swigged at his soda, feeling pretty good about how things were going. He and Shane were beginning to forge a bond, and Beth's relationship didn't seem like it was going to be an issue for long. Every time the guy called, Beth ended up looking hurt or upset.

Perfect. I'll let good ole Mitch dig himself a hole, while I turn on the Dempsey charm.

Cole was reveling in the thought of winning Beth over, when he noticed Shane staring at him. But he wasn't smiling.

"What's wrong?"

Shane just shrugged as he pushed his fork around on his plate.

"Is it girl trouble?"

Shane shook his head.

"If it's because your mom's upset, I'm sure things will—"

"It's not that."

"Well, by the powers of deduction, I guess that only leaves me."

When Shane didn't deny it, Cole cursed under his breath. "Fine. What did I do wrong?"

Shane didn't answer, but continued to play with the leftover food on his plate.

"Come on, Shane, I obviously ticked you off somehow. Just spit it out."

Shane stewed a moment longer, before making eye contact with him. "Did you ever love my mom?"

Cole swallowed hard, not expecting Shane's question to be so to the point. He lowered his chair to the floor and rested his elbows on the table, his hands clenched together.

"I thought I did." He hung his head, knowing he had to choose his words carefully. "But I was young and stupid; the thought of being tied down scared me to death. So I ran."

Shane twisted his napkin in his hands, his eyes in his lap. "Then how could you . . ." his words caught in his throat, "how could you hurt someone you loved?"

Cole felt all the air being sucked out of the room. How could he answer him? How would he explain to Shane the actions he'd taken that night? The night he'd left Beth in a heap on the barn floor, caring only about himself and his future?

Finally, he lifted his eyes to Shane. "I was drunk."

Shane looked away.

"I know that's no excuse for what I did. I was a coward; I only cared about myself. I never meant to hurt Beth. But when she cornered me in the barn, and threatened me, I just lost it."

"She was pregnant with your kid. You didn't think leaving was going to hurt her?" Shane's tone was indignant as he refuted Cole's explanation.

"I told you, I was young and stupid. We didn't know anything about raising a kid. I thought she would get a—" he stopped short of saying it.

"An abortion?" Shane finished for him.

The reality of the situation was like a noose around Cole's neck. He was staring into the eyes of the child he had wanted destroyed—that he thought would've been better off never existing.

"I'm sorry, Shane. What can I say? There's nothing I can do to change the past. I screwed up; I know that now. I see that when I look at the fine young man you've grown in to, and the incredible woman Beth has become. I've missed out on so many things because of my selfishness. My only hope is that it's not too late."

Beth sat in the shadows of the stairwell in utter disbelief.

When she heard Shane and Cole talking about the ranch, she decided not to interrupt, wanting to hear what Shane would say. She was thrilled beyond belief to hear a hint of excitement in his voice. She couldn't help but feel hopeful.

Then, their conversation turned serious.

Beth held her breath as Shane asked Cole about the feelings he'd once had for her. She fought tears when Shane was faced with the reality of Cole's actions so many years ago. She didn't know what to think or what to believe.

Was Cole serious? Was he truly sorry for the choices he'd made? Did he really think they could have a future together?

Silently, Beth stood and walked back to her room. She collapsed across her bed pushing the palms of her hands into her eyes, trying to suppress the tears that pooled there all too often lately.

Why am I being so emotional? I know better than to believe anything Cole says. He's a manipulator, a schemer. He's only saying what he thinks Shane wants to hear.

Well, I know Cole better than that.

It's not going to work on me.

Chapter Fifty-Four

Cole had been at the Diamond-J for three weeks, yet Beth had never told Mitch. She had made two more attempts, but neither had been successful.

The first time Beth worked up the courage to tell Mitch, their phone call was cut short. Their conversation consisted of the customary: *How are you? I miss you. I love you.* But before Beth could launch into her practiced speech, Mitch was called back to the set by an irate director.

The second time Beth prepared herself to explain the situation—and defuse any and all of Mitch's concerns—the static on the line was so great, Mitch hung up twice and called back, trying to secure a clearer connection. Three times during their phone call Beth readied herself for the difficult discussion. Each time she began, Mitch talked over her, unable to hear a word she was saying.

Completely frustrated, Beth flippantly told Mitch there was no sense in calling if their conversations were always going to be interrupted or relegated to: *Can you hear me? What did you say? Repeat that.* However, the instant the terse words were out of her mouth, Beth apologized—assuring Mitch she wanted to hear from him no matter how short the call or how many times they were interrupted. Unfortunately, the negative vibe hung like a dark cloud over the rest of their conversation, never completely going away. They asked each other benign questions and replied with one-word answers. It most definitely was not the right mood to say: *Oh, by the way, Cole is here—has been for a few weeks—but don't worry, I have everything under control.* So, Beth decided not to tell Mitch at all, convinced the timing would be better after Cole was gone.

Never, in a million years, could Beth have predicted that three weeks later, Cole would still be staying at the Diamond-J. When the days turned into weeks, her window of opportunity to calmly explain the situation to Mitch was long gone. Beth knew if she tried to tell him now, he would only get upset.

Beth nervously laughed to herself—even though the situation was far from funny. *Who am I kidding? I passed 'upset' weeks ago. Mitch would be livid. He would feel lied to and in a sense, betrayed.*

Doing what she could to justify her deception, Beth constantly reminded herself there was nothing Mitch could do from over a thousand miles away. To tell him would actually be worse than keeping it from him, at least that's how she soothed her nagging conscience. Beth knew she was playing a dangerous game of situational ethics, viewing her choices through a skewed lens of gray. But no matter what—one thing was clear—she was in a lose-lose situation.

Convinced the matter would be better handled face-to-face, Beth stuck to her decision to wait until Mitch got home. She would be able to gauge Mitch's reaction by the look in his eyes, not the silence at the other end of a telephone call. Cole would be long gone by then, so any threat Mitch might have felt would be gone as well. They would be able to discuss the situation in the past-tense where it belonged.

Of course, that wasn't the way Uncle Charlie saw it. She'd had more than one argument with him, reminding him not to say anything to Mitch about Cole's presence, assuring Charlie she knew what she was doing. He always voiced his disapproval. Loudly. But in the end, he agreed not to say anything to Mitch without Beth's consent.

Shane was easier to persuade. Since he was the one responsible for their current situation, he was more than willing to keep quiet. Besides, he barely talked to Mitch at all. Maybe a few words before handing the phone over to her, but other than that, Shane was wrapped up in his own little world.

The conversation she'd had with Mr. Carter proved to be the most awkward. Beth knew he had forged a bond with Mitch, and she was putting him in a difficult position. She explained there was more to the situation then she cared to share, and politely asked him not to interfere. He agreed, begrudgingly. But was quick to remind Beth, he wouldn't lie. He wouldn't bring the subject up for conversation, but if Mitch got wind of Cole's presence and asked him a direct question, he would answer if truthfully.

But, in the quiet of night, when Beth lay in bed trying to sleep, the real reason she hadn't told Mitch haunted her. She was afraid—afraid if she told him while he was gone, there was a chance he wouldn't come back. Each night, with tears in her eyes, Beth denied those fears, convinced she was doing the right thing for both of them.

So, day after day, when Mitch called, Beth veered their conversations to safe topics, explaining all that was going on at the ranch—minus Cole. She talked about the time she spent with Kat improving her barrel racing technique, and how proud she was of Shane and his new take-charge attitude. Beth told Mitch what a great job Josh and Dustin—the ranch hands Uncle Charlie had hired—were doing picking up the slack while Shane was in school. Mitch wasn't thrilled when he found out they were only nineteen and twenty. He immediately voiced his concern, not wanting a repeat performance of Brett and Rusty, but Beth assured Mitch that wasn't a problem. Josh and Dustin were good kids who loved ranch life and treated her with respect.

When Beth had exhausted all she could say about her day—careful to side-step anything to do with Cole—she would turn the tables on Mitch and ask about his day.

He explained how they had to shoot the same scene over and over again because of the director's OCD tendencies. Beth listened, but only heard what Mitch *wasn't* telling her . . . the amount of time he was spending with Kara Kensington. Beth's mind reeled with conjured up images of them together. She wanted to believe nothing was going on between Mitch and Kara, but her insecurities bloomed because of her own deception. *You're hiding Cole from Mitch, what's to say Mitch isn't hiding Kara from you?*

As much as Beth tried to convince her inner voice that the two situations were completely different, her thoughts always returned to the basics. Both of them were spending time with people they once loved. No matter how much that person had hurt them, it didn't invalidate the feelings they had once shared.

Lord, help me to trust!

Cole stayed busy while keeping his distance from Charlie. It didn't matter how hard he busted his butt to convince the old man he had changed; Charlie was belligerent and rude, and made it very clear he didn't like having him around. Travis wasn't any better, so Cole worked with Dustin and Josh until Shane got home from school. Then, the two of them spent time together before dinner.

Beth did her best to make herself unavailable to him. She rode with Charlie during the day, then disappear into her office or bedroom at night. She made polite conversation with him over dinner—obviously for Shane's sake—and exchanged a few words at breakfast, but other than that, Beth made herself scarce.

Three weeks Cole had been at the Diamond-J, yet Beth still ignored him. Cole knew, if she'd just let her defenses down and give him a chance, he could stir in Beth the passion that had once existed between them.

Cole smiled as he rode toward the house. *Maybe I'll get that chance today.*

Beth was working in the small, backyard vegetable garden, Charlie nowhere in sight. Glancing at his watch, Cole knew Shane would be home soon. So, if he hoped to get even a few minutes alone with Beth, he'd better hurry.

Cole took Midas to the barn, quickly put his tack away, and headed for the house. Walking around to the back, Cole leaned on the clapboard siding and watched Beth unnoticed.

She was beautiful.

The Beth he had known before was a girl, but the Beth that stood in front of him now was all woman. With jeans that hugged her curvy shape and sun-kissed arms that glistened in the afternoon sun, Beth was incredible to look at. Dream about. Want.

Clenching the garden hose with her knees, Beth filled the channel between two rows of carrots while pulling the hat from her head and swiping at the sweat on her brow. After tucking a few wisps of hair behind her ear, Beth placed the hat back on her head. As she bent to tug at the weeds growing alongside a row of tomatoes, Beth swung the garden hose to the side, oblivious to Cole's approach.

"Hey!" he shouted as he jumped back, but it was too late. Beth had doused him from buckle to boot.

Beth righted herself and turned to Cole. When she saw his water-streaked jeans, she laughed.

"Oh, so you think it's funny? Well, let's see how funny it is when the tables are turned." Cole lunged for the garden hose still in her hand.

Beth straight-armed him, holding the hose out of his reach, all the while laughing.

"You're asking for it, Beth." Cole threatened, even though he was unable to hide the amusement in his tone.

"Don't be such a baby. It's only a little water. You're not going to melt."

"Oh yeah?" Quicker than Beth could react, Cole had her around the waist and pulled her against his chest. He reached for Beth's outstretched hand as she fought, begged, and laughed—all at the same time. In an instant, Cole had the hose turned on Beth, soaking her from head to toe. But she didn't give up. With her right hand on the hose, she twisted the stream of water back on him.

Turning in circles as they each fought for control, their feet became tangled in the hose that snaked around them. Stumbling backwards, Beth fell with a squeal—Cole landing on top of her.

Their laughter ceased the minute they made eye contact, but Cole couldn't move.

"Cole!" Beth protested as she wriggled her arms free and pressed her palms to his shoulders. "Get off me!"

"Don't!" he gasped. "It's my back; I can't move."

"I'm serious, Cole. Get off of me now!" She yelled, struggling harder to separate them.

"Stop it!" he shouted in pain. "Just give me a minute!" Cole forced his words through teeth clenched tight.

Cole laid his head to Beth's chest for just a second, preparing himself for the pain. Moaning, he planted his forearm on the ground and gingerly rolled to one side, allowing Beth enough room to scoot out from under him. As soon as she was clear, Cole collapsed, prone on the ground, not caring that his face laid in the muddy soil.

Beth knelt beside Cole, breathing hard, not knowing what to do. It was obvious from his distorted face, this was no prank. He was clearly in an incredible amount of pain. Pushing her dripping hair behind her ear, Beth asked, "Cole, what can I do?"

"Just give me a minute." He winced.

Cole lay very still, his breathing labored. When he finally tried to move, he slowly rolled over—moaning and grimacing—until he rested on his back. When Cole looked up at Beth, he smiled that charismatic smile of his. "I must've died and gone to heaven."

"Dang you, Cole," she slugged his shoulder causing him to flinch. "I thought you were really hurt." She got up and walked away.

"Beth, come on, you've got to help me."

She stalked to the side of the house and twisted the spigot handle. When Beth turned back around, Cole was still lying motionless in the mud. She waited for him to give up the ruse, but he just laid there with his eyes closed, taking deep, even breaths.

"Cole, just get up. You look ridiculous."

"Believe me, I would love to, but I can't."

Beth begrudgingly walked back to where he was lying. She crossed her arms against her chest and hovered over him, water dripping from her hair. "Cole, if you're not hurt, so help me, you will be when I get done with you."

Cole had to chuckle at Beth's threat, even though it caused him pain. She looked so intimidating, all five-foot-three of her, dripping wet and streaked with mud. "Beth, I promise. As much as I enjoyed our little tumble, I'm being serious."

She released her arms. "Then what should I do?"

"Just give me a minute."

Slowly, Cole rolled on to his stomach. It took a few more minutes before he could pull his knees up under him and balance on all fours.

"Bring that chair over here," he grimaced, pointing to the patio furniture to the side of the porch.

Beth quickly got the chair and positioned it next to his shoulder. Again, it took a moment before he could move. When he did, it was slow, the grunting and groaning involuntary. Beth held the chair as he inched to his feet. Cole stood for a moment, leaning on the chair, perspiration running down his neck. His breath was labored, his face muddy, his wet jeans clinging to his legs. He looked like crap and felt even worse.

"Can you help me into the house?"

Beth stood alongside him, her arm around his waist. He lifted his arm to rest it on Beth's shoulders, hating that he was leaning on her so heavily. With a few slow steps, Beth walked him to the bottom of the stairs. Gripping the banister with his free hand, Cole inched his way up the steps. Slowly, they made it through the mudroom and to the kitchen. Standing at the foot of the stairs Beth asked, "Do you want to rest a moment before tackling the stairs?"

"No, I'd better keep moving."

The stairs proved to be quite daunting. Cole leaned on Beth more and more as they neared the top. The pain was incredible, but he gutted it out all the way to his room. Beth pointed him toward the side of the bed when he stopped her.

"I need to get these clothes off and take a shower."

Beth looked up at him with irritation.

"Come on, Beth, I'm filthy. Just help me to the bathroom and get my boots off. I'll do the rest."

Cole watched as Beth pressed her lips together—the way she did whenever she was frustrated—but she helped him anyway.

Pulling his boots off proved to be difficult. Cole leaned against the sink, holding on to the rim while Beth yanked and wiggled the worn leather loose.

When he looked at himself in the mirror, Cole felt like he was going to puke. His skin was ashen and there was no color left in his lips.

"Cole, you look awful. We need to get you to a doctor."

"I'll be fine," he snapped, fumbling with the buttons on his shirt.

"How can you say that? You can't even walk. Let me call the—"

"No!" he raised his voice, then apologized. "There's nothing they can do, Beth. It's a spasm. It will go away. Just help me get my shirt off."

Beth looked at Cole's shirt, unbuttoned and grimy, his tank undershirt stretched across his well-defined chest. She stared at him, knowing he was plotting something.

"Come on, Beth, I can barely move. Don't look at me like I'm trying to seduce you."

She turned from Cole, trying to hide her embarrassment. It was true; he was in a lot of pain and could barely move. Not exactly the tools for a seduction.

Sighing, Beth conceded. "Turn around."

Reaching up, she pulled his shirt from his shoulders and dragged it down his well-defined arms. Beth wadded it up and tossed it in the sink while Cole yanked at the hem of his t-shirt, pulling it free from his jeans. When he crossed his arms—to pull his shirt over his head—he grimaced and cursed.

"Will you give me a hand?"

Cole had pulled his undershirt up around his torso, but that is where his ability left it. Beth stretched the wide armhole around Cole's elbow—freeing one arm—then pulled it up and over his head, and dragged it down his other side.

When Beth heard the screen door downstairs snap shut, she twisted around, listening for Shane. When she turned back, to say something to Cole, he had already unfastened his belt buckle and was pulling on the zipper on his jeans.

"Cole, you're crazy if you think I'm going to help you with your pants."

He cocked one brow and grinned—momentarily looking pain-free. "As fun as that sounds, I thought maybe Shane could help me."

"Good idea," she said mockingly.

Beth walked through the bedroom and met Shane in the hall. He glanced over her filthy clothes, but before he could ask, she explained, "Cole had a little accident and needs your help."

Shane dropped his backpack there in the hall and followed her into the guestroom. Beth watched as Shane sized-up the situation. Cole stood in the bathroom half dressed, filthy, with a painful expression etched on his face. Shane then looked at her—mud-splattered and dirty. Beth could almost hear the wheels turning in Shane's head, the assumptions he was making.

"Cole fell outside causing his back to spasm. I had to help him upstairs," she quickly explained, leaving out details that weren't necessary. "He needs to take a shower and get some clean clothes on. I did as much as I could but . . ."

Beth didn't finish, figuring the situation spoke for itself. "Anyway, I need to get cleaned up, too. Do you think you can handle Cole if I go take a shower?"

"Yeah," Shane said, with as much sarcasm as one word could hold. "I think I can handle him."

Chapter Fifty-Five

Shane turned to Cole once his mom had left the room. "So, are you going to tell me what *really* happened?" he asked as he helped Cole with his pants."
"I tripped and fell over the hose," Cole replied nonchalantly.
"That doesn't explain why my mom is as dirty as you are."
Cole leaned on Shane as he stepped over the edge of the tub. "Let's just say she got tangled up with me."
Shane looked at Cole, seeing amusement in his expression. "Let me guess . . . she broke your fall?"
"Something like that." Cole smiled as he slowly pulled the shower curtain closed. "Do me a favor and turn on the water."
Reaching through the shower curtain, Shane twisted the cold-water handle full force.
"Dammit, Shane! Turn it off! Now!"
Shane quickly reached in and turned the hot-water handle, laughing quietly to himself. "I thought you could use a little something to cool off."
"Thanks, a lot! But shock therapy I can do without!"
Feeling agitated, Shane sat on the toilet seat and waited for Cole to finish. He knew what his dad was doing. He'd watched him for weeks and had seen the way he looked at his mom, watching her out of the corner of his eye, moving near her in the kitchen when she was making dinner or breakfast.
Shane felt his emotions divided between what he had wanted as a child and the friend he'd found in Mitch. As a kid, Shane always dreamed of the day his father would come home to him and his mom,

apologize, and the three of them would live happily ever after.

But Shane wasn't a little boy anymore.

He now knew the rest of the story.

Cole didn't just leave for the rodeo. He hurt his mom both physically and emotionally before taking off. She was a single mom at the age of sixteen, never really having a life of her own.

Then Mitch showed up out of nowhere. Though Mitch and his mom had locked horns that first week, their feelings for each other had grown into something special. Shane smiled, remembering how happy his mom looked when she finally admitted she was in love with Mitch.

But, she wasn't the only one who had grown attached to him. Shane felt the connection as well. Sure, Mitch had been a royal pain-in-the-butt when he first arrived, trying to tell him what to do and what not to do, but Shane grew to appreciate Mitch's honesty and straightforwardness. He was the first adult to talk to him without treating him like a kid. Shane considered Mitch a friend—a good friend. He was a great guy who loved his mom.

At least, Shane thought Mitch loved her.

Shane wasn't sure what was going on between them. It seemed like every time his mom got off the phone with Mitch, she was upset. Shane didn't ask about their conversations, but she certainly didn't look happy.

Maybe Hollywood wasn't completely out of Mitch's blood? Fast cars. Fast women. Loads of money. He could've missed it more than he thought he would. Maybe he won't want to come back?

Shane thought a moment longer.

Maybe mom and Cole could make it work?

They still could have a happily ever after. All three of them.

Beth showered, trying to wash away the confusing feelings stirring inside her.

She loved Mitch. She knew she did.

Then why is it every time Cole and I lock eyes, I feel emotions I thought were buried a long time ago?

Buried because of his abuse.

Buried because of his betrayal.

How could those feelings survive years of hate?

Watching Cole with Shane, seeing the admiration in her son's eyes when his father spoke with him, the forgiveness Shane so willingly extended to Cole—even though he was the one hurt most by his father's desertion—all added to the perplexity Beth was dealing with.

That, along with the lack of communication she had with Mitch.

Beth let the hot water beat against her neck and shoulders as she tried to sort through her jumbled feelings. Every time Mitch called he was either tired or in a hurry. Beth hated when the first words out of his mouth were, 'I don't have a lot of time to talk but . . .' Or, he tried to carry on a conversation with her, but was clearly distracted. Beth couldn't help but wonder it Kara was the reason for his distraction.

Of course, Mitch wasn't the only one to blame for their strained conversations. The self-loathing Beth felt, knowing she was keeping Cole's arrival from Mitch, wasn't very conducive to enjoyable chit-chat. She had to watch everything she said, and one time she had to hurry to her room when Cole and Shane walked into the house in the throes of laughter. Mitch heard the commotion and asked about it, giving Beth the perfect opportunity to come clean. But instead, Beth out-and-out lied. She told him she accidentally hit the volume button on the TV remote, then quickly changed the subject.

What will Mitch think when he finds out Cole's been here for several weeks and I never bothered to tell him? Will he be mad? Disappointed? Jealous?

Beth was afraid to find out.

Stepping from the shower, Beth felt clean but not comforted.

She yanked on a pair of jeans and fumbled for something heavier than a t-shirt. She was chilled from her go-around with Cole and the garden hose and needed something to ward off the cold. Or was it her confused feelings, spinning inside her that caused goose bumps to raise on her arms?

Beth grabbed a light-weight, brown turtleneck from her closet and pulled it over her head. She dragged a brush through her hair before walking out into the hall almost running into Shane.

"How's Cole?"

"Grouchy," Shane answered as he grabbed his backpack from where he'd dropped it in the hall.

"Where are you going?" Beth asked as he swung the pack over his shoulder.

"To Kat's to study. We have a Lit test on Friday."

"Wait a minute, what about Cole?"

"He said he wasn't going to be very good company and not to hang around for his sake," Shane headed down the stairs, yelling. "I'm going to have dinner at the Carter's. I'll be home by eleven."

Beth tossed her head back and closed her eyes. *Great! Now I have to play nursemaid.* With a huff, she turned and walked to the guestroom. Cole's door was ajar, but she knocked anyway. "Cole, are you decent?"

"Yeah," he groaned.

Beth swung the door open to find Cole sprawled out, face down across the bed, wearing nothing but a pair of boxer shorts.

"I thought you said you were dressed?" she snapped.

"No, I said I was decent," Cole groaned, his words barely audible. "Come on, Beth, don't be such a Girl Scout. It's not like you haven't seen me—"

"Yeah, well, that was then and this is now."

Cole didn't argue; he just lay completely still, closing his eyes against the pillow.

"How bad is it?" she asked.

"Bad."

Beth walked around the bed and knelt down so she was eye level with him. "How long does it usually last?"

"Sometimes twenty minutes, sometimes hours."

"Is there anything you should be doing? I can get you a heating pad, ice, or . . ." Beth thought about the liniment—remembering the day she had rubbed it on Mitch's shoulders. *Nope. I'm not going there.*

"Ice."

"Then I'll get you an ice pack."

"Okay, I guess that will work."

"What do you mean, *you guess*? You just said you needed ice."

"Yeah, well, but a pack doesn't . . . never mind."

Beth huffed, doing nothing to hide her agitation. "What?"

"I'm supposed to massage ice against my muscles, not just lay it there. Twelve minutes with ice, then twenty minutes without, but that's okay. An ice pack is better than nothing." He sounded unconvincing.

"Cole, don't hem-and-haw. Just tell me what you need."

"At home, I use a frozen water bottle, but anything round would do."

"How about a tube of ground beef?"

"That would probably work."

"Okay, I'll be right back."

"Bring some Ibuprofen with you. A lot."

In the kitchen, Beth removed a loaf of ground beef and a gel ice-pack from the freezer. Opening the cupboard alongside the refrigerator, she shook six Advil into her hand, filled a glass with water, then grabbed a bendy straw from the drawer.

When Beth returned to the guestroom, Cole hadn't moved a muscle. "Here," she squatted down alongside the bed, "this is twelve hundred milligrams." Beth pushed the six small brown pills against his clenched lips, then held the glass of water by his chin. Bending the straw so Cole could reach it, she watched as he took a couple of sips before backing the straw out of his mouth.

"Thanks," he said as water drooled onto the pillow.

"Okay, now what do I do?" Beth begrudgingly asked as she stood with the roll of beef in one hand and the ice pack in the other.

Cole swiveled his left arm from under his pillow and twisted it around to the small of his back. "I need you to massage right here. Use the loaf like a rolling pin, but not too hard because I need to get used to the cold first."

JUST AN ACT

Beth sat down on the edge of the bed, trying to ignore Cole's exposure and his muscular form. She moved and fidgeted until she found a comfortable position. Sitting with her left foot tucked under her and her right leg dangling off the side of the bed, Beth carefully touched Cole's skin with the frozen beef.

He winced immediately, his muscles contracting.

"Sorry." She removed the frigid loaf from his back.

"It's okay. I just need to get used to the cold."

Beth glided the loaf across his back for a second time, and even though Cole flinched and grimaced, she didn't stop. It only took a minute or two for her to fall into a comfortable rhythm. *Okay, this isn't so bad.*

When she reached the halfway point, Cole sighed, "How about working small circles at the center of my back, like a mortar and pestle?"

Even though Beth wanted to tell Cole exactly where he could put his mortar and pestle, she bit back the acerbic catchphrase on the tip of her tongue and complied.

With her arm aching and her fingers frozen, Beth switched hands. When the awkward position proved to be uncomfortable, she got up and moved to the other side of the bed.

"Beth, if you're getting tired, you can stop."

"No, I only have three more minutes," she said, looking at the clock on the nightstand.

When she watched the last minute click off, Beth stopped and straightened up from her hunched over position. Stretching out her sore muscles, she asked, "Now what?"

"We wait for twenty minutes, then do it again."

"Okay, I'm going to put the loaf back in the freezer so it stays hard."

Cole didn't acknowledge her; he just laid there, his eyes closed and his color pale.

When Beth returned a few minutes later, Cole's steady breathing let her know he'd fallen asleep. Moving to the corner of the room, Beth curled up in the over-stuffed chair and closed her eyes.

"Beth, you don't have to sit with me."

She opened her eyes to see Cole staring at her.

"Just come back in twenty minutes."

"What can I accomplish in twenty minutes? Besides, I'm tired, too. I'll just rest here until it's time to torture you again. She closed her eyes and nestled further into the comfort of the chair."

The quiet had almost lulled Beth to sleep, when Cole said, "I never told you how sorry I was to hear about your father. He was a good man."

Hearing the genuineness in Cole's tone, Beth opened her eyes and replied, "Thank you."

"That must have been hard. I know how much you loved him . . . and how much he loved you."

Beth found it difficult to speak, her emotions too close to the surface. Cole closed his eyes, respecting her silence, which she appreciated.

When she felt she could talk without falling apart, Beth said, "I was mad at God for a long time. I thought He was punishing me for what we had done."

"And now?"

"Now," she shrugged, "I know life isn't always going to be fair. Things happen—like losing Pandora and breaking my leg. But I have to remain faithful. I have to balance what I don't understand about God's plan, with what I do know about God's character. He loves me, cares for me, and most importantly, He'll never walk away from me. That doesn't mean I still don't question His tactics at times. But without my faith, I think I would've lost hope a long time ago."

"So, do you believe in second chances?"

Beth looked at Cole, knowing what he was getting at. "I don't think God gives up on us, if that's what you mean." She knew it wasn't, but was hoping Cole would leave the subject of *them* alone.

"So, you think God can forgive me for running out on you and Shane?"

"Yes," she said with assurance.

"And what about you, Beth . . . can you forgive me?"

JUST AN ACT

Beth's heart twisted. She didn't want to forgive Cole. She wanted him to feel the same pain she had felt, but each day he spent with Shane—every time she heard them laughing or talking together—a little more of her hate crumbled away.

"I'm sorry, Beth, that wasn't fair of me. It's just that . . . these last few weeks have been so good. I just thought . . . I don't know, I guess I was hoping you would . . ."

"Cole, don't." Beth looked at him, but his eyes were so deep, so mesmerizing, she had to turn away. Standing, she walked over to the window, staring out at the field that stretched before her. "We can't go back, Cole. Too much time has passed, too many things have changed."

Out of the corner of her eye, Beth saw Cole slowly push to his feet, groaning with every inch. He walked over to where she was standing, his muffled grunts of pain marking his steps. He stood right behind her, but she didn't dare turn around.

"You shouldn't be up; you'll hurt yourself even more."

"I'll take my chances." He placed his hands on her shoulders, turning her around. "Look at me, Beth."

Slowly, she raised her eyes.

Cole stood in front of her, his brawny physique just inches away, his strong hands gently stroking her arms. She was overwhelmed with confusion—the physical attraction she felt for Cole was still so incredibly strong. When he cupped her jaw and began caressing her cheek with his calloused thumb, her mind told her to pull away, but her body remembered how good it once felt to be in his arms. Desire danced in Cole's eyes, his gaze almost hypnotic.

Almost.

Beth had to close her eyes to extinguish Cole's allure, then willed herself to take a step back. "I don't know what you expected when you came here, Cole, but whatever we had was over a long time ago."

"So, are you telling me, if this Mitch guy wasn't in the picture, you'd still feel the same way?"

Beth looked at him, spurred by the hurt she had endured for so many years. "Cole, do you know how many nights I cried myself to sleep after you left? Even after you hurt me, I wanted nothing more than for you to come back to the Diamond-J, say you were sorry, promise you would stay, and love me and our baby. I convinced myself you were just young and scared, that you really didn't mean to hurt me, you just needed some time to think. I still loved you, Cole. God help me; after everything you did, I still loved you."

Cole started to say something, but Beth wasn't finished.

"When I went to see you in Wichita, after Shane was born, you treated me like I was nothing more than a buckle bunny, looking for a cowboy to ride. That's when you broke my heart. Not when you beat me, not when you left me pregnant with your child, but when you looked at me like I was nothing but a cheap, two-bit whore."

Cole swallowed hard. Beth wasn't sure if it was emotion or anger distorting his features. Either way, she didn't care. It was time he took responsibility for his actions.

"I swore then and there I would never give you a chance to hurt Shane like you hurt me. For a while, it wasn't an issue. Then my father died, creating a void in Shane's life. He no longer had a father figure to look up to. That's when the questions started. At first, they were easy. Shane asked if I knew where you lived, why you left, and if you were coming back. I kept my answers simple, praying he would let it go, but as Shane got older, he only became more inquisitive. You were an obsession to him, an obsession that started to drive a wedge between us. Shane became belligerent toward me and resented Uncle Charlie's silence, knowing he knew the truth. Then Shane started talking about what he would do if he ever found out who you were. He wanted to confront you and make you own up to your mistake."

Beth glared at Cole, needing him to understand the gravity of the situation.

"Did you hear what I said, Cole? Shane thought he was a mistake, and no matter how many times I told him he was a gift from God, Shane referred to himself as a mistake. Your mistake. I couldn't handle it any longer, so I lied to him. I told Shane you never even knew he existed. I shouldered the blame and told him it was my fault you left. I was hoping that would put an end to it, but it only made things worse. Shane became even more resolute to find out who you were."

"So, why didn't you just tell him?"

"Because I was terrified what you would do. You beat me up when I cornered you, Cole, and that was before you hit the big time. I could only imagine what you would do if a cocky teenager approached you and started throwing accusations around, jeopardizing your stellar All-American reputation. I wasn't willing to take that chance."

Cole massaged his temples, then dragged his hand down his face.

"That's it? You have nothing to say for yourself?" Beth asked, angered by his silence.

He shook his head and shrugged his shoulders. "You're right, Beth, about all of it. I was a kid; I was selfish. There's no excuse for the way I treated you. All I cared about was making it big, having lots of money, and being number one. But I've grown up since then. I've had time to reflect on my decision to walk away, realizing what a horrible, horrible mistake I made. I can't just say I'm sorry. There's no way a few words can make up for all the hurt I've caused you. But, I've changed, Beth. I have no intentions of hurting Shane or you. I know I can never make up for the time we've lost, but I would like to make the best of the time we have now."

Beth cleared her throat and crossed her arms against her chest. "I won't stand between you and Shane because he finally has what he's always wanted—a relationship with you. But as for me, I've moved on."

"But you never answered my question, Beth. If you weren't involved with someone right now, would you give us a second chance?"

"It doesn't matter because I *am* involved with someone. Someone who loves me. Someone who has seen me through some difficult situations and didn't pick up and leave just because things got tough."

"Then where is he now?"

Cole's question sliced clear through to her heart, poking at Beth's insecurities.

"It's been twenty minutes," she said abruptly. "You need to get more ice on your back."

When Beth returned, Cole immediately apologized for being so pushy.

"Just forget it, okay? What's done is done. We can't go back and rewrite history. Besides, I have other things I need to do. I can't play nursemaid to you all day. Here, you need to take care of yourself," she said, handing him an ice pack before turning and walking away.

Chapter Fifty-Six

Cole was up early the following morning, feeling a little stiff, but at least he wasn't flat on his back. Beth was making breakfast when he came downstairs. She glanced his way, but chose not to speak to him.

He inhaled deep. "I've always loved the smell of breakfast," he said, then chuckled. "Remember the time we rode out to the east pasture to watch the sunrise? We tried cooking eggs over an open fire and toasting bread in that wire contraption. We ended up with burnt crumbs and runny eggs. Breakfast wasn't great, but as I recall, we spent our time satisfying *other* appetites."

Beth blushed, even if she refused to comment. Cole just smiled as he crossed the kitchen and poured himself a cup of coffee.

He stood behind Beth, leaning against the counter, taking every opportunity to be as close to her as possible. Because, even if she wasn't willing to admit it, he was convinced she still had feelings for him. Even after Beth's lecture last night, Cole was sure—given enough time—he would be able to wear down her defenses. Especially, if the so-called boyfriend continued to be a no-show. All Cole had to do was keep reminding Beth of the good times and let the chemistry between them do the rest.

When he turned to take a seat at the bar, he caught a glimpse of Shane's ball cap peeking out from around the corner.

He was spying on them.

Cole smiled to himself. *Okay, Dempsey, you have an audience. Choose your words carefully.* He took a seat, then cleared his throat, wanting to make sure Shane heard every word.

"I know last night was confusing for you, but I'm not sorry it happened. It's obvious the feelings we have for each other are strong, and I'm glad we were able to explore those feelings. I know our current situation isn't without its issues, but I promise you, Beth, we can work it out."

Beth turned to him looking perplexed, but before she could offer a rebuttal, Cole cut her off.

"Good morning, Shane."

Shane cringed. Cole knew he was standing there.

He had just washed up in the downstairs bathroom when he heard his parents talking in the kitchen. He pressed closer to the wall and listened, shocked by what Cole was saying.

What did he mean he wasn't sorry it happened?

What happened?

When Shane left last night, Cole was face down on the bed in pain. But the way he was talking, something had happened between him and his mom. And what did Cole mean when he said he was glad they were able to *explore their feelings*?

Shane didn't know, but he couldn't keep lurking in the hallway. He walked around the corner, took a seat at the bar, and tried to act casual. "Smells good, Mom."

"Well, there's plenty." She stacked pancakes and a couple of sausage links on two plates, then slid them in front of him and Cole.

Shane waited for his mom to sit down, but she just folded a pancake around a link and ate while she cleaned the kitchen. She seemed agitated.

"So how was your evening with Kat?" Cole asked.

"Great! We studied for our Literature test and then went for a ride after dinner."

"Horseback?"

"No, quads."

"Sounds like fun. But then again, even torture is bearable when you're in the presence of someone special."

His mom spun around and glared at Cole, then tossed the kitchen towel on the counter. "I have some cleaning I need to do." She turned to him and smiled. "Have a good day at school. I'll see you when you get home." After she disappeared upstairs, Shane turned to Cole and asked, "So, what happened between you two last night?"

"Who said anything happened?"

"I overheard you talking," Shane spoke as he chewed. "I just got the feeling something might have happened between the two of you."

"And how would you feel about that?"

Shane thought for a second, then looked at Cole. "I don't want to see my mom get hurt."

"I have no intentions of hurting Beth."

"But what about her and Mitch?"

"What about them?"

Shane watched as Cole swigged his coffee.

"You don't care that she's already in a relationship?"

"Look, Shane, I'm just letting you know that as much as your mother wants to deny her feelings for me, they're still there. She showed them to me last night. I don't know how serious she is about this Mitch guy, but I'm not going to let that stop me in my pursuit of her."

Shane heard something in Cole's tone that bothered him. He couldn't quite explain it. He couldn't tell if his father was talking passionately because he still had strong feelings for his mom, or possessively, because he felt he had some sort of claim to her and he wasn't willing to let go.

Shane didn't say anything. He just finished his breakfast and left for school.

Beth busied herself around the house, catching up on chores. It was the most productive way she knew of to work off her pent-up frustration. Cole had disappeared after breakfast. Beth didn't know where he had gone, she was just glad to have him out of her hair.

After working for hours cleaning ceiling fans and baseboards, shower tiles and kitchen grout, Beth had a late lunch of cheese and crackers, before deciding to go outdoors where it was a little cooler.

She swept the front porch and cleared the cobwebs from all the eves, then went around pulling off window screens, careful to keep them in the right order. Propping them up against the back porch, she reached for the hose to spray them off.

As soon as Beth squeezed the nozzle, her mind's eye replayed the tangled hose incident with Cole. She couldn't help but laugh, then just as quickly pulled her lips tight and sulked—wanting to forget the incident ever happened. After spraying the screens, she left them to dry.

Now to tackle the windows.

Grabbing the large aluminum ladder from the toolshed, Beth leaned it against the house. Arming herself with a spray bottle and a few sheets of newspapers, she went to work on the windows. Beth was almost done with the north side of the house when she saw Cole walking her way. She glanced at her watch, shocked to see it was already four o'clock.

"Should you really be up on a ladder with your leg so weak?"

"I'm fine," she huffed as she stretched to the furthest point of the window.

"You know . . . you don't have to put yourself in danger just because you want to avoid me."

"I'm not avoiding you. This is cleaning that needs to get done before the weather turns cold." Beth climbed down from the ladder and walked around the back of the house to see if the screens were dry. Cole followed her like a devoted hound dog.

"I can put those away for you."

"I can do it."

"Come on, Beth. Let me feel useful."

"Fine," she said as she stacked them carefully. "But you have to put them away in the same order they are now. Don't mix them up. Each window is a different size, and if you get them out of order, it will take me forever to put them up next Spring. So don't get them screwed up."

"Wow, when did you get to be so bossy?" Cole teased.

"When I became a mom."

Their eyes met for a moment before Beth disappeared around the other side of the house.

Cole had just finished putting the window screens in the shed when he heard Beth scream. Bolting around the corner, Cole saw Beth on her hands and knees, the ladder laying on the ground.

"Beth! Are you all right?"

"I'm fine!" She stood, brushing the dirt from her clothes, her right eye blinking profusely.

"Beth, what's wrong?"

"I've got something in my eye," she said as her lashes continued to flutter.

"Here, let me look." Cole pulled Beth close. "Lean your head back."

She did what he said but kept pulling and rubbing her eyelid.

"Beth, I can't see with your hand in the way."

When she dropped her hands to her sides, her eye immediately squeezed shut, tears running into her ear. Cole gently pried her eyelids apart and saw the tiny fleck of paint that was causing the problem. "I see it. Now hold still." Carefully, Cole pressed the tip of his pinky to the orb of her eye.

Beth flinched. "Did you get it?"

"I'm not sure," Cole said as he looked at the minuscule chip of paint on the end of his finger. "Let me look again."

He took a step closer, his face so near to Beth's lips, he could feel her breath against his cheek. Cole lifted her eyelid, no longer having to look for the fleck, but not wanting to give up their connection. When Beth staggered slightly, he wrapped his arm around her back and pulled her closer still.

Beth opened her eyes and looked into his.

"I think I got it," he whispered.

She quickly took a step back. "I think you're right." Beth opened and closed her eyes a few times, wiping the tears from her cheek. "Thank you."

"Believe me, the pleasure was all mine."

Beth felt her skin heat up as Cole smirked and walked away.

"Holler when you're done, so I can put the rest of those screens away for you."

"I can do it myself!" Beth shouted back, angry at Cole for being such a jerk, but angrier still that she'd been such an easy mark.

After putting the rest of the screens and the ladder back in the shed, Beth watched Shane pull into the yard. She could tell by the look on his face something was wrong. *Oh boy.*

"What's wrong?" she asked as they climbed the steps together.

"Nothing."

"That wasn't very convincing," she said, pulling the screen door back, then following Shane into the house. He set his backpack on the dining room table and walked to the refrigerator.

"Did something happen at school or between you and Kat?"

"No, nothing like that."

"So, *there is* something bothering you."

He popped the soda in his hand and took a long swallow.

"Come on, Shane, what's up?"

"When was the last time you talked to Mitch?"

His question surprised Beth. "I talked to him last night for a few minutes. Why?"

"Did he say how things were going?"

"He said they were having long shooting schedules and that he didn't have a lot of time to himself. Why?"

Shane just shrugged.

"Is that what this is about? You miss Mitch?" Beth smiled, feeling a sense of relief. From his solemn expression, she had expected something more serious. "Come on, Shane, Mitch told us it would be like this."

"But doesn't it bother you?" His voiced rose in frustration. "He has to get days off once in a while. You would think he could fly home for a few days if he wanted to."

"But Mitch told us he wouldn't. He doesn't want to chance the paparazzi following him. If reporters found out about us, they'd set up camp outside our gates. Mitch explained all this. Why are you so upset?"

Shane toyed with the zipper on his backpack. "I just don't like it."

"I don't like it either, but there's nothing we can do about it. Mitch will be home soon. You'll see."

She tousled Shane's hair like she used to when he was just a boy, but somehow in the last few months he'd changed from a boy to a man.

Beth watched as he carried his backpack up the stairs and disappeared around the landing.

When Shane got to his room, he closed the door, unzipped his backpack, and pulled out the entertainment magazine. Splashed across the cover was a picture of Mitch and his beautiful co-star, with the caption "On Again."

Shane balled up the magazine and tossed it across the room. He gritted his teeth while running his fingers through his hair. Pacing, it took all the self-control he could muster not to put his fist through the wall.

How could you, Mitch? How could you? Mom trusted you. I trusted you. But it was all just a lie.

Shane continued to pace, his chest pounding so hard he thought it would explode.

Maybe Cole is right.

Chapter Fifty-Seven

Another three weeks had crept by since Mitch left for Hollywood, each day proving to be more difficult than the one before.

Even though Beth continued to defend Mitch to Shane, she was struggling. Several nights she'd cried herself to sleep when their phone conversations were cut short by a late-night shooting schedule or one of Mitch's PR commitments. She hated when the first words out of his mouth when he called was, 'I can't talk too long because I have to . . .'

There was always something, something more important than talking to her. Beth told Mitch—on more than one occasion—that she felt like an interruption in his life rather than a priority. But every night, Mitch assured Beth how much he loved her and that the next few months were only a drop in the bucket compared to the time they would have once filming was done. And each night, she hung up the phone wanting to believe him.

But last night, Beth was inconsolable. When Mitch told her he wouldn't be home for Thanksgiving, she'd fallen apart. The studio arranged for him and Kara to ride in the Macy's Thanksgiving Day Parade, to keep the buzz surrounding the movie alive. Mitch apologized to Beth a hundred times and explained how he'd gone straight to the president of the studio to get out of the commitment. Unfortunately—because of a personal appearance clause in his contract—he was stuck.

Beth was heartbroken. Not because Mitch wouldn't be home for Thanksgiving, but because she felt their connection slowly coming undone.

And then there was Cole.

Not only was he playing the part of super dad—spending as much time with Shane as possible—he was also acting the part of the hopeless romantic, doing his best to win Beth back.

Cole had taken to making dinner twice a week, insisting Beth worked too hard and deserved a break. Along with Shane as his sous chef, Cole had come up with some pretty comical concoctions. But it wasn't the meals that mattered; it was the relationship Beth saw growing between Shane and his father.

Then, flowers and small gifts magically appeared every few days. Beautiful bouquets, boxes of chocolates, even a bottle of perfume—the fragrance Beth had worn when she and Cole were together. Beth told him he was only wasting his money, but in suave, Cole-like fashion, he assured Beth she was well worth it.

He was even doing his best to get on Uncle Charlie's good side—though Charlie would have none of it. In fact, her uncle had pulled Beth aside and given her the what-fors when he saw the personal attention Cole was showing her. Uncle Charlie warned Beth she was playing a dangerous game, allowing Cole to stay while keeping Mitch in the dark. His words echoed in her conscience from time to time.

"Remember, Beth, he's a violent man with a very short fuse, especially when he doesn't get his way. Letting him stay is sending the wrong message. If he thinks you're toying with him, the real Cole is going to come out, then things will get ugly fast."

Beth was angered every time she replayed Uncle Charlie's heated reprimand. Not only had he treated her like a child—accusing her of lacking common sense—he had basically called her a tease.

But was she? Was she letting Cole believe what he wanted because she was angry with Mitch?

Daily, Cole told Beth how beautiful she was, what an amazing businesswoman she'd turned out to be, and what an incredible job she'd done raising Shane. His compliments were endless and over the top. Beth just laughed, assuring Cole his flattery would get him nowhere. But down deep it was still nice to hear.

Cole's strategy didn't stop with compliments and gifts. He also orchestrated opportunities for them to be alone together. He would volunteer to help Beth with kitchen clean-up, then use the tight quarters as an excuse to brush up against her or hover over her shoulder to speak quietly into her ear.

Also, under the guise of gentlemanly behavior, Cole would hold the door open for her when entering the house, then follow behind her with a light touch to the small of her back.

Though Beth had told Cole a hundred times his charms and charisma no longer worked on her, he would just smile and say, "I told you I've changed." He insisted more than once she was seeing the new and improved Cole Dempsey.

He was being nice. Kind. And at times, he reminded Beth of the cowboy she'd fallen in love with. She wanted to believe Cole had really changed. Really cared. Even so, every once in a while, Beth would recall what Cole had said the day he arrived. *Remember, Beth, I will play dirty if I have to*. But he hadn't. Not really. Maybe he'd manipulated a few conversations, and gotten hot-tempered a couple of times, but for the most part, Cole was doing everything he could to earn Shane's approval and his respect.

Beth began to wonder . . . if given enough time . . .

Coming down the stairs after dinner, Beth heard Cole and Shane talking. She couldn't quite make out what Shane said, but Cole's words came through loud and clear.

"Don't be sore with your mom, Shane. She has every reason to keep me at arm's length. Beth has years of hurt built up, and I don't blame her. I only hope she'll eventually see how much I still care about her—about us. We deserve to be a family. Sooner or later, she'll see that I'm right."

Cole's words bounced around in Beth's head like a ricocheting bullet. *She'll see that I'm right.* It was as if she'd been hit with a bucket of ice water. His tone. His words. It was the reality check Beth needed. Cole hadn't changed in the least. He was still a master manipulator. But hearing him use his powers of persuasion on Shane was like a knife to the heart. She hated herself for even thinking of giving Cole the benefit of the doubt.

Beth waited until she heard the screen door shut before continuing down the stairs. She watched Cole rinse out the ice cream bowls he and Shane had used, then put them in the dishwasher.

"Where'd Shane go?"

Cole turned around as he dried his hands. "He went to see Kat. I told him I didn't want to cramp his love life and let him know he didn't have to spend all his free time with me."

"How self-sacrificing of you."

"What's that supposed to mean?"

"Nothing." Beth snatched an apple from the countertop bowl and went to the living room. Grabbing the television remote from the coffee table, she clicked it on before sinking into the couch cushions.

"Beth, what's wrong?" Cole asked as he walked into the room.

"You. You're what's wrong. I overheard you talking to Shane. Every word, every sentence out of your mouth is manipulation. You haven't missed a beat, you know that. You still sound as convincing as ever."

"Did you ever stop to think that maybe the reason I sound so convincing is because it's the truth?" Cole sat on the edge of the chair, his elbows resting on his knees. "I know you've had a hard time forgiving me for what I did, but if you would just give me another chance, I know I can make things right."

"That's not going to happen, Cole." She continued to click the television remote, refusing to look at him.

"But Beth, we had something good together. I know I blew it, and I'll admit I . . ."

Beth stopped listening to Cole, her attention riveted to the television. There, on the screen in front of her, was Mitch and Kara Kensington side-by-side on a red carpet, a microphone held in front of them by an entertainment reporter. Mitch was beaming, tuxedo-clad, smiling his million-dollar smile. Beth quickly turned up the volume, missing the reporter's first question, only hearing Mitch's answer.

"What can I say, Kara's amazing."

Beth couldn't believe what she was hearing. She leaned in closer to the television as if that would give her better clarity.

"So, this must feel like déjà vu for you two, hitting the red carpet as a couple again?" The reporter smiled as she tipped the microphone back toward Mitch.

"Beth!" Cole hollered, making her jump, snapping her head in his direction. "I'm pouring out my guts over here, while you're glued to the television set."

She looked at Cole for a second, then quickly turned her attention back to the TV, but it was too late. Mitch and Kara were already walking away, the interview over, the reporter preying on the next celebrity couple to walk her way.

"Beth, what is your problem?" Cole barked.

She jerked to her feet, tossing the remote on the table. "Nothing," she said, walking out of the room.

"Where are you going?"

"It's chilly outside. I need to put a blanket on Althea."

"Wait, I'll go with—"

"No! I don't need you following me everywhere I go!"

"I just thought I could help with—"

"I told you, I don't need your help! I don't need *anyone's* help!"

Beth rushed out the front door, crossing the yard before Cole could see her crying. She hurried through the barn to the door on the other side. Pushing it open she gasped, releasing the cry inside her. Flinging her apple as far as she could, she clutched on to the fencing rail and sobbed.

This isn't happening. This can't be happening. I trusted you, Mitch. I trusted you.

Cole was headed for the front door when the phone rang. "Hello?" he answered.

After a moment's hesitation, a male voice asked, "Charlie? Is that you?"

"Charlie's not here. Did you want to leave a message?"

"No! I don't want to leave a message! I want to know who this is!?"

Cole stood up straighter when he realized who he was talking to. *The boyfriend. Perfect.*

He cleared his throat as he smiled to himself. "This is Cole Dempsey. Were you looking for Shane?"

Cole relished the silence, imagining the shock on the guy's face. *That's right, buddy. I'm here, and you're not.*

"Let me talk to Beth!"

"I'm sorry, she's not available at the moment. But I would be glad to give her a message."

"I don't want to leave a message! I want to talk to Beth. Now!"

"Listen, buddy, she's not too thrilled with you right now. If I were you, I'd—"

"What are you doing there? So help me, if you've hurt Beth or Shane—as God is my witness—I will tear you limb from limb."

"Hey! If anyone has hurt Beth, it's you! Stringing her along, the way you have. Clearly, whatever you two had together is over. But don't worry, I've given Beth a strong shoulder to cry on. She doesn't need you anymore. The three of us are doing just fine."

"Let me talk to Beth! You filthy son-of . . ."

Cole listened as he was called every name in the book.

"Wow, I can see why Beth was hesitant about you. She would never allow such language to be used around her son. Or should I say, *our* son."

"So help me— Let me talk to her!"

"Why would I do that? You've hurt her enough. Besides, Beth's already in bed for the evening. My bed."

"Why you—"

"And don't bother calling back." Cole hung up the phone, grinning with a keen sense of satisfaction.

You lose.

As soon as he stepped away from the counter, the phone rang again. *Now, we can't have that all night, can we?* He chuckled to himself as he detached the cord from the back of the phone. *There.*

That should do it.

Cole went to the barn looking for Beth, still wondering what had set her off. When he saw the backdoor slightly ajar, he poked his head out to find Beth sitting against the fence line. She was huddled together with her legs pulled up to her chest, her head resting on her knees.

He squatted down close to her and gently stroked her arm. "Beth, what's wrong?"

"I'm a fool—that's what's wrong," she stuttered between sobs.

"You're not a fool, Beth. But I don't understand what happened. I mean, one minute you're sitting in front of the TV doing your best to ignore me, and the next, you're flying out of the house like a fox with his tail on fire. Clearly, I said something to upset you, but I don't know what?"

What do I say? The man I love is superstar Simon Grey and look, there he is in the arms of another woman.

"You didn't say anything wrong, okay? It's me. I'm my own worst enemy." Beth palmed her eyes and wiped her tears. "I'm an idiot—that's what's wrong—and I have lousy taste in men. Uncle Charlie was right. I'm too gullible for my own good."

"Beth, why are you being so hard on yourself?" Cole scooted closer, wrapping his arm around her. "The problems we had were my fault, not yours. You're not gullible. You're caring and loving. It's what makes you so special."

Beth turned, looking into Cole's eyes, wanting to believe she was special, that she wasn't a fool. She watched as his stare moved from her eyes to her lips. His calloused thumb came up to brush the tears from her cheek, then gently stroked her mouth.

"I'll spend the rest of my life proving to you how special you are, if you'll only let me," Cole whispered as he slowly leaned forward.

Beth knew he was going to kiss her, but did nothing to stop him. She was angry at Mitch and wanted to hurt him just like he had hurt her.

Cole's lips were warm and soft. Beth kissed him back, wanting to feel for him what she had when she was younger.

When she pulled back, he smiled.

"Now, come on, it's too cold out here to be sitting on the ground." He stood and extended his hand to help her up. Tugging Beth to her feet, Cole held her against his chest, and looked at her with eyes full of passion. "I love you, Beth. You know that, right?"

Beth froze. Those were Mitch's exact words before he boarded the plane for Hollywood. *What am I doing? Mitch might not be in love with me anymore, but I'm still in love with him.*

She took a step back, shaking her head. "I can't do this, Cole."

Beth turned to walk away but he caught her by the arm. "Wait." Cole pulled her back to stand in front of him. "We belong together, Beth, can't you see that? The three of us—you, me, and Shane. We deserve a chance."

"Our chance was sixteen years ago, but you chose to walk away. That was then, and this is now. You have another life, another family. We can't go back, Cole. Too much has changed."

"No." He held her arms firmer. "I don't believe that. You let me stay all this time. If you didn't have feelings for me, you would've made me leave long ago."

"I let you stay for Shane's sake, not for mine."

"But Beth, can't you see . . . our son brought us back together. We're meant to be together. It's what he wants. It's what I want."

"But it's not what I want!" she shouted.

"Don't say that!" He shook her hard, causing Beth's head to snap back.

"Cole, you're hurting me." When she looked into his eyes, Beth was terrified by what she saw. Passion had been replaced with rage—a rage she knew all too well. "Cole, please let me go," Beth whispered, trying to diffuse the situation.

"No!" He shook her again. "I'll never let you go. Don't you get it? You and Shane belong to me."

Cole pressed his lips hard against Beth's, muffling her protest. When she twisted her mouth free, she gasped, "But I don't love you!

I love Mitch!"

He pulled back like he'd been jolted by an electric charge. Beth was sure Cole was going to hit her, but instead he just laughed.

"He ran out on you, Beth. Why can't you see that? Oh sure, he calls you, but he's only stringing you along. Your so-called boyfriend has moved on." Cole shook his head, as if scolding a child. "Silly, naive little Beth, if he loved you, he would've been here instead of me."

She struggled to break free of his hold, but Cole clamped his hands even tighter around her arms.

"Don't fight it, Beth. You know you love me. Your kiss told me so."

"No. You're wrong. I was hurt and angry."

"I don't think so." Cole shoved her against the side of the barn, pinning her arms to her sides. "I'm done playing games, Beth. I belong here, and you belong to me."

Beth began to cry. "Don't do something you can't undo, Cole. Think about Shane. Do you really want to jeopardize your relationship?"

"I'm only claiming what's mine."

He crushed his lips against hers while Beth tried to wrestle free. Letting go of her right arm, Cole slipped his hand under her t-shirt, making his intentions clear.

Oh God, he's snapped! Help me. Please God, help me.

With her right hand free, Beth shoved at Cole's chest, trying to push him away, but she was no match for his frenzied strength. Realizing she had to use whatever tactics necessary, Beth reached for his face and dug her fingernails into the flesh of his cheek. Cole hollered and instinctively brought his hands up to his face.

The second he let her go, Beth sprinted into the barn. Slamming the heavy door closed, she backed away, picking up momentum as she did. When Beth turned to run, she stumbled over some bailing wire, sending her spread-eagle to the straw-littered floor. Hearing the large door swing open behind her, she hurried to get to her feet. With her sights set on the yard, Beth ran.

JUST AN ACT

She was only a few strides from the open door when Beth felt the weight of Cole's body come down on top of her. Rolling her on to her back, Cole straddled her legs. Screaming, Beth swung her arms violently, landing several punches against his already bloodied face.

Grabbing her arms, Cole pinned them over her head, while his other hand pulled a knife from his boot. With the snap of the blade, he pressed it to her chest. Beth felt a pinch, then a trail of warmth as blood trickled to her neck.

"Why did you have to fight me, Beth? Why did you have to make this so difficult?"

"Think about what you're doing," Beth cried hysterically. "All Shane wanted was a father he could be proud of. And now look at what you've done. You've proven to him what a horrible, violent man you are. You've ruined everything, Cole! For Shane. For you. You've ruined it all."

"I haven't ruined anything!" he shouted. "Do you really think I care about some bratty teenager? Come on, Beth, all I care about is your land. The Diamond-J is a gold mine. Since my divorce is going to cost me a small fortune, I'm going to need something to fall back on.

"I planned on marrying into it, but this will work, too. Shane will inherit the Diamond-J after you're gone. Of course, we both know he couldn't care less about the ranch, and the memory of his mother's tragic accident will make it even easier for him to let it go. As his father, I'll help him handle his grief and manage his financial dealings—naturally, with only his best interest in mind." Cole smiled. "I'll have the Diamond-J deeded to me in no time."

Beth couldn't believe what she was hearing. From the minute Cole had shown up, everything he had said and done was a lie. The only reason he was there was because of the ranch.

Panic surged through Beth as her mind scrambled for something to say. Cole was clearly beyond reason but she had to try.

"Cole, please don't do this! You can walk away right now! I promise, I'll never tell anyone about tonight. Ever!"

"Why should I walk away when I'm so close to getting what I

want?"

"Because you'll never get away with it. Do you really think you can kill me, then concoct a story that's plausible enough that you won't look guilty? Even if Shane believes you, Uncle Charlie and Mitch will know you had something to do with it. Especially when the ranch ends up in your name."

Beth began to squirm, but Cole pressed the knife to her chest, forcing her to lay still.

"But you forget how persuasive I can be, Beth. These last few weeks are a perfect example. Shane believes I'm madly in love with you, and that I'll wait patiently for you to love me in return. And you, even with all your doubts about me, you believed I was here to forge a relationship with Shane."

"You're right, we did. Shane and I believed you. But Charlie and Mitch won't."

Cole shrugged. "It doesn't matter what they believe. Without proof of my involvement, the authorities will categorize your death as a tragic accident. I'll explain to them how you went to the barn to blanket your horse but never returned to the house. When I went to see what was keeping you, I found you on the floor of Althea's stall, crumpled in the corner, your neck broken. It will be horrible for Shane, but in time, and with me by his side, he'll eventually get over you."

Beth shuddered, then shrieked when she felt the blade of the knife cut her again.

"We could've avoided this, Beth. All you had to do was give me a second chance. I'm sorry it has to end this way."

In a split second, Cole leaned forward and pressed his forearm across Beth's neck, pinching off her air supply. With her hands free, Beth did everything she could to fight him off, but was no match for Cole's strength. Her vision blurred and her chest burned. As she choked on what she was sure would be her last breath, a shot exploded in the barn.

She looked at Cole hovering over her, his face contorted in shock. Then Beth noticed a small trickle of blood oozing from his lips right before he collapsed on top of her. Gasping for the air she was deprived of, Beth struggled to get out from under the weight of Cole's body. Panting, she sat back on her heels, watching as a circle of red swelled across the back of Cole's shirt.

Motion out of the corner of her eye startled her.

That's when she turned and saw Shane standing in the doorway.

A gun in his hand.

Chapter Fifty-Eight

Beth scrambled to her feet and rushed toward Shane. He dropped the gun on the ground, tears streaming down his face. Wrapping her arms around him, she turned Shane, so he couldn't see Cole's body.

"How did you know?" Beth cried.

"Mitch called the Carter's."

Confused, she took a step back and looked at Shane. "But how did Mitch know?"

"He called the house. Cole answered. Mitch said he knew something was wrong, so he called the Carter's looking for me." Shane looked at her and sobbed, "I told Mitch to leave us alone, that he had hurt you enough."

"Why would you say that, Shane?"

"Because his face is all over those celebrity magazines and the Internet, him and that Kira woman. The headlines say they're getting back together."

"Why didn't you tell me?"

"Because I didn't want to believe it. Then when Mitch called and told me the things Cole had said to him, I thought he was lying—that he was jealous because Cole was here and he wasn't. I told Mitch to leave us alone. Then I hung up on him."

"Then what made you come home?"

Shane shrugged. "I don't know. I guess I just needed to see for myself that everything was okay. But when I heard you scream, I freaked out and got the gun from Mitch's truck. I didn't plan on using it; I just wanted to scare him so he would leave you alone. But when I saw what he was doing and heard what he said . . . I . . . I pulled the

JUST AN ACT

trigger."

Shane turned, looking over his shoulder, but Beth quickly turned his face back toward her.

"What was I thinking?" Shane sobbed. "I could have hit you. I could have shot you instead of him."

"But you didn't," she looked into her son's eyes—seeing torment and anguish. "Listen to me, Shane." She waited for him to focus on her. "You saved my life."

"But I killed my dad."

Shane groaned and started toward Cole's body, but Beth stopped him and held him tight.

"Don't, Shane. There's nothing you can do."

Just then, the Carter's truck roared into the yard. Hank, Tim, and Tom piled out of the front seat, each one with a shotgun in hand. From the opposite direction, headlights beamed across the field. Without even stopping to open the gate, Uncle Charlie burst into the yard, splintering the wood in all directions. He screeched to a halt, leapt out and ran to where Beth held Shane. Pulling them into a bear hug, he held them tight. "Thank God you two are all right."

When Uncle Charlie finally released them, Beth took a step back.

"Beth, you're bleeding?"

She looked down at the blood on her shirt, not knowing if it was hers or Cole's. "I'm okay." Beth turned when she saw Hank walk from the barn, his shotgun at his side. He made eye contact with Charlie and slowly shook his head. When he pulled a heavy tarp from the back of his truck, Beth knew.

Cole was dead.

Uncle Charlie glanced at the gun lying near the barn door, then back to her and Shane. "What happened?"

Putting a protective arm around Shane, she cleared her throat. "We need to call the police." Beth took a few steps toward the house. "But first I need to . . ." she took a few steps toward the barn, then turned abruptly toward the house, "but I need to . . ."

Charlie stopped her with an outstretched arm. "Beth, it's okay. I'll call the police. You and Shane need to go inside."

"But I—"

"No, Beth, you need to be with Shane right now. We'll take care of things out here."

Beth looked at Shane. He stood remarkably still, his eyes fixed on the barn. "Come on, let's go inside." She reached for his arm to move him toward the house but his feet were unmovable. "Shane, come on," Beth urged him again, but he continued to stare at the barn.

He was in shock.

Standing in front of him, Beth reached up to cradle his face. "Look at me, Shane." She waited for him to make eye contact. When he did, the emptiness in his stare chilled her. Stroking his face, Beth whispered, "Shane, you did what you had to do."

"I killed him. I killed my own father."

"No, Shane. You protected me from a dangerous, violent man. A man that never would've been the father you deserve. You didn't kill him; you saved my life. Cole's responsible for his own death."

She didn't know how much Shane heard, but this time, when she tugged on his arm, he turned and followed her into the house.

They sat on the couch for some time. Beth continued to console Shane, reassuring him he did what he had to do, but her words seemed inconsequential. She sounded strong and confident as she spoke, but inside she was terrified. Shane was only sixteen. What was going to happen to him? Would the police believe he was defending her and that he had no choice? What if they found out about his shooting incident with Mitch? Would they just assume he was a delinquent kid and not listen to what they had to say?

When Uncle Charlie came to check on them, Beth quickly told him what happened. Not everything, but what was most important. He held her close, assuring her everything was going to be okay. But in her heart of hearts, Beth knew things were far from okay.

Sitting with Shane, she held his hand tight, contemplating how close she'd come to being killed. *God, I know you protected me, but please, protect Shane. He needs you right now.*

The next time Beth chanced a glance at the clock, she was shocked to see nearly two hours had gone by. Shane sat in a numb silence beside her, unable to move. *What was Uncle Charlie doing? And what about Mitch? Did he know what was happening? And if so, why hadn't he called?*

No longer able to sit, Beth got up from the couch and walked toward the kitchen. That's when she noticed the strobe of blue and red lights flickering through the front window. The police. They were there. *But why hadn't anyone come to talk to them?*

Even as Beth was thinking it, Uncle Charlie walked through the front door accompanied by a uniformed officer and a man wearing a pair of jeans and a camel-colored blazer. The officer removed his hat while the man in the blazer glanced around the house.

Beth found his perusal intrusive.

Uncle Charlie crossed the room, looking panicked. "Beth, honey, your shirt? Your head?"

She looked down, surprised to see the red stain had grown. "Umm, I'm sure it's just a scratch. I'll be—" she coughed, trying to clear the rasp from her throat, but it only hurt more. It felt like she'd swallowed a thousand needles.

"But you have a knot on—"

"Uncle Charlie!" she snapped, biting back the pain. "I'm fine. A couple of scratches are the least of my worries right now."

"But Mrs. Justin, if you're injured, we—"

"It's *Miss* Justin." She looked at the man in the blazer. "And I'm fine."

He nodded in consolation, then took a second before introducing himself. "Miss Justin, I'm Detective Hanes and this is Officer Reynolds. We'd like to ask you and your son a few questions regarding what happened tonight."

Beth nodded, then moved toward the living room where Shane was sitting on the couch. "Shane, this is Det. Hanes and Officer Reynolds. They need to ask us some questions."

Shane looked at her scared and afraid. "Mom, your voice?"

"It's okay. I'm just a little hoarse."

Beth found it hard to keep her composure. *Please God, don't let anything happen to Shane. This isn't his fault.* "Shane, we need to answer some questions for the police, but don't worry. I'll be right here. All you need to do is tell them what—"

"Actually, Miss Justin," Det. Hanes interrupted. "It would be best if we talk to you two separately. Your Uncle can stay with Shane if you'd like, unless of course, you feel the need to have an attorney present?"

Beth's heart stopped. "A lawyer? But we didn't do anything wrong. I mean . . . Cole . . . he . . . he said he was going to kill me and make it look like an accident. If Shane hadn't . . ."

She turned to Uncle Charlie for help. "It wasn't our fault."

"Miss Justin, please," the detective softened his tone. "I don't want to upset you. I know you and your son have already been through a very traumatic ordeal tonight, but I still need to know exactly what happened."

Beth didn't know what to do. "Uncle Charlie?"

"It's okay, Beth," he said as he pulled her into a hug. "You two have nothing to hide. You go on; I'll stay with Shane. Then it will all be over."

"Miss Justin, where can we talk?" Officer Reynolds asked, startling her from behind.

"Aah . . . my office."

"Are you going to be all right, Shane?" Beth asked. "Uncle Charlie will be right here, okay?"

Shane nodded, but she could see fear in his eyes. He no longer looked like the strong, determined young man he'd become of late. Instead, she saw a scared little boy trying to look brave.

Officer Reynolds followed Beth into her office, closing the door behind them. She took a seat in front of her computer while he pulled out the chair that was tucked in the corner. Looking at her shirt, he asked, "Are you sure you're okay, Miss Justin?"

"I'm fine," she said, her hands shaking in her lap. "I mean, as good as I can be, considering."

"Is it painful for you to speak?"

"It hurts a little, but I'll be fine."

"Okay, then I need you to tell me what happened as you remember it."

Beth took a few deep breaths, not knowing where to begin. She tried to recall the chain of events as they happened and where it had all gone so terribly wrong. "I was upset when I went outside . . ."

Shane felt the cushions shift as Uncle Charlie took a seat next to him. "It's going to be okay, Shane. Just tell Det. Hanes what happened."

Shane looked at the detective, standing with a small notebook in hand.

"Why don't you start by telling me where you got the gun?" Det. Hanes asked.

"From Mitch's truck."

"Who's Mitch?"

"My mom's boyfriend."

"Is it Mitch's gun?"

"No, it's . . ." Shane looked at the detective and swallowed hard. "It belongs to a friend of mine."

"Then what was it doing in Mitch's truck?"

Closing his eyes and rubbing his forehead, Shane realized how bad it was going to sound, but he knew he had to tell the truth. "Mitch took it away from me . . . after I shot at his truck."

The detective glanced up from his notepad, exchanged looks with Uncle Charlie, then back to Shane. "Maybe you better start by telling me how you obtained possession of the firearm."

Chapter Fifty-Nine

Beth paced, feeling anxious. Officer Reynolds had stepped out of her office a while ago, but asked her to stay put. *What's taking so long? Please, God, be with Shane. Don't let Det. Hanes try to trip Shane up like Officer Reynolds did me.* Beth knew it was probably procedure to ask the same questions repeatedly, to see if the person's answers would change. But Shane was in shock. He could easily get confused, misunderstand a question, or get angry if he thought they didn't believe him. *Be with him, Lord. Protect him.*

Beth sunk into her office chair and doubled over, feeling sick to her stomach. Cole's words replayed in her mind—words filled with anger and hate. *He didn't care about Shane . . . or me. He just wanted the Diamond-J. He was willing to kill me, and destroy Shane's life, all for a piece of land.*

When Beth could stand it no longer, she left her office and walked into the living room, just as Det. Hanes and Uncle Charlie were getting to their feet. Shane was still sitting on the couch, his eyes red, his cheeks wet. Beth looked at Det. Hanes and instantly knew something was wrong.

"What is it?" she asked.

"Miss Justin, I need a little more time to question Shane. I think it would be best if I do it down at the station."

"What? Why?" Beth rushed to Shane's side and sat with him, wrapping her arm around his shoulder. "I don't understand."

"Miss Justin, Shane is involved in a homicide—a homicide he committed with a handgun he previously used in a criminal act."

Beth started to cry. "I know how this looks, but Shane isn't a bad kid. He was protecting me. Why can't you see that?"

"Miss Justin, I understand, but I still have a homicide to investigate, and now I have to decide if a weapons charge needs to be filed as well." His tone, though somewhat compassionate, was firm.

"But Shane's a minor."

"Yes, but because of the seriousness of the crime—if this case was to go to trial—he could be charged as an adult."

Beth felt like she was going to pass out, or throw-up—or both.

"Look, Miss Justin, your best option is to work with me on this. If I have your full cooperation, I can keep things moving through the system pretty quick—starting with Shane coming to the station to make an official statement. I will need yours as well, but first, I need you to go to the hospital and have your wounds examined and photographed. Mr. Justin, can you drive her?"

"Yes, of course."

"No. That's not necessary. I'm fine," she said stubbornly as she wiped tears from her cheek. "I want to be with Shane."

"Miss Justin," Det. Hanes said pointedly, "having your wounds photographed is in Shane's best interest. It's proof there was a struggle and Mr. Dempsey meant you physical harm. It's evidence that corroborates Shane's use of deadly force."

"It's okay, Mom." Shane stood. "Everything will be okay. I know I did the right thing."

Beth stood, wrapping her arms around him, knowing she had to be strong for her son's sake, not fall apart in front of him. "It's going to be okay, Shane," she rasped. "The police are just doing their job. You'll come home with me tomorrow. I know you will."

"I know, Mom," he answered as he took a step back. "I love you, and don't worry. I'll be fine."

Beth watched as Officer Reynolds led Shane outside. Det. Hanes was saying something to her but she wasn't listening.

"Miss Justin, did you hear me?"

She shook her head. "No. I'm sorry, I didn't."

"Someone from the police department will meet you at the hospital. She'll collect evidence and be with you during your exam.

You'll want to bring a change of clothes with you, and please, don't wash your hands or face, or even brush your hair until after the exam."

"Fine," Beth whispered, her voice all but gone.

After grabbing a pair of jeans and a t-shirt from her bedroom, she and Uncle Charlie walked to his pick-up in the yard.

Looking around, she saw that Shane was already gone. *Be with him, Lord. Keep him strong.*

Det. Hanes was standing near the barn with a man wearing a black jacket with POLICE emblazoned across the back. He was deep in conversation as the other officer talked expressively with his hands. Just as Beth turned to climb into the truck, a gurney carrying Cole's body was rolled from the barn. She shuddered and brought her hand to her chest, and for the first time, Beth felt pain.

Pulling at her t-shirt, Beth saw two gashes on her chest. She remembered Cole pricking her with the knife, but the other cut must've happened when he collapsed on top of her, pinning the knife between them. She hadn't felt it.

Climbing into the truck, she laid her head back and wept.

"Hang in there, Beth. Remember, God is on our side."

After arriving at the hospital, Beth insisted Uncle Charlie drop her off. Though he argued, Beth's mind was made up. Shane was the priority. She needed Uncle Charlie to be with him.

"I'll meet you at the police station when I'm done," Beth said as she slowly climbed out of the truck.

"How? You won't have a vehicle."

"I'll call a cab or see if a volunteer can drive me. I can take care of myself, but I need to know Shane's not alone."

Beth didn't give Uncle Charlie a chance to object; she hopped out, slammed the truck door, and walked toward the E.R. entrance.

Once inside, Beth checked-in at the front desk, assuring the nurse her injuries looked worse than they were. She was handed a clipboard of information to fill out—which Beth tried to do—but her mind just wouldn't cooperate. She wasn't sure how long she'd been waiting when a nurse called her name. Beth stood on shaky legs and followed the nurse to an examination room.

"I was treated by Dr. Cummings just a few weeks ago. Is he working tonight?"

"I'm sorry, Miss Justin, but Dr. Cummings is on vacation. Dr. Thomas is the physician on duty."

Beth took a seat on the exam table so the nurse could perform the perfunctory tasks. Blood pressure. Temperature. Heart. Lungs. "Are you experiencing any nausea, headache, dizziness?"

"No." She lied.

When the nurse was done, she pulled a cotton gown from a side drawer and laid it on Beth's lap. "Miss Justin, you'll need to disrobe completely and put on this gown—opening in the front. A representative from the police department will be here shortly. Once she arrives, the doctor will perform the examination."

"This won't be necessary," she coughed, referring to the gown. "The only wound I have is right here," Beth said, pointing to her bloody shirt.

The nurse looked at her sympathetically. "Miss Justin, you were physically assaulted. Most likely, you have other wounds you're unaware of, like the bump on your head, and the bruising on your cheek and around your neck."

Instinctively, Beth reached for her neck, wincing at the pain.

"The doctor will need to do a thorough examination to document those wounds and any others." Smiling, the nurse opened the door. "Someone will be with you shortly."

And then she was gone, leaving Beth alone.

Setting her change of clothes on a chair in the corner, Beth slipped on the gown as instructed, glad it was large enough to crisscross over her chest. She folded her dirty clothes and held them on her lap while she sat on the edge of the paper-covered table. She waited and waited—her eyes fixed on the clock on the wall—convinced she'd been forgotten when she heard a slight tap on the door. A woman wearing a navy windbreaker, who looked to be in her late thirties, stepped inside the room. She smiled politely as she closed the door.

"Miss Justin, I'm Jenny Armstrong. I work with the police department and will be present during your exam. I'm here not only to document your assault but to help you with any questions you might have."

"I don't think any of this is necessary," Beth cleared her throat then winced, frustrated that no one was listening to her. "All I need are a few Band-Aids."

"I know you've been through a devastating event—and this will feel like just one more violation—but trust me, pictures are extremely important in cases where a physical assault needs to be substantiated."

Beth watched as Jenny pulled several items from a backpack. Digital camera, small box, paper bag, gloves. The woman set the backpack on the floor, pulled on the latex gloves, then shook out the paper bag.

"Are those the clothes you were wearing when you were assaulted?" she asked, pointing to the pile on her lap.

"Yes."

She put them in the bag, then sealed it shut. "Which is your dominant hand?"

Perplexed, Beth wasn't sure she heard right. "Excuse me?"

"Are you right-handed or left-handed?"

"Left-handed, why?"

Jenny set the small box on the exam table next to Beth, revealing several plastic vials.

"What are those for?"

"I need to test for gunshot residue."

"But I didn't shoot him."

"It's just standard procedure," Jenny explained.

Do they think I shot Cole and I'm letting Shane take the blame? That's it. They think I'm sacrificing my son to protect my own neck.

Beth's anger grew as she watched Jenny systematically daubed the fingers on her left hand with the little plastic vials. Not only was Jenny testing for residue, she was trying to catch Beth in a lie. Even though Beth knew the tests would come back negative, she couldn't help but feel threatened.

"Miss Justin, are you experiencing any difficulty breathing?"

"No. It hurts to swallow, and I can't seem to clear my throat."

"You were lucky."

Beth looked at her. "Sorry if I don't share your opinion."

"I apologize. I didn't mean to minimize the ordeal you suffered, but it could've been worst."

Beth knew that all too well.

Jenny finished what she was doing by running what looked like a simple square of gauze over Beth's hand, then put it in a small plastic box, squeezed a dropper of liquid on it, pressed the lid in place, and set it on the counter behind her. She gathered the vials together, put them in a plastic bag, and set the bag next to the box.

"You think I shot Cole," Beth stated as if it was fact.

"No, Miss Justin. Like I said, it's routine."

"But I didn't—"

Beth was interrupted by a tap at the door.

Without waiting on an answer, a man in green scrubs and a white doctor's coat walked in. "Miss Justin, I'm Dr. Thomas. I'll be performing your exam today."

Though the doctor gave her a quick smile, he seemed cold and impersonal. From the moment he pulled on his latex gloves, he was all clinician and procedure.

The first thing he did was trim her fingernails—gathering the clippings into a small bag and handing it to Jenny. Then he started his exam. Pointing out the bruising on her wrists, Jenny moved in close with her camera and clicked off several pictures. This continued with every scratch and abrasion until he examined the bruising on her neck.

His expression changed slightly, and for a split-second Beth saw a hint of concern in the doctor's eyes. Or was it compassion? Whichever it was, it didn't last long. Before Beth could take her next breath, the doctor unceremoniously pulled open her gown, exposing her chest and upper body.

Humiliated, Beth lay with her eyes closed, while Jenny clicked several more pictures, and the doctor stated the length and depth of each laceration on her chest. When Dr. Thomas pressed on her ribs,

Beth winced, but explained that the pain was from a preexisting fall. Instantly, she relived that night. Tumbling to the ground. Pandora's grunts and cries. *One nightmare after another.*

After pointing out a few bruises on her lower leg, the doctor once again tugged open Beth's hospital gown and pressed his fingers against her upper thigh.

"That's enough!" Beth snapped as she pulled the gown closed, thankful she'd left on her underwear. "I wasn't raped, and I think you have plenty of pictures to prove I was physically assaulted."

The doctor stepped back without saying a word and looked at Jenny. "Is there anything else you need?"

"Just your official report when you're done."

"Okay. Then I'll go ahead and treat these wounds."

Beth watched as Jenny picked up the little plastic box she had set aside earlier. After scrutinizing the piece of gauze inside, she put the box in the bag with the rest of the vials, then moved to Beth's side.

"What are you doing?" Beth asked.

"Staying with you until the doctor is done." Jenny smiled, then squeezed Beth's hand.

Dr. Thomas used three stitches to close up the larger of the two lacerations on her chest, then taped a square of gauze on top of it. "You need to keep this dry for a few days," he said, before moving on to her other wounds—most of which he was able to clean up and treated with ointment. "The bruising around your throat will be tender for a few days and your voice a bit distorted, but I don't anticipate any long-term effects." Before leaving, he scribbled a prescription for pain medication, then exited with a quick good-bye over his shoulder.

"His bedside manner could use some improvement," Jenny chuckled as she gathered her things. Beth didn't say anything. She just sat up on the exam table and waited until the room stopped spinning.

"Miss Justin, are you sure you're okay? Maybe you should stay overnight."

"No. I'm fine." Beth slid from the exam table, making sure her legs were underneath her before reaching for the change of clothes on the chair. She still felt wobbly but didn't want to waste any more time at the hospital. She needed to get to the police station.

She needed to be with Shane.

"Miss Justin, I'm sorry for all you and your son have been through. I'll be praying for you both."

Beth wanted to cry at the kindness in Jenny's tone but knew if she did, she would never recover. "Thank you. I appreciate that very much."

"Are you sure you don't need any help?"

"No. I'll be fine."

After Jenny left, Beth realized she was far from fine. Listening to Dr. Thomas catalog her injuries made them more real—and with that realism came pain. Her neck felt like it was in a vice, the knot on her forehead felt like someone had embedded a golf ball under her skin, and the cuts on her chest burned like she imagined a branding iron felt to a new calf.

Beth dressed slowly—having to stop between garments in order to regain her strength. Pulling on her boots was a monumental feat, forcing her to rest before she could stand without keeling over. When she finally stepped toward the door, Beth was startled by her reflection in the small mirror hanging on the back of it. The bump on her head and the swelling and discoloration of her cheek made her face look lopsided and out of proportion. She quickly opened the door, needing the image to go away before it made her throw-up.

Beth walked down the hall to the emergency entrance. When she looked at the clock above the doors—and saw that it was a few minutes past midnight—she panicked. Shane had been taken to the police station hours ago.

I have to get to him.

I have to make sure he's all right.

Pushing the round button on the wall to activate the electronic doors, she waited for them to open, and was stunned to see Mitch standing on the other side.

Rushing to her, Mitch wrapped his arms around Beth, enveloping her with his strength, whispering in her ear, "It's going to be okay,

Beth. Everything is going to be okay."

Beth collapsed against Mitch's chest, her tears turning into sobs of anguish. He slowly led her over to one of the waiting room chairs, eased her down, then squatted in front of her. When Mitch pushed back the hair from her face, his reaction confirmed how bad she looked.

"Beth, talk to me. Tell me you're okay."

She looked away, not knowing what to say. Beth wanted nothing more than for Mitch to hold her, but the picture of him on the red carpet with his co-star, reignited her anger and reminded Beth their relationship was over.

"What are you doing here?" she whispered as she wiped the tears from her cheeks and sat up straighter.

"I called Charlie the minute I landed. He told me he was at the police station with Shane, but that I should come here to be with you."

The police station. "I need to go." She stood abruptly, almost knocking Mitch over as she walked toward the exit.

"Whoa," he got to his feet and followed her through the sliding glass doors. "Beth," he shouted, but she continued to walk aimlessly through the parking lot.

"Beth . . ." he caught up with her and grabbed her arm, gently pulling her close, "where are you going?"

"I need to get to the police station. I need to be with Shane." She tried to step away, but Mitch wouldn't let her go.

"Beth, I'll take you, just calm down."

"Calm down?" She shook her arms free from his hold, angered Mitch didn't understand the gravity of the situation. "Calm down? Shane is being questioned by the police. He might be charged with murder—the murder of his father—and you want me to calm down?!"

Mitch reached for her again, but she took a step back.

"I don't understand, Beth. Why was Cole at the ranch? Better yet, why didn't you tell me?"

Her deception stabbed at Beth's conscience, but only for a second. After all, Mitch had deceived her as well. She glared. "What does it matter. You were gone. And from the looks of it, you picked up right

JUST AN ACT

where you left off."

Beth tried to storm away, but Mitch wouldn't let her. He grabbed her by the arm and pulled her close. She winced, causing him to soften his grasp. "Don't do this, Beth. You can't believe the things you read in rag magazines. They're not true. I told you that before I left."

"But I saw you! I heard you tell the reporter how great Kara was. I'm not stupid, Mitch. I saw it with my own eyes."

"So, you're saying you don't believe me. You think I cheated on you, is that it?" Mitch looked at Beth with a fierceness she hadn't seen before. "Is that why Cole was at the ranch? You thought I was screwing around so you decided to even the score with—"

Beth slapped his face, furious Mitch had the audacity to accuse her of the very thing he'd been doing.

He hung his head while rubbing his jaw, then looked at her. The hurt in his eyes matched the sting in her hand, but Beth didn't care. He deserved it.

She turned and started back toward the hospital entrance.

"Where are you going?" Mitch hollered after her.

"To call a cab."

"You don't need a cab! I said I would take you."

Beth watched Mitch get into a pick-up truck and rev the engine to life. Screeching out of the parking spot, he pulled up alongside of her, skidding to an abrupt stop.

She climbed in and slammed the door, not caring how she got to the police station, just knowing that's where she needed to be.

"Where is it?" he asked in a monotone voice.

"Head out the driveway," she winced, clearing her throat. "Then turn right."

"Beth . . . are you o—"

"I'm fine."

"But your voice, you sound—"

"I can't talk about this right now, Mitch. Just get me to the police station."

Beth gave Mitch directions as he drove but said nothing else. When they pulled into the station, she was shocked to see a crowd of people hovering near the entrance. "What's going on?"

"It's the media. They must have found out about Cole."

Beth sat unmoving, gripped by panic. Thinking nothing of his own celebrity status, Mitch hurried around to her side of the vehicle and opened the door. It took only a second for the media to recognize Mitch. And when they did, they rushed toward his vehicle like a horde of locust.

Chapter Sixty

"Come on, Beth, I've got you." Mitch pulled her from the truck amid the glaring lights and caustic questions being hurled at them by the media.

Wrapping his arm around her shoulder, Mitch walked purposefully toward the front doors of the police station, Beth's face tucked against his chest. An officer held the door open, then quickly shut it behind them. When Beth glanced over her shoulder, she saw video cameras and telephoto lenses still trying to get a shot of Mitch through the glass door.

"This way." An officer directed them down the hall, away from the prying eyes of the paparazzi. After they were ushered into a small conference room, Mitch pulled her into an embrace, and whispered close to her ear. "Are you okay?"

She nodded slowly.

"Don't listen to them, Beth. They're grasping at straws."

The media's questions were vicious and their accusations outrageous. They accused her of having a sixteen-year relationship with Cole and asked if she was the real reason his marriage was in shambles. She heard phrases like: *an act of passion, a tryst gone wrong, a jealous rage.* They accused her of pulling the trigger and allowing her son to take the fall. Then they hurled questions at Simon Grey, wanting to know his involvement, and if, in fact, Cole's death was the result of a lover's triangle.

"Mitch, I'm so sorry." Beth looked up at him, realizing in that instance, the anonymity he'd worked so hard to obtain was gone.

"Hey, don't worry about me," he said as he rocked her in his arms.

"I'm used to this kind of stuff."

"But what are you going to do? How are you going to explain why you're here?"

"I don't need to explain anything. And if I choose to talk to them, I'll tell them the truth."

Before Beth could ask him what the truth was, Det. Hanes walked into the room and closed the door. He looked directly at Mitch, scrutinizing him, before extending his hand. "I'm Det. Hanes."

"Mitch Burk," he offered.

Hanes' brow rose slightly.

"Mitch Burk is my real name, but most people know me as Simon Grey."

"The movie star. The one who pulled the disappearing act," the detective clarified.

"Unfortunately, yes."

"Great!" Hanes cursed under his breath. "A rodeo star *and* a celebrity. All I need is a bearded lady to have a full-blown three-ring circus on my hands."

Beth ignored the detective's rant. "When can I see Shane?" All she cared about was seeing her son—making sure he was okay, but Mitch didn't let Hanes off the hook that easy.

"Listen, *detective*, this is hard enough on Beth. Maybe you wouldn't mind dialing back the sarcasm a little."

"Hey," he pointed a finger in Mitch's direction, "I have a job to do. I would appreciate you keeping your opinions to yourself. You might be high and mighty in Hollywood, but in my station, you're just another civilian."

"Then maybe I need to get my lawyer down here to make sure Beth's case is handled without prejudice," Mitch taunted.

"Do what you want. It's not going to change the way I do business. Now, if you don't mind, I have a case to work." He turned to her, his demeanor softening. "Miss Justin, your son is with your uncle. I can take you to see him now. Then we're going to need to get your statement."

Beth nodded.

Hanes turned back to Mitch, keeping his tone business like. "You're welcome to wait, but this could take a while."

"I'll wait," Mitch said with defiance.

Beth turned to him. "You don't have to, Mitch. Uncle Charlie is here and I just need to see Shane."

"I said I'll wait."

Stepping closer to him, Beth noticed for the first time his reddened cheek where she'd slapped him. Brushing the back of her hand against it, she allowed her fingers to linger, but only for a second before dropping her hand to her side. "It was nice of you to come all this way, Mitch, but you don't have to stay. Shane and I are used to handling things on our own. We always have and always will. You have other people to consider, other responsibilities."

"But—"

"Mitch, it wasn't going to work out. I guess I always knew that." Beth pressed a tender kiss to his lips. "Good-bye," she said, before hurrying through the open door where Det. Hanes was waiting for her.

When Beth saw Shane in a cell with Uncle Charlie, she gasped and turned to Det. Hanes. "You've arrested him?! You said you were only going to question him!"

"Miss Justin, Shane is not under arrest. He needed a break. I wanted him to be able to lay down if he wanted to. The door isn't even closed."

"I'm sorry." She glanced at the open doorway. "I didn't mean to snap like—" Beth didn't bother to finish her apology. When she saw Shane stand up, she rushed to him, and hugged him tight.

"I'm okay, Mom, really. Det. Hanes has been treating me just fine."

"Are you sure?" she whispered.

"Yeah, Mom, I'm sure. But what about you? You sound—"

"I'm fine. Don't worry about me."

After spending a few minutes with Shane—him assuring her several times that he was okay—Beth was led to a small room with a table, two chairs, a pad of paper, and a recorder. Taking a seat across from Det. Hanes, she watched as he pulled off his blazer, looped it across the back of his chair, then sat down. "Miss Justin, do I have your permission to record this interview?"

"Yes."

Det. Hanes pushed a button on the recorder, then repeated the question. "Elizabeth Ann Justin, do I have your permission to record this interview."

"Yes."

"Just to be clear, Miss Justin, you are not under arrest, neither are you being detained. You understand that even though you have not been Mirandized, anything you say is admissible in court. Is that correct?"

"Yes."

"You have agreed to speak without an attorney present. Is that correct?"

"Yes."

"And you understand, that you are under no obligation to answer any questions. All answers are voluntary and you may terminate this interview at any time?"

"Yes."

"Very good. Then, would you please recount for me the events leading up to the shooting death of Colton James Dempsey."

Beth explained to Det. Hanes everything that happened from the moment she left the house—upset after seeing Mitch's red carpet interview—to the minute Uncle Charlie and the Carters arrived in the yard. Det. Hanes didn't interrupt; he just jotted down notes as she told her story from beginning to end. Though Beth tried to maintain her composure, by the time she was done, tears streamed down her face. She had lived through a nightmare—the facts even hard for her to comprehend. Cole had intended on killing her, and would have, if Shane hadn't shown up when he did. Beth could still see the shock in Cole's eyes after the shot rang out. She could still feel the weight of his body when he collapsed on top of her. But nothing compared to the horror of seeing Shane standing by the barn door.

A gun in his hand.

When Beth was done, Det. Hanes flipped back his notepad to the beginning and asked her some follow-up questions. He was pretty direct, sometimes harsh. He probed heavily regarding the nature of her relationship with Cole, even insinuating that the altercation had started as a lover's quarrel and escalated when Cole found out Beth was involved with another man. But it didn't matter what Det. Hanes said. Beth's story didn't change. She was telling the truth. Cole had suffered some kind of mental break. He was delusional—insisting she and Shane belonged to him. And when Beth refused to concede, he turned violent.

Finally, Det. Hanes turned off the recorder and sat back in his chair.

Letting out a deep breath, Beth's shoulders sagged with exhaustion. "Are we done?"

"Yes."

"Now what?"

"I need to do some follow-up interviews to corroborate the statements you and Shane have given me."

"I don't understand." Beth stared at him, dumbfounded.

"Your uncle already gave us his statement while you were at the hospital, but I have to interview Tim, Tom, and Hank Carter since both you and Shane stated they were first to arrive at the scene. But I also have to interview Curtis Hamilton and Mitch Burk."

"Curtis and Mitch? Why? They have nothing to do with this."

"Shane stated that he got the gun in question from Curtis Hamilton. He also admitted to using that same gun a few months back in an incident that involved Mitch Burk."

Beth wilted, her head nearly dropping to the table. "Please don't tell me Shane's future depends on Curtis Hamilton. The kid is a lowlife delinquent with parents as screwed up as he is."

"Actually, I know Curtis quite well."

Beth looked at him, horrified. *Please, God, don't let Curtis be a family friend or distant relative of Det. Hanes.*

"And I would have to agree with your characterization of him. Curtis has been getting into trouble since the age of ten."

Beth sat up straighter. "Then why bother talking to him? Why allow anything Curtis says to be used against Shane?"

"Because, Miss Justin, I still have a job to do. This is a homicide we're talking about, not a petty crime. Procedures need to be followed. And because this case involves a minor, and not one, but two celebrities, the media will be watching and critiquing how it is handled."

"But Shane can come home while you do these interviews, right?"

Det. Hanes looked down at his notepad, then at Beth. "Miss Justin, please, let me explain. Shane is—"

"You're going to arrest him, aren't you?" she cried. "But he's just a boy. He doesn't belong in jail with other criminals—men who are perverts and killers. At least let him go to a juvenile facility. Please don't—"

"Miss Justin," Det. Hanes raised his voice slightly. "I'm on your side. Just give me a minute to explain."

Beth stopped, unsure if she'd heard right. "You think Shane is innocent?"

"Of homicide, yes. I believe Shane acted out of fear for your life. However, even if it was justifiable, there are procedures that still need to be followed, which includes interviewing people who witnessed the crime or can corroborate a suspect's statement. That's what I intend to do as quickly and as effectively as possible."

"Okay," Beth wiped tears from her face and asked, "What does that mean for Shane?"

"I would like for him to stay here overnight."

"Overnight? In jail?"

"No. Not in jail. He would be staying voluntarily—and with your permission—for further questioning."

"But why would I agree to that? Shane has been traumatized enough. He needs to be home with me, not subjected to a night in jail."

"Miss Justin, let me put it to you this way. A man is dead. I can't just let Shane walk out of here without examining all the evidence and interviewing the witnesses. But that's going to take a little time—

JUST AN ACT

time I won't have if you force my hand."

"I'm not trying to force your hand, detective. I only want to do what's best for Shane."

"As do I. So, if Shane stays here voluntarily, I can hold off on an arrest, which includes sending him to a juvenile detention facility. Because, Miss Justin, once things are set in motion, there is a timetable and protocols that needs to be adhered to. But, if I can hold off on an arrest until I have Shane's file ready for the D.A., I'm confident no charges will be brought against him."

"Really? And that's all legal? Holding him, I mean, without arresting him?"

Det. Hanes shrugged. "I admit, it's a little unorthodox, and my actions could be called into question if things go south. In fact, you could charge me with coercion if you wanted to and most likely end up with my badge. But, Miss Justin, I'm willing to take that chance because I believe Shane is innocent. I just need time to gather all the information necessary for the D.A. to make a well-founded decision. I plan on talking to the Carters ASAP. Then, I will pay Curtis a visit. After I have everyone's statement—and as long as none of those statements contradict each other, I will give it to the D.A."

"But what about the media? Like you said, they're circling like vultures. What if the D.A. decides to grandstand—to make a name for himself?"

"Convicting a sixteen-year-old boy of homicide because he was in fear for his mother's life is not the kind of case a D.A. wants to build his career on. Besides, I know Donald Butler. He's a fair man."

"And you don't think the media will influence his decision?"

"No. Like I said, Donald's fair. But . . ."

"But what?"

The detective drug his hand down his face, clearly debating if he should answer her question.

"Please, detective, if you have any doubts, you need to tell me. I need to know what we're up against."

"Okay," he let out a deep breath, "the only issue I see as a possible obstacle is Cole Dempsey's character."

"What do you mean?"

"Well, up until a few months ago, his reputation was squeaky clean. He's a pillar in the rodeo community—has been for years—and everyone knows him as the All-American Cowboy. It might be difficult for the D.A. to ignore Cole's proven character and replace it with that of a homicidal maniac."

"But Cole was arrested for assault with a deadly weapon."

"Yes, but those charges were dropped."

"But it shows he has a violent streak."

"Miss Justin, it was one instance, not a streak. And, if I remember correctly, the man who charged Cole later stated it was a misunderstanding and apologized for *his* actions."

Beth sighed. "So, you're saying Cole's charisma is stronger than the facts?"

"No. You asked me what you might be up against. That's the only factor I see as a problem. Again, as long as the rest of the statements I gather coincide with the ones I already have. As I said before, Donald Butler is a fair man. Not only do I believe he will decide in Shane's favor, I'm certain his decision will be swift, once presented with all the facts. Donald will want to send a clear message to the media and anyone else who's watching, that he is confident about his decision, and that it was made without reservation."

"Okay," Beth whispered, swallowing the pain. "Can I be the one to explain to Shane what we're doing and why?"

"Of course. I'll even go with you—in case he has any questions."

Det. Hanes stood and moved to the door, his hand resting on the handle. Beth scooted her chair back and started toward him when she felt her body sway. She reached out for the table to maintain her balance, but it was the detective's arm that steadied her.

"Miss Justin, are you going to be all right? Maybe you should go back to the hospital, just as a precaution."

"Of course I'm not all right! But I need to be strong for Shane."

She moved around him, out the door, and started down the hall. When she reached out for the wall, the detective's hand came alongside her and held on to her elbow, helping her balance. He led her to where Shane was being held and stayed with Beth while she explained why he wasn't going home.

Mitch sat with his head bowed, praying. *God, I know Beth is hurt and confused. I know her trust has been shaken again, and she's afraid. Please help her see that I love her. I would do anything for her and Shane. Don't let her push me away. Help her see that I am here for her, and I have no intention of leaving.*

When he heard the door open, he stood. Seeing the way the detective was holding on to Beth, Mitch rushed to her side. Hanes took a step back.

"What's wrong?" Mitch asked Beth as he steadied her.

She said nothing.

He looked at the detective for a straight answer.

"She's exhausted and in quite a bit of pain," Hanes explained.

"What are you still doing here?" Beth asked Mitch. "And where is Uncle Charlie?"

"Charlie went home to take care of the ranch. He'll be back in the morning." He turned his attention to the detective. "What now?"

"Actually, I need to ask you a few questions."

"Me? I wasn't even there."

"This involves the roadside incident that happened a few months ago."

Mitch huffed. "Are you kidding me? It was a teenage prank. Shane's sitting in jail and Beth is near collapse, but you want to take the time to talk about something completely unrelated? If you're trying to build a case against Shane, you're wrong. He's a good—"

"Mitch, it's okay. Just talk to Det. Hanes," Beth said, her voice shaky and thin.

"Can't this wait until tomorrow? I need to get Beth some—"

"Please, Mitch. Talk to him now. The faster Det. Hanes can get his investigation over with, the sooner the D.A. can make his decision."

"What about Shane?"

"He'll be staying here tonight."

"Why?" Mitch glared at the detective, then looked at Beth. "They can't hold him. They either have to charge Shane or let him go. I'm calling my lawyer and—"

"It's okay, Mitch. I agreed to it," Beth said as she lowered herself into one of the chairs against the wall. "I'll wait here until you're done."

"Mr. Burk," the detective addressed him as he held the door open.

Mitch was conflicted. Beth looked horrible, and he hadn't been allowed to see Shane. He couldn't imagine why Beth agreed to let him spend the night in jail, but it was clear he wouldn't find out until after he answered the detective's questions.

Chapter Sixty-One

After answering the detective's questions, Mitch returned to the small conference room. Beth was sitting in the corner, eyes closed, head leaning against the wall—a thin grey blanket draped over her shoulders. It matched her complexion except for the black and purple on her cheek, forehead, and neck.

Mitch squatted down in front of her. "Beth," he whispered. She sighed, grimaced, then forced her eyes open. "Let's go. We'll come back in the morning." Beth looked around, getting her bearings, then Mitch helped her to her feet. They started toward the door, Mitch holding Beth close.

"You don't want to go out there." An officer stopped him in the hallway. "There has to be at least fifty reporters and cameramen crowding the parking lot. You won't get a hundred feet."

"But it's the middle of the night," Beth said, stunned.

"That doesn't matter to the media," Mitch snapped. "It wouldn't matter if they were in the path of an oncoming tornado. They're not going to leave until they get their story." He looked at Hanes to see if he would offer some help.

"Tell them I will be out in ten minutes to make a statement," he instructed the officer.

He nodded then headed to the lobby. Hanes turned to Mitch. "While I'm talking to the press, you two can go out the back."

"But my vehicle is out front."

Hanes thought for a moment. "Okay, this is what we're going to do."

Det. Hanes pushed open the glass doors and took his place front and center among the pandemonium. He crossed his arms against his chest, a folder clutched in his hand. Voices shouted above voices. Questions were lobbed at him from all sides, each one louder than the other; every reporter vied for his attention. Microphones were shoved in front of him and blinding lights shone in his eyes.

Some of the questions were so bizarre, so far-fetched, Hanes wanted to walk away and leave the media to their sensationalized speculations. But he knew the escalated noise would aid Beth Justin and Mitch Burk in getting away without being mobbed. So, he just stood there, unmoving, waiting for the roar to dim.

When most of the shouting subsided, Hanes cleared his throat and said, "I have a prepared statement regarding the death of Colson James Dempsey."

The crowd hushed further.

"We were summoned to the Diamond-J ranch at approximately 5:54 p.m. by a 911 call. When we arrived, we found Mr. Dempsey had been fatally shot. He was pronounced dead at the scene." An audible gasp rose from the crowd. "We have a suspect, along with his sworn confession. He is a juvenile, so we will not be releasing his name at this time."

Hanes looked up from the file he was referencing and saw over the heads of the reporters his personal vehicle pulling into the front parking lot, no lights on, unheard over the low rumblings of the crowd. He watched as Beth Justin and Mitch Burk slip from the backseat and into a black pick-up truck.

"I will answer a few questions at this time."

Instantly, the reporters began shouting out their questions, the noise once again at a fevered pitch.

One reporter shouted above the others. "What is Simon Grey's involvement?" Everyone quieted, waiting for his response.

"He's a friend of the family," Hanes answered.

Once again, they shouted their questions, but Hanes did nothing to silence them. He allowed the reporters to vie for his attention as he watched the pick-up truck across the parking lot, quietly roll in reverse.

"Is it true the Diamond-J is really a rehab facility and that's why both Cole Dempsey and Simon Grey were there?" a reporter from one of the major networks shouted.

When the crowd quieted, waiting for his response, a reporter in the back yelled, "Simon Grey is leaving!" Instantly, cameras, reporters, and blaring lights turned toward the parking lot. The mob hurried to catch up with the truck, photographers sprinted to get a picture of Simon Grey and his passenger, but it was too late. The vehicle roared out of the driveway before anyone could catch up to it. A few photographers jumped into their vehicles with the intentions of following them, but a squad car exited the parking lot right on their tails. They would be pulled over and cited the minute they exceeded the speed limit.

Beth was wide awake and giving Mitch directions as he switch-backed through town to avoid being followed. When they were satisfied no one was tailing them, she gave him instructions to a quaint roadside motel. It was after three in the morning, so of course, the place looked dark, except for the glowing "vacancy" sign and a small desk lamp in the office.

Beth approached the front desk and rang the bell on the counter, embarrassed because of the late hour. She heard feet shuffling in the adjoining room and a low voice saying he'd be right there.

Benjamin Smith dragged himself to the front counter, perched a pair of glasses on the end of his nose, then looked up. "How can—" He stopped mid-sentence, his mouth hanging open.

"Hello, Mr. Smith."

"Well, I'll be," he said as he blinked the sleep from his eyes. "Elizabeth Justin, what kind of trouble have you gotten yourself into?"

Beth had known Benjamin Smith for as long as she could

remember. He'd been a close friend of her dad's and was a godly man with a quiet countenance. He and his wife had managed The Traveler's Motel for decades.

"Why, it's all over the news," he continued as a frown creased his face. "Those reporters are saying you had yourself two beaus and things got out of hand. Now, the misses and I know that's not the Elizabeth Justin we've watched grow up, so they must be telling tales. You would never behave the way they're prattling on."

"Thank you, Mr. Smith. It's nice to know not everyone is going to believe what they hear."

"You don't sound too good, Missy."

"Just a sore throat." Beth raised a hand, casually covering the bruises on her neck as she glanced over her shoulder to where Mitch was waiting in the truck. She turned back to the kindly old man and smiled. "Mr. Smith, I need a room."

"All righty." He turned to the antique pegboard behind the counter and pulled a key from the hooked labeled "7", then flipped a switch that added a bright red "No" to the vacancy sign in the window.

"I also need a favor," Beth said as he handed her the key. "Reporters might come looking for us, and you see how vicious they can be. Would it be possible to park our truck in your garage?"

"Sure thing. Anything for Jack's little girl."

"Thank you, Mr. Smith. You don't know how much I appreciate this."

Beth slowly climbed back into the pickup. "Drive around to the back of the motel. Mr. Smith is going to let us park in his garage."

Mitch circled behind the small house attached to the motel and waited while Mr. Smith pulled out his older model Pontiac, then pulled his truck inside.

Mr. Smith stood alongside the house in his pajamas, slippers, and a robe. As Beth approached him, she could tell his demeanor had changed. Of course, it was the middle of the night, and he was standing outside in his bathrobe, talking to someone he hadn't seen in at least a decade.

"I don't have another room, Missy, but you're welcome to stay with me and the misses."

When he glanced over her shoulder to watch Mitch walking toward them, his bristly attitude made more sense. He was only trying to protect her virtue.

"That's okay, Mr. Smith, Mitch and I have a few things we need to discuss. One room will be fine." She tried to assure him with a smile.

"I know who he is, Elizabeth, you don't need to lie to me." His words were razor sharp.

"But Mr. Smith, Mitch *is* his real name. Simon Grey is just his stage name. I would never dream of lying to you."

"Even so, it's not right for you to share your room with him. It's not proper."

"Mr. Smith, I assure you, my virtue is not in danger."

Beth only had to think of the way Mitch looked standing next to Kara on the red carpet to convince herself that what she'd once had with Mitch was over.

"Ready?" Mitch asked as he joined them by the back porch.

Mr. Smith glared at him before disappearing inside his house.

"What was that for?" Mitch asked as he fell in step beside her.

"Mr. Smith is old-fashioned. He doesn't think we should be sharing a room. But I assured him we don't have that kind of relationship. Not anymore."

Beth saw the hurt in Mitch's eyes, but she didn't care. She wanted to hurt him, just like she'd been hurt by his red carpet appearance.

She stumbled slightly as she hurried across the gravel parking lot, but Mitch was quick with a steady hand on her hip, guiding her the rest of the way.

Once they were in the room, Beth sunk to the edge of the bed, beyond exhausted. However, she and Mitch had a few things to clear up. When Mitch finished bolting and locking the door, he turned around.

"You never answered my question." Her words were cold, void of feeling. "What are you doing here?"

"As soon as I got off the phone with Shane, I chartered a plane."

Beth looked aside. "You didn't need to do that. This doesn't concern you."

"What is wrong with you, Beth?" he snapped, then lowered his voice. "Why are you treating me like yesterday's garbage?"

"Me treating you?" she flared, then coughed. "I saw you with Kara. I listened as you told the whole world how wonderful she is. Give me a little credit, Mitch. How stupid do you think I am?"

"Obviously pretty stupid if you don't know by now how much I love you."

"Get out!" She barked, her tone raspy and raw. Hurrying to the door, she unlatched it before yanking it open. "I don't need your insults or your help. You can go back to the make-believe world you live in. I'm a little busy dealing with reality—the reality that my son might be charged with—" her voice broke from emotion.

Mitch took a step toward her, but she stopped him. "I don't need your pity, Mr. Grey. Save it for your fans."

"Stop it!" he shouted. "Just stop it!"

Beth could see his eyes were red and beginning to swell with tears. Slowly, he moved toward her, reached for her, but dropped his hands to his sides. She watched a tear slide down his cheek.

"I love you, Beth. I love you more than I can say. I haven't stopped thinking about you, not one minute since I've been gone. You've got to trust me. Please don't push me away."

Beth looked at the emotion in Mitch's eyes. She didn't know what to think. Her heart was his—she'd given it to him. It was his to hold or to break. But her mind . . . her mind fed on her insecurities, her weaknesses, her mistakes. Deep down inside, Beth was convinced she didn't deserve happiness and was a fool to think Mitch could really love her with all of her flaws and shortcomings. A tug-of-war raged inside her.

She closed her eyes. *God, I don't know what to do or what to believe.*

Trust.

Beth heard the single word as clearly as if it had been spoken out loud. She wanted to trust—both God and Mitch.

JUST AN ACT

But what would it cost her?

Mitch looked at her as if his life was hanging in the balance.

She couldn't help herself. *God, please don't let me down.*

Reaching for Mitch's hand, Beth laced her fingers in his. Pressing his palm to her cheek, she felt his warmth and sighed. "I want to trust you, Mitch, really I do. I just don't know—"

He pulled her close. "Then let me say it again. I love you, Beth." Mitch rocked her in his embrace, stroking her hair. "I will never stop loving you."

"I love you, too," she sobbed. "I just can't handle getting hurt again—having one more person leave me."

"I'm never going to leave you, never again. I'll be right here whenever you need me."

Mitch cradled Beth's face in his hands, his eyes searching hers for assurance. Gently, he pressed his lips to hers. Beth accepted his kiss, tasting salty tears—not knowing if they were hers or his. Slowly, Mitch pulled back, brushed his thumb across her lips, then stared into Beth's eyes. "I don't know what I would've done if you had made me leave."

"And I don't know what I'll do if you ever go."

"I promise you, I'm not going anywhere."

Mitch held Beth for some time but could tell by the tremors in her legs, she needed to lie down. Scooping her up in his arms, Mitch carried her to the bed. Beth sank into the worn quilt and clutched on to Mitch's hand as he stood to walk away. "Don't go," she whispered, her eyes almost closed.

"Don't worry, I'm not going anywhere."

Chapter Sixty-Two

Mitch lay alongside Beth, watching as she slept, unable to take his eyes off of her. Seeing her bruised and battered body caused his mind to conjure up one horrifying scenario after another. Not knowing what had happened was driving him crazy, but he couldn't bring himself to wake her.

Exhaustion had consumed Beth the minute her head hit the pillow. Even though she slept fitfully—wincing and moaning each time she moved—it was important she get what rest she could. God only knew what the day would bring, and Beth would need every bit of strength she had to face it.

It had been a couple of hours since they arrived at the motel. With every minute that went by, Mitch's irrational imagination slowly eroded at his sanity. Wondering.

Beth moaned, then rolled onto her side, grimacing. When she opened her eyes, Mitch saw fear, shock, and emptiness. He couldn't wait any longer. He needed to know. "Did he rape you?"

Her mind fuzzy, Beth closed her eyes, cataloging what she knew. *Mitch was home. Shane was in jail. Cole was dead.* Opening her eyes, she looked at Mitch stretched out next to her.

"How long was I asleep?" Beth asked, sounding like she had a bad case of laryngitis.

"A couple hours."

Slowly, she pushed herself to a sitting position—biting back the pain—then tipped her head back against the wall. "What time is it?"

"Almost six." Mitch sat up next to her.

Beth was quiet as she rolled her head from side to side, then winced when she pressed her hand to her chest.

"Beth, you didn't answer me. Did Cole ra—"

"No. I've got bumps and bruises, but nothing that won't heal."

"But your voice?"

"It hurts to swallow."

"Beth," Mitch sat so he could look into her eyes. "What happened? What was he doing there in the first place?"

"He came to visit Shane."

"Only Shane?"

She looked away, realizing everything Cole had told her was a lie.

"Why didn't you tell me?" Mitch asked, his voice strained.

"Because there was nothing you could've done. You were over a thousand miles away; I didn't want to upset you."

"So, you knew it would upset me, but you let him stay anyway."

"I didn't have a choice, Mitch," She coughed, feeling the pain. "If I had forced Cole to leave, he would've convinced Shane to go with him. I didn't trust him. So I figured I was better off having Cole on the ranch where I could keep an eye on him."

"So did he come on to you?"

She looked at Mitch and answered calmly, "He tried, but I handled it."

"Handled it how?"

"I told him I wasn't interested, that I was seeing someone else."

"And he stopped, just like that?" Mitch did nothing to hide his belligerence.

"No, he didn't stop, but that didn't change my feelings."

Beth thought about the kiss she'd exchanged with Cole, and how she had wanted to hurt Mitch. Beth admitted to Det. Hanes she had kissed Cole back because she was hurt, but had also told him she'd put a stop to it or at least she had tried.

Beth knew she needed to be honest with Mitch. After all, it was in her report.

"Mitch, when I saw you on television with Kara, I was hurt and confused. I stormed out of the house because I didn't want Cole to see me crying."

Beth tried pulling her knees to her chest but her ribs protested. Sighing, she rested her head back against the wall.

"Cole found me behind the barn crying. He didn't know why I was so upset but tried to console me anyway. And . . . and I let him."

"You let him?" Mitch asked, confused.

"I kissed him," Beth blurted out, in a hoarse whisper. "I was hurt and angry. I wanted to get even with you for what I thought you were doing with Kara, so I let Cole kiss me. The minute I did, I knew it was wrong. I pulled away from him and told Cole I was sorry . . . but he didn't stop."

"What happened?" Mitch asked, his complexion drained of color.

"He tried convincing me that he and I were meant to be together. Cole said if you loved me, you would've been there with me, and I was a fool to think you were coming back."

"You told him who I was?"

"No. He just figured you were some lowlife guy who skipped out on me."

Beth glanced at Mitch but quickly looked down at the worn comforter.

"Then what happened?"

"He came completely unhinged. I got away from him once, but he overpowered me in the barn. He pulled a knife from his boot and told me he was going to kill me." Beth shuddered at the memory, reaching for her neck. "That's when Shane shot him. It was horrible, Mitch. Shane was standing there, stunned . . . horrified . . . and—"

Mitch gently pulled her against his chest. "It's okay, Beth. It's going to be okay. The only thing that matters now is you and Shane."

Chapter Sixty-Three

Beth woke to the sound of running water, Mitch no longer beside her. The bedside clock let her know another hour had slipped by. Slowly, she lowered her feet to the side of the bed, her entire body protesting. Reaching for her cell phone, she dialed.

"Uncle Charlie, it's me. No, it sounds worse than it is. I'm with Mitch. I just called to say I think it would be best if you stayed at the ranch instead of coming to the station." Beth couldn't get the picture of Uncle Charlie from the previous night out of her head. He had looked haggard like he had aged twenty years from all that had happened. She was concerned for his health, not knowing how much more his aged body could take. "I would feel better knowing you're at the ranch—taking care of things. If the media shows up, I want them kept at a distance. Please, do this for me. Thanks, Uncle Charlie. I'll keep you posted."

Beth disconnected the call, convinced he probably saw through her excuse, but was glad he didn't fight her on it.

Looking down at the discolored marks on her arms, Beth felt for the bump on her head. It was still tender to the touch but some of the swelling had gone down. She unbuttoned her shirt and pressed at the piece of gauze on her chest, trying not to think about what would've happened if Shane hadn't come home when he did, or Mitch hadn't returned at all.

"What are you thinking?"

Beth gasped, then swallowed against the pain. She quickly fastened the buttons on her blouse before turning around. Mitch stood shirtless, his jeans low on his hips as he ruffled a towel through his wet hair. Beth watched as the muscles of his arms flexed against the motion.

"I . . . uh, I was just thinking . . . uh . . . about what would've happened if Shane hadn't . . .you know . . ." Beth shook her head trying to clear the ghastly thoughts. "Never mind." She got to her feet. "I need to wash up."

Mitch pulled her to his bare chest. "Everything's going to be fine." He stroked her back tenderly, his hands reassuring and strong. Beth could feel the droplets of water on his back as she held him tight. The warmth of his skin against her cheek was comforting, his words soothing and encouraging. She wanted to believe Mitch, but she knew better. Even with Det. Hanes in their corner, there was still a very good chance Shane would be arrested and charged.

"I've got to get cleaned up," Beth whispered as she reluctantly pulled away from Mitch's embrace and dragged herself to the bathroom.

Even though she'd only been awake a few minutes, the day was already weighing on her like a mantle made of stone.

Mitch reached for the television remote and clicked it on. He surfed the channels looking for the morning news, stopping when he saw a picture of himself and Cole Dempsey flash across the screen. It was one of the news-gossip shows that reported more gossip than news, and usually walked a fine line between truth and fabricated rumors.

"We have breaking news concerning the Cole Dempsey shooting that you're not going to believe," the in-studio reporter said from where she sat behind an acrylic desk with large pictures of him and Cole on the screens behind her. "We go live to Meredith Andrews in Triune, Kansas."

The field reporter held the mike with the show's logo on it and spoke into the camera. "That's right, Rebecca, I'm standing outside the Triune Kansas Police Department where just minutes ago Donna

Dempsey, estranged wife of Cole Dempsey, was ushered inside by an unidentified man."

The news feed cut from the reporter to canned footage of a petite blond and a man in a black suit walking briskly across the parking lot and into the station. The woman was wearing dark glasses and walked with her head down, while the man alongside her held her by the elbow and led the way to the front door. They were assaulted with questions as they walked through the maze of reporters; she refused to look up or answer. The picture cut back to the reporter as she continued live.

"We know the Dempseys were in the middle of a messy divorce—citing irreconcilable differences—and that just a few weeks ago, Cole Dempsey was involved in an altercation with his ranch foreman, Daniel Brewer. Though the charge of assault with a deadly weapon was dropped, rumors of a supposed affair between Donna Dempsey and Brewer have yet to be confirmed. However, we *have* been able to confirm that Cole Dempsey had previous ties to the Diamond-J Ranch where he was shot and killed last night. Sixteen years ago, before his rodeo career began, Dempsey worked on the Kansas cattle ranch and quite possibly had a romantic relationship with Elizabeth Justin, the current owner of the Diamond-J."

"What the—" Mitch muttered, taking a deep breath, preparing himself for what else the gossip hounds had dug up.

"So, Meredith, are you saying because of the break-up of his marriage, Dempsey sought out a prior love interest? Or, is this a relationship that's been ongoing for sixteen years?" the anchorwoman asked.

"How long their relationship has gone on is unclear. However, if there was, in fact, a relationship when Dempsey lived on the ranch, Elizabeth Justin would've only been sixteen at the time."

"Wow! If that's true, it would definitely rock the pedestal Dempsey's fans have put him on for all these years."

"Oh, but there's more. The minor who is being held in the shooting death of Cole Dempsey is Justin's *sixteen-year-old* son."

The anchorwoman gasped. "Are you saying there's a possibility that Cole Dempsey was shot and killed by his own son?"

God, no. Mitch stood and began to pace.

"Of course, we can only speculate at this time, but the puzzle pieces are quickly falling into place."

"This is a shocking revelation, Meredith, but what about Simon Grey? How does he play into all this?"

"Well, according to Det. Samuel Hanes' statement last night, Simon Grey was characterized as a family friend. But, we have since found out that Simon Grey was at Elizabeth Justin's side during her recent hospital stay following a riding accident. According to our source, their relationship appeared to be far more than just friends."

Mitch sunk to the edge of the bed, his head spinning.

Beth walked out of the bathroom to see Mitch sitting on the end of the bed, his eyes glued to the television set. "What is it?" she asked as she moved closer to the bed.

"Beth . . ." Mitch tried to say something, but she waved him off, listening for herself as the reporters continued.

"You know what they say, life is stranger than fiction. This could, in fact, be a lover's triangle that ended with deadly results. An ex-lover, a movie star, and a woman they both wanted. But the tragedy here is Ms. Justin's son might pay for her indiscretion if he is found guilty of murder."

"That would be tragic, but Meredith, but back to Donna Dempsey. Do we know why she is there?"

"Well, Rebecca, speculation is rampant as to why Mrs. Dempsey is here, but this could be "the woman scorn" factor. If it's true Cole Dempsey was leading a double life, I can only wonder if his wife is here to exact her pound of flesh. Public humiliation is a strong motive for revenge. If she feels her divorce settlement is in jeopardy, you can be sure she'll be looking for someone to blame. This is Meredith Andrews, live in Triune, Kansas. Back to you, Rebecca."

"Thank you, Meredith," the reporter at the acrylic desk smiled at

JUST AN ACT

the camera. "That's the latest in the Cole Dempsey murder investigation. We will switch back to Meredith Andrews when new information becomes available."

Beth sunk to the bed. "Murder? They're reporting Cole's death as a murder?" She turned to Mitch. "What happened? What did they say? They're going to try Shane as an adult, aren't they? They're going to try to convict him of murder."

"No, Beth, that's not going to happen."

"Then why would they say that if it isn't a possibility?" She kneaded her forehead, ignoring the pain of her injury. Beth began to pace, feeling like a caged animal cornered by others. "Det. Hanes lied to me, didn't he? They aren't going to consider our statements at all? They're just going to brand Shane a murderer and lock him away? What about Cole? He was going to kill me. I have the bruises and cuts to prove it. Why aren't they talking about that? Why aren't they reporting the truth?"

"Stop, Beth."

Mitch reached for her but she stepped away from him, anger replacing her fear.

"They're reporters, Beth. They sensationalize everything."

"Sensationalize! They're not sensationalizing anything! They're lying!" Beth wiped the tears from her eyes and sat to pull on her boots. "We need to get over there. I need to be with Shane."

Beth braced herself for the madness as Mitch pulled into the police station parking lot. They were barraged by cameras and questions before they could even get out of the vehicle. Mitch hurried around to help Beth out of the truck—drawing her close to him—shielding her from the reporters and the cameras. Questions assaulted them from every direction. Some were ugly and distasteful but the comments regarding Shane's involvement caused the fear inside Beth to race out of control.

When they reached the top step of the police station, the door automatically opened, an officer holding it, so they didn't have to stop. Once they were inside, Beth let out a gasp, realizing she'd been holding her breath the entire time they crossed the parking lot.

She and Mitch were ushered down the hall to the same small conference room they'd been in the night before. When the officer opened the door for them, Beth was shocked to see Donna Dempsey sitting off to one side, her perfectly manicured fingers laced together and resting atop her crossed legs.

Beth took a breath.

Though Mitch had warned her Cole's wife had shown up at the station, Beth hadn't been prepared to meet her face-to-face. She could only assume Donna Dempsey was there to make sure someone paid for her husband's death. Why else would she have come so far?

Beth didn't notice the man in the corner until he stepped forward with an extended hand. "Hello, I'm Andrew Harris, Mrs. Dempsey's attorney." He shook Beth's hand and then Mitch's.

Beth watched a puzzled look cross the attorney's face when Mitch introduced himself.

Mitch was quick to clarify. "Simon Grey is my stage name. My real name is Mitch Burk."

"I see." He smiled. "It's a pleasure to meet you. I really enjoy your films. I was surprised to hear about your disappearance. I figured it was just a publicity stunt. I guess it paid off; you've been in the news for months."

Beth disliked the man instantly. He acted cavalier, as if they had met in a restaurant, not a police station where her son's future hung in the balance.

"This is Donna Dempsey," the lawyer turned to the impeccably dressed woman. Mrs. Dempsey stood and extended her hand. Beth took it out of decorum.

"I wish I could say this is a pleasure. Unfortunately, we both know that isn't the case." Donna Dempsey spoke from behind her dark glasses.

"No, it isn't." Beth responded, wanting to drop to her knees and beg the woman to understand what Shane did and why. "Mrs. Dempsey, please, you've got to under—"

An officer walked into the room, interrupting Beth.

"Mrs. Dempsey, Det. Hanes will take your statement now."

No, Beth wanted to shout. She needed to talk with the woman first, make her see, make her understand, but it was too late. Donna Dempsey was escorted down the hall with her lawyer.

"She's going to demand charges are filed, isn't she?" Beth looked at Mitch, panic coloring her words.

"We don't know that."

"Then why is she here? Why does she have her lawyer with her?" Mitch sighed. "I don't know."

Beth walked out of the room, to a desk where an officer was sitting, his thick fingers plucking away at a computer keyboard.

"I want to see my son," Beth demanded.

She was led to the holding cell where Shane had spent the night. He stood when he saw her coming.

"Can I go inside and sit with him?" she asked the officer.

"Just a moment." He took a few steps away from her and spoke into the microphone attached to his shoulder. A short minute later, a female officer walked toward her.

"Miss Justin, I need to search you before you go inside the cell."

"But Shane isn't under arrest. Ask Det. Hanes. He's here voluntarily."

"I understand that, Ma'am, but we still have procedures that need to be followed."

"But I could demand you release Shane right now and walk out of here with him if I wanted to."

"Ma'am, would you like to wait until Det. Hanes is available?"

Beth didn't want to wait. She had the sinking feeling something terrible had happened during the night. She needed to be with Shane to make sure he was okay.

Stepping around the corner with the woman, Beth allowed the officer to do an extensive search. The humiliation meant nothing, as long as she was able to see Shane.

When Beth walked back to the holding cell area, the male officer unlocked the door and allowed Beth to step inside. *Why is the door locked? It's not supposed to be locked.* She threw her arms around

Shane and held him tight. Beth didn't speak; she just held him.

"It's going to be okay, Mom," Shane consoled her.

Beth was surprised by the strength in his voice. She stepped back, her hands latching on to Shane's. He wasn't pale like he'd been the night before and he no longer appeared afraid. Instead, he looked strong . . . calm even.

"How are you doing, Shane?"

"I'm doing fine, Mom, but your neck and your cheek . . ." Shane's countenance changed as he studied her injuries. "I can't believe he did that to you."

"It looks worse than it is." Beth tried to smile, not wanting Shane to worry.

"But your voice. You can barely talk."

"But it doesn't hurt that much. I'm more worried about you."

"I'm fine, Mom, really I am."

She was confused. How could he be so calm, so 'fine' when in a matter of hours, he could be charged with murder? "I don't understand, Shane."

He led her to the cot against the wall and took a seat.

Beth sat, staring at Shane.

"Mom, what I did was justifiable."

"But what if they don't see it that way?"

"Then I'll have to go through the process. Even so, I'm convinced that's not going to happen. I did nothing wrong."

"How can you be so sure?"

Shane didn't know how to explain it—because he wasn't even sure he understood it himself—but something had happened last night. When he had thought he would go crazy from claustrophobia and fear, he cried out to God for help, and He gave it. Not only did God calm his anxieties but He stayed with him throughout the night. Shane spent the night talking with God. And as absurd as it sounded, God had spoken back.

"Because, Mom, God knows the truth, and He's not going to let me be punished for something I didn't do."

Beth couldn't believe what she was hearing. Even though she had raised Shane to believe and trust in God, as he had gotten older, Shane's belief had waned. But now . . . now he spoke with calmness and assurance, confident that God was by his side.

She was speechless.

Shane reached for her hand and gave it a squeeze. "Believe it or not, Mom, I have been listening. You've taught me since I was a little boy that God is in control. You told me all the time that He loves us more than we can imagine. I never understood how you could love God so much when he allowed horrible things to happen to you. But somehow . . . last night . . . I felt it. I really felt as if God was right here with me, reminding me He was in control and all I needed to do was trust in Him. Somehow it seemed simple . . . to trust. I mean . . . what else could I do? I understand now that I'm in God's hands. I just have to be strong enough to deal with whatever the world throws at me. But, at least I won't have to deal with it on my own."

Chapter Sixty-Four

Beth walked back to the conference room where Mitch was waiting. She was sure it was the stunned expression on her face that brought him to his feet and to her side.

"What's wrong, Beth? What happened?" Mitch asked.

She shook her head in amazement. "It's Shane."

"What about Shane?" he asked, looking panicked. "Did something happen to him? Is he okay?"

She looked into his eyes and smiled. "I can't believe it, Mitch. It's incredible!"

"What's incredible? What are you talking about?"

"Shane. He said he spent the night talking with God and now understands what it means to trust—to trust in God."

Mitch gently cupped her face in his hands, his thumbs wiping the tears from her cheeks. "What did you expect? Shane's watched you since he was a little boy."

"But I've struggled with trust my whole life. How could he see something in me that wasn't there?"

"It was there, Beth." Mitch smiled. "You've shown him what it means to live out your faith even when life gets tough. You never doubted God, you just had a hard time trusting people. Shane's a great kid, Beth." Mitch looped his arm around her shoulders and pulled her close. "He's going to be okay."

Beth had almost convinced herself everything was going to be all right, then Donna Dempsey and her lawyer walked back into the conference room. Instantly, fear and doubt rushed over Beth, drowning out the assurance she'd seen in Shane's eyes.

JUST AN ACT

"I've got to talk to her, Mitch. I've got to make her understand what happened."

Walking over to where Mrs. Dempsey stood, Beth said a quick prayer. *Help me, God. Help me make her understand.*

"Mrs. Dempsey," Beth tried to sound strong, but her raspy voice was barely more than a whisper. "I don't know what Cole told you about us . . . about me . . . or Shane. Or maybe he didn't . . . tell you, that is . . . not that there was anything . . ." Words tumbled from Beth's mouth, none of them making any sense.

"I know who you are, Ms. Justin. I've known about you for some time."

"Oh." Beth was surprised. She just assumed Cole had spent the last sixteen years of his life denying she and Shane even existed.

"Cole told me his son contacted him and wanted to meet. He was looking forward to it. Of course, I knew it was because he was looking forward to seeing you again."

Beth couldn't read the woman's expression since her dark glasses hid her eyes. "Cole's interest was in Shane, Mrs. Dempsey. The relationship we had was over a long time ago."

"Or so you thought."

"I don't understand."

"He never got over you, Ms. Justin. But he was smart enough to stay away. Cole knew his career would be over if anyone found out about his love child. So, he married me—the rodeo queen—to improve his image. Oh, our marriage was good for a few years. We have two precious little girls to show for it. But when he got drunk, all Cole talked about was you, and how I would never measure up."

Beth heard the chill in the woman's tone. Clearly, she was hurt and angry. But was she vindictive? Would she really let Shane pay because of the way Cole treated her?

"Mrs. Dempsey, Cole was not the golden boy of the rodeo circuit when I knew him. Our relationship was not something I wanted to repeat."

The woman looked away.

"He beat me, Mrs. Dempsey. He beat me the night he left. Cole knew I was carrying his child but that didn't stop him. That's the Cole Dempsey I knew. And last night, he intended to kill me. When I told him I loved someone else—that there could never be anything between us—Cole attacked me."

Beth broke down, unable to hold back her emotions. "Shane was only protecting me. He had no intentions of shooting Cole. He wanted to believe in his father. Shane wanted to build a relationship with the man he had dreamed about his whole life. But when he saw Cole put a knife to my throat, Shane shot him."

Beth took a moment to control her crying, before continuing. "You have to believe me, Mrs. Dempsey. Shane didn't mean for this to happen. It was a horrible, horrible accident. But please . . . don't make Shane pay for Cole's actions. He's been through enough already."

Beth saw a tear slip from beneath the woman's glasses before she removed them. Finally, Beth was able to see Donna Dempsey's eyes. She expected to see hate and scorn. Instead, she saw sadness and compassion. Beth watched as the woman's gaze traveled from the welt on her forehead to the bruising around her neck.

"I believe you, Ms. Justin."

Beth was stunned, sure she had heard wrong.

"That's why I'm here. Det. Hanes contacted me last night, not only to notify me of Cole's death, but to ask if Cole had ever been abusive or violent. With Cole dead, it was a secret I finally felt safe enough to share."

The woman took a deep breath, as if needing to gather enough courage to speak.

"Cole had taken his anger out on me on more than one occasion. I tried to leave him a hundred times, but he threatened me. He told me he would take the girls away from me if I made trouble for him." She stared at Beth intently. "He threatened my life, just like he did you. When he shot at Daniel, I finally had the leverage I needed. Daniel and I were not having an affair, but Daniel knew about Cole's violent streak. He'd found me on more than one occasion after one of Cole's rampages. Daniel wanted to press charges as a way of keeping Cole away from me. Instead, we struck a deal. Daniel would drop the charges if Cole agreed to a divorce. Hoping to save his career and his reputation, he agreed."

Beth didn't know what to say. She had thought Donna Dempsey was the enemy, that she'd come to Triune to get revenge for Cole's death. But instead, she wanted to help. Beth reached out for the woman, embracing her. "Thank you. Thank you so much," Beth sobbed.

Beth took a step back and wiped the tears from her face—trying to regain her composure.

Mitch extended his hand. "Thank you, Mrs. Dempsey. We appreciate the time you took coming here on Shane's behalf."

"I knew it was the right thing to do. Very few people know the Cole I knew . . . that Ms. Justin knew." She looked at Beth as if somehow they were bound together because of the secrets they had kept. "I didn't want your son to be just one more person victimized by Cole Dempsey."

"Donna," he attorney interrupted. "We really need to be going."

She looked at her watch and gave Beth an empathetic smile. "I'm sorry for the pain Cole caused you. I hope things go well for you and your son."

"Thank you," Beth replied.

Mrs. Dempsey looked at Mitch. "I wish we had met under different circumstances, Mr. Grey. I'm a fan . . . as silly as that sounds." She blushed slightly. "Will I be seeing you in the movies anytime soon?"

"One more time, that's all."

"That's a shame."

"Not for me." Mitch smiled and turned to Beth. "I found what I've been looking for my whole life. I have no intentions of letting her go."

Chapter Sixty-Five

Mitch held Beth's hand as they sat in the police station conference room, her eyes fixed on the wall clock, watching each excruciating minute tick by. Det. Hanes had completed his interviews by midday, and as promised, finished his final report as quickly as possible.

The D.A. had arrived hours ago, introducing himself and offering his sympathies to Beth—acknowledging the ordeal she'd suffered.

It had buoyed her feelings regarding the man's character, but as time crept by, she realized his solicitude was a polite gesture, and would have no bearing on how he would decide Shane's case.

Beth and Mitch took turns sitting with Shane, and Beth called Uncle Charlie hourly to let him know they were still waiting. Mitch had finally silenced the television that hung on the wall, no longer able to listen to the sensationalized statements being reported by the media. He promised Beth his lawyer would be filing defamation suits against each and every reporter who mishandled the facts, but she didn't care. They could say whatever they wanted as long the D.A. based his decision on the truth.

Around eleven thirty, Shane said he was tired and wanted to rest. So, Beth returned to the conference room and sat with Mitch. Minutes before midnight, Beth got to her feet, no longer able to sit still.

"It's taking too long. We should have heard something by now. The D.A. has had plenty of time to read our statements, study the crime scene photos, and the photographs of my injuries. Donna Dempsey's statement proves Cole's abusive nature and that he'd threatened her life on numerous occasions. What more does he need?"

"He has to be thorough, Beth. The national media is speculating about everything. He has to make sure he has all his bases covered."

She twisted her hands as she continued to pace.

"Beth, you need to sit down. Exhausting yourself is not going to help anything."

She took a seat alongside him—trying to get comfortable—wincing when she moved wrong.

"You never told me the extent of your injuries. You're limping, and you keep holding your side. I can see the bump and bruises, but what else aren't you telling me?"

"My leg and my ribs are just a little sore . . . and I have a few stitches, but that's it."

"Stitches?"

"It was just a small cut." Her hand subconsciously pressed against her blouse. Mitch's eyes drop to her chest. When his eyes came up to meet hers, they were filled with regret.

"I should have been there. None of this would've happened if I had stayed."

"Mitch, none of this is your fault."

"It wouldn't have happened if I had been there."

"It wouldn't have happened if Shane hadn't invited Cole. It wouldn't have happened if I had told him he couldn't stay. But it happened, Mitch, and there's nothing we can do about it but pray. Pray the D.A. sees this for what it is. A horrible, tragic accident."

As if on cue, the door opened. "Miss Justin, the District Attorney is ready to speak with you," the officer said.

She got to her feet, her legs feeling like brittle sticks as she moved toward the door.

"Can I come with her?" Mitch asked.

"That would be up to Miss Justin."

Beth reached for Mitch's hand, squeezing it tight as they walked down the hall. The D.A. stood as they entered the small office he was using. He shook hands with Beth and Mitch, his grip firm, his eyes direct.

"Have a seat." He motioned to the two chairs that sat side-by-side.

The three of them sat, the D.A. lacing his fingers together, resting his elbows on the desk. "Miss Justin, I know this has been difficult on you. How are you feeling?"

"I'll let you know in a few minutes."

He smiled. "Good enough."

With a serious expression on his face, he looked at the papers on his desk and shuffled them around. "I want you to know I've studied the evidence extensively. As you well know, the media—along with other news agencies—have already weighed in on this case. Even though they had no basis for their theories. I can assure you, anything outside of this file," he raised the folder and set it back down, "had no bearing on my decision. Det. Hanes' report was clear and concise, and in my opinion, left no room for conjecture. With that said, I'm ruling the death of Colson James Dempsey as justifiable homicide."

Beth heard what he said but wasn't sure she understood what it meant. She looked at him, searching for more information.

"Miss Justin, it is my judgment that your son acted out of fear for your life. There will be no charges filed against him."

Deep sobs shook Beth's body as she covered her face with her hands. Mitch dropped his arm across her shoulders, rubbing his hand up and down her arm.

Relief consumed Beth, making it difficult for her to gather her composure. Finally, she raised her head, barely able to focus through her tears. "Thank you." Her voice was husky, more with emotion than pain. "I don't know what else to say."

"You don't have to say anything, Miss Justin. The evidence was clear. I'm sorry my decision was slow in coming, but I'm sure you can understand the immense scrutiny this case will receive. Because of the media attention it has garnered, I couldn't leave room for error or hearsay."

The D.A. stood and smiled. "I believe there is someone here who needs a ride home."

She turned to see Shane standing in the doorway. Beth hurried to her feet and wrapped her arms around him, holding him tight, crying all over again.

"Come on, Mom. It's okay."

It took a moment before Beth stepped back from Shane and wiped the tears from her face.

Mitch stepped forward and put his hand on Shane's shoulder, then enveloped him in a bear hug. Beth watched as Shane embraced Mitch in return and thanked him for sticking by them.

As the D.A. stepped around the desk, Shane stuck out his hand. "Thank you, sir."

The D.A. accepted his handshake. "You're welcome."

"Can I go home now?"

"Not just yet."

Beth tensed. "What do you mean, not yet?"

"I need to make a statement to the press first, let them know I won't be filing charges. Then you'll have to walk the gauntlet for yourself." He looked at Beth and Mitch. "My suggestion would be that you make your own statement. What I have to say doesn't explain how Mr. Grey is involved. Unless you want the continued rumors, it would behoove you to set the record straight."

"What about the gun?" Shane asked the D.A. "Det. Hanes told me I could be charged with possession of a stolen weapon and discharging a firearm in public."

Beth, Mitch, and Shane looked at the D.A., waiting for his answer. "Shane, I'm dropping it. I think you've been through enough." He eyed him sternly. "Don't make me regret my decision."

"No, sir." Shane responded with respect.

Mitch, Beth, and Shane waited inside the police station while the district attorney took his place in front of the media circus.

Beth couldn't hear what he was saying but it didn't matter. Shane was free to go home, and the three of them were more than ready to get on with the rest of their lives.

Chapter Sixty-Six

Beth lay awake, curled on her side as the rising sun was just beginning to thaw the frost on the small bedside window. She clutched the blanket under her chin, warding off the chill of the morning air. She replayed the events of the past six months like scenes from a movie. Hollywood screenwriters had nothing on her. Her life had been filled with one dramatic episode after another. Beth closed her eyes, pushing away the bad, only wanting to dwell on the good.

Mitch had been released from his movie deal, citing personal hardship. Lexmar agreed to a cash settlement that took a healthy chunk of Mitch's holding, but he didn't care. Jerry argued with the agreement, wanting the insurance company to pick up the tab, but Mitch was more than willing to pay. He wanted to start his new life with no ties to the past.

Beth had officially taken the ranch off the market only to find out the interested buyer was none other than Mitch himself. He'd made his offer and asked for more time, knowing Shane was waning about moving. He figured if Beth had an impressive offer in the wings, she wouldn't do anything rash. It had worked.

Shane no longer wanted to move from the Diamond-J. The excitement of the last few months had shown him a stable home, family, and love was enough for him—that and a certain redhead.

Beth felt Mitch stretch next to her, right before he draped his warm, muscular arm around her and pulled her close against his chest.

"Merry Christmas, Mrs. Burk," he whispered in her ear before dotting her neck with kisses.

"Yes, it is," she answered with a smile, feeling the heat he always stirred inside her. Beth tried to move toward the edge of the bed, but Mitch held her tight.

"Where are you going?"

"I need to make breakfast."

"I think I can stave off hunger until lunch . . . well, at least for food."

"Mitch!" she said with slight exasperation.

"What? Can't I tell my wife how much I crave her?"

It amazed Beth, how with just a few words Mitch could render her speechless. She turned around and snuggled close, finding Mitch so intoxicating she couldn't remember what they were talking about.

Mitch smirked. "Breakfast, Beth . . . we were talking about breakfast."

"I know what I was talking about." She gave him a nudge, trying to regain her footing. "Shane and I have always made it a tradition to have a big Christmas breakfast. No gifts can be opened until we're done eating and the kitchen is clean."

"Then I guess I'm breaking tradition because I already have all the gift I need." Mitch lowered his mouth to hers and consumed her with a kiss so passionate, Beth knew breakfast would have to wait.

"I love you, Beth," he spoke breathlessly. "And I will spend the rest of my life doing whatever it takes to show you how much I love you."

"I know how you can show me," she said softly as she outlined his lips with her finger.

"Tell me," he spoke with an English accent, waving his hand around with dramatic flair. "Anything for Lady Elizabeth. Anything she asks, it will be given to her. Name your request, my lady. Tell me what it is you want and I shall give it to you."

Beth laughed at his theatrics, then turned serious. She stroked his face, overwhelmed by the love he gave her.

"Beth, what is it?" Mitch asked. "Tell me what it is you want."

A warm smile creased her face. "A daughter."

ABOUT THE AUTHOR

Tamara Tilley writes from her home at Hume Lake Christian Camps, located in the beautiful Sequoia National Forest. She and her husband, Walter, have been on full-time staff at Hume for over twenty years. Tamara is a retail manager and an active book reviewer. You can read her reviews on her blog at http://tamara-tilley.blogspot.com. Along with reading, spending time with her grandkids, and crafting cards, she loves connecting with readers at www.tamaratilley.com. Or on Facebook at https://facebook.com/tamara.tilley.author.

CPSIA information can be obtained
at www.ICGtesting.com
Printed in the USA
LVOW10s0020240517
535560LV00016B/1952/P